THE FIRST TEN

BY
JAMIE MATHIESON

To Ele,
For everything

Contents

An Introduction

"USED to be a TV writer, apparently," said D.I. Fosse.

D.I. Hirsch nodded, looking in through the one-way mirror at the suspect.

He was cuffed to the table, alone in the interrogation room. He'd resisted arrest, according to the report. A bruise, blooming on one cheek, was crowned with an open cut and the socket of one eye was gradually darkening.

And he was smiling.

A distant smile of reverie at odds with his current situation. His fingers tapped out a playful rhythm on the table before him.

No, not tapping. Typing.

Ink-stained fingers moving over a keyboard that only he could see.

"You think he's good for it?" said Hirsch.

In answer, his partner tossed across a bulky item in an evidence bag. Hirsch caught it awkwardly and peered closer. It resembled a book, home-made by the looks of it. Thick string stitches held a cardboard cover around a wad of paper. The title was in broad black letters across the cover: THE FIRST TEN.

"What's this? A confession?" said Hirsch.

Fosse shrugged.

"Ten stories in the book," he said.

"So our ten corpses?" said Hirsch.

"Just a coincidence," said Fosse. Did he really believe that?

Hirsch pulled on latex gloves and carefully removed the book from the bag. There was a lot of red ink on the cover. At least he hoped it was ink. He put the book carefully down on his desk, as though it were a bomb.

"Anyone tried reading it?" he asked.

"Cover to cover," said Fosse. "Last night."

That was odd, thought Hirsch. Fosse could have delegated that task to any number of low-ranking officers. He didn't look tired either, his eyes bright and energised.

"Page-turner was it?" said Hirsch.

"They're just stories," said Fosse. "No smoking guns, as far as I could see. I don't think he's our man,"

"What are the stories about?" said Hirsch.

Fosse looked hesitant and Hirsch was abruptly taken with the conviction that he was lying. That the book was filled with damning details, the boasts of a mass murderer.

The moment passed as quickly as it had come. Fosse opened a buff folder and began to read.

"UFOs," he said, "parallel worlds, ouija boards, lobotomies--"

"Lobotomies?" said Hirsch.

"You know, when they…" Fosse mimed scissors cutting across his forehead.

"Yeah, I know what they are," said Hirsch. "Just an odd topic for a story is all. So no serial killers confessing their crimes?"

"Well…" said Fosse, awkwardly. "There are a *couple* of serial killers. And a woman chained up in a basement,"

"Jesus. You're saying that's *not* a smoking gun?" said Hirsch.

"Doesn't fit the profile," said Fosse blankly.

Hirsch felt unsettled once more. Something about Fosse, the book - hell, this whole situation - felt off.

He decided to change tack.

"What shows did he write for?" said Hirsch. "On TV?"

"Well, the big one was *Doctor Who*," said Fosse.

"Isn't that for kids?" said Hirsch.

"Debatable," said Fosse "The demographic split--"

"This sure isn't for kids though, is it?" said Hirsch, tapping the book.

"No," said Fosse. "It really isn't. He's got swearing all over the shop. Sex, torture--"

"Jesus," said Hirsch. "Well, good job no kids will ever read it,"

"Yeah," said Fosse. "And if any tried, I would definitely warn them away,"

"Definitely," said Hirsch.

They sat without speaking for a second, the only sound the white-noise hiss of the rain on the concrete outside.

"You should read it," said Fosse.

"What?"

"Belt and braces, you know," said Fosse. "I might have missed something, some detail that puts him in the frame,"

Strictly speaking, it was doubling up the work. There was no need for both of them to read it, but Hirsch found himself nodding.

"Just to rule him out," he heard himself saying.

He picked up the book again. It felt heavier than he remembered.

He was simply reviewing a piece of evidence. There was nothing else happening here.

He was aware of Fosse watching him, nodding, a distant smile on his face.

Hirsch opened the book. The first story was called *Eviction Day*. He began to read:

"*My name is Father Julius Montague and for the past thirty-three years…*"

Eviction Day

"MY name is Father Julius Montague and for the past thirty-three years I have been working directly for the Vatican as an exorcist."

Said just like that, as though it were the most normal thing in the world. Thinking about it later, Cathy decided it was the voice that sold it: authoritative, deep and resonant. In short, it sounded as though it belonged to someone else, which was ironic, considering the subject matter.

She had been unloading the weekly shop from her trolley into the back of the car when she saw him approach. Up until then, the morning had been nicely mundane. At that time of day, the supermarket had been mostly empty, and once she'd got the items on her list, she'd allowed herself a little time off, wandering the aisles without purpose. She'd opened the ice cream freezer, enjoying the billow of cold air, then studiously compared the flavours, as if she was actually considering buying some. She'd then lucked out with her cashier, who she privately thought of as the best one: no small talk, quick at scanning.

And now this.

At first glance, Cathy took him for a homeless man and inwardly winced when she realised she wouldn't have finished loading the car by the time he reached her. Were there no staff nearby who could intervene?

"Excuse me. I apologise for approaching you this way, but I

come with a dire warning."

He had a slight European accent. Spanish perhaps? She continued to load the trunk. Only two more bags to go. Eye contact could set him off, so she didn't make any. She braced herself for the inevitable pivot to issues of money or food.

Then he introduced himself and said he was an exorcist.

Cathy turned and looked at him properly for the first time.

A matted grey beard framed a haggard face lined with wrinkles so deep they read like scars. A tan that spoke of years without shelter, summers spent day sleeping in parks. Tangled grey shoulder-length hair and a mouth with nothing but missing or discoloured teeth. He was wearing a black suit a size too large over a similarly baggy blue sweater. Cathy was willing to bet they both came from charity shops.

She decided her initial reading of him had been correct. He was homeless and plainly had significant mental issues. She thought she'd kept her face blank, but the man reacted as though he could read her mind. He gestured apologetically to himself with the air of a man who only wore this body on wash day.

"I apologise for my appearance. I learned long ago that the physical is fleeting, but I sometimes fear I abuse the notion."

He smiled, but there was a desperation there.

All the bags of shopping were now in the boot. Cathy closed it and began to walk to the driver's door. He stepped closer and the smell of his body washed over her - a repellent mix of stale sweat, urine and alcohol, with a grace note of tooth decay.

"Please. Listen to me. I have spent so long fighting with the damned that I…"

His voice broke and something in his eyes made Cathy feel for him. Whatever mental issues he was fighting were very real to him. He was in genuine torment.

His voice fell to a whisper, conspiratorial.

"I hear them all the time now. Their chatter in the air. I don't want to, but I do."

Cathy had her keys in one hand. Two of them protruded through gaps in her fingers, ready to punch him if he should grab for her.

"And they are excited. Excited at the possibilities of your husband's new machine. The empty soulless bodies it will provide."

Cathy drove home and parked in the garage. There was a pile of cardboard boxes still in there, unopened since the move. Black marker pen declared their destination: WORKSHOP, CELLAR, SHED. She turned off the engine as the roller door hummed and clacked closed behind her. It shut off the sunlight like a descending curtain, reducing the room to near darkness. But Cathy didn't get out of the car. Not yet. Her window was open and she could hear a tick of cooling metal from the engine.

The priest, if that's what he was, hadn't mentioned her name. Or Tom's. Cathy wanted to believe that it had all been random. That the priest would have said those words to any other potential convert he found in that car park. No doubt had Cathy continued to listen, rather than hurrying to escape, his spiel would have soon moved on to issues of joining his church, or cult, or whatever it was he was actually peddling.

Cathy wanted to believe all of that, but didn't for a second.

The priest had known that Tom made machines. That he was making a *new* one. He didn't need to name him.

So where did that leave us? What should she tell Tom? *"Honey, you know your new machine? Turns out it's actually a gateway to hell."*

There was a concussive thump and a flash of light that Cathy had been braced for, but she still jumped. The vase of flowers had gone from the glass platform, literally disappearing in a cloud of dust.

Cathy turned and peered across the wide bay of the factory floor. Inside the assembler tank, she could see the vase again, magically teleported fifty feet and slowly sinking inside the viscous goop within. Pumps were already working to clear the unused fluid. By the time Cathy reached the tank it had been fully drained and the sad, sodden flowers had come free of the vase, now both resting against the filtration unit set into the floor.

She turned to find Tom crouching on the glass platform where the flowers had begun their journey, running the dust left behind through his fingers. It made Cathy uneasy. Surrounding him were hundreds of thin barrels, all aiming at the focal point of the platform. She'd been informed that they were customised electron microscopes, but to her eye they looked more like rifles in some futuristic firing squad.

"So that bit measures the original?" she said.

He nodded. "Down to the smallest molecule. And then the assembler prints an identical copy."

Cathy nodded, trying to look as if she understood.

The machine had grown significantly since she last saw it. Cathy was fairly sure an interior wall had been removed to accommodate the new sections. Vast snakes of ductwork had been suspended in the rafters, just above the pigeon nets. These, in turn, connected to humming refrigeration units. Cathy vaguely remembered Tom complaining about something overheating a few weeks ago. This looked like quite the solution.

The outer shell of the building itself had barely been modified and still bore the scars of its previous life as a tyre factory. Curling safety posters with Fifties fonts, mysterious scorch marks, rusting girders and cryptic spray-painted initials on flaking brickwork. There was also a pervasive smell of burning rubber. All acting as a bizarre anachronistic shell for the sprawling mass of cutting-edge technology Tom had assembled.

A bank of servers was connected by a trunk of cabling to the twin hearts of the machine - the glass platform firing squad that Tom called the recorder and the tank of viscous goop that he called the assembler. Access was provided by a series of metal gantries suspended several feet above the factory floor.

"So if you're just measuring it, why does it disappear?" asked Cathy.

"Measuring weakens it."

Cathy knew him well enough to know he was dumbing it down for her and raised an eyebrow. Tom, in turn, knew Cathy well enough to be suspicious.

"Why the sudden interest?" he asked.

"Just tell me."

Tom shrugged and began to explain, but he looked irritated and Cathy could tell he was no longer holding back with the techno-babble. He wanted her to get confused and leave like she always did, so he could get on with his work. She stubbornly did her best to follow.

Apparently, measuring anything with the kind of deep molecular precision that Tom was attempting would, by necessity, destroy it in the process. The molecular bonds were weakened enough to turn it literally into dust.

However, this was kind of irrelevant, as a perfect copy would appear almost instantly in the assembler.

"So it's not really a teleporter at all."

Tom could tell she was trying to wind him up. There was a time when he would have rolled his eyes and smiled wryly. Perhaps played along, shot back something witty. Today he just stared at her.

Cathy was reminded of a day shortly after they first moved in, when the factory was just an echoing cavernous space, home to nothing but pigeons and mice. She'd found a plank covered in pigeon shit and chased Tom around the factory floor with it, both of them weak with laughter.

Revisiting that memory felt like watching two different people.

She made herself a cup of tea in the little refreshments area he'd set up and Tom got back to work. She blew on her tea and noticed that, at some point, he'd added a microwave to his little mini kitchen. One less reason to return to the house.

This was always going to be part of the deal. Tom had warned her fairly early in their relationship. To do what he did, to achieve all he had achieved, he needed to get lost in the work, at the expense of every other aspect of his life. He might appear catatonic and ignore her, for hours or days at a time, as his mind was consumed with some problem or other. He could become manic once the solutions had come to him, working around the clock to bring them into the world. Missed meals and empty beds would become the norm.

And they had. She'd endured it all and even joked about being a science widow with her friends, because ultimately she understood it was a cycle. He would eventually return to her with a new patent or device or theory; they would spend time together for a while, enjoying the fruits of his labour, until his eyes glazed as a new problem took hold and the cycle began again.

The machine had been different.

The machine had consumed him in a way that no previous project ever had. They had purchased the factory, with their new house conveniently situated beside it, just over a year ago. Since then, the nights Tom spent in bed beside Cathy had dwindled to the point where she was actually startled the last time she rolled over and found him there.

She sipped her tea and watched him work, elbow-deep inside a conduit, an array of tools beside him. She wished he would surface and come back to her, if only for a little while. A couple of days of the old Tom back would fix everything, surely.

She asked him how far away he was from copying a person.

Tom blinked and frowned in her direction. Cathy could tell his mind was elsewhere. She repeated the question. Tom nodded, then considered, staring off into the middle distance.

"Months. Maybe years," he replied.

"But you'd do it? With a person?"

Tom had an incredulous look on his face.

"That's always been the ultimate aim. Imagine having one half of the machine in London and the assembler in Tokyo. Instantaneous travel."

"But the original person would be destroyed. Dead. Only the copy would end up in Tokyo."

Tom sighed and started explaining it to her again as though she were a child. The copy would be identical, down to the smallest neuron within their brains. All their memories would be preserved. They would even remember stepping into the machine.

But it wouldn't *be* them, thought Cathy. It would be a copy. And if there is such a thing as a soul, that wouldn't be copied at all.

Cathy washed and dried her mug, said goodbye to Tom and left the factory.

There was a small yard between the factory and the house. When they first moved in, Cathy had planned to perhaps fill it with potted plants and a climbing trellis. She imagined that with some judicious planting and a bench or two, it could become a green refuge and make up for the property's sad lack of a garden.

Ultimately, her plans came to nothing. Work on the house had consumed her attention and the yard had instead become a dumping ground for Tom. Every time she passed through it, it seemed there was more junk on either side of her path. Stacked breeze blocks on pallets, coiled wire on spindles and rusting metal frameworks under flapping tarpaulin. By this stage, there was only a narrow snaking pathway between the slouching piles of discarded material.

Usually, Cathy didn't give the yard much thought at all, beyond a vague regret as to what might have been. It was simply the route she took to visit Tom, that was all. But this evening, as the sun set and the shadows grew larger and deeper, she didn't like the yard at all. The darkness felt oppressive and the pools of rainwater stained red with rust looked like blood. She told herself she was being ridiculous and overcompensated by whistling as she passed through it.

Only when the door to the main house was closed behind her did she release the breath she didn't realise she'd been holding.

That night Cathy dreamed.

In the dream, she was at a party with Tom, who was celebrating that he'd managed to teleport people, but Cathy knew what had really happened. The teleported people had actually been killed by the machine and copies made, copies without souls. Demons had possessed these soulless bodies and taken them over.

In the dream, Cathy was walking through the party holding a gun, intending to kill any demons she could find. But there was no way to tell them apart from normal people. Everyone she met smiled pleasantly and behaved cordially, eating pizza and drinking wine. Some of them asked if she was alright.

She recognised Mrs Landry, the manager from the local Co-op. Her roots were showing and she was wearing bifocals and false eyelashes. Cathy could tell she was a demon, so she put her gun to Mrs Landry's forehead. Mrs Landry was still smiling and explained that if Cathy got it wrong, she was a murderer.

Tom appeared at her elbow and said he had a present for her. He didn't seem to notice the gun or care. Soon it had disappeared. Tom said he wanted her to be teleported. He said it didn't hurt at all. Then Cathy realised that Tom wasn't Tom anymore. There was a demon controlling him.

Cathy tried to get away, but realised that she was the only one at the party who hadn't been teleported. The only one with a soul. They all turned on her and she found herself being dragged towards the machine. She begged, screamed and thrashed in their grip, but it was no use.

The machine had teeth and the face of the priest from the car park. It opened its mouth to swallow her.

Cathy awoke soaked with sweat, her legs tangled up in the bedding.

It was 2am. The other side of the bed was empty.

She changed into fresh pyjamas and padded downstairs, turning on every light as she went. She left the kitchen in darkness as its windows faced the street. There was enough light from the hall to see what she was doing.

She let the tap run for a while before filling a pint glass with water. She drank it all standing before the sink, staring out into the street. She allowed her thoughts to drift, trying not to think about the dream.

Just like theirs, the houses across the street were all built in the 1920s and peppered with art deco features. They were originally home to the workers in the former tyre factory that now served as Tom's workshop. She wondered if any of the workers or their offspring still lived there.

She thought ahead to her plan for tomorrow. There was a

layer of white gloss to apply in the back bedroom then that room was complete. The tiler had finished their en suite shower a few days ago, which should be dry by now. Furniture needed to be moved out of storage and back into the snug. And then...

And then the house would be finished and Cathy would have nothing else left to do.

She felt ungrateful for even thinking that way. Three years ago, Tom had pointed out that she didn't need to work anymore, that his invention patents were earning more than enough to justify her giving up her job at the care home. She'd resisted at first - it didn't feel fair to rely upon his money. But then Tom had smiled and said he didn't think of it that way. He said he was paying to see more of her, and that without the job she'd be happier.

And she was happier, at first. Cathy had never defined herself by her job, had never thought of elderly care as her career. It was a stop-gap at best. But with it gone, she was increasingly troubled by a lack of purpose. She'd tried to deflect it with various hobbies and projects over the years. The latest was the renovation of their new home. She'd spent the last few months overseeing the installation of flecked granite counter-tops and walk-in showers, all of which would very soon come to a close. Leaving her facing the question she'd been avoiding: exactly who am I?

And the answer she feared the most was: Tom's wife. Defined only by her relationship with a brilliant scientist, while her own light grew ever dimmer.

A motion from across the street caught her eye, an urban fox trotting by. He stopped then ran back the way he'd come. Cathy idly wondered what had spooked him, then spotted the priest standing under the tree.

Cathy took a step back in shock. She was certain she was virtually invisible, the kitchen must have seemed in near darkness from the outside. Nevertheless, the priest reacted by nodding politely as though they'd just been introduced at a dinner party. He then pointed towards the park and began to stride in that direction. En route, he beckoned slightly in her direction, an invitation to join him there.

Cathy watched him until he was out of sight.

She stood for perhaps a full minute in the half-light of the kitchen, staring sightlessly out of the window. Then she went back upstairs, changed clothes and went out to meet the priest.

She was thankful he'd not gone any deeper into the park. He was sitting on a bench near the swings, only a few feet from the outer gate, well lit by streetlights. As she drew closer, she could see that he was sitting at one end of the bench, an implied invitation for her to sit at the other. Cathy ignored it and walked over to stand facing him, with perhaps fifty feet between them. She kept her hands deep in the pockets of her jacket - one hand holding pepper spray, the other a short paring knife.

"What do you want?" she asked, but there was no force in her words.

"To stop demons from consuming the world of the living," he said, hands wide, palms out, as though it were the most reasonable thing in the world.

"You sound like a crazy person," said Cathy.

"And yet here you are. You could have stayed inside, called the police. You did neither," he said, watching her carefully. "I think you are coming to believe. To see the danger I spoke of. The danger in the machine."

Cathy could think of a handful of scathing retorts, but she said nothing.

After a while, she asked: "How did you know about it? The machine?"

"The voices in my head told me," he replied with a smile, then his smile faded. He considered then leaned forward, his voice softening, as though afraid of being overheard.

"For over thirty years, I have fought the entities you know as demons. Hundreds of them perhaps. Driving them out of the bodies of innocents. Doing battle like this, curses you with a certain... *sensitivity*, over time. In the early years, I would hear the odd whisper of their voices in certain dark places. Now, it is almost constant. A tireless chatter on the edge of hearing. It is there that I first heard of your husband's machine."

"What did they say?" asked Cathy.

"That it is a machine that can make empty bodies. That it could be a way in. A way in for *all* of them."

Cathy thought again of her dream. The party where she alone had a soul. She imagined the machine running day and night, pumping out soulless bodies for demons to inhabit.

She shook her head, as if to deny the image. This was insanity. It was just a dream. So he knew about the machine. So what? Tom was hardly secretive. One of his colleagues at the institute could have mentioned it within earshot of this so-called priest. It happened to dovetail nicely with a couple of his delusions and here we are.

She realised that the priest was talking again and tried to focus.

"Tell me," said the priest, "do you rent your home, or own it?"

It was such a bizarre question in the circumstances. Cathy was momentarily taken with the idea that this was the priest's grift finally exposed. He was after the house.

"We've got a mortgage," she replied.

He nodded, pleased with the answer.

"Then you take care of your house. You know that any improvements you make, you will feel the benefit of. Not the landlord, not some future tenant. So you paint the rooms, maintain the roof, keep the gutters clear."

Where was he going with this? None of it was helping Cathy's very real fear that she was in her local park at 2am, talking to an alcoholic with mental issues.

He leant forward, finally getting to the point.

"It might help if you think of demons as the most selfish, vindictive tenants in the world. When they move into a body, they pay no deposit, they know they will in all likelihood not be there very long. So they run that body into the ground. They take a certain kind of... *perverse delight* in ruining it. I have seen the possessed gouge out their own eyes and eat them. And worse. So that when the true owner returns, he finds he cannot walk, or see, or make love. Do you understand what I am telling you?"

Cathy felt sick. She understood. She still didn't know if she believed, but she understood.

"Say I believe you. And everything you're saying is true. What then? Destroy the machine?"

The priest shook his head sadly. "The knowledge of how to rebuild it would still exist in your husband's mind."

Cathy stared at the priest. "Are you suggesting that I kill my husband?"

Cathy returned to the house half an hour later. She showered before retiring, as though washing off evidence of some infidelity. Tom's side of the bed was still empty. She slept fitfully and, in the morning, went over to the factory with a tray of breakfast: eggs, bacon, coffee and fresh orange juice.

She discovered Tom sitting in the centre of the deconstructed shell of the assembler. Components and tools lay around him in a fan. His clothes and hands were covered in dark grease stains and he was feverishly manic. He explained that he'd had a breakthrough with the molecular injector. This time Cathy could tell he wasn't trying to lose her, but he was so excited that he did anyway. Thoughts tumbled out of him in a torrent of half-sentences, acronyms and shorthand terms. Apparently, quantum entanglement had always been crucial to the interaction between the recorder and assembler, but never before had he realised how pivotal it was to the operation of the machine as a whole.

When did he last sleep?

It turned out, surprisingly, that he had. He must have done, as he was claiming that the breakthrough came to him in a dream. (He had a sleeping bag in there for "power naps" - another reason to not return to the house.)

Cathy deposited the breakfast tray in a gap on his desk and made encouraging noises whenever he paused for breath. She wondered - not for the first time - if she slowly backed away and left the room, would he just keep talking?

He had pivoted now to praising his own subconscious mind for the insight it had gifted him. And in such a novel way, not through metaphor or surreal imagery, but through a chorus of whispering voices.

The face of the priest looked at peace in death. His mouth had the hint of a smile, hair combed back from his face with a neatness Cathy had never seen in life. She knew that the photograph had been taken on a metal mortuary table, but something about the lighting made her think of a prep table in a kitchen.

Cathy stared at the photo for a few seconds, frowned and decided to change her story.

"No wait, I *do* know him. Well, recognise him. He came up to me in a supermarket car park the other day, mumbling something about demons."

The two police officers shared a look. Cathy thought she could read what it meant. They knew damn well he'd spoken to her in that car park. Probably had CCTV footage of it.

The officers were both sitting on the sofa opposite, sinking into it. Cathy liked that it slightly robbed them of their authority. The drawn-looking one, who had introduced herself as D.I. Welling, took back the photograph and nodded sagely.

"But you've no idea why he was interested in you?" she said.

"To be honest, he seemed insane. You say he had my address?"

"Scrawled on a note in his pocket. When he died."

"How did he die?"

Another shared look. Cathy thought this one meant: should we tell her? She pushed the issue.

"I mean, should I be worried for my safety? Do you think he was murdered?"

"The details of his death you might find… distressing."

"I want to know."

"He either threw himself, or was thrown from, the top of a multi-storey car park."

Cathy did her best to look scathing. "If you'd spoken to him for five seconds, you'd think suicide the far more likely option."

She hoped that by patronising them, implying they were

idiots, they might be irritated enough to want to prove her wrong and provide more details.

The tactic worked and then some. D.I. Welling looked indignant and leant forward with a sour look. Even before the officer spoke, Cathy could tell she hoped her words would be upsetting.

"Before he jumped, or was thrown, he had been forced to eat, or had eaten of his own volition, seven of his fingers. And his own tongue."

Years ago, in the early days of their relationship, when Tom was still trying to impress her, he had explained to Cathy the idea of Schrödinger's Cat. A creature neither dead nor alive until the lid of its box is opened and reality is forced to decide which option is true. (There was also something in there about quantum theory and the act of observing, which Cathy didn't follow, but she thought she got the gist.)

Cathy felt like that cat right now.

One, and only one, of two stories could be true.

The machine was just that. A machine. It was also brilliant, groundbreaking and could, in theory, change the world and make both Tom and Cathy rich beyond her wildest dreams.

But it was still just a machine.

The priest had clearly been insane. He had somehow overheard details of its construction and they had fuelled his own obsessive fantasies. Fantasies that then caused him to self-mutilate then take his own life.

Or…

The machine could end the world. If Cathy allowed it to be completed, it would become a gateway for thousands of disembodied demons to pour through, to defile and torture and kill, spreading like a plague. They had already killed the priest and were currently whispering in Tom's ear, guiding him to complete the machine, way ahead of schedule.

Cathy felt herself flipping between blind panic at the oncoming potential apocalypse and shame at her own gullibility, as the two versions of reality struggled for supremacy in her mind.

If the doomsday scenario was true and she did nothing, she would be damning humanity. If the innocuous scenario was true and she overreacted, she risked jeopardising not only years of Tom's work, but probably her marriage. If only there were some middle ground she could tread, some insurance she could take out against damnation.

Something a little less severe than murdering her own husband.

When Cathy had raised that idea with the priest, he had just stared at her evenly and calmly before nodding slowly, turning the idea over in his mind, as though it were something he had not considered until that point.

He was not a very good actor.

And now, for some reason, the idea of killing Tom kept resurfacing in her mind. At first, it was a notion she recoiled from. Even if she came to fully believe the priest's story, she could never bring herself to do that.

Could she?

Like a hangnail she couldn't resist pulling, she kept returning to the thought. She finally succumbed to it, telling herself it was a purely intellectual exercise. It didn't *mean* anything. Not really. It was all just theoretical. Just thinking it through didn't commit her to any action.

So…

How would she do it?

Poison? Knife? Could she make it appear like an accident? A burglary gone wrong?

Once Cathy was past her initial revulsion, she was surprised at the ease with which she found herself planning her husband's demise. Elaborate, detailed fantasies grew in her mind with each retelling, usually as she lay in bed alone at night, trying and failing to sleep. She concluded that poisoning Tom and burning down the factory was probably the way to go. This option would destroy the machine and had a nice bonus of removing any evidence of foul play.

She then pictured how she would behave in the inevitable police interviews ("He was obsessed with his work. Safety was never really something he thought about. I don't know what I'm going to do without him.") and finally imagined using the money from the insurance to buy a nice country property, perhaps a barn conversion. She could live there alone, maybe with a couple of spaniels for company.

She noticed that the part of the plan she kept returning to in her mind was what should have been the grace note: collecting on the insurance and moving into her new home. She found herself going into ridiculous detail over the internal décor of the barn: tile patterns, curtain colours, a dining suite she'd seen on a makeover show. At first she thought she was just enjoying the mental process of interior design, but she knew in her heart of hearts that it went deeper than that.

The reason she kept returning to that part of the fantasy was that she was picturing a life without Tom. And enjoying that picture.

Father Hampton smiled benignly and nodded, arms clasped behind his back like some minor royal. He looked around the warehouse at the immense sprawling sections of the machine.

"Very impressive," he said, as if viewing a new cancer wing.

Cathy didn't know what she'd been expecting, but it certainly wasn't this.

Getting another priest to look at the machine had been relatively easy. She had googled the number of the nearest Catholic Church, St Marys, the one she passed every time she went to her gym. The secretary fielding the priest's calls was very good at deflecting, but once Cathy mentioned a potential donation of ten thousand pounds, Father Hampton's schedule opened right up. Tomorrow at noon? Perfect!

Ten minutes before he was due, Cathy had watched the priest park a Renault hatchback across the street and check a small notebook as he looked up at their house. She saw the thought cross his face - this does not look like the house of someone with ten thousand pounds to spare.

He was perhaps thirty, but his high eyebrows and plump cheeks made him seem much younger. He'd grown a neatly trimmed beard, which Cathy read as an attempt to add age and gravitas. It didn't really work.

Cathy decided he was probably of a generation that didn't even believe in hell or demons anymore. She wondered if that would matter.

She'd welcomed him in, made him tea and discussed trivial standards such as the traffic on his ride over and the weather. In person, he was charming and affable, but Cathy could sense his impatience and doubt, so she threw in a mention of how profitable several of Tom's patents were. As though a switch had been flipped, the priest relaxed. The money was coming, he just had to smile and nod a little longer.

Under the pretext of a house tour, she led him through the yard and into the factory. Cathy had briefly considered arranging the priest's visit for a time when Tom was out buying supplies or the like, but the idea seemed hopelessly optimistic. Tom never seemed to leave the side of the machine anymore.

As they entered, Tom was lying under one of the trunks of cabling connected to the server farm, spanner in hand. He barely looked up as Cathy introduced the priest. She'd prepared a whole spiel about donating to worthy causes to explain Father Hampton's presence, but it didn't matter. She could see from Tom's glazed look that his focus and interest had switched from them utterly. Cathy felt certain she could have introduced the priest as her new lover without Tom reacting at all.

Cathy had hoped that the presence of a priest so close to the machine would trigger something. Quite what, she didn't know. Some supernatural event that would finally settle the question of the machine in her own mind. But nothing happened. No poltergeist activity or demonic chanting. All she heard was a soft but distinct gurgle from Father Hampton's stomach that they both studiously ignored.

Weren't the demons supposed to be watching, all the time? Wouldn't they see the priest as a threat? She didn't know the rules, that was the problem. She even tried to goad them by asking the priest to say a blessing over various bits of the machine. He complied, looking a little embarrassed, then they both left after saying goodbye to Tom, who grunted in their direction without looking.

They returned to the house and Cathy produced the promised cheque from the ceramic pig in the kitchen. Father Hampton graciously accepted it, although Cathy felt a little ashamed of the hoops she'd made him jump through.

As she watched the priest return to his car, she wondered if it had been money well spent. Surely, had there been any truth to the whole demon scare, something would have happened. Hadn't she just proved the whole thing to be a sad delusion? Couldn't she just relax now?

Cathy was loading her car with shopping and the dead priest was standing beside her, as before. Only now, some of his fingers ended in stumps. He noticed her trying not to stare and apologised for his appearance. His words were garbled but Cathy somehow understood him. She remembered that the demons had made him eat his tongue.

That would explain the blood bubbling on his lips.

He told her that she needed to hurry and she did her best, ramming the shopping bags into the car, but he shook his head and seemed upset. She sensed that wasn't what he meant. He gripped her shoulder and Cathy felt it.

"It's happening now," he said.

Cathy awoke in the darkness, knowing intuitively that something was very, very wrong. She could still feel the priest's grip on her shoulder. She turned on the bedside light. The other side of the bed was empty.

She pulled on her dressing gown and slippers and headed for the factory.

The day after the police visited and told her about the death of the priest, Cathy had started to wear a silver crucifix on a chain around her neck.

It had belonged to her late mother, and although Cathy knew

it had held no sentimental value to her in life, she just couldn't bring herself to sell it or give it away. It had been following her from move to move over the past eight years, along with another couple of boxes of her mother's possessions that fell into the same category: kaftans, chunky costume jewellery and bangle earrings. None of which she would ever wear and none of which she could ever part with.

She told herself that she started to wear the crucifix in preparation for the visit from the new priest, as part of her Catholic pretence. But that wasn't the whole story.

She wore it because she thought it might protect her from the demons.

She wore it because, if Tom got possessed, it might prevent him from dragging her kicking and screaming into the machine. And, failing that, she hoped that it would render her newly copied body possession-proof.

All magical thinking of course. All superstitious nonsense.

She usually took the crucifix off before she slept and on the night of the dream, she was halfway across the yard before she remembered it. She thought she'd left it on her bedside table and considered going back then realised she was holding it after all. She could feel the sharp points of the cross inside her fist. She must have snatched it up, half-awake.

She'd forgotten her phone, though, so couldn't use it as a torch to light her path. The yard was reduced to a series of dark looming columns. She knew they were just discarded material, but was suddenly taken with the fancy that they were demons queuing, awaiting their turn to be born.

As she drew closer to the factory, she could hear the rising whine of the machine. She'd heard it enough times to know what it meant. A test run. Something was being teleported. Something was being destroyed and copied. She knew Tom had moved up to testing live subjects. Rats. Rabbits.

He'd said he was weeks away from human tests.

He'd said it wasn't ready, that the risks of errors were too high.

Even before Cathy opened the door, she somehow knew that he'd lied.

A billow of warm air washed over her as she crossed the threshold. The smell of hot metal, rotting food and body odour. He'd been alone in here too long. Why had she let it get this far?

She caught a momentary glimpse of the naked form of Tom crouching on the glass platform of the recorder. He had a distant look on his face. He met her eye as she reached the gantry and she raised an arm, began to say something, but she was too late.

There was a familiar concussive crack and Tom was consumed in light, burning the image on to Cathy's retinas.

Then the factory was plunged into complete darkness.

The breakers had tripped again. They sometimes did after a test. Cathy could hear the descending whine of motors and fans powering down all over the factory.

She called Tom's name. He didn't answer.

Back-up generators were kicking in, lone lightbulbs gradually flickering on here and there. Cathy could soon make out the glass platform of the recorder again. It was now home to a large pile of dust.

Tom, she thought. That dust used to be Tom.

A new noise. The churning of the drainage pumps from the assembler tank.

Cathy turned to face it. That section of the factory was still unlit. She heard the hatch of the tank opening in the darkness.

My husband is dead, thought Cathy.

Her eyes were adjusting to the darkness. She could just make out the silhouette of a figure climbing out of the assembler, see the sheen of fluid from the tank on his skin.

More lights flickered on, illuminating the new Tom.

He was standing naked, perhaps thirty feet away, fluid dripping from his body. He smiled at the sight of Cathy.

"It worked," said the copy of her husband. The empty copy with no soul.

"Well done love," said Cathy.

She had one hand behind her back. Wrapped around her knuckles was the silver necklace with the crucifix held tightly in her fist.

The new Tom reached for a nearby towel and began to dry himself. He noticed that Cathy wasn't coming any closer and looked in her direction.

"Something wrong?" he asked.

Cathy shook her head, her smile brittle.

Then Tom frowned and let the towel fall. He held up his hands and looked at them curiously, as though seeing them for the first time. Perhaps he was. Perhaps a demon had just entered him. Perhaps Cathy was witnessing the moment it took over.

He turned and looked at Cathy again then smiled, slowly and widely. It could have been a smile of scientific victory. It could also have been the smile of a predator locating new prey.

He began to walk slowly towards her.

Then he started to scream.

There were two ways to interpret what happened next. The first was that Tom had made a mistake somewhere in his calculations. He had used himself as a guinea pig far too early in the development of his invention and was now paying the price. Some error in the formulation of his new molecules had made them unstable.

That was one explanation and it certainly fit most of the facts.

Most of them.

Another explanation was that the fluid in the assembler, from which his new molecules were composed, used a large tank of sterilised water as a base. A tank of water that Cathy made sure Father Hampton blessed on his brief visit. Just insurance, she'd told herself.

Tom's new body was literally constructed from holy water.

Cathy assumed that demons would have a hard time possessing such a body.

But, as she watched Tom convulse and burst into flame, his skin bubbling and hissing, she found herself calmly thinking, "They're giving it a bloody good try."

He stumbled towards her, his screaming face a mask of flame, arms outstretched and twitching. She could smell his hair burning. She had always hated that smell.

She tried to back away, but had nowhere to go, cold metal pipework at her back. He was still coming. Her thoughts felt abstract, far away.

She wondered what it would feel like to be embraced by a burning man.

He stopped around five feet from her and fell to his knees. She could feel the heat of the inferno he had become, taste the acrid tang of his burning flesh in the back of her throat.

She noticed she was holding out the crucifix.

When did she do that? Was the cross keeping him at bay, or had his pain simply become too great to keep walking?

His scream died in his throat, trailing off to a liquid gurgle as he slumped on to his side and lay still. The flames all across his body were still burning brightly.

She hoped he was dead, for his sake.

His new position allowed the fire to lap against a duct of rubber pipes and plastic wiring. Fresh flames and thick gouts of smoke began to rise.

With his still-burning body slumped off to one side, Cathy could leave, in theory. There was enough space on the gantry for her to hurry by. But she had seen this movie. The villain that you think is dead never is. If she tried to run past, a charred hand would snake out and grab her by the wrist or ankle.

But she had no choice, the fire was really taking hold now. Flames were licking up the wall to the joists above. Burning rubber had dripped through the gantry and on to a stack of wooden pallets below.

Cathy took a deep breath and ran. She was primed and ready to lunge aside from the inevitable attack.

It never came. She hurried by. He didn't move.

She left the factory, locking the door behind her. The flickering firelight in the windows made the shadows in the yard jump, made the piles of junk look like they were moving. Cathy decided they were her friends now and that this was their victory dance.

She made it to the house and turned.

Thick black smoke was billowing through gaps in the corrugated roof and windows, most of which were alive with orange light. She heard something collapse within. A groan of expanding metal and glass smashing.

So, who was she now?

The widow of a brilliant man?

A gullible fool who bought into a troubled priest's fantasy?

No. In a moment of diamond-perfect clarity, she saw exactly who she was.

She was the woman who had saved the world.

She sat on the kitchen step and watched the factory burn.

Goliath Is Waiting

MY involvement commenced with a phone call at 2.30 am the night of the crash. My mobile was configured to only ring during the night if called by a handful of numbers, most of which were family.

This was not a call from my family.

Three hours later, I was facing proof we are not alone in the universe and wishing I'd worn my wellies.

Base camp was a little village of tents and prefabs unloaded from lorries. The sound and fumes of diesel generators filled the air. Shouted orders. Floodlights illuminating the drifting rain.

We were all shivering in the drizzle, maybe a dozen of us: theoretical physicists, linguists, metallurgists, even sign language experts. Some of us had met before, called out on other nights to false alarms, but the body language of everyone on site told me this was the real thing. As they gave us our jabs and issued our hazmat suits, the soldiers were as professional as always, but there was a nervous energy, a wildness to their eyes.

They had already seen the ship.

I was technically there because of my qualifications in biology, but as usual I felt like a fraud. My field was brimming with scientists eminently more qualified than me. Understand me, this isn't false modesty. The only reason I was called, the only reason I was *ever* called, was because of my own stupidity and laziness.

Let me explain.

When I was twenty-four years old, I wrote a paper for my masters degree on the topic of theoretical exobiology. It was, and I quote, a "speculative rumination on the effects of differing environmental pressures on the potential forms of extra-terrestrials". Which was a long-winded way of saying: what might aliens look like?

In choosing this as a topic, I thought I was saving myself a ton of work. Aliens were theoretical. There was nothing concrete to research. In addition, no one could disprove my conclusions on these theoretical beings. I figured I could wax lyrical for a few thousand words, cite some worthy sounding studies on deep-sea vent sulphur creatures and the effects of low gravity on astronaut bone density and coast to a B minus.

The paper got an A. It also got the attention of the intelligence community, was widely circulated at NASA and, by the time I graduated, was part of a briefing pack for first contact at the CIA.

I was utterly unaware of any of this until I was contacted by Her Majesty's government a year later and informed that, seemingly without any choice in the matter, I was now at their beck and call 24/7, should, say, a UFO happen to crash in the centre of The New Forest.

All because I thought writing about aliens would save me work.

Once we were all suited up, we were informed that it was apparently too far to walk, so we were directed to a couple of Humvees. They didn't have headlights on and the drivers were wearing night-vision goggles, which was disconcerting. As we set off, I asked our driver if this was for security reasons and he didn't answer. He didn't even look at me.

We drove for twenty minutes in pitch darkness, before another oasis of floodlights told us we'd arrived. Another village of tents, this time pitched beside the ship. We all got our first look at a craft from another world.

Frankly, I was expecting something bigger.

It was roughly the size of a three-storey building and sat at the end of a long muddy trench it had gouged as it landed, a deep scar running through the centre of the forest that I realised we had just driven down. Most of the trees had been flung aside, but some had been pushed before it, forming a tangled lattice of pines. It now sat in the centre of that nest like some otherworldly egg.

In the days that followed, the nickname that came to stick was "The Teardrop", which was roughly accurate, as far as it goes. The ship was bulbous and spherical at one end and tapered to a fine point. It never looked like a teardrop to me, though. It looked like the massive skull of a bird. The tapering point I saw as a gigantic beak. Large indented domes, deep scollops in the hull stared back at me like empty eye sockets.

We all clambered out of our Humvees and they U-turned and left, disappearing back into the darkness. No one came to greet us. We watched the activity around the ship. Workers with chainsaws were cutting away some of the more precarious-looking trunks from the nest of debris. Others were erecting tents or putting down walkways. All ignoring the miracle in their midst.

As we drew closer, I noticed a bank of floodlights directed at a jagged breach in the hull, perhaps twenty feet across. Hazard tape on poles bordered a path leading right up to it. I was expecting some kind of briefing or instructions but a Major in a hazmat suit spotted us and simply gestured for us to follow him as he strode into the ship.

The alien was fifty feet tall and appeared to have been killed in the crash.

A metal strut the size of a tree had impaled him through the centre of his chest, pinning him to his chair. The jagged tip of the strut had impacted with sufficient force to pass through his chair and the bulkhead behind it. Clear viscous fluid had pooled around his seat. We assumed it was his blood.

We stood staring up at the alien for quite a while. It towered above us. Everything did, the whole ship designed for the use of creatures many times our size. All the control panels were way out of reach, simple doorways loomed like cathedral archways. The psychological impact was subtle, but we all remarked upon it later. It left us feeling infantilized, brought back in our minds to a time when we were all helpless children.

The alien had thick overlapping bone plates reminiscent of an armadillo. His feet were bare and three-toed, each toe ending in something like a hoof. The top of his head was flat and crested with a wedge of bone that looked like the prow of a ship. He didn't appear to have facial features as we understood them. The later autopsy revealed that his eyes and mouth were retractable. When not in use, they nestled safely behind another cluster of bone plates. The same was true of retractable tentacles at the end of his arms, which ended in fearsome clubs at all other times.

I tried to apply the cold logical principles of evolution to the features I could see. There was no conclusion to be drawn from the alien's appearance other than the fact that it had clearly evolved on a world with fearsome predators and perhaps a different gravity. That was all. The fact that it had piloted a ship to another world spoke of a highly evolved intelligence. This was no mindless brute, in the same way that our canine teeth and sharp fingernails didn't make us automatically aggressive.

All of these well-reasoned arguments rattled around my conscious brain - but another, deeper, instinctive part of me was fighting the urge to flee. I simply couldn't imagine this creature holding out a hand in greeting or conversing calmly. I could, however, quite easily imagine it rising from its seat and bludgeoning us all to death.

The chamber we were standing in was largely spherical and the only room in the ship, taking up the majority of the interior space. There was only one other seat in the entire vessel and it sat empty beside the corpse. Once these factors - along with the adjusted scale - had been taken into account, it began to feel less like a landing craft and more like some sort of escape pod.

The chamber was swarming with technicians and soldiers. They had already constructed scaffolding and a raised walkway around twenty feet from the ground, allowing them to examine the various control surfaces within reach of the alien. We were invited to walk up the ramp to join them.

One of the technicians was excitedly examining what I initially took to be a monitor screen cracked by the girder that killed our giant friend; but as I drew closer, I realised that it was actually the glass wall to some sort of box, six feet across. The interior seemed familiar, at least in principle. It was a terrarium, a transplanted cube of soil, rocks and foliage from another world. Purple fronds and bristling blue cacti artfully placed around undulating sand.

Quite why it was part of the control panel of an escape pod wasn't immediately clear.

I was the first to spot the other alien. That it had gone unnoticed until then was hardly surprising - it was comparatively tiny, perhaps the size of a hamster, and its fur was exactly the same shade as the sand. It was also clearly dead, the back half of its body crushed by the girder, which had concertinaed most of the terrarium's roof.

In many ways, it looked like a conventional earth creature, perhaps some distant offshoot of the squirrel family. Had I been told that this species had been discovered in some remote corner of the Amazon, I would have accepted it. Large eyes, here half-closed in death, over a bulbous snout, its front legs ending in delicate three-fingered paws. Short sandy fur with a darker mottling along the spine, which we discovered, on freeing the back half of his body, led to a long bushy tail.

We mused a little over the reason for the presence of the terrarium. Was it purely decorative? Some wag suggested that perhaps the big fella liked his food fresh. Some of us laughed.

I didn't. It seemed just as likely as anything else.

The Major called us down from the gantry. He said he had something else to show us.

Aside from the breach in the hull we had entered through, there was only one door in or out of the chamber. It was open to the night, sixty feet high and around thirty wide. As we approached, I noticed that it was cordoned off, technicians on their knees carefully working in the mud outside. I soon saw why.

There was a clear set of huge three-toed footprints leading away from the ship.

There had been a survivor.

The soldiers had set up a line of floodlights following the footprints fifty feet until they reached the edge of the river. They did not reappear on the other side.

There was quite a gap between each footprint and they were definitely deeper at the toe than the heel. Assuming our survivor was the same height as their dead companion, they'd been running. I later read a twelve-page report that came to much the same conclusion, in a hundred times the words.

I wish they hadn't been running. I wish they'd been staggering. Running implied vitality. Running implied purpose.

But running could also imply fear, and who wouldn't be afraid? They'd just crashed on an alien world, their shipmate had been killed on impact. They were probably hiding in the woods not far from here, listening terrified as we picked over the corpse of their companion. I tried to bring that image to mind, to picture a living version of the impaled giant cowering and hiding, but somehow I couldn't.

The footprint analysis I later read also mentioned, almost as an afterthought, that several much smaller pawprints had been found meandering around the larger footprints. These matched the tiny dead creature we found in the cracked terrarium.

Our giant survivor had not been alone.

We spent the next three hours studying the crash site, cataloguing, measuring and speculating about every aspect of the creatures and their craft. We were then ferried back to base camp for decontamination and lunch before being returned to the crash site for another three hours of the same.

We were dimly aware of other activity in our peripheral vision. At daybreak, dogs had been brought in and set to search the woods, along with infra-red drones. At one point, I was pulled aside and asked if I could make a back-of-an-envelope estimate of the larger creature's running speed, based upon its speculated biology and length of stride. I didn't ask them exactly what they meant by "speculated biology". My calculations led to a large circle on the map of its potential location, growing wider with each passing minute. There was another set of circles based upon the idea that the alien had been washed downstream.

No one asked for an estimate of the smaller creature's speed.

Well aware of the danger of decomposition, an entire group had a priority of packing the giant in ice until it could be removed for autopsy. At some point, it was given the codename of GOLIATH, which felt a little on the nose to me. The smaller rodent was codenamed DAVID, which read like a lazy afterthought.

Night found the more fortunate of us checking into B&Bs in neighbouring villages. I was not amongst that group, instead being instructed to pick one of the bunks in a mass dormitory at base camp. I slept fitfully, my dreams filled with visions of Goliath rampaging through the camp, overturning cars as it roared.

I awoke to TV news bulletins filled with an obvious MOD cover story, a fairly blatant attempt to keep people out of the woods. Apparently, a top-secret spyplane had crashed containing several cannisters of a potent bioweapon. One nice touch was the idea that exposure to this toxin could cause hallucinations. No, you didn't see a fifty-foot monster, you got poisoned. Here, take this cure and go home.

By the way, where did you see the monster?

By the end of the next day, the corpse of Goliath had been cut from the chair, packed into a huge refrigerated crate and removed from the crash site by means of crane and articulated lorry.

The corpse of David travelled with it, inside a glorified coolbox.

Given my specialism, I left with them, travelling in a convoy with six other biologists and geneticists. We were told we were being taken to the nearest military base with the relevant facilities to allow autopsy and biological analysis. That was the last time I saw the ship in one piece.

Three storeys of concrete and glass office block were bordered by a well-maintained lawn and a modest car park. A sign proclaimed the company to be HELLING DATA: "Your Memories, Safe In Our Hands." Across a service road was a large warehouse, bristling with air-con units, which I assumed to be its server farm. I could see smiling staff in white shirts and pencil skirts enjoying their lunch in the open-air cafeteria.

I genuinely thought we'd taken a wrong turn.

Our Goliath convoy had left the motorway twenty minutes ago and had been whipping through countryside, I assumed en route to a military base of parade grounds and barracks. And now this.

Our MOD minders ignored all our questions, as usual, and instructed us to disembark. We were led into a small service lift, which - to our surprise - went down rather than up and continued to descend for an alarming length of time. We emerged, blinking, on to a floor that felt like a private hospital. It proved to have laboratories stacked with enough high-end analytical equipment to put CERN to shame.

The company above was a front, of course, with no military links on paper. They were effectively the guardhouse for the twenty floors below that did not appear on any blueprints.

We explored our new home and were all just marvelling at the efficiency of the whole operation when someone pointed out that there wasn't a room anywhere on our entire floor big enough to contain the corpse of Goliath.

Ultimately, the only space big enough for our needs proved to be the third floor "vehicle storage bay", a greasy car park lined with jeeps and trucks covered in tarpaulins. We ferried up whatever equipment we could and the crate containing Goliath was brought down to us by means of a truly impressive cargo lift that I was informed could carry a tank.

By contrast, we conducted the autopsy of David on a small metal table around three feet wide.

Before we opened the Goliath crate, we sealed it in a clear plastic tent to avoid any risk of contamination. Portable refrigeration units blew icy air over the body as we worked.

I say "we", but I did none of the actual dissection. As someone with supposed dazzling insight, I was made part of the team collating and analysing the autopsy data as it came in. I pitched in, moving equipment when it was needed, but most of my working day was spent running the mass spectrometers and watching video feeds of the autopsies.

The two corpses had recognisable DNA, which shocked all of us. Not only that, but the DNA was composed of the usual four bases: adenine, cytosine, guanine and thymine. The geneticists immediately began arguing about the likelihood of this. Either all life everywhere could only evolve down the same narrow route that would lead to DNA as we knew it, or we were looking at something else.

Their biology also followed rules we were very familiar with. Recognisable digestive, nervous and circulatory systems, lungs, heart and brain, although sometimes of a surprising number. Both bodies had two hearts and brain tissue dispersed in small clusters throughout.

Most of the surprises we found in the body of Goliath. The bony armour plates covering its skin were found to have been infused with a titanium alloy, as was its skull. It was wearing armour that it could literally not take off. One of our military overseers asked if the armour could deflect a bullet. We told him we genuinely had no idea. Once the plates had been cut from the body, he took one of them with him to test at their firing range. He returned some time later, looking ashen. He wouldn't reveal the results of his tests, but insisted that we provide him with a diagram indicating any gaps in the plating on the creature's body.

The gaps we did find contained more surprises. Sleek thorns were discovered embedded deep under the skin in any area that wasn't armoured. The purpose of these thorns wasn't immediately clear until deeper cuts revealed a pressurised gas bladder beneath each thorn. One of them was accidentally triggered, resulting in the thorn being ejected at speed, shattering an overhead light.

I tried to keep an open mind, tried to view these discoveries dispassionately. But it became harder and harder to reconcile the idea of peaceful explorer with the body lying before us. And there was another living specimen out there somewhere, somehow managing to avoid our best efforts to locate it. Hiding. Waiting.

Additional teams arrived. We began to work in shifts, which made a lot of sense. The impulse was to work until you dropped, but nobody wanted errors due to fatigue. At the end of the first day, I assumed we would be sleeping at barracks on another floor, so I was surprised when our military minder led us all up and out of the base.

We were taken by minibus to the centre of the nearby village of Croworth and informed that we had all been allocated separate cottages. Our confusion must have been evident, but our minder did little to alleviate it, simply handing us our keys and telling us he would return for us in eight hours.

We soon came to realise that, despite appearances, the entire village of Croworth was actually the dormitory for the base we had just left. It was wonderfully idyllic on the face of it, with rows of thatched cottages built in rings around the focal point of the village green, which was in turn bordered by the black-beamed King's Shilling pub, corner shop and post office. It felt like a little slice of calm normality to return to after a day spent studying the innards of creatures from another world. Several of us began to make a habit of enjoying a pint in the beer garden that overlooked the village pond before retiring.

It was all fake, of course. The village didn't exist until 1955 and our thatched cottages all had concrete walls. We were the only civilians for miles and our smiling bucolic bar staff were actually military police in disguise. I kept expecting to bump into Patrick McGoohan.

Still, it was a damn sight better than a bunk bed underground.

Two months went by. Both David and Goliath had been autopsied to destruction. Every cell, bone, fluid and organ had been harvested, catalogued and analysed to the best of our ability, before being forwarded to other specialists. We could feel the labs winding down as we ran out of things to usefully do.

I had actually got as far as starting to arrange transport back home when I became aware of a commotion. Soldiers and scientists were running past my lab and I overheard one of them excitedly repeating, "We've caught it! We've caught it!" I followed immediately. I had visions of a huge cage in our dissection bay containing the living Goliath, spitting with rage. Instead, I found a group gathered around a table in our main lab.

And there, sitting calmly in a small perspex cage, chewing happily on a poppy seed, was a living, breathing David.

We had a substantial programme of tests primed and ready to go for just such an opportunity. In addition, it turned out that a team of animal behaviourists had apparently been living in the village, sequestered on standby for the past two months. They joined our team within the hour.

We had just taken blood and stool samples when I was informed by the MOD that I was to be temporarily reassigned. The timing seemed very odd until I realised that they wanted my "unique perspective" on the location where the creature had been found. I protested, in vain, and was soon leaving the base in a lorry full of hazmat suits and containment tents, along with several other similarly irritated scientists.

Our destination turned out to be Wythenshaw Police Station in Manchester, two hundred and fifty miles away from the crash site, which was something of a surprise. Some of our colleagues were already on site, preaching the familiar gospel of chemical leak to keep the station clear. We smoothly took over and began isolating the rooms we were told had contained the creature. There was also a group of very nervous policemen not used to being on the other side of an interrogation table.

The story of how the creature came to wind up there is long and complicated. It's a sequence of events I obviously wasn't involved with at all, but which can be pieced together with a fair amount of certainty from police reports and witness statements.

Approximately six miles east of the crash site, there is a former dairy farm belonging to a man called Roger Twitchell. The farm had been in his family for at least three generations, but recent money troubles caused by Roger's gambling habit had led him to turn over most of his milking sheds to the cultivation of several highly profitable cannabis strains.

Two days after the crash, Roger was, by his own account, in the middle of "quality control" of one of his latest batches, lying on a recliner and gazing idly out through bay windows of the farmhouse at his garden. It was at this point that he noticed "a very unusual looking squirrel" raiding his bird feeder.

The squirrel was still there when he entered the garden half an hour later to refill the feeder. As he drew closer, he noticed that it appeared to be pregnant and completely unfazed by his proximity. He fed it directly from his fingers then reached out to stroke it.

Twenty minutes later, he found himself lying on his back in the centre of the garden, having just experienced one of the most profound and euphoric trips of his life.

None of us had any idea. I suppose that's where the scientific method falls down a little. Our contamination protocols were so rigorous, I don't think any of us had breathed the same air that surrounded the David corpse, let alone stroked its fur with our bare hands. The idea was unthinkable.

Oh sure, we'd studied the fur through a microscope, noticed that each follicle was hollow and filled with fluid, which had then been extracted for later analysis. We'd even noted the sharp needle-like points at the end of each hair, theorising that this was perhaps part of a defensive mechanism. But that was as far as it went. We'd had so many other wonders to ponder in the bodies before us.

Roger regained consciousness in the middle of his garden. There was no sign of the creature that had caused his trip anywhere near the bird feeder. Nevertheless, he went inside to find a suitable cage and some marigold gloves. The creature returned an hour later and was quite happy to be handled and placed in the cage.

It gave birth that night on Roger's dining room table. A litter of ten. Roger then made a phone call to Ian Legrand, his usual contact in the cannabis supply chain. Upon hearing Roger's tale of the narcotic squirrel, Mr Legrand assumed that he was either winding him up or tripping on something else. Either way, he saw no reason to hurry over and refused to visit any earlier than his scheduled day.

In the interim, Roger continued to provide food to the mother and her litter. He also began to remove his marigolds at regular intervals to stroke the mother through the bars of the cage. His later account of the highs he experienced are florid and verbose. Suffice it to say that the quality and strength of the euphoria did not appear to wane in the intervening days.

Ian Legrand visited the farm five days after the call. At Roger's insistence, he stroked one of the new litter and, after recovering from his trip, agreed to purchase one. Roger refused to sell him a breeding pair and Ian had to be satisfied with a single male, which he purchased for one hundred pounds.

The next part of the story unfortunately relies on speculation, as Ian Legrand's contacts higher in the cannabis chain remain unknown to us. However, we can reasonably assume that they fully realised the commercial possibilities of his new acquisition, mainly because of the team of heavily armed criminals that descended on the farm less than a day later, relieving Roger, at gunpoint, of his entire stock of creatures.

Within six weeks, police reports in both Manchester and Liverpool began to mention a new drug appearing on the streets. It took the form of a tiny square of what was initially taken to be fabric and was known by the street name of "mink".

They were breeding and skinning the creatures.

A few days later, a live specimen was taken in a drugs raid, along with several hundred squares of harvested fur. Photographs of this mystery creature were sent up the chain, and, at a certain point, happened to cross the desk of someone with sufficient clearance to have seen photographs from the crash site.

Within a few hours, the captured creature was in our lab and I was standing in the station that had recovered it.

Our rigid contamination protocols around the David corpse suddenly felt ridiculous. How many hundreds of people had already been exposed to either a living specimen or samples of its fur? Nevertheless, lacking any other ideas, we sterilised the areas of the police station where the creature had been stored. We also passed around the Official Secrets Act, made sure that any more creatures the police recovered would be sent our way, and set off back to our bunker.

I returned to discover that precious little new information had been gleaned from our live specimen. The animal behaviourists had tested the creature at length and concluded that, in terms of intelligence, it was slightly dumber than a cat. Frankly, after seeing footage of the tests, I thought they were being generous. When it wasn't eating or defecating, it seemed to spend most of its time staring off into the middle distance. Some half-hearted attempts had been made at communication, but it tried to eat any flash cards left in its cage.

I wondered if it was affected by the narcotic in its own fur. It would explain a lot.

The story finally broke in the media. The focus in the report was not the animals, but instead the squares of their fur - this new mystery drug sweeping the north. The MOD swept in with gagging orders, but the problem by this stage was too large to be brushed under the carpet. Mink squares were appearing everywhere, from nightclub toilets in Edinburgh to stockbroker parties as far south as London.

The creatures initially existed in something of a bizarre legal grey area. As aliens, their very existence was highly classified, yet they were now a common fixture in the illegal drug trade of the country. Ultimately, a very tightly worded bill was rushed through parliament, making possession of the creatures or derivatives thereof illegal, without mentioning their extra-terrestrial status at all.

A week after we received our first live specimen, we received four more, also recovered in a raid. Within a fortnight, we had seventeen of them. They kept coming at regular intervals until it got to the point that we were running out of room and they were diverted to other facilities.

It was around this time that we stopped calling them Davids. Having both male and female specimens, it didn't really scan anymore. Taking our cue from the drug dealers, we started calling them mink.

Given the speed with which the criminal underworld had managed to establish factory farming, we had our suspicions about the length of their breeding cycle. We sought permission to confirm this by allowing several of our pairs to breed. In normal circumstances, I've no doubt that request would have been denied, but common sense prevailed. We were playing catch-up, after all.

Our mink gestation period, from conception to birth, took roughly eight days. For comparison, a brown rat has a gestation period of twenty-two days. Our mink had litters of between six and eleven pups, significantly less than that of a rat, which can have litters of between eight and eighteen. However, the female brown rat reaches sexual maturity and is able to reproduce eleven weeks after birth.

Our mink reached sexual maturity within two weeks.

If those numbers don't terrify you then you're not paying attention.

They certainly terrified us. Given average litter size and an equal gender split, two mink could become one hundred and seventy in just over seven weeks.

Their potential for exponential growth was horrifying.

We passed our findings on, trying to stress the need for swift action, for containment, but it didn't really feel as though we had their full attention. Everyone we spoke to in the chain of command was much more concerned with our Goliath findings. Had we discovered any new weaknesses that the soldiers could exploit? Did we have any ideas about how it could have remained hidden for so long?

On one level, we understood their reticence to shift focus. I remember how powerless I felt, staring up at Goliath, impaled on its throne. We knew that teams of heavily armed soldiers were still regularly searching the woods around the crash site. We also saw, in a report not intended for our eyes, that high frequency radio transmissions of unknown origin had been picked up nearby. The hope was that the living Goliath was calling for help. The worry was that it was calling for reinforcements.

But we all felt that they were watching the wrong ball. We drafted strongly worded letters outlining the very real threat of a mink plague, delivered them in person and waited in vain for a response. Our final pints of the day at the King's Shilling rapidly turned into long maudlin drinking sessions punctuated with predictions of doom. We sarcastically toasted the future and waited for the other shoe to drop.

The flat bed of the lorry steadily rose up like a hinge as the hydraulics hissed. Pouring out, tumbling in a torrent, came thousands of tiny mink bodies. As soon as the lorry was empty, it rumbled away, flat bed descending back into place as it went, ready to receive another load. The bulldozer moved in, blade fully down as it scraped the pile into the new pit, freshly dug this morning, four feet deep and twenty feet long. It was already half-full of dead mink.

Parallel to this, dozens of other trenches were visible, staggered at regular intervals. Some were already blazing, billowing smoke. Others contained nothing but smouldering ash. The whole site was shrouded in smoke, the setting sun reduced to a pale orange disc.

I stood on a small hillock to one side, watching the operation. I was in full hazmat gear and felt like a tourist. None of the workers I could see had any protection beyond a cloth facemask.

Living mink were dotted here and there all over the site. Some were obvious survivors of the poison gas that had clawed their way out of the pits and seemed bewildered and close to death, twitching and trembling. Others were much more sprightly, no doubt locals. The workers ignored them as they busied themselves incinerating the creatures' brethren.

For their part, the healthy mink also seemed oblivious to what was happening. Some of them were drawn to the heat of the fires, basking like cats in their glow. A passing worker casually kicked one into the inferno. I tried to follow its progress but it was lost in fire. The nearby mink didn't even flinch.

The workers all moved with a practised efficiency, but there was a slump to their shoulders, a look of defeat in their eyes. I wondered how long they'd been working, how many thousands of mink they had burned.

I turned to my driver and we both climbed back into the jeep. Wordlessly, we drove out of the site, following the empty lorry back towards town.

It had all happened much as we predicted, and then some. Less than six months ago, we had all sat around in that beer garden predicting doom. And now that doom had arrived.

The collapse in the mink fur trade was the first domino. Our contacts in the police had informed us that, barely months old, it had been superseded by rival up-and-coming dealers breeding and selling live mink. The original gangs had avoided this, as it was such a short-sighted strategy - once a customer had a live mink, they never needed to contact their dealer ever again. But the short-term profit to be made was too tempting for some.

The animals were soon in the hands of the public, a dirty secret hidden in sheds, garages and attics all over the country. Like any other pet, they could now be abandoned or escape, and their phenomenally short breeding cycle came as a shock to many. Cardboard boxes full of mink pups began appearing in lay-bys and, in short order, in woods and fields up and down the country.

Taking their cue from the British government, possession of mink had been made a criminal offence in most countries. Customs forces were vigilant, doing what they could to stop the spread of both the drug and the creature. It didn't matter.

Squares of mink were soon reported on both the continent and in the US. They were lagging slightly behind us, but they soon caught up, as the trade in live creatures lead to their escape and proliferation.

After that, it was just a matter of brutal mathematics to bring us here.

The wheat field had been stripped bare. The road bisecting it was alive with the creatures, but most of them scattered in our headlights. Others just blankly stared at the jeep until we ran them down.

We reached the outskirts of town as night fell. Workers were shovelling dead mink from the foot of an electric fence. They stopped and watched us as we passed. We were waved in through a high metal gate and drove over a cattle grid covered in electrified mesh.

The streets were deserted, evacuated before the extermination crews moved in. Each house we passed inside the fence had a sign on the door proclaiming that it had been cleared of mink. Some of the windows were still sealed with hazard tape.

The crews were expanding the fence as they cleared. We could see them working within a second cordon, huge plastic tents covering each house as they pumped in the gas. Other teams were conducting controlled burns of gardens and verges, or shovelling dead mink into piles, which a JCB would then scoop into the back of a lorry.

I wondered about the man hours all this was taking, the cost to keep the fences running.

Thank God they didn't burrow.

It's possible we could have come back from this. If it was just their breeding cycle to contend with, maybe we could have prevailed. But that isn't what finally brought us low.

There was a clue hidden in plain sight, in the police report concerning the very first man to encounter the mink, Roger Twitchell. The marijuana farmer who found what he took to be a pregnant squirrel on his bird feeder.

The summation of the police report mentions armed criminals forcibly taking his stock of mink at gunpoint. But if you read the full report, as I have, you discover that that isn't exactly what happened.

He fought them.

Even though they were armed and he wasn't, he fought them. So they shot him in the leg. Then he got up and tried to fight them again. So they broke three of his ribs and one of his arms. He kept coming. And, lest you should be tempted to read this as some misguided altruistic attempt to save the lives of those poor mink, by his own account it was nothing of the sort.

They were taking his drugs away and he really didn't want that to happen.

Remember, this is after just six days of exposure, six days of contact high from their fur. After which a man without so much as a criminal record, let alone one for violence, was prepared to blindly rush into battle with no thought for his own safety, all in the name of safeguarding his next fix.

Understand, by necessity, what follows is all anecdotal evidence. It would have been nice to have the luxury of a long peer-reviewed study, with test subjects and control groups, but things went south too quickly for that to ever be an option.

Here are the facts as we came to understand them.

The drug dose delivered from a square of the minks' fur was reasonably addictive, seemingly on a par with cocaine. However, a dose from the fur of the living animal had a level of addictiveness for which we simply had no comparison.

It varied from person to person, but it seemed that around sixty to seventy per cent of people would be addicted after just one hit. Craving for a new hit would occur approximately an hour later. During that time, the addict often felt compelled to do nothing at all but wait beside their mink. All other desires could well leave them. There appeared to be a component of the drug that actively suppressed normal, rational thought in the period between highs. We read shocking reports of emaciated addicts starving to death only feet away from fridges full of food.

All of this paints a very grim picture for the risk-takers who chose to get high using the mink. But there were thousands of people who became unwitting addicts. It's worth remembering that these were creatures that appeared to have no natural fear of humans. They would happily approach anyone they saw and allow themselves to be stroked. With our woods, hedgerows and soon even our parks and gardens rapidly filling up with them, accidental addiction became a very real possibility.

As soon as the true measure of the hazard was appreciated, public service warnings were made, alerting people to avoid the creatures, to cover their skin, their hands, their legs.

All too little, all too late.

Social media was overflowing with heartbreaking stories, tragic litanies of accidental addicts. Dog walkers in parks, ramblers, outdoor workers, parents confiscating mink from their teenage children. All now addicted and inseparable from their living fix.

We drove on through the deserted streets, our headlights picking out looted shops, burned-out cars. Things collapsing. The only other intact vehicle in sight was an ambulance and, lacking any other destination, we headed towards it. It was parked beside a bungalow with peeling paint and blankets over the windows instead of curtains.

Two dead-eyed medics were wheeling out a body bag strapped to a gurney. I hoped they were dead before the gas was pumped in, but I doubted it. More likely, they hid from the exterminators as they searched, ignoring their calls and warnings. Anything but surrender their mink. Surrender their high.

We drove past the ambulance without slowing down. We reached the perimeter fence, turned and drove along it. We were soon approaching the original gate. Just before we reached it, all the street lights went out. Another power cut. A shout went up and we heard diesel generators kick into life.

The fence was still on. For now.

We passed out of the gate and headed back towards the bunker.

The number of people addicted to mink worldwide was very hard to estimate. Accurate statistics were hardly a priority in a global crisis, but for every addict there would be families whose lives were massively disrupted as they struggled to care for these new strangers in their midst. The ripple effects were incalculable.

Power cuts were becoming more and more common. There was some debate as to their cause. The idea that a huge amount of power station staff - far above the normal percentage - had become addicted, seemed unlikely. One theory was that the problem wasn't the plants themselves but the infrastructure, the power lines and substations, all of which required maintenance from engineers in the field, who would have been exposed to the first wave of mink before warnings had been issued.

Whatever the reasons, every time the lights went out, I found myself counting the seconds until they came on again. And every time, the number I reached was higher.

I asked my driver to drop me off at the King's Shilling. I had nothing useful to report to my MOD paymasters. My little fact-finding mission had uncovered nothing that we didn't already know. Besides, I seriously doubted they'd even noticed my absence. The focus within the bunker had totally shifted to any and all methods of destroying the mink. Pathogen and viral specialists now prowled the corridors, discussing myxomatosis and contagious sterility. Labs that had been taken up with cute little side projects, like observing mink sleep cycles, were now devoted to their extinction.

I ordered a pint of bitter and, as I entered the beer garden, discovered that I was not the only scientist taking refuge there. Haskins was around forty, lithe and dressed in a hooded top and combat trousers. I'd never seen him in anything else and I understood that he liked free climbing in his spare time. That was the limit of my knowledge about the man.

My path had not crossed with his often, as his specialism was 3D simulations of things, such as the crash trajectory of the UFO. As I understood it, his most recent project had been an attempt to create a computer simulation of Goliath's gait, based upon the muscular and skeletal data we had gleaned.

I nodded hello and was going to take a different table, but he beckoned me over as though we were old friends. As soon as I sat down, it became abundantly clear that he was morbidly drunk. I attempted to excuse myself, but he was having none of it. He plainly needed to unburden himself to someone and I was to be the unlucky recipient. Much of what he was saying seemed to centre around the Goliath simulation, which apparently couldn't be made to work. I offered a couple of platitudes about teamwork and believing in yourself, but he seemed determined to self-flagellate so I tuned him out.

It was then that I noticed the mink. It was sitting in a copse of trees around twenty feet away, staring blankly into the middle distance.

It shouldn't have been there at all. Our little fake town was one of the first to fence itself off. It had been assumed that a house-to-house search was unnecessary, given our usual level of security. It seemed that that assumption had been a little premature. Someone would have to be alerted.

I stood and was about to make my excuses, but Haskins didn't even pause in his flow. He wasn't even facing me anymore, looking off to one side, eyes unfocussed, rambling something about the bones of the dead Goliath. Apparently, he'd been sent incorrect figures for the creature's bone density from another department and they totally broke his simulation. The numbers were so low that its skeleton wouldn't have been able to support its weight in Earth's gravity. Someone had obviously screwed up somewhere.

I walked towards the mink. I would have to pass it on my way to the bar anyway. I wanted to see if it was alone. I noticed that it appeared to be using a twig to scratch in the dirt, which was unusual but not unprecedented. Tool use had been witnessed in mink if food was at stake, when their problem-solving abilities seemed to suddenly improve. They had been observed using rocks to rip open garbage bags.

As I walked over, something about Haskins' words began to trouble me. The bone density figures would have been checked and rechecked before they left that department. And even if the incorrect figures were sent, alerting them and obtaining the true figures would have taken one phone call. But Haskins was behaving as though the sky was falling. Drinking like a man trying to forget.

The mink appeared to be gouging a series of small trenches into the earth. Perhaps in search of worms. Something about the shape of the trenches rang a bell.

A slow feeling of dread began to settle in my gut.

I knew why Haskins was drinking. I knew what he'd figured out.

The bone density figures had been accurate. A living Goliath couldn't even stand erect on Earth without breaking his legs. Which begged the question: what had been hiding in the woods? What had we been searching for all these months?

I realised what the mink had been gouging in the mud with its stick and it all fell sickeningly into place. A crashed UFO that had been nothing of the sort. A dead giant that had never even lived, designed and built by committee to do nothing but fill us with fear and distract us from the real threat until it was too late.

The mink paused in its work and looked directly at me with a steady calculating gaze, the pretence of stupidity finally dropped. They had won. There was no longer any need for subterfuge or deception. And, as a final twist of the knife, they wanted to show us exactly how easily we were fooled.

Because there, carved into the soft earth, was a perfect replica of the huge Goliath footprints that had led humanity off the cliff.

The power cut out again and the lights in the beer garden flickered and died.

I stood in the darkness, counting.

Trolley Dash

THE last thing Suki's father ever said to her was: "Stay out of sight."

Then he went out to face the looters, who killed him.

They didn't do it immediately, though. They questioned him for a little while. Suki couldn't hear all of it, just the odd word echoing around the car park. Her father was talking the loudest and Suki was certain it was for her benefit. He lied, said he was alone and asked if they had room for him in their group. He didn't sound like her father. He was putting on an act, pretending to be a weak, wheedling man. A man who was no threat to anyone.

Thinking about it later, Suki wondered if his act had worked too well. If they'd believed his act of being no threat to them, and therefore of no use either.

Suki heard a crunching of glass below her. A couple of the looters searching the supermarket. Would they be able to guess where she was? Was this hiding place theirs? She did her best to stay still and quiet and soon heard the footsteps move back outside.

"Anyone else?" said the leader.

"Dead bloke in the back. Been dead a while," came the reply.

A short while later, there was a noise like something heavy being dropped and a cruel laugh went up from the group. Her father stopped talking. Then the truck's engine started up and

Suki heard it driving away.

Suki tried to imagine that her father had been allowed to join the group. That he was going to sneak back later with food and water that he'd stolen from them. She took comfort in that idea for a little while, but she knew she was lying to herself. She knew what the noise she'd heard meant and what she would see if she came out of hiding and looked out into the car park.

She waited until an hour had passed then lowered herself down from her hiding place above the shelves. She walked carefully to the front of the supermarket, trying to avoid the broken glass. Even before she reached the windows, she could see her father's body. It was around fifty feet away, near the jumble of trolleys and the burned-out car. He was lying facedown with a dark stain on his blue shirt. His coat was missing. They must have taken it, thought Suki.

It was a big risk, but Suki had to be sure. She walked carefully out through the sliding door with no glass in it and hurried to her father's side. If her father had still been alive, Suki didn't know what she would have done. There were no hospitals or ambulances to call anymore. But her father's face was whiter than she'd ever seen it and his eyes were open and staring, which Suki knew meant you were really dead. He was lying in a large puddle of blood that already had a film of dust on it.

Suki ran back inside the supermarket, climbed back up into her new hiding place and thought about what to do next.

Looters had totally emptied the supermarket. Suki and her father had searched it when they first got there. Every tin, every bottle, every packet had gone. All they'd really left were the adverts for things that weren't there anymore, that would never be there again. Big cardboard cutouts of smiling people enjoying food.

Suki could understand why the food had been taken, and the books and magazines too. You didn't need electricity to read. But they'd taken all the blu-rays and games too. Her father said that maybe the electricity would come back one day, and when that happened the looters could play the blu-rays or sell them.

As her father had said all that, Suki had been looking right at him. She could tell that he didn't believe it. It was another lie to protect her. Suki wondered when she'd first started noticing them.

Probably the morning after Geraldine hit.

Geraldine was the name of the asteroid that had ended the world. For a while, the news had said that Geraldine was going to just miss the Earth, but there would be pretty lights in the night sky. Suki had got excited at the idea. Katie Donaldson at school said her brother had a telescope and that Suki could come round and watch.

Then the news realised they'd got it wrong and it was going to hit after all. The messages on the news got very serious. Geraldine was over a kilometre wide, which didn't sound very big to Suki. She'd walked over a kilometre across the South Downs many times. But her father explained that it was travelling so fast that it would make a massive crater and throw up a lot of dirt, high in the air. So much dirt that it would blot out the sun for a long time. And that was why people were so worried.

It was due to crash somewhere in China called Ordos, which was over seven and a half thousand kilometres away, as the crow flies, which is less than by roads. Suki looked it up on the internet.

When Geraldine was due to hit, Suki's father made them both go into the cellar and lay under a mattress, with earplugs in. Suki could still hear the noise through her earplugs. It was like the loudest thunder in the world. They stayed down in the cellar for the whole night because the sound was travelling around the world, over and over. Every time it came back, it was quieter, but it was still loud enough to make Suki jump.

When they came out in the morning, all their windows were broken, but so were everybody else's. Her father made a joke about it being good business for glazers. Suki asked him when they were going to get them fixed. Her father said he was sure they'd get round to it eventually, but Suki could tell he didn't believe that.

That was the first time Suki realised her father was lying to protect her.

He spent the morning dismantling the garden decking to turn it into boards to cover the windows, measuring and sawing and nailing. Suki helped, carrying the planks into the house.

Mrs Curran, from two doors down, asked if Suki's father could help her board up her windows too.

He replied, "If you can find me the wood. This is barely enough for us."

Mrs Curran watched them for a long time. Then she started to walk back to her house. Suki could tell from her shoulders that she was crying. Suki knew she lived alone. She probably didn't even own a saw.

Once the house was secure, Suki's father went out to try and get food. He came back an hour later with nothing. He said that the supermarket was closed, but he had a new cut on his knuckle. They started rationing the food they had, but her father always made sure that Suki ate more than him. Even so, Suki was always hungry. They also filled every pot and pan and bucket with water, "just in case".

The TV seemed to be just news now. Any channel that wasn't felt wrong. Some channels were showing comedies full of people laughing. Suki thought: I can tell this is in the past. They don't know what's coming, none of them. They wouldn't be laughing if they did.

The dirt and dust caused by Geraldine was in a huge cloud moving slowly around the world. Within a couple of weeks it had reached them. Days were always dim now, the sky a dirty yellow. You could look right at the sun and it didn't hurt anymore.

The news said that the cloud would be around for years. That it would kill crops. That there wasn't enough food in storage. People were getting angry, asking why governments hadn't planned for this. There were films of riots, all looking weird because of the yellow sky.

One morning, Suki woke up and her father was emptying the freezer because the power was off.

It never came on again.

The water turned brown in the taps then stopped. They

started drinking from the pots and pans.

And every day they had less and less food.

A month after the power went off, Suki's father woke her in the middle of the night pointing the wind-up torch. He told her to get dressed because they had to leave. Suki had a lot of questions, but her father told her she had to be quiet. He said they were in danger.

They left through the back door and went down the garden to the back gate. They had two rucksacks filled with all the food and water they had left. It wasn't much at all.

Suki could see that some of the other houses on the road were on fire. She wondered if that was the danger, if the fire was going to spread all the way to their house. But then she heard people laughing on the road. The sound of a truck engine. Someone singing.

Suki's father told her later that he'd spotted looters going from house to house, breaking down doors, taking whatever they wanted, then burning down the houses. Bad people with no police to stop them.

They hid in the back garden of a house on Yarrow Road, which backed on to theirs. Suki had been in this garden before, maybe a year ago, to get a rounders ball back. Her father had come with her, which embarrassed her.

She remembered the man who lived here was fat and friendly and had started listing famous cricketers from the past, even though they'd been playing rounders. Her father had nodded and smiled, but Suki didn't recognise any of the names. Suki wondered if the man was still inside. All his windows were still broken.

They crouched in the damp grass, listening. Ten minutes later, they heard someone break down their front door. Even though they weren't inside, Suki still felt scared. Twenty minutes after that, she could see the flickering orange of fire through the cracks in their window boards.

They watched their house burn down as dawn broke.

They had a small breakfast in the garden, then, once it was

light enough to not use torches, they headed towards town. Her father still had keys to his offices. Maybe they could hide there.

Suki wanted to ask him if there was any food there, but didn't say anything.

On the way into town, they saw three bodies. One in a ditch, one in a car and one in the middle of the road. Suki's father told her not to look at any of them.

There was dust over everything, which her father said was either bits of Geraldine or from the crater in China. Suki was too hungry and scared to find it interesting.

There were also lots of cars blocking roads, like barricades. One sign said: "LOOTERS KEEP OUT - THIS ROAD HAS GUNS."

They nearly went right past the supermarket. Even from the road, they could see the shelves were empty, but Suki badgered her father to go in. Maybe there was some small bit of food in there, something the looters had missed. So they went inside and searched it - but, as they feared, everything had gone.

Suki thought the stock room smelt of rotting food, but it was a body, lying in the corner, face grey and blotchy. He was wearing the uniform of the store. Suki wondered if looters had killed him.

Suki's father said they should leave.

They were just about to go when Suki spotted something on top of one of the shelves. They couldn't see what it was from the ground. Her father started climbing the shelves but they started to creak and wobble. He was too heavy, so Suki climbed up instead.

Her dad handed her the wind-up torch so she could see what it was.

It was a rat trap.

Suki was about to come down, but she noticed there were faint footprints on top of the shelves. Someone else had been up there. Her father said she could follow the footprints, but they stopped after a while. Suki thought the person must have climbed down, but then she noticed a grille on the wall. She shone the torch through and could see a narrow gap between the breeze block walls. When she tilted her torch down, she saw a sleeping bag and some clothing. Someone had built a little person-nest in the gap.

Suki pulled at the grille and it hinged open. She climbed in and searched the space. There was a rucksack full of newspapers, a pile of clothing, another wind-up torch, some toilet roll and a few packets of mints. But no real food.

It was a good hiding spot, but it was somebody else's. Maybe they'd be coming back soon.

Maybe they should leave.

Suki was about to climb down when they heard the truck pull into the parking lot.

Both Suki and her father froze. Suki turned off the torch.

They could hear voices. Were they going to come in? Was this the same people who burned down their house?

Suki's father could have climbed the shelves, but they might have collapsed, might have made noise. Instead, he took off his rucksack, handed it up to Suki and said, "Stay out of sight."

Then he went outside to die.

Suki spent three days in her new hiding spot. It didn't exactly feel safe, but it was a much better option than outside. Anyone coming into the supermarket would have to step on broken glass, which she felt sure she would hear. The new sleeping bag smelled of old sweat, but it was warm at least.

She worried at first that whoever had left the footprints might return, but then she thought to check the shoes of the dead man in the stock room. They looked about the same size as the prints on the shelf and had the same pattern. She could have made sure, but couldn't bring herself to pull a shoe from the corpse to compare. She dusted the prints away and threw the rat trap into a corner so that no one could follow the same clues to find her.

She cried a lot on the first day, for her father and, if she was honest, for herself.

She was hungry all the time now. She'd doubled her rations, taking her father's share, but it didn't really make any difference. A lot of what was left didn't really classify as food in her mind:

stock cubes, flour, hard uncooked pasta. All of which made her even more thirsty.

She began to sleep a lot, losing track of time, becoming confused as to whether it was day or night. Now, even at midday, the sun was little more than a dim candle in the sky.

She didn't know what she was going to do when her food and water ran out.

There was a small message scratched on to the bricks within the hiding space. Suki only spotted it on the second day. It read *"The needle skips here."* Suki assumed that the dead man had made it. It reminded her of the phrase "The buck stops here." It had the same rhythm.

She wasn't sure what either of the phrases meant.

She tried to read to fill her time. Her rucksack had been packed in a hurry and still had some old homework and a book in it. It was one of her favourites, *The Gibbous Gate*, the story of a brave girl lost in a haunted mansion. The problem was she knew the book too well. It felt like a lot of effort to wind up a torch to read something so familiar.

She ended up turning to the rucksack full of newspapers collected by the dead man. It was boring adult stuff, but at least it was new. She understood most of the words, but she got angry reading about people arguing over petty things that didn't even exist anymore. Political parties and conferences and debates. She wanted to shake them all and tell them they were wasting time.

Most of the papers mentioned Geraldine somewhere. They were mainly papers from a time just before people realised the full danger, meaning the articles were small and hidden deep inside. There were a few papers near the bottom of the pile with front page headlines from after the danger was realised: "ASTEROID WILL HIT" and "NUCLEAR WINTER WARNINGS". There were neat little illustrations of the predicted impact zone and dust cloud to follow. Suki wondered about the person that drew them. Did they realise it would be their last job? Did they have tears in their eyes as they drew?

Suki drifted in and out of sleep. Once or twice, she awoke with a start, convinced that she'd heard glass crunching, that someone had come into the supermarket. But then an hour would pass with her listening intently and she'd decide that it had been a dream.

One morning, she awoke shivering. The temperature had dropped overnight to the point where her breath formed clouds in front of her. Her father had said that the dust blocking sunlight would cause the world to cool eventually, but she didn't think it would happen so soon.

She emerged from the hatch intending to go to the toilet in the stock room, but then stopped when she saw what had happened to the car park.

Overnight, a massive quantity of dust had settled over everything, in some places a foot or two deep. It looked like the town was now in the middle of a desert, with sweeping drifts of dust gathering against walls and in corners.

She could no longer see her father's body.

Something else was different, but at first she couldn't figure out what it was. Eventually, she realised that no birds were singing.

She looked out into the car park for a long time, then went into the stock room to pee.

She'd been going in the opposite corner to the dead man, which made her feel brave, but she always had to point her torch at him. She couldn't go with his corpse hidden by darkness. She kept worrying he might move, which she knew was silly, but she had to watch him anyway. As a result, she'd begun to track his gradual decay over the days: his lips pulling back from his teeth, his cheeks hollowing.

Today when she entered the stock room, she thought someone had stolen the body and left the clothes behind, an idea that scared her more than any corpse. But, as she drew closer, she realised that the body was still there, it had just withered and shrivelled, shrinking down within the uniform. His eyes had gone, the hollows of the sockets exposed, the skin now like leather, tight over the bones. He still smelled, but now it was less offensive, more like a compost heap.

She kept her torch pointed at him as she peed, thinking about how much he'd changed overnight, then returned to the hiding spot. She stuffed newspaper inside her clothes to keep out the cold and worked out her rations. She estimated that she had four days left before the rucksacks were totally empty.

Two days later, she awoke to find most of the dust had gone.

She assumed there had been some great unheard wind in the night that had blown it all away. It was also a lot warmer, the same wind presumably clearing a path for a bit of sunshine to get through.

Then she saw the body in the stock room and realised that wasn't what had happened at all.

He was still dead, plainly, but his flesh had all now returned. His face was plump, his eyes back in his sockets. It was hard to gauge, but he looked and smelled much as he had the first time she'd seen him.

Suki returned to the hiding place and thought for a very long time.

Suki knew what vinyl records were because Jane Wilton's dad had owned a record player. Suki and Jane had spent an afternoon playing old records and dancing and laughing in her lounge. She also knew that knocking the record player would cause the needle to jump out of the groove and the song to skip a little, like fast forwarding a song on a mobile.

The needle skips here.

The message scratched into the wall of the hiding place. A clue to what was happening.

The first time the needle had skipped, it had jumped ahead to a time when the dust was deep, when the birds had all died and the body in the stock room had almost rotted away.

Then, last night, the needle had skipped again. Back to a time when there was very little dust and the body was back as before.

Suki knew what time travel was. There were plenty of kids' books and shows featuring it in some form. Even Harry Potter had it in one book, she seemed to remember. She supposed it had just never really interested her as an idea. History, for the most part, she found quite boring and, by most accounts, was a lot smellier than now, so going back to see it held no appeal. Similarly, the future in kids' stories always seemed to be full of aliens or robots, both of which appealed to her even less than time travel.

But it was happening to her now. It had happened twice already. Part of her found the idea ridiculous, but whichever way she turned the facts in her mind, she came to the same conclusion.

The needle was skipping.

It was happening. It was real.

And, amazing though it was, she was still starving to death.

She was so hungry and weak, she was finding it hard to think, but one thing was clear - all the versions of the supermarket she'd seen so far were of no use to her at all. Slightly different details but the same empty shop with more or less sunshine, more or less dust. But no food at all.

What she really needed was a thriving supermarket, back how it used to be before Geraldine. She imagined awaking to that scene. Lights back on, aisles full of produce. Just picturing it made her mouth water.

Was there any reason that couldn't happen?

The needle, or whatever you wanted to call it, had already jumped forward then back again, months at a time. Surely there was no reason it couldn't jump back even further, to a supermarket that could actually help her.

She knew it was wishful thinking, but she was desperate. She decided to behave as if this impossible, wonderful dream was definitely going to happen.

She walked through the shop, reading the signs at the end of each empty aisle. Where would she go first? The sensible answer was tins, maybe tinned fish and then bottled water. But all Suki could think about was chocolate. It felt so long since she'd eaten any.

She abruptly realised that her hunger was blinding her to

other possibilities. If she actually did find herself in a full
supermarket with lights and shoppers, wouldn't that mean that
her father was alive again?

Couldn't she just run home and warn him?

Or would the needle skip again before she got there, and drag
her back to a dead world? She didn't know any of the rules, that
was the problem.

As a compromise, she decided that if the jump into the past
actually did happen, she would try to warn her father, but only
once she had a full rucksack of food on her back.

Just in case.

With this decided, Suki began to plan in earnest for the
needle skip that might save her life. It felt a little like madness,
training for something that felt so unlikely. Nevertheless, she
began to memorise the layout of the shop and plan a route
between all the aisles she wanted to visit. Tinned goods, aisle
three. Bottled water, aisle twelve. Crisps and nuts, aisle five, facing
sweets and chocolate, aisle six. She also started wearing an empty
rucksack at all times. She didn't want to waste any time at all if it
happened.

The next two days passed in a woozy delirium of desperate
hope. By the time she washed down her last mouthful of food she
not only knew the product types and numbers of every aisle, but
a good percentage of the product names on the shelves. She was
as ready as she would ever be. It had to happen now.

Three more days passed.

Suki had just under a pint of water left. Her father had told
her once that you could live for weeks without food but only days
without water. She was trying to ration herself to a couple of
swigs a day. Headaches were almost constant. She drifted in and
out of consciousness. Every now and again, she would emerge
from the hiding place and walk like a zombie around the route
she had planned, imagining all the food she would take.

There was a voice in the back of her head telling her that this
was all pointless. That she had wasted what little food and time
she had hoping for an impossible dream. That she should have
tried to go somewhere else while she still could.

But it was too late now. She barely had the energy to climb up and down the shelves to get in and out of the hiding place anymore.

Either the needle would save her, or she would die here.

The next day, the needle skipped again.

For the first time, Suki was down in the supermarket when it happened. She was mindlessly shuffling down her favourite aisles, mumbling the names printed on shelves of food that she was gradually coming to accept she would never see again.

She felt a pressure in her ears followed by nausea. She closed her eyes and staggered, holding on to a shelf for support. The feeling passed and she was about to dismiss it as just another symptom of her starvation when she glanced out into the car park.

The dust was back in force.

Perhaps even deeper than before. The buildings beyond seemed to have crumbled under the weight, sharp fingers of metal girders raking the dirty yellow sky.

Suki almost laughed at the sight.

She was further from food than she'd ever been. The needle mocking her. Proving it could take her far away in time, just not in the direction she needed.

How far in the future was she? Months? Years? Was anyone still alive?

She walked out to stand just inside the shattered doorway, looking out at the silent landscape. Maybe she should just give up. Walk out into this dead future, trudge back to the blackened ruins of her house and die there. Something about that felt more appealing than wasting away here, waiting for a miracle that would never come.

She even took a step out of the building, her first since the day she arrived. She stared down at her trainer as it sank down into the dust. It would be so easy to just keep walking. Another step, then another, all the way home.

She turned to look back into the supermarket. Was it to say goodbye? She was certain she had heard no noise, but whatever the reason, she turned and viewed the empty shop, the passing of time visible even here. A couple of shelves near the back had collapsed, and others were sagging, brackets visibly rusted. Elsewhere…

Suki froze and looked back at the central aisle.

Halfway down it, there was a dog.

It was totally motionless, staring at Suki with unnerving focus. One eye was a milky cataract, a full moon glinting in the darkness of the aisles. The breed she couldn't guess at. Something tall and rangy, maybe a greyhound mix. Most of its fur had gone, its skin a mass of scars, speaking of a multitude of unseen fights. It was also plainly starving to death, with deep gaps between its ribs and a pelvis in clear outline through its skin.

The idea that this had ever been someone's pet seemed laughable.

Suki felt as though she were facing the final survivor of some vast unseen competition for survival. In its wake, hundreds of desperate starving people, all now gnawed bones.

They stared at each other for a long moment. Suki had the primal instinct to flee out into the car park, but knew that the dog would be on her back in moments.

Her only chance was to get back inside and somehow climb up out of reach, but between Suki and the shelves were thirty feet of parallel cash registers and bare tiles.

How fast could she run thirty feet?

How fast could the dog?

She pictured running in her mind's eye, reaching the shelves in time, maybe even climbing up a little.

Just before the dog's jaws clamped around her ankle.

The only thing in her favour was the fact that the dog was down an aisle. If Suki took a few steps to her left she would be out of its eyeline.

She reached into her pocket for one of the wind-up torches.

And ran.

Firstly, she sprinted to her left, losing sight of the dog almost immediately. She heard its claws clacking on the tiles as it began to race towards her. Suki darted down behind one of the checkout counters, simultaneously throwing the torch down the aisle facing her.

She heard a satisfying clatter as the torch bounced down the aisle. A second later, she watched the dog fly past, slamming into the shelves as it skidded on the turn. She had seconds before it realised its mistake.

Suki kept low and scurried along the back of the checkout counters, then headed down the aisle nearest the wall. She could hear her own heartbeat pulsing in her ears. She began to climb the shelves.

Two steps up, she began to feel dizzy.

She knew that passing out now would mean death. She forced herself to hold on, pushing through the nausea to keep climbing. Almost there. She closed her eyes with the exertion.

When she opened them again, everything was white.

All the lights in the supermarket were on. She was halfway up a shelf filled with packets of pulses and beans, spilling and toppling around her as she climbed. She looked numbly around.

The supermarket was full of food.

The needle had saved her. Finally.

Suki was still shaking from the chase with the dog, but told herself it couldn't hurt her anymore. It was trapped months, maybe years in the future. It had been the final guardian she needed to face before the needle would let her through to her reward.

She re-examined her last thought and realised it was nonsense.

She was becoming delirious.

She forced herself to climb down from the shelf and took a deep breath. She'd trained for this. She was almost spent, but this was the opportunity she'd been waiting for. She gathered her last reserves of energy and mentally called up her map of the supermarket. She realised that she hadn't even planned to visit this aisle.

She stumbled to the registers, already removing the rucksack from her back. The front doors were intact, metal shutters pulled down. It felt like night time. Suki hadn't heard a sound to indicate that anyone else was in the building.

She hurried to aisle three, tinned goods. Enough food to feed her for months, years. She began to methodically pile tins inside the rucksack. Beans, spaghetti, tuna. Within a minute it was already a struggle to carry it.

She hadn't thought about weight at all. Stupid.

Some of the tins made her pause. Brands she knew well, but something about the typefaces felt wrong. Off somehow. What did that mean? She forced herself to ignore them. There was no time for mysteries. She didn't know how long she had.

Next, bottled water, aisle twelve.

She hefted the rucksack onto her shoulder by one strap and stumbled to the end of the aisle, off balance. There was usually a cardboard stand there, cartoon rabbits advertising an animated film called *The Hutch Bunch*. Today it had gone, replaced by a pyramid of gravy tins. Next to that was a cardboard cutout of a mother type with a Princess Diana hairstyle pouring the gravy.

So this was a time before *The Hutch Bunch*. That was all it meant. But how far before? The gravy woman's clothing did look very old-fashioned. Suki wanted to say from 2000.

She decided she didn't really care. As long as she could still eat the food.

She hurried past the gravy pyramid and had a moment to register a snarling blur of motion as the dog leapt, its momentum knocking her sprawling on to her back.

Suki struggled to get away, but the dog's jaws were locked on to her, its head thrashing back and forth. Suki was screaming, close enough to smell the decay on its breath, the stench of pus in badly healed wounds. In the midst of her terror, she felt a flicker of indignation. The dog had travelled with her! How was that fair?

But she felt no pain. She realised that the rucksack had saved her for the moment, the dog's teeth tearing and gouging through the fabric and padding. Tins bounced and rolled as it thrashed on top of her.

Suki mourned the loss of her bounty but let the rucksack go, wriggling free of the strap and rolling to one side. She scrabbled to her feet.

The dog realised something was amiss almost immediately. It had not survived this long through dumb luck. It ceased its attack on the rucksack and propelled itself towards Suki. She had begun to run but turned, tried to kick it and failed as it was already leaping.

Its jaws locked around Suki's upper arm and she fell again.

She felt pain then as the teeth took hold and the dog began to wrench it's head back and forth, tearing into her sleeve and arm. The warm wetness of her blood soaking through. She became aware that she was screaming as she punched the dog in the face over and over with her free hand, but it felt as though she were watching another person.

It wouldn't let go. She was going to die.

She felt dizzy but this time recognised it for what it was.

The needle was about to jump again.

A lucky blow hit the dog in the eye and it yelped, releasing its hold and backing away, but it was immediately tensing for another leap.

Then the lights all died, the supermarket winking out of existence.

Half an hour later, Nigel Dremmel stood in the very same aisle, confused.

He'd been awoken at 3 am by an alert from the silent alarm indicating that motion had been detected inside the store. Nine times out of ten, this was down to a trapped bird or the like, especially seeing as none of the alarms on the outer doors or windows had been triggered. The last time this happened, he turned over and went back to sleep, only to wake up to a written warning.

So this time he duly dressed, cursing under his breath as he did so, and drove to the supermarket only to discover what appeared to be evidence of a robbery in progress. A grimy rucksack half-full of tins abandoned next to evidence of a scuffle and - was that blood?

He locked himself in the office, called the police and rewound the CCTV.

Suki had never really thought about visiting the monument.

It had been part of her local landscape since the day she was born and if she thought about it at all, it was in terms of traffic problems it could cause on certain days, or the annoying tourists it attracted.

It had always been there - right on their doorstep, less than a mile from their house - which was probably the reason why it had never appealed. They could have gone at any time, which made the whole thing seem a little commonplace. It felt more like a direction you would give someone - *turn right at the monument and keep driving* - than somewhere you would actually visit.

But it had been all over the news in the run-up to G Day, which made it seem kind of cool again. So, one lazy Saturday morning, long after the hubbub had died down and the visitor numbers had dwindled, her father put down his tablet and announced that he'd bought tickets and that they were finally going. So they did.

They walked there, of course, although there was a huge car park. They took photos of the Traveller statue and looked at all the artefacts in the visitor centre. Suki's father even badgered her into doing all the lame interactive sections with him, which made them both laugh. Then they browsed the gift shop and had lunch in the restaurant, where Suki had banoffee pie.

Suki knew most of the story already. Everyone got taught it in school, which was probably why she found it all a little dull. Someone worked out that more people had seen footage of the Traveller on YouTube than had watched the moon landing. Suki had even watched the unedited version with the full dog fight, although her father said she was way too young and told her off when he found out.

They had the same CCTV clip on a loop in a cinema in the visitor centre. The scary bits had been edited out, but it was kind of cool to see it on a big screen. So, Suki and her father sat together and watched the Traveller arrive from the future, fill their rucksack with food from the supermarket before fighting the dog and disappearing.

Even on a big screen, the resolution was terrible. The cameras in the supermarket thirty years ago had been pretty bad. Even if the Traveller hadn't been wearing a hood on his coat, Suki thought his face would have been about three pixels wide.

Or her face. No one was really sure.

They were definitely a child, though. That was what the experts said, although Suki thought it was pretty obvious. When she first heard the story, she'd liked it because it was about a child who did something incredible, even though they didn't mean to. It made her feel that she might do something incredible one day too.

In a glass case next to the cinema, they had the original ripped newspaper pages from the future that had fallen from the Traveller's jacket in the dog attack. The theory was they'd been using it for insulation. The fact that there was enough information on those pages to warn the future about Geraldine was pure luck.

Another lucky piece of the puzzle was the security guard at the supermarket who checked the CCTV and recovered the newspaper pieces. They had a grainy interview with him looking awkward and proud, but Suki and her father only watched the beginning of that.

There were other sections in the visitor centre covering the Geraldine space missions and the technology used to adjust the asteroid's course, but Suki and her father skipped all that too. The news had been full of the same footage on G Day (the day the asteroid should have hit Earth, but didn't).

Suki's favourite bit of all was the actual supermarket, of course. There was a glass-walled corridor leading visitors through the aisles and an echoey recording recounting the story. Again. They had dummy empty boxes on all the shelves identical to those from the day.

The section where the Traveller and the dog had disappeared were walled off, though. The recording explained that there was a medical team on twenty-four-hour stand by to tend to the Traveller's wounds, if and when they ever came back. They didn't mention what they'd do if the dog returned.

Suki hoped they would shoot it, but didn't say that out loud.

On the way home, Suki's father explained that there was another theory about where the Traveller had gone. The idea was that, because the Traveller dropped the newspaper, they changed the future, and that's why they disappeared. They'd ceased to exist.

Suki didn't like that idea. It felt so unjust. The Traveller had saved the world. They deserved more than that. They deserved some sort of reward.

That night, they played scrabble on the long wooden table in the den. Suki's father won by ten points, but Suki didn't mind at all.

Your Chain Has A Radius

YOU awake in pain, which shouldn't really be a surprise after a night out with Tess.

It's the mother of all hangovers, a dark pulse of pain behind the eyes. Did you really drink that much? You don't remember, which in itself is a neon warning sign. Moving feels like it would be painful, opening your eyes doubly so, so you're content to just lie there and take stock. What exactly did you *do* last night?

The plan was cocktails at The High Life. Did you even make it there? You stopped at The Crown for some reason. Oh that's right, Tess was stalking an ex - you remember that much - but you didn't find him. What you did find was a table of medical students, celebrating something, bright-eyed and fizzing, all idealistic and charming.

There was one in particular, was his name Clive? Beautiful eyes. He was twenty, only five years younger than you, but it felt like so much more. So you lied about your age, then lied about your job. Said you were on a gap year. Tried to come off as spiritual and worthy. Hoped he would kiss you.

They had a karaoke slot booked. Private room. Some of the group weren't keen on you tagging along but by that point you were too drunk to care. Duetting on "Single Ladies", soloing on "Jolene". Inflatable guitars to mime with and cowboy hats. More drinks. And then a wave of jealousy as you caught Tess snogging Clive.

Did they leave together? Of course they did.

That's the way it always goes with Tess. Waking up in pain.

The rest of the night has gaps. Did you get an Uber home? Or risk the walk through the park? You have no idea.

You know you have work today. That's something you do remember. You usually open up on Saturday mornings, but you swapped shifts with Stacey because you're not an idiot. You have the whole morning to rehydrate and get yourself presentable, then it's eight hours of the joy that is Burger Palace. All fixed smiles and "That'll be coming right up", desperately hoping that your tips will cover the rent. The smell of old grease permeating your skin.

Sudden nausea. Don't think about the grease.

You'll be on with Lily, which means more tips all round. Funny how that works. Lily gets a lot of tips because she's beautiful. She doesn't even milk it. Her smiles are as brisk and as business-like as she can make them, conversation rarely straying beyond the orders. And she still makes double what you do.

You still wouldn't want to swap places with her, though, because the price of those tips seems to be a huge side order of harassment. For every customer happy to tip well and leave there seems to be another three who think that a tip entitles them to her phone number. You've heard Lily's "letting them down gently" speech so many times, you think you could repeat it verbatim. You've also noticed that she delivers it with a counter between her and the customer, with a clear line to the lockable office.

Some men do not take rejection well.

Still, she's pleasant enough company and she pulls her weight, which can't be said for everyone working there.

Your mind drifts back to last night. How *did* you get home? You didn't think you were *that* drunk. Your headache is begging to differ and you gradually become aware of another pain in the mix. A dull ache at your wrist. Did you fall on it? Wouldn't be your first mystery drunken injury.

You blearily open your eyes and hold up your hand.

It's bound by a bright steel manacle attached to a thick chain.

84

Without any conscious thought you find yourself scrabbling, trying to get up, get away, get out. The chain pulls taut, attached to a bracket on the wall and you are stopped dead, whiplashing, pain flaring in your wrist. You should stop then, but panic has taken hold. You're sobbing, crying, pleading, pulling at the chain with all your might, bare feet sliding on the dirty concrete floor. An animal unable to understand the trap it now finds itself in.

A barrage of impressions as you look wildly around. The low-ceilinged room, bare concrete walls and floor, no windows, the only light from a bare lightbulb, the smell of damp and mould, the filthy mattress beneath you.

The dark crushing realisation that this may well be the room you die in.

Leonard Deakin did not consider himself a serial killer.

He understood that technically he matched the criteria, being personally responsible for the torture and murder of almost thirty people, but the narrative he had constructed around those deaths framed them as necessary evils that had no doubt saved lives.

In his own mind he was, in short, a hero.

Here is the form his heroism took. He would go driving on a motorway, usually the M25. He would drive passively, following the speed limit and only changing lanes when overtaking. And he would wait for the universe to provide him with his quarry.

It didn't usually take long, especially around rush hour. Everyone seemed to be in such a hurry and so quick to anger. But his parameters were very specific. He was not interested in people changing lanes without indicating or leaving insufficient stopping distance. He was only after the really dangerous drivers. People texting at ninety miles an hour. Tailgating bullies recklessly overtaking. Brake checkers. One or more of those boxes ticked and he would begin to follow, the start of a pursuit that would more often than not end with someone zip-tied to a chair, breathing their last.

Leonard genuinely viewed his kills as a public service. He reasoned that if his victims were allowed to live, their dangerous driving could well lead to fatal accidents. Indeed, he had been witness to just such an accident less than a year ago. He had been following his latest quarry down a dual carriageway when they had aggressively overtaken a van, misjudged the distance involved and caused a multi car pile-up, which he later read had left five people dead.

The quarry in question had kept driving, completely unscathed and apparently oblivious to the carnage in their wake. Leonard had managed to drive around the knot of mangled and burning cars before continuing his pursuit. He finally caught up with them around an hour later and peppered their torture with passive aggressive admonishments about the quality of their driving and the crash they had just caused. By the time they breathed their last, they had been left in no doubt that the world would be a much safer place with their passing.

Today found Leonard twenty minutes into his latest pursuit. The quarry had initially drawn his attention by drifting slightly out of their lane, a minor offence that he would have usually overlooked. However, a closer inspection had revealed that the cause of this sloppiness was the driver casually scrolling through their phone with only one eye on the road.

This simply would not do. They would have to go.

The moment Leonard chose a new quarry, he would immediately begin noticing things about their vehicle that confirmed both the correctness of his choice and poor quality of their character. He recognised it for the confirmation bias that it was, but enjoyed it nonetheless. Of course, their back window was filthy and they were driving a piece of shit hatchback with a dented side panel. Each new detail spoke to a series of poor life choices that had culminated here and now, with death fast approaching in their rear-view mirror.

After a few junctions, the hatchback left the motorway and was soon speeding down a country lane, open fields and knots of woodland whipping by. Leonard did his best to stay far enough behind to not arouse suspicion, but then lost sight of the car altogether. Cursing his caution, he sped up, then realised they must have turned off. He U-turned then slowed beside the most likely option, a long tree-lined drive with a sign proclaiming that it led to "Mullins Farm".

Leonard turned onto the drive and gingerly drove down it, his van barely moving. A series of stables and outbuildings dominated by a large farmhouse hove into view and Leonard stopped. He could see the hatchback parked beside the farmhouse, the driver unloading shopping from the boot.

Leonard was fairly certain his approach had gone undetected - the drive was bordered with high banks and thick bushes between the trees - but he turned off his engine anyway. He watched his quarry for a moment, his first good look at the man he intended to kill.

He was perhaps forty, balding and gone to seed, beer belly under camouflage-green body warmer. Leonard wondered if he would plead for his life, mention family that would miss him or pass out from the pain.

Leonard became aware that he already had an erection.

No one else emerged from the farm to help bring in the shopping, which of course confirmed nothing. Leonard always behaved as though others were inside until certain.

The man closed the boot and carried the final bags inside. Leonard took his chance to study the farmhouse a little more closely. It was Georgian and double-fronted with bay windows. He could imagine it had looked quite grand in its day, but everywhere he looked he saw neglect - further confirmation of his quarry's poor character. A broken gutter sagged in one corner, no doubt the cause of a spreading green stain on the white plaster below. A cracked pane on an upstairs window had allowed the wind to pull through the corner of a curtain. It fluttered like a pennant, a grimy flag of surrender.

Once his quarry was dead, perhaps the house would be renovated. Sold on to new owners, probably at a discount because of the horrific way the previous owner died. Leonard found himself imagining these new owners, no doubt people of much higher moral fibre, fixing all the problems he could see with gusto, returning the house to its former glory. The idea made Leonard oddly happy. He could see it clearly in his mind, the sequence of events that he was about to set in motion.

Leonard climbed into the back of his van and began to prepare. He had developed a very precise choreography for the initial contact, which he slavishly adhered to. It had been honed and refined over dozens of kills and had proven its efficacy time and again.

It began even before he reached the house. His van was transformed by the simple addition of a long magnetic panel to the side proclaiming him to be a "GAS ENGINEER". His clothing became an all-in-one overall, gloves and fluorescent vest, all of which helped sell the lie, but also kept his DNA from the scene.

He also operated on the assumption that his every move was being observed from the moment he arrived. He had a phone to his ear as he stepped out of the van, halfway through a weary call to a fictional superior.

He didn't even have a chance to ring the doorbell, the door already opening as he approached. He barely glanced at his quarry, holding up a finger, turning away as if for privacy, but speaking just loud enough to be overheard.

"Yeah, poor ventilation," he said. "Milking shed. No. He lost a couple but he's insured. OK. I'll let you know."

Leonard was very proud of this part of his script. A short alarming story, trimmed and gutted to the bare minimum, with the added bonus of making the listener feel smart for decoding the gaps.

Leonard finally hung up and turned to face his quarry with an apologetic look. Up close, he was surprised at the man's height. From a distance, Leonard had seen a beer belly and associated that with a short man, but he now realised that his target was well over six feet tall. It would be quite the workout to move him once unconscious.

Leonard held up an ID on a lanyard that had taken him two hours in Photoshop to create.

"Sorry about that," said Leonard. "We've had a batch of faulty gas cannisters sold in this area. Caught quite a few leaks. Can I ask, have you smelled anything?"

The address was rural enough for Leonard to be reasonably

sure that they weren't connected to the gas network. It would be self-contained tanks all the way. Even so, he was more than a little relieved when the man's answers confirmed it.

"No. Nothing like that," said the man. "Have they killed some cows?"

"Afraid I can't discuss that," said Leonard. "Data protection. I don't want to alarm you, but is there anyone else inside you've not checked on in a while?"

"No. No-one but me," said the man.

Tick. The quarry was alone. Leonard could see a row of muddy shoes and boots in the hall, but they all looked the same size. He held up a gas sensor. Eighty-four pounds on e-Bay.

"Just to be sure, I need to sweep this over any cannisters you own--"

"No. There's no gas here," said with a flicker of panic.

He'd already started to slowly close the door. He really didn't want Leonard inside. At a guess, he had a greenhouse full of weed somewhere close. Leonard mentally shrugged. He'd allowed for this. His script smoothly shifted to a contingency branch.

"Listen. I don't want to be here, you don't want me here. But if you die or your farm goes boom, I get it in the neck. Now I could call the police, force the issue, but I don't need the paperwork."

At the mention of the police, the slow steady closing of the door ceased.

That must be a big greenhouse.

Leonard held out the sensor.

"You can do it."

"What?"

"Just hold it next to your cannisters and bring it back to me. I don't even have to come in."

The man gingerly accepted the meter.

Leonard activated the bluetooth switch in his pocket and the taser hidden inside the gas meter's handle delivered fifty thousand volts straight into his quarry's palm.

He shuddered and fell backwards into the house, forced into

gripping the taser by the spasm of his muscles.

Leonard calmly stepped into the house and closed the door behind him.

The manacle around your wrist is a thick band of steel attached to a much older chain. The links are as thick as your finger, connected to a looped bracket set into the brick that looks like it was made to hold livestock.

Your chain has a radius, a half-circle centring on the bracket. It leaves scratches on the concrete floor when you move. There are already marks there that you didn't make.

The implications make you want to vomit.

You are not the first. Someone else made those marks, chained here before you. Someone else lay here on this filthy mattress and begged and cried into the silence.

How long were they here? How long before he tired of them?

You discover crusted blood and a tender lump on the back of your head. A blow to the head you don't remember taking. From the park?

Irrelevant now.

You're still wearing the clothes you went drinking in. Mostly. No sign of your shoes, handbag or jacket. Your white jeans have grass stains. Your sequinned top is ripped. You remember choosing it as you planned the night, hoping it would catch the lights of the bar, maybe draw someone's eye. You desperately want to be that girl again, head nodding along to her pre-party playlist. Part of you hates her for her naivety.

This room smells of death. You are down with the dead things now.

There is a bucket to one side. Next to the bucket is a toilet roll. The roll is half-used. You stare at the roll for far too long. How long does it take to use half a roll? How many days? Is that how long they survived? Or was this the last roll of many? How long will you survive? Will that roll still be here when you're gone?

What are you prepared to do to stay alive?

There is nothing within your reach except the bucket and the mattress. The room is long, the ceiling low, the air damp. You think it's a cellar. The only light comes from a bare bulb fifty feet away. It's next to a brick staircase leading up out of sight. You can just see the bottom slice of a closed door. Next to the staircase is a pile of boxes half-covered in tarpaulin. Most of the walls and ceiling are covered in what look like egg boxes, something you don't understand.

Your mind keeps forcing you to replay the events of last night. Searching for a way out, a version that ends a different way. This time you call an Uber. Or your brother. Or your father. Anything but the shortcut through the park. Anything but this.

You imagine enduring your father's irritation and judgement with a big dopey smile on your face, because you know that you'll soon be safe and warm in your own bed. Yes, Dad, I'm a disappointment and a screw-up, and I'm deep in debt - who isn't? But I am alive and it's so, so sweet.

You consider screaming for help, but worry that it might anger your captor.

You use the bucket. You feel dehydrated, weak. You lie down again on the mattress. A broken spring digs into your back. You shift your weight to avoid it.

You picture the springs, coiled in a row. Like snakes. Like soldiers. Their bayonets ready to impale you.

You feel heady, delirious.

You imagine your predecessor lying here, avoiding the same broken spring. You run your hand over the mattress. There's a ragged hole, a sharp metal point standing proud.

You dig into the mattress and push it down around the spring, feeling its shape. Almost without thought, you begin to pull at it, bending it, distorting it. The sharp tip cuts into your fingertips. You keep pulling, the spring now slick with blood. Something gives and a noise like a plucked string sounds, but the spring is still attached. You grip it with your fist, ignoring the pain, and pull with all your might. It moves slightly but doesn't come free. You try again, shuddering with the effort, but to no avail.

You sag, panting, and release the spring.

You start to cry, huge sobs racking your body. You look at

your shaking fingers, now smeared with blood, deep cuts in two of them. You wrap some toilet roll around the wounds, wincing as the blood blooms.

What did you hope to accomplish? Even if you had worked the spring free, what then? Use it as a weapon? Use it to pick your manacle? You wouldn't know where to start.

Something has fallen from the toilet roll. You almost discount it as a rogue sliver of toilet paper, but something makes you pause. You pick it up. It's the size and shape of a flattened cigarette. A single sheet, folded multiple times and tucked back into the roll. You carefully unfold it.

The lettering is spidery and tiny. You read:

"I cannot take any more. I try to escape. To blind him. If I die I will be free. Remember me - Alice Sallow".

You re-read the message over and over, then sit staring at it, unseeing. A message from your predecessor. The woman who lay here before you.

Why did she even bother to leave it? How could she be so sure there would be another after her to find it?

The realisation, when it comes, almost overwhelms you.

She left the message because, just like you, she knew she was not the first.

This was usually Leonard's favourite part of the kill. That moment when his quarry realised that all the threatening, bargaining and pleading in the world was not going to save them. At that point, something changed in their eyes. He had seen it happen, time and again. A light going out. A stillness. A deadness.

Leonard liked to think that it was hope leaving them.

And in that moment, Leonard felt he could see the real person at last. The bedrock of their character, with all the false protective veneers stripped away. All the social niceties and bravado and ego. All gone. All burned away in the face of the unavoidable fact - this man is going to kill you and there is nothing that you can do about it.

As much as Leonard liked to justify his behaviour in terms of the lives saved on the road, those quiet moments with his victims were his real reward. The moments of complete dominance and surrender.

Not today, though. He somehow doubted that he would ever reach that moment with his current quarry.

The process began conventionally enough. Leonard turned off the taser and used the few seconds of the man's reeling insensibility to inject him in the arm with a mild sedative. Once he was out, Leonard began his inspection of the house. This was primarily to ensure they were alone, but he always found other people's houses interesting. The clues they left to how they lived.

For its size the lounge off the hallway was minimally furnished to the point of oddness. A single battered leather armchair faced a flatscreen TV connected to a Blu-Ray player and a game console. There were empty picture hooks and faded rectangles on a flock floral wallpaper. Water-damaged brown velvet curtains half-closed in the bay window.

The next room was the exact opposite. Furniture and furnishings piled high without care. Folding beds, dining chairs, boxes of bedside lamps. A couch had been shoved atop a dining table, its legs leaving deep gouges in the dark wood. All covered in a thick layer of dust.

There was a framed photograph of a schoolboy lying on the floor. Leonard picked it up. It was his quarry, the set of the jaw was unmistakable. He looked defiant and surly. Angry at the photographer. At the world.

A narrow path led through the piled debris to the kitchen. A kettle had just finished boiling. The hob was filthy with congealed food, the sink fetid with unwashed pots. Flies circled lazily.

Leonard was going to guess the man lived alone.

The new shopping had yet to be put away, the bags sitting on the counter top. Lots of microwavable meals for one. Spirits.

There was a utility room beyond. Washer. Dryer. A door leading to an overgrown garden. Another door, padlocked, leading where? A larder? A cellar?

Upstairs told a similar story. Only one room was in use, the bed unmade. All the other rooms were either empty or being used as storage.

Leonard returned to his van to get his toolbag.

Ten minutes later, his quarry was sitting slumped in a wicker-backed dining chair in the centre of the living room. Plastic zip ties held him to the chair by his wrists and ankles. There was also a belt around his chest holding his torso to the backrest, a measure Leonard began to adopt after a writhing quarry once managed to headbutt him.

Leonard injected a stimulant, then went to sit in the armchair opposite. A few seconds later, he heard the telltale change in breathing that indicated consciousness. Leonard coughed politely. His quarry's eyes flicked open. Leonard read aloud from the wallet in his hand.

"Trevor Padget. Or do you prefer Trev?"

Trevor just stared at him. No fear, which was interesting. Well, that would come soon enough. Leonard tossed the wallet aside.

"Well Trev. I'm afraid you've been a bad lad."

"Have I really?" he rumbled.

Leonard was annoyed. Interruptions could make him lose his place.

"You have. And it can't carry on. But I want you to know why I'm doing this, before you die."

"*Die* is it? You think you're going to kill me? Little shit like you."

Trevor had the body language of someone arguing in a pub car park. He obviously needed reminding of his situation. Leonard sighed theatrically, leaned over and reached into his toolbag, satisfied to note that Trevor was watching him intently. He rummaged around, then held up the gardening secateurs.

Still no fear. A kind of bored resignation, which *was* surprising. The appearance of a tool usually prompted begging, threatening, bargaining. Questions at least. Who are you? Who sent you? But Trevor was giving him none of that.

Leonard carefully approached the chair and tightened the extra zip tie he had fitted just below Trevor's elbow to serve as a tourniquet. He then firmly gripped Trevor's left hand and snipped off his little finger with the secateurs. The finger bounced on the carpet. There was very little blood.

Leonard stood back, expectantly.

Trevor was breathing hard through his nose, like a bull, staring up at him with loathing, but still no fear.

It didn't matter. It would soon come. It always did.

Leonard was almost back to the chair before Trevor spoke again.

"Uneven," he muttered.

"What was that?" said Leonard.

"I said it's uneven. You need to do the other hand."

Chin pushed out. Defiant. Eyes burning with hate.

For a moment, Leonard just stood there, trying to process. This was unprecedented. Of course he was bluffing. It was bravado, nothing more. An attempt at a power move doomed to fail. At the last moment, he would back down.

Surely.

Leonard moved back towards Trevor, tightened the tourniquet below the right elbow, moved the blades of the secateurs around the little finger - and paused. Waiting for Trevor to speak, to crack, to back down.

And Trevor just stared up at him, a half-smile on his lips.

"Problem?" he asked.

Leonard squeezed the secateurs decisively and another finger fell to the carpet.

"There you go," said Trevor. "That wasn't so hard, was it?"

He was smiling wide now. Encouraging. Supportive. Knowing he'd won that round.

Leonard backed away. He wondered if what he was feeling was showing on his face. He tried to recalibrate. He had the power here, for fuck's sake.

But for the very first time with any quarry, Leonard felt afraid.

He sat back down in the armchair and put the secateurs back in the toolbag. He then began to rummage around, making a big show of deciding what tool to use next, buying himself time. He needed to get back on track, back to the script.

He selected a hunting knife and tapped it to his chin as though considering, then tossed it back into the bag. He sat back in the chair and steepled his fingers, a pose he was very fond of.

"I'm here to make the world a safer place. Because believe me, it will be a hell of a lot safer with you gone. With your death, I will be saving lives. I followed you today, you see. Saw you veering all over the road. Looking at your phone while driving. And it's only a matter of time--"

Leonard was surprised to hear laughter. It began as a low chuckle, but soon Trevor was roaring, head back, chest heaving.

"You're here because of my fucking *driving?*"

Leonard sat in stunned silence and watched as Trevor rocked in his chair with laughter. The rest of the script he had planned suddenly seemed trite and irrelevant. Even his grand mission to make the roads safer faded in his mind, revealed as the façade - the excuse - that perhaps it always was. In that moment, Leonard acknowledged a truth about himself. It had always been about control, always been about inflicting pain on others. That was always the point, everything else was just a means to that glorious end. And right here and now, all he could think was how good inflicting pain on this man would make him feel.

Leonard reached into his bag for the battery-powered sander.

"I am going to live."

You say it aloud in the silence. Your voice cracks and wavers, unconvincing even to yourself. A pep talk in the face of futility.

You can smell your own armpits. Your mouth is dry, your lips cracked.

How long have you been here? How long until he returns?

You wonder how many girls he has taken over the years, how many he has killed. You feel the weight of your shared history. You are one of them now, part of an unseen sisterhood. The image of them blooms, vivid in your mind. Standing together, watching silently, looking down on you. With what? Pity?

No. Hope.

Hope that you'll be the one to get away. Hope that you'll be the one to take their memory out into the light.

You realise you're hallucinating. Your eyes are open, but you can see them, the girls who came before you, standing silently in the empty cellar. Watching. Waiting.

Of course. They can't leave. Can't leave until one of them escapes.

You close your eyes and when you open them again, they are gone.

You're exhausted and dehydrated, your thoughts are fragmented, feverish. You tell yourself that the girls were never there. That their hope, their need for you to escape isn't real. You try to put it out of your mind. But you can't. Maybe you don't want to. Because you recognise the truth at the heart of it and the engine that it gives you.

You have to fight, not just for your sake, or theirs. You have to fight for the future girls he will take if you don't.

You take an inventory, for what feels like the hundredth time. Everything you have, everything you can reach. You even turn the mattress over to see if you've missed anything, but there is nothing new or useful.

Lacking any better ideas, you continue to work to free the broken spring. You've taken off your sequinned top and are using it to protect your fingers, switching hands when you tire. Your eyes glaze as you work. You stop thinking. You're a machine that twists and pulls and strains.

As you work, you realise you're staring at the toilet bucket. Something drawing your eye. It's a second before you spot it.

The bucket is plastic but the handle is metal.

You gingerly reach out, hands shaking. The handle unhooks with ease.

You stare at it. A thin curved metal rod, around a foot across.

You experimentally put it to the lock of your manacle. It's too big to even fit into the keyhole. Weirdly, you're relieved. You don't know the first thing about picking locks.

So. A weapon then? You mime stabbing and slashing at the air. The rod feels slick and unstable in your palm.

Could you stab him with this? Wait until he comes for you and then...

Stab him where? The throat? The eye?

Could you bring yourself to do that?

Yes. You think you could.

Having the will is one thing, but this isn't a knife. It's a thin rod of metal. So much could go wrong.

You hold up the handle again, squinting. How else could this help you? Tentatively, you tie it to one sleeve of your top, thinking. Holding on to the other sleeve, you toss the handle like a hook.

You look across at the tarp-covered pile of cardboard boxes near the stairs. How far away are they? Thirty feet?

They could be empty. They could contain nothing but useless crap.

You have no other ideas.

You take off your jeans. You use the sharp edge of the spring to punch holes, which you then pull wider, tearing the length of the leg. You repeat the process at three-inch intervals. It's slow and awkward. The hems and the waist are tougher. You use the spring to pick at the stitches. Eventually your jeans are reduced to thin strips of denim.

As you begin to knot them into a rope, you notice your hands shaking with cold. You're now wearing nothing but your underwear, the mattress damp against gooseflesh. You clench your teeth and carry on. You repeat the process with your top. More strips, more rope. You add them to the denim, tightening each knot.

It's finally ready.

You take a deep breath and toss the rope and hook towards the boxes.

It clatters on the concrete, ten feet short.

You stare at the hook for a long time. You realise you're crying silently, tears dripping from your chin.

You slowly pull the rope back in and sink down on to the mattress. You could just sleep. No one would blame you. You tried really hard. You gave it your best shot but there's nothing else you can do. You simply have no more cloth.

A woman's voice whispers from the darkness: "Yes you do.

You have the mattress."

You're hallucinating again. There was no voice. It's your subconscious, that's all.

But she's right. You have the mattress.

You stand up, wipe your eyes and begin again. You work into the hole around the broken spring, pulling, tearing. You manage to create a long rip from one end of the mattress to the other. You use the bucket handle to punch other holes to enable more rips.

Dust rises from within the mattress, sticking to the tears on your face, the cold sweat on your body. You cough and spit.

You farm more fabric from the face of the mattress and add it to your rope. Strip after strip. The springs are exposed. You can't sit on it anymore. You're kneeling on the floor, chafing your knees.

That *must* be long enough.

You tighten the knots, stand and toss the hook again.

The rope is now long enough, but your first throw is poor. The hook lands next to the nearest box. You carefully pull it back and throw it again. It lands on the box but doesn't find purchase, clattering back across the floor. You throw it again. And again. And again.

The hook lands perfectly, catching within the partly open lid. You gently, ever so gently, pull on your rope.

The box moves.

It slides gradually, magically across the floor towards you. You keep the pressure steady. Soon the box is close enough to touch.

You take a deep breath and open the lid.

Dusty clothing. Which is something. More fuel for rope.

Blouses and skirts and…

A sick sinking feeling. A realisation.

Not just any clothing. Women's clothing. And there is *so* much of it.

A sob racks your chest but you push it down. Focus.

You search through what pockets you can find. All empty. Digging through the trophies of past victims. You feel sick at the implications of each garment. You select a light blue sweater and pull it over your head and one arm. The chain prevents you from fully wearing it. You say a silent thanks to the former owner.

You can still smell her perfume.

You gather up your rope and try again.

The process is easier this time. You manage to snag the next box with just a few throws, but it's heavier, harder to pull over, and when it arrives you discover why. Inside are a few half-used tins of paint and a bundle of stained rags. Useless.

You gather up your rope and are just about to throw it at the next box when you hear the screaming.

It's very faint, just on the edge of hearing, but it's there. You think it's a man, but you can't be sure.

Once you're past the shock, your first shame-filled feeling is one of relief.

He's busy with someone else.

But for how long?

You begin to speed up your throws. Again. Again. You snag the tarpaulin and it flops away, revealing more of the boxes. Your next throw lands right inside one of them. You carefully pull. The cardboard wall of the box bulges, but the box stays put. It's heavy. You pull a little harder, as hard as you dare. The box doesn't move. You attempt to whip the rope, to flick the hook back out of the box. Something rattles, but it stays inside. Caught on something. You whip it again. Nothing.

The screaming stops.

How can the silence be more terrifying?

You pull the rope harder than you ever have before.

There is an abrupt tearing noise and the rope snaps, fifteen feet away.

On autopilot, you wind in what you can. You stare dumbly at the wad of fabric in your hands. Part of your top was the weak link. Can you make a new hook? You have lots of clothing for new rope. Do you even have time? The paint tins, maybe using them as a hook somehow. You pull a tin out and see a glint of metal from within the wad of stained rags. You pick up the wad. There's something within. Something heavy.

You unravel what looks like a large metal syringe, around two feet long. You recognise it as a sealant gun, loaded with a half-used plastic cannister. You have one just like it under your sink, bought to fix a leaking shower. Could this be your new hook? The plunger has a metal handle, almost as thick as your finger, with a curved end.

The silence upstairs continues. You sense you don't have time for any of this. You wish the screaming would begin again, then hate yourself for the thought.

Whatever you're going to do, you need to do it now.

You look to the chain holding you there, the hooped bracket on the wall. Almost without thought, you push the plunger's thick metal handle into the bracket. Using it as a lever, you pull with all your might. The body of the gun twists and distorts and the handle gouges into the plasterwork below the bracket, fragments falling, but the bracket doesn't move. You can feel the gun cutting into your palms but you keep pulling. It's this or death and you want to live. Oh God, you want to live. The handle skitters across the wall and you stagger as purchase is lost.

You reposition and try again. You begin shuddering with the effort, black spots on your vision. The sealant cannister splits, white toothpaste-like sealant oozing. Blood is dripping from your hands to the floor. You stop again, panting. It's not working. You need more leverage. You brace one foot against the wall and pull your lever down again, teeth clenched. You feel close to passing out. You haven't got any more to give. You're sobbing, still pulling, but your strength is slowly ebbing. I'm sorry. I tried. I really did. But I can't--

You are not alone. You feel other hands slide along your arms to join you at the lever. So many hands. You don't look over your shoulder. You know whose hands they are.

One last hallucination before you go. Why not?

You pull with everything you have. With everything they have lost.

You hear a crack. You think it's the sealant gun breaking.

You fall backwards as something gives way. You find yourself lying on your back, panting, in a cloud of dust.

Free.

If there was a skill to torture, and Leonard liked to believe that there was, it was finding that sweet spot where immense pain was being inflicted and yet the subject was in no danger of passing out. That was always the balancing act. Too much pain, too much blood loss or shock - all could lead to an unconscious quarry, which was frankly of no use to anyone.

In Leonard's early blundering days, he had gone in too hard too early, all blowtorches and power drills out of the gate. The sessions had been intense but far too short, leading in some cases to the quarry's death before Leonard was sated. He'd found it intensely frustrating.

This, in turn, had lead to six months of intensive research on the theme of pharmaceutical pain management and ultimately to his current day job of hospital porter. He spent his days pushing patients down endless linoleum corridors, doing his best to blend in, and, whenever the opportunity presented itself, stealing drugs.

He'd initially thought this would be a challenge and, for his first few weeks, did nothing but carefully monitor the hospital's security systems, before realising that he was massively over-thinking things. His job already made him practically invisible and most people looked right through him. This, combined with overworked staff, only too eager to pass the buck and lighten their load, meant that incorrect paperwork and lanyards could all be overlooked with the right combination of feigned ignorance and blank stupidity.

He soon had a growing selection of pharmaceutical tools at his disposal. The capture and subduing of his quarries became a much more civilised affair, as did their torture. He now viewed their level of consciousness, and indeed pain, as dials that he could control with some precision.

That had all gone out of the window with Trevor, of course.

Leonard had wanted to demolish him. To break him. To make him suffer and scream and beg. So he had gone in hard and fast, using endgame techniques that he usually only reserved for the last few minutes of his sessions.

And Trevor had stayed silent, defying him, staring him down

and grinding his teeth as his blood flowed and his flesh burned. Several times, Leonard was sure he'd pushed it too far, that Trevor was about to pass out, but he never did.

He was soon enduring a level of pain that Leonard had previously thought impossible. All in total silence.

Leonard found it unnerving.

Time began to lose meaning as he hunched over Trevor, working on the ruined body beneath him. Sweat ran down his nose to drip into the wounds he was creating.

It had begun as a battle of wills, a challenge to his dominance that he had to answer, but now he just wanted it to be over. He was sickened by the smell of the dying man beneath him, repulsed by the torture that was usually such a source of joy. At this stage, he just wanted to kill him and leave. The only thing stopping him was his own pride.

He told himself that all he needed was one scream. Just one tiny scream and this could all end. But he was fast running out of options. The only techniques left to him were so extreme they would probably kill him.

And then Trevor opened his mouth and started to wail.

It was like the sun coming out. Leonard stood back and enjoyed the moment. He wasn't even touching him now, hadn't for a good few seconds, but the screams kept coming. Hoarse and raw, spittle flecked with blood. Screams that spoke of complete ruin.

He was broken and it was glorious.

Leonard sat back in the armchair and enjoyed the show.

Eventually, Trevor passed out, slumped in his chair, and Leonard considered what to do next. Usually, he would deliver the *coup de grâce*, douse the body in bleach and leave. Usually. But there was nothing about this quarry that felt usual.

Everything about Trevor's behaviour and his responses had made Leonard uneasy. How many people would awake tied to a chair, facing death, and simply shrug? Trevor had looked resigned, not surprised by the situation at all. He *had* been surprised by Leonard's reasons for visiting him. Which meant what?

Which meant he had done something else. Something else worth killing him for.

Part of Leonard wanted to simply end him, leave and never look back. But he could sense he was not seeing the whole picture and knew it would play on his mind if he left things unresolved.

He picked up Trevor's wallet from where he'd tossed it and began going through it a little more carefully. Driver's license, bank cards, loyalty cards for coffee shops, receipts for groceries. It felt banal, perhaps studiedly so, much like his own wallet. He threw it aside again. Did he really expect his secret to be that easy to find?

Trevor's smartphone also lay on the floor. Leonard had briefly examined it at the beginning, but it required a passcode. He pictured himself trying to torture the code out of Trevor. Getting a scream out of him had nearly killed him. He tossed the phone aside.

When Leonard had arrived in his persona of gas engineer, he had sensed resistance from Trevor. He hadn't wanted him inside his house and he certainly hadn't wanted the police involved. But there was nothing Leonard had seen within that indicated obvious illegal activity. Perhaps there was something in the outbuildings. Perhaps. He'd already been through every room in the house hadn't he?

No. He hadn't.

There was one door he hadn't opened. Off the utility room, wasn't it? Padlocked.

Who padlocks a door inside their own house?

He approached Trevor's slumped form and began to search his blood-soaked pockets for keys.

You genuinely have no idea what to do next. You gaze dumbly through a cloud of dust at the fist-sized hollow in the wall that once held the bracket. You're still manacled to the chain, but it now swings free, ending in a jagged chunk of masonry. You gather it up into your arms like a baby. You're free, in the cellar at least. Your impulse is to run to the steps, to the door, but it's bound to be locked.

Isn't it?

You take two steps towards the stairs then look down at your hands. They're bleeding freely, leaving a dripped trail wherever you go. You wind the rope around your hands as makeshift bandages. You feel dizzy. Breathe in. Breathe out.

The moment passes.

You set off towards the stairs again. It feels surreal crossing the floor so easily. It's been unthinkable for so long. You pause, looking up the stairs at the door. White painted wood, yellowed with age. You picture your tormentor waiting on the other side of it. What if he hears you trying it? What if you leave blood on the stairs?

He can't know you're free. You instinctively know that's your main advantage. Trying a door that you know in your heart is bound to be locked is too big a risk.

You return to the mattress and the chaos you've created. You imagine him entering and seeing all this.

You need to reset the room.

You drag the two boxes you've snagged back to the pile near the staircase. You take off your borrowed jumper and put it back in the clothing box. You say a silent thank you. To all of them.

You retrieve the other half of the rope and check inside the heavy box that broke it. It's filled to the brim with more paint tins. Magnolia and Apricot. Do you have time to search the other boxes? It feels a risk but they've been your goal for so long. You quickly flip open the lids. Sacks of plaster. A sewing machine and spools of thread. Folded fabric mottled with mould. Dozens of metal coathangers. Any one of them would have seemed a miracle an hour ago. You take one on impulse.

You drag the tarpaulin cover back over the boxes and pad back to your mattress, scuffing away any drag marks, blood drips or footprints as you come. You grunt as you flip your mattress to hide the side you destroyed. The effort makes you feel dizzy again. It's worse this time. The room spins and your legs give way. You fall face-first on to the mattress, panting.

You know that if you pass out, it's all over.

Eventually, the room steadies. You sit up carefully and

struggle to think. What have you missed?

The chain is an issue. As soon as he gets close, he'll see the hole where the bracket should be. You drag the mattress against the wall, bend it up into an L shape to cover the hole and your stash of potential weapons. You shove the end of the chain in with them. You allow yourself a moment's rest.

How long since the screaming stopped? Ten minutes? More? The idea that he would be coming for you next - what was that based on, other than fear? There was no real logic to it, was there? He could be doing a million things up there. Part of you wonders if all this panicked effort is for nothing. You could be left here alone for hours. You're just coming to terms with that idea when you hear the bright, brittle noise of keys beyond the door.

He has come for you. Your time is up.

Leonard had an entire subset of personal rules and best practices devoted to the topic of killing innocent people.

Generally speaking, he would do everything he could to ensure that his quarry and his quarry alone suffered at his hands. The moment he discovered they were not alone, assuming he had not yet assaulted them, he would stay in his persona of gas engineer, wish everyone a good day and retreat. The main focus would then become surveillance, to ensure that the quarry could be later abducted alone.

Once the quarry was restrained, however, a whole new set of parameters took over. Leonard was very fond of his freedom, a freedom that witnesses could well jeopardise. His freedom was also necessary to continue his mission, which he believed was saving dozens of lives. This made the death of innocents, although regrettable and, of course, a last resort, very easy to justify.

They were unfortunate collateral damage. That's all.

Most of the time, the innocents that crossed his path did so because the quarry had lied about being alone in the house, for sometimes inexplicable reasons. He had killed sullen teenagers, terrified flatmates, confused bedbound grandparents and, in one case, a secretary that he was fairly sure the quarry was having an affair with.

And now, it seemed, he would have to kill a girl chained to a wall.

He almost didn't find her. The bunch of keys he found in Trevor's pocket initially seemed promising, but none of them were the right shape for the padlock. Leonard then checked the kitchen drawers and looked in vain for convenient hooks near the mystery door, before finally resolving to break the padlock off somehow. He'd just started his search for a crowbar when he came to his senses. He was spending too long on this. True, the farm was isolated and Leonard doubted he would be disturbed, but he had already gone way past his self-imposed time limit for the kill.

He had just resolved to leave when his eye was caught by something glinting behind the shopping bags on the kitchen counter. A whole other bunch of keys, just idly tossed there. Mainly for mortise locks, some large and rusting - for outbuildings perhaps - but nestled amongst them were a couple that Leonard thought might do the trick.

Thirty seconds later, Leonard was standing in the cellar and staring at the girl he would now have to kill.

His heart really did go out to her, though. She looked as though she hadn't been having a very nice time down here. She was perhaps twenty five, but her eyes were much older. Her skin was filthy, dried blood smeared on her arms. Bleached blonde bob matted and tangled. He wondered how long ago Trevor had abducted her.

Didn't bear thinking about.

She watched him intently from her seat on the stained mattress, knees drawn up protectively to her chin. Leonard could see the chain on her wrist, which led out of sight behind her. He could estimate her reach based upon the scratches on the floor. Even so, he kept his distance. Something about her made him wary.

If Leonard had just killed Trevor and left, how long would she have survived down here? Trevor didn't feel like a man with many visitors. It didn't take a lot of imagination for Leonard to frame his killing of the girl as a mercy, saving her from the stagnant nightmare of starvation.

She should be thanking him really.

Still, he had solved the mystery of Trevor, which was something. In hindsight, his behaviour seemed riddled with the tells of a killer. Leonard strongly doubted that this girl was his first. At least she would be his last. Leonard would make sure of that.

Leonard unconsciously puffed out his chest. This had been a very good day. Ridding the world of a serial killer, not to mention the mercy killing of an innocent girl who would have starved to death without him.

He was quite the hero.

He would need his toolbag. He turned to leave, already musing over the best weapon for the job.

You don't know what you were expecting, but it wasn't this.

The face of a bank manager. A parking warden. Slicked back hair and a trimmed moustache. An overall and a fluorescent vest. He's here to read the meter and cut your throat. Because there is blood spattered there, glistening on his gloves and chest. Blood from the man who screamed. But his face shows kindness and sympathy. A facsimile of human emotion to hide the black hole.

You wonder if his expression changes when he cuts.

He's not holding a weapon you can see, but he's bigger than you and you're so, so weak.

He's frowning now, as though irritated by your presence. It's not an expression you like. He steps nearer and you shrink away in fear. You're not sure how much is an act. You're braced for him to come closer. One more step, that's all.

Then he turns and walks away.

No. He can't leave. You're moving without thinking, grabbing your weapon of choice from behind the mattress and lunging toward him. But you're clumsy and ungainly, almost falling before you're even on your feet.

He's still moving, not looking back, twenty feet away. You can tell that he's completely dismissed you. You're finally up and running towards him now, closing the gap. But it feels like an eternity. You feel so slow and the gap between you is so wide.

The rattle of your chain gives you away just before you reach him and he begins to turn. He has an expression between wry amusement and irritation, the look of someone about to ward off a charity clipboard. This changes to shock as he realises just how close you are. He has time to hold up one arm before the wide arc you're swinging with the paint tin connects to the side of his head. The impact dislodges the lid, magnolia spraying over both of you.

You knee him in the groin and he goes down.

You straddle him and scrabble for the bucket handle hook at your waistband. He's groaning beneath you, half-conscious, blood welling from a deep gouge on his temple and mixing with the white paint on his face. Raspberry ripple, you find yourself thinking. Raspberry ripple. You begin to repeat it to yourself as a mindless mantra. A distraction to avoid thinking about what you're doing as you press. The. Hook. Deep. Into. His. Eye.

He screams, high and desperate, and claws at your face. You wrench your head away. He grabs a handful of your hair. You press the hook deeper and hear a crunch. He spasms and releases your hair. Everything is suddenly still.

You feel a growing warmth beneath your thighs and realise he's pissed himself.

You pull yourself to your feet and look down at his sprawled body. You feel nothing but relief. It's over. It has to be. You have so little left in the tank.

Behind you, the staircase leading up to the open doorway and freedom.

You begin to climb, one step at a time.

There is a beige landline phone mounted on the wall of the kitchen. No one has landline phones. Not anymore. It won't be connected. You pick it up and put it to your ear.

You hear a dial tone.

You dial 999. The handset is now smeared with blood. You don't know how much of it is yours.

"Emergency services, which service do you require?" A woman's voice. Clipped and efficient.

You speak in a monotone. You haven't the energy for anything else. You tell them you've just killed a man who had chained you up in his cellar. You say that he killed other girls. They ask where you are. You have no idea. Surely they can trace the call.

There's something in the woman's tone that sounds sceptical. She has so many questions and you have so little energy. You release the handset and leave it swinging. Her voice is now tinny and distant.

You've done enough. They will come.

You become aware you're cold. How long have you been cold? Your hands are shaking. There's a row of coat hooks beside the back door. You stand staring at them. The hooks are beyond full, strata upon strata of clothing. On the top layer, you can see a waxed jacket, a parka and a transparent plastic raincoat.

You select the parka. It's enormous on you, ending below your knees. You have to roll up the sleeves to use your hands. Your chain gets in the way. You keep forgetting you have it. You thread it through the sleeve and tuck what you can in a pocket.

You find a cupboard full of dusty pint glasses. You take one to the sink. You fill it with water and drink. It's the best drink of your entire life. You fill the glass again. The second drink is just as good.

Through the window you can see a barn, fields and woods beyond. Are you in the country? Thoughts are so hard to hold on to, skittering across your mind. You stare at the view for a long time. The sky is brooding with clouds. You can also see a rusting trailer piled with breeze blocks and the sagging shell of an abandoned greenhouse, smashed panes choked with weeds.

You think it might be the best view you've ever seen.

You could just wait here for the police, with your tap and your view, but the smell from the sink is making you nauseous.

You move further into the house.

There's a framed picture of a schoolboy lying on the floor.

You don't think it's the man you killed. He looks angry. You wonder what happened to him. How his photo wound up here.

Then you reach the room with the dead man tied to the chair.

You stand and stare at him for quite a while. You count how many fingers he has left. How many lay on the floor. It doesn't add up to ten. You wonder idly where the missing finger has gone.

Are you in shock? Is this what shock feels like?

This must have been the man screaming, you think. How could you have forgotten about him? Your thoughts feel like someone else's, distant and faint.

He is hard to look at but you force yourself. You're not sure why. Perhaps to honour him, in some perverse way. You want to tell him that his screams saved you, spurred you on. But he cannot hear you. So instead you stare at his ruined body and bear witness to how he was broken.

Were the girls who came before you tied to this chair? Would you have ended up here, had you failed?

Then the man in the chair opens his eyes and looks at you.

You take a step backwards in shock. How can he still be alive? He blinks at you in confusion. He must be terrified.

"He's dead. We're safe," you say.

You see him process that. A brief smile flickers. Relief? He still looks wary. He tries to move in his seat then notices the zip ties, as though for the first time. He looks from them to you with meaning.

Of course. You need to cut him free.

Your first thought is to search the kitchen for a knife but you're not thinking clearly. You've already noticed the toolbag but didn't want to look too closely. Now it's imperative. You crouch and begin to search through the jumble of tools. Some of them are still sticky with his blood. You tamp down your revulsion.

You become aware of him watching you. Why should that matter?

All the blades you find risk cutting him in the process of freeing him. You finally find some scissors.

Up close, you can smell him. A warm, heady mix of sweat and blood. His breath is sweet with decay. It repulses you. You tell yourself it's not his fault. You probably smell just as bad. So why does it matter?

Why do you want to run?

You carefully slide the lower blade of the scissors between his skin and the zip tie on his left wrist. You snip it off, then repeat the process on the right.

His hands are free. He reaches for the belt holding him to the chair, but it's tied at the back. You move around the chair and untie it. He slumps in the chair as the belt is released. He looks so weak. What's next? His ankles. You crouch to cut the zip ties there.

He looks down at you. You're suddenly aware of his size.

"Water," he says.

You nod and hurry back to the kitchen.

You choose another dusty pint glass from the cupboard and fill it.

You hear a tinny distant voice. It's the phone, still connected to the police. You pick it up and ask them to send an ambulance, then let it hang again. You can hear them asking more questions, insistent, annoyed.

You head back, glancing again at the photo of the schoolboy as you pass. Such angry eyes.

You walk back into the room, carrying the water carefully. He's sitting up in the chair, rubbing his wrists. He seems much more alert. Suspicious.

"Who were you talking to?" he asks.

"They're sending an ambulance," you reply.

He nods and holds out both hands for the water. He only has two fingers and a thumb on one of his hands.

You stand beside him as he drinks, holding out a steadying hand in case he drops the glass. As he drinks, he is watching you carefully. Up close, his face suddenly seems familiar. His smell envelops you again. And again, you have the instinct to run.

You notice a fresh pink scar below one eye, perhaps only weeks old. Easy to miss with all his fresh wounds. You wonder what could have caused it. A centimetre higher and it could have been his eye. Could have blinded him.

Blinded him.

He finishes drinking and you hold out your hand to accept the empty glass. He hands it over with a grateful smile. He's reaching behind himself for something.

The realisation is almost there, the truth about this man, links gradually swimming into focus. The familiar face in the photograph. The woman who came before you and vowed to blind her captor. Even before they are fully in place, your instinct takes over.

You bring back the pint glass and smash it into his face with all of your might.

He roars and lunges forward, arm thrusting. There is a flash of bright metal. A hunting knife. But you're already moving, leaping headlong out of his reach. The knife slashes through empty air, but he's rising, still coming. You're on the floor, scrabbling for the tool bag.

It's closed. He must have closed it when you left the room. There's no time.

You try to roll away, but you're not quick enough. His kick lands in your midriff. You feel something snap with a flash of pain. A rib? You keep rolling away, but he's striding across the room, keeping pace. You feel your chain become dislodged, hear it rattle as it hits the floor. Metal and masonry whipping free. It threatens to tangle you.

You run out of space, hitting the wall and he's upon you, lunging with the knife. It punches through the parka and you feel it connect, slicing through your side, but the coat is so baggy he's misjudged his thrust. You feel the vibration as the point embeds into the floor below you. His face is looming above you, blood spattering down, shards of pint glass still embedded in his cheek, in his eye. He's shouting, roaring, but he's beyond words now.

You grab the hand holding the knife, trying to keep him from withdrawing it, but he's too strong. He pulls it further out and goes in for another thrust. In desperation, you grab at the blade and try to twist it aside.

The knife comes out of his hand.

It was his missing fingers that saved you. He looks confused, not used to their absence.

And you slash his throat open with one hard swipe of the knife.

His arterial blood sprays, drenching your face. You taste the salt iron tang of it. He stumbles backwards, hand pressed to his throat, blood flowing freely through what's left of his fingers. He flops down against the facing wall, sitting awkwardly. You can see the pulse of his blood slowing, his eyes dimming. In his last moments, he looks across at you and meets your eye. He considers you then snorts a laugh as if to say: I can't believe it was you. I can't believe it was you that killed me.

You watch the light die in his eyes, but they're still fixed on you.

You continue to meet his gaze, long minutes after his death.

In The Forest
Lay A Body

IN the forest lay a body.

In life, the body had been called Tolland Coyle. In death, his body had been dumped unceremoniously behind a pine tree, leaving his limbs twisted into a position that would have been quite painful, had he still lived. As it was, his body lay undiscovered for hours in a position that would have elicited sympathetic winces from any witnesses.

Tolland Coyle had lived a wholly unremarkable life in most respects. In many ways, his death was the most interesting thing about him. He held a historic distinction, which went totally unnoticed at the time, of being the first human to die more than a million miles from Earth. For his body, the pine tree it lay behind and the forest itself were all sealed beneath a geodesic Plexiglass dome - one of many bolted to the hull of a ship currently moving out of the solar system at thousands of miles an hour.

The ship was called the Terra Firma, a name chosen - according to the promotional brochure accompanying it's launch - because it was "evocative of a hope that humanity will find new lands to call our home". The brochure had lots of inspiring pictures of glittering space stations and brave astronauts staring off into the middle distance. Nowhere in the brochure did the words "dying planet" or "desperate last hope" appear.

Tolland's body had lain in close to perfect darkness for just over four hours. At six in the morning, the UV lamps set in the ceiling of the dome were turned on, gifting the forest the illusion of daylight. Five minutes later, the sprinkler system embedded just below the forest floor activated. Pulsing jets of water soaked Tolland's bright orange jumpsuit, his arms and his face. Had he been alive, he might have flinched or shivered. As he was dead, he did neither. Droplets of water settled on his unblinking eye.

The first person to find the body of Tolland Coyle was called Mary Cranmer. Her official job title was Floral Technician, which was the fancy space term for a gardener. Her job title had originally been just that: gardener, but was changed to something "more befitting the ambience of the mission" after a long, terse and ultimately insulting email exchange between the staffing co-ordinator and the project hiring manager.

She had just begun her morning rounds, weeding, gathering dead leaves and inspecting the plants and trees for any signs of disease or parasites. She was wearing a dark green jumpsuit and pushing a large trolley containing a rake, shovel and refuse sacks.

She spotted the body of Tolland Coyle at ten past eight. It was obvious, from the twisted position of his limbs, ghostly pallor of his face and gaping wound in his neck, that he was quite dead. Mary, however, did not immediately raise the alarm. Instead, she wheeled her trolley right past the body and continued on her rounds for a further ten minutes.

As she went through the motions of her duties, she thought carefully about what potential benefits and pitfalls might be attached to finding the corpse. Could she be blamed in some way and have her competence questioned? Or would she be praised for her diligence?

This was the way she viewed most major decisions, on a balance sheet of possible pros and cons. She was, in many ways, a supremely selfish person, viewing everything purely in terms of her own gain. This aspect of her personality she wisely kept hidden, having realised long ago the ill will it could cause. Instead, she acted selflessly and altruistically in all matters of little consequence, only revealing her true nature over larger issues. A dead body certainly felt like just such an issue.

She ultimately concluded that not finding the body on her rounds could make her appear incompetent. There was also the potential to milk the event for emotional capital. Finding a body was quite a traumatic event, after all. It could surely be leveraged into time off, or perhaps even compensation.

Thus decided, she returned her trolley to the body, performed a double-take so pronounced that it would have convinced anyone watching that she was the murderer, then ran off to raise the alarm. There was a much quicker way to alert others, via her wrist-mounted tablet, but she rejected this method out of hand as being far too impersonal. Ideally, she decided she needed to make a scene, so she hurried out of the forest dome in search of an audience.

In the connecting corridor, she found several crew members striding by en route to their work stations for the day. The first few she deemed too low status for the news, their menial ranks given away by the flashing on their jumpsuits. She finally settled on a middle-aged man wearing the distinctive black jumpsuit of the officer class.

"A body!" she wailed. "In the forest!" and fell to her knees.

Dr Joseph Polker's first thought, when he saw the running woman, was that she was late for work. It was such a mundane old-school term, but it could still happen, even out here in space. Her green overall was a problem, though. It meant she worked in the botanic section, which she seemed to be running away from, rather than towards. Another couple of nails in the coffin of his theory came when she babbled something about a body in the forest and collapsed at his feet.

The doctor felt something akin to relief. The shapeless, nameless disaster he had dreaded for as long as he could remember was finally happening.

Dr Polker's official title was Exo Liaison. There were several crew members with this title on board, all with differing specialisms. The "Exo" stood for exobiology, which was a fancy way of saying "alien". On paper, their role was to welcome and facilitate any contact with an alien intelligence. Most of them had training in diplomacy, protocol and language analysis.

Dr Polker had training in none of these things.

The remit of his colleagues in the Exo Liaison division could be described as to hope for the best. Dr Polker's job was to plan for the worst. As there had thus far been no confirmed contact with alien life, his training consisted mainly of briefings on theoretical methods by which a malevolent alien intelligence might infiltrate, kill and - in some cases - consume the crew. The possibilities ranged from the mundane (hacking the ship's systems, direct military attack) to the exotic (intelligent soundwaves, nanotech spacecraft the size of a pin, hypnotic messages hidden in a fast-spinning pulsar). All of which might give the most stable of characters a little paranoia, but this new information did not alter Dr Polker's outlook one iota.

Since the age of seven, when he witnessed his mother collapse and die from a brain embolism, he had viewed the world as essentially chaotic. Humanity might attempt to impose order and structure, but these were all fragile façades. He went through life braced for the splintering of those façades, for a maelstrom of death and ruin to swirl in and obliterate everything.

The climate disaster that was fast claiming the Earth hadn't depressed or horrified him. Instead, he was filled with a sense of vindication. He had been right. Chaos was always waiting, clawing at the door. And now, on this last desperate mission to escape to the stars, he was filled with just the same sense of futility. Something would go wrong. Something would claim them all. Some force of nature or alien influence, or even just a stupid overlooked error in the math keeping them alive, would suck the air from their lungs and cast their brittle bodies spinning out into the dark.

It could well begin small. With, say, a single body found in a forest...

Within ten minutes, the body had been cordoned off and the captain, Stefan Pace, was crouching to view it with what he hoped was an expression of sufficient gravity. His knees were hurting. He was flanked by his deputies, the closest thing that the ship had to a police force.

"Everything needs maintenance," said Captain Pace, standing carefully. His knees made a clicking noise as he did so.

He was explaining to Dr Polker why a particular server had been offline last night. For six whole hours. This was the server that collated the video feeds from every single surveillance camera on the ship. Had it been online, they would have been able to follow Tolland Coyle's final hours in crisp hi-def from a variety of angles. As it had been offline, they had absolutely nothing.

That wasn't strictly true. Dr Polker had gained a new aspect to his ever-present sense of dread.

Just looking at the body, Polker couldn't imagine this was suicide. Which made the timing of the server maintenance feel very convenient. Surely, either the killer had been aware of this planned downtime or had arranged it. Which significantly narrowed the potential suspects and included most of the people currently clustered around the body.

"I'll want to be there," said Dr Polker, "for the autopsy."

"I think we can rule out aliens, don't you?" said Captain Pace.

"No sir," said Dr Polker. "That would be my job. After the autopsy."

Captain Pace met his gaze. Technically, Polker was correct, which was the worst kind of correct.

"Of course," said Captain Pace. "Protocols must be observed. Good catch."

He said *good catch* with exactly the same tone and facial expression as one might say *fuck you.*

Mary Cranmer, of course, played no part in the subsequent investigation. After pointing out the body, she was led out of the domed forest and into a small barely furnished office nearby. There she was brought sweet tea and a blanket, as though she'd run a marathon or survived a car crash. Through the window of her new room, she watched a procession of high-ranking crew members enter and leave the dome, before the body itself was brought out in a sealed crate.

Eventually, a man that Mary had never seen before entered her room. Usually, jumpsuits would give some clues to rank or department, but his was plain with no identifying braiding or colour. He introduced himself as Mr Culver and sat opposite. He had a pale, thin face, no hair at all, two distended veins on either side of his forehead and a perpetual frown. He could have been anything from thirty to fifty. Technically, he did all the right things - offering sympathy, recommending counselling and time off - but he didn't blink enough for Mary's liking. She began to feel like a problem he needed to solve.

Mr Culver revealed that the dead man had had a variety of emotional issues, including a messy breakup that his team hadn't realised had affected him quite so severely. Mary was initially confused until she realised that suicide was being implied.

"But his throat was missing," she blurted out, and almost immediately regretted it.

Mr Culver stopped speaking and sighed. He looked as though he was considering his next words very carefully.

"Shock can do strange things to a person's memory," he said. "In this instance we are one hundred per cent sure that Mr Coyle took his own life."

Mary could still see the body clearly in her mind's eye. The ragged void beneath his chin. They were saying that was self-inflicted?

Mr Culver leaned forward.

"Morale on board ship is very important," he said. "For that reason I would advise you to keep any other… narratives, to yourself. Do you understand me?"

Mary nodded slowly. She understood him perfectly.

The body of Tolland Coyle lay on a table in the medical bay. His clothes had been removed, photographed and sealed inside plastic bags. Ironically, he looked a lot more comfortable now than he had twisted up behind the pine tree, although his chest now bore a large Y-shaped scar, stretching from shoulder to shoulder and down to his groin.

Dr Polker had watched the autopsy. It was hardly his field of expertise, but what little he did know caused him concern before the surgeon made a single incision. He knew that without a heart pumping it, blood will tend to settle into the lower parts of the body, leading to light-red discolouration, known as liver mortis, beginning as little as an hour after death.

Every inch of Tolland Coyle's body was as white as chalk.

The surgeon performing the autopsy was professional and curt, dictating into a hanging microphone, but Polker could sense his unease. The evidence was pointing to murder, that much was clear, but something else had happened here. Something calculated and perverse.

"In my professional opinion, he's been bled," said the surgeon.

He was washing his hands and forearms in a large sink after the autopsy, speaking over his shoulder. The room was too small to contain anyone else, so the captain was leaning in. In the treatment room beyond, two of the captain's deputies were eyeing Dr Polker uneasily. They'd been given the job of investigating the death and viewed him as an unnecessary annoyance.

"When you say bled--" began the captain.

"As you would a pig," said the surgeon, and mimed swiping across his throat.

"They hang them upside down, on the farm. Then cut their throats. Gravity and the pump of the heart does the rest."

"So all of his blood...?" said Polker.

"Ninety per cent of it. Just gone," said the surgeon.

In common with most people, Mary Cranmer had, over time, constructed a mental model of the universe. It was an uneven patchwork of her own experiences, absorbed media, supposition and pure fantasy. She was, of course, utterly oblivious to this process. As far as she was concerned, the version of reality she held in her mind and the one she observed were identical.

One of the central pillars of belief in Mary's view of the

universe could be summed up with the phrase *"the bosses are on the take"*. Meaning that any figures of authority you encounter are usually corrupt in some way.

Although this aphorism was supremely cynical and so broad as to be almost meaningless, Mary had yet to have it disproved. For over the years, she had, quite coincidentally, been subordinate to a string of adulterers, embezzlers and - in one memorable case - the moonlighting head of a local drug distribution hub.

In each case, she had uncovered their secrets, after months of subtle and steady investigation, then used them as leverage for either promotion, a pay rise or transfer to a better location.

Following that pattern of behaviour had ultimately snagged her a position here, on humanity's escape rocket to the stars. To find that the bosses were still just as corrupt a million miles from home was no surprise to Mary at all. Just as she always did, she decided to investigate the corruption with a view to using it to her own advantage.

Tolland Coyle had plainly not killed himself, however much Mr Culver would wish it were so. Perhaps the officers were putting that out as a cover story while they investigated his murder. Giving themselves breathing room, or hoping to put the killer at ease.

But Culver's attitude felt wrong. Everything about their meeting hinted at something darker. Something was being covered up, which, as always, Mary saw as an opportunity. The idea that pursuing this might be foolhardy or reckless did not even cross her mind. It was just the way she did things. Her bosses had secrets, Mary dug around until she found them and then negotiated a reward for her silence. That was how the world worked.

She had been given three days' compassionate leave after the discovery of the body. It was the unspoken assumption that she would spend most of those days in her quarters, but technically she had the run of the ship. She returned to her quarters to change, leaving behind the tell-tale green of her Floral Tech jumpsuit in favour of neutral tactical trousers and T-shirt.

While she was changing, her wrist tab chimed. Invitations to book an appointment with the ship psychiatrist, a couple of supportive messages from the captain and the head of her section. They all felt like form letters. "We're very sorry you had to go through the trauma of *insert details of trauma here.*"

Mary headed for the protein vats, which were situated in the aft section of the ship. No one had volunteered the information, but she knew that Tolland Coyle had worked there from the orange of his jumpsuit. The section wasn't called "protein vats", of course. Its official title was "Provision Supply", but Mary didn't know anyone who called it that. It was the place where the food for the ship was grown in huge vats of nutrient-rich slurry, composed mainly of fungus.

Its actual recipe was a proprietary secret, intellectual property of the Uniten Corporation. Most things on the ship were, as the Terra Firma was eighty per cent corporate-funded. It was the only way to build the ship in the first place. So many of the ship's essential systems relied upon technology developed in privately funded labs: the fusion core, the cryo bays, even the paint on the hull. Uniten held the lion's share of patents, so they were effectively in charge, a telling microcosm of a similar power shift back on Earth.

From the forest domes to the vats was a good ten-minute walk, which was mainly taken up with negotiating airlocks. Technically, she wasn't doing anything wrong, she told herself. People deal with trauma in different ways. She shouldn't be victimised because her coping mechanism happened to be going for a walk.

The corridors she passed through offered stunning views on either side. The windows were actually an illusion created by holographic tiling. Years of research had shown that levels of stress and anxiety on a spaceship could be massively reduced by the simple measure of introducing a good view, usually of somewhere lush and green.

This was a conclusion that surprised absolutely no one involved.

So the walls that Mary passed sold the convincing illusion

that she was actually on a covered walkway suspended above the Amazon basin, or a forest of giant redwoods, or one of the great lakes, rather than in a sealed bubble of metal and oxygen hurtling through the void.

Of course, as is often the case, the marketing department couldn't leave a good idea alone. So every single view was also dominated - and arguably therefore ruined - by a huge floating advertisement. This would have been bad enough, but as the price of promotion in such an exclusive location was exorbitantly steep, the only items it made sense to advertise were high-end luxury goods: SUVs, diamond wristwatches and the like. None of these items was for sale on the ship, or indeed could ever be purchased by the crew, given that this trip was one-way. No one would be returning to Earth to buy luxury cars or yachts any time soon. In addition, an argument could be made that the pursuit of exactly those kinds of luxury items had led to the climate collapse that made this mission necessary in the first place.

The upshot of all of this was that introducing holograms of relaxing views had backfired massively, as they now elicited anything from mild irritation to incandescent anger. Some sections of the ship had campaigned to turn them off altogether, but were informed this wasn't viable as the advertisers had paid a lot of money to place those ads. To sell them all those items they could never buy.

Even without the advertisements, it's doubtful that Mary would have looked out of the windows. She'd always classed holograms as fiction and therefore irrelevant. She kept her focus on the real sections of corridor as she passed through them, colour-coded to match the jumpsuits of their workers: green for botanics, yellow for propulsion and finally orange for provision supply.

The aft canteen was virtually identical to the one in the stern. Bolted-down chairs and tables in grids with food dispensers ranged along one wall. At this time of day, it was almost deserted, with just a few orange and yellow jumpsuits dotted around. Mary poured herself a coffee and took a seat. Her plan was to seek out and talk to the dead man's colleagues. Surely news of his death would have reached them by now. Would they be given compassionate leave, as she had been? Would they return to their quarters, or seek comfort from others? Perhaps in a communal area, such as this?

On the way here, Mary's plan, such as it was, had seemed to have some merit. But now, sitting in the virtually empty canteen, she felt foolish. None of the people in orange jumpsuits seemed particularly upset. She could see smiles and overhear laughter. They either hadn't been told of the death or didn't particularly care.

She was about to leave when a further knot of orange jumpsuits entered. Immediately, she knew that they were friends of the dead man. There were four of them, all with slumped shoulders, leaning on each other for support. Two of them appeared to have been crying recently.

Mary greeted each new sign of grief with a growing sense of elation.

The group moved to a table furthest from any other crew and began to talk in low voices with earnest expressions. Mary stood and approached. On the way over, she did her best to mimic their body language, lowering her shoulders, slumping. She tried to imagine what it was like to care about someone else. How it might feel if they died. The group looked up as she drew closer.

"Did you hear about Tolland?" said Mary.

She decided that people in shock wouldn't say much, so she kept her lies short. She said she'd known Tolland back on Earth, that they'd only met a couple of times since they left. She needn't have worried. No one had any follow up questions. They were all still reeling with news of his "suicide". Apparently, the method hadn't been specified, but they'd been told he was found in one of the forests, which led them to assume he'd hung himself from a tree.

Mary didn't correct them. She didn't say anything else. Once she'd been accepted as one of his friends, she was allowed to sit at their table and simply ignored. She just listened as his colleagues struggled to cope with the news. There had apparently been no warning signs at all, which is often the case with murders passed off as suicide. It seemed that Tolland had been jovial, sociable and well-liked. Platitudes were wheeled out, such as "It's always the ones you least expect" and "Just goes to show, you can never truly know someone."

Mary found all of this intensely frustrating.

She was hoping that at least some within the group would have questioned the lie they'd been fed, but there wasn't even a flicker of resistance. She supposed it was understandable. No one would ever think there could be a murderer on board. Every crew member had undergone rigorous psychological screening, for obvious reasons. They were all going to be stuck together on this ship for a very long time. Anyone with insufficient mental stability or, say, murderous psychopathic tendencies, would presumably have not made the cut. Which was a lovely theory as far as it went, but Mary was self-aware enough to realise that she registered at some point on the sociopathic spectrum.

Their filtering obviously wasn't all it was cracked up to be.

She had hoped that the group would provide her with some new avenue of investigation, or a fact about Tolland that would hint at the truth of it all, but thus far all she was getting from them was banal anecdotes about what a nice man he'd been and their useless grieving. The single fact that even remotely piqued Mary's interest was that he'd recently started work in a different section of the protein vats. It was the only thing in his life that appeared to have changed recently.

"He always said he was really happy in his work," said Mary carefully. She was simply rephrasing what one of his colleagues had said, which made the statement safe enough.

"Do you think I might be allowed to visit his section?" she said. "It might help me come to terms with it, to accept that he's actually gone."

Dr Polker walked much the same route as Mary towards the protein vats. He too avoided the views, but for very different reasons. He found them laughable, a denial of the truth about the Earth. How many of those locations were now underwater, or burning? He would have been happier if they'd shown a real-time view of the devastation they were leaving behind. A vindication of his world view, instead of this pantomime.

Like Mary, he also believed that Tolland Coyle had been murdered, but Polker had the advantage of being assured as much by a highly respected surgeon. The method of killing, though. That, in his mind, was still open to debate.

Almost all of the blood in the body had been missing, which not surprisingly led the surgeon to the conclusion that he had been hung upside down and bled out, like some animal in a slaughterhouse. But there were a few problems with that theory. There had been no visible bruising from the rope or cord presumably necessary to hold him aloft in such a fashion. No traces of blood in his hair, which Polker imagined would have been soaked if the surgeon's theory was true.

He was surprised that no one pointed out these obvious holes in the theory, but kept his thoughts to himself. The wound itself was also an issue - a ragged tear that the surgeon stated was not caused by any blade. Polker found himself musing, if it was not gravity that had drained him, then could the cause have been a simple difference in pressure? They were, after all, surrounded by a complete absence of it.

He pictured a micro meteorite, puncturing the hull. A small rupture surrounded by jagged metal. Sudden massive suction pulling Tolland towards it, ripping open his throat then holding him there as the vacuum of space drained his body. In his mind's eye, he could see the blood, spinning away from the ship in vast frozen sheets.

It had a certain bizarre plausibility, but upon closer examination, Polker's new theory was just as shaky as the surgeon's. It required a hole in the hull and a sudden catastrophic drop in pressure to somehow remain undetected by any systems, followed by a speedy repair of the same hole, again unnoticed by anyone. In addition, Tolland's body was found in the centre of one of the domed forests, far from any outer bulkhead. Which meant that even if the vacuum of space had claimed his blood, someone had found his empty lifeless body, rejected the logical idea of raising the alarm, instead deciding to carry the body into the forest and hide it behind a tree.

As part of his role as Exo Liaison, Dr Polker had been trained to think laterally. He'd also been exposed to so many outlandish, but apparently scientifically sound, potential ways that an alien intelligence could, in principle, infiltrate the ship that his definition of the word "impossible" had taken a hell of a battering. No doubt partly because of this, there was an unthinkable idea rattling at the bars of his rational mind. It had been on the edge of his thoughts since the autopsy, but he had been determined to work the problem through logically before allowing it centre-stage. His rational options exhausted, he finally examined it.

All the potential scenarios explaining the death of Tolland Coyle were complicated and unwieldy, apart from one. It was a very simple explanation that fitted all of the facts of his death. The only problem was that it required Polker to accept the existence of a mythical creature.

The explanation was this:
Tolland Coyle had been killed by a vampire.

Mary had never had reason to visit the protein vats. Once this was over, she doubted she ever would again.

The ship's architects had plainly done their best to make the section aesthetically pleasing. Lots of tasteful lighting and sweeping curves, but it felt like a disguise, or an apology. This was a room where large vats of slurry were cooked and processed on an industrial scale. It wasn't sexy or dynamic. It was essentially a factory, where dull, sweaty but ultimately vital work was done.

It also stank. A sickly mix of yeast and warm mushroom, with a sharp note of decay from somewhere. If someone had walked by with a dead rat on a shovel, Mary would not have been surprised.

The dead man's work station seemed much the same as any other in the wide production bay. One of his colleagues explained to her how Tolland's duties used to be to stir the raw fungal matter into the vats. He'd recently been moved to the cutting section, where the cooled and solidified provision, looking much like tofu, was cut and sealed for later consumption.

Mary couldn't see anything worth killing for in his new position. It was one of the many menial jobs on board ship, somewhere on the gruelling scale between replacing the air filters and cleaning the sewage recyclers. True, it involved a computer-controlled blade, which could feasibly have sliced open his throat, but the idea that someone would then run the risk of carrying the body all the way to the forest felt ridiculous.

Mary was about to call it a day and return to her quarters when she overheard one of Tolland's colleagues comforting another, which had been par for the course over the past half hour. But something about this was different, a detail that leaped out at Mary.

The woman being comforted had apparently been due to go on a date with Tolland. Her name was Jen, she was in her late twenties and looked haunted. Dark hollows beneath her eyes, lips compressed into a thin line, hair bleached blonde and pulled back. She had said the least of anyone there, which Mary supposed was understandable.

Drawn to this intriguing new detail, Mary approached and steered Jen with a couple of innocent questions. Apparently, the date would have been their first, but he never showed up. She assumed he'd had second thoughts, only to discover the awful truth this morning.

Mary was watching Jen very carefully as she said this. It reminded her of something she'd not thought about for a very long time. When she was a teenager, she'd gone through a phase of watching true-crime documentaries. At the time, she'd been expecting genius-level serial killers with puzzle-riddled motifs, but instead she found herself watching sad little crimes of passion committed by idiots. She remembered the weary detectives, sick of the media's obsession with random serial killings. They said that ninety-nine per cent of the time, your killer is someone you know. Husband. Wife. Boyfriend.

Or girlfriend.

There were precious few places on board the ship to take

someone on a date. The forests were one. It wasn't strictly allowed, but people turned a blind eye. Perhaps he had turned up for their date after all. Perhaps they'd taken a late-night walk through the forest. Perhaps he'd then got a little too handsy and Jen had defended herself. A little too well, as somehow Tolland had ended up with a ragged hole beneath his chin.

As theories went, Mary had heard worse.

"Had you decided where you were going to go? On your date?" asked Mary innocently.

Jen responded with some vague tale about viewing the stars through one of the observatories. It sounded rehearsed and Mary was barely listening. She'd heard enough, because for the merest fraction of a second after hearing the question, Jen had flickered panic.

Mary was sure she had found her killer.

Dr Polker was wearing the black jumpsuit of the officer class, which meant that anyone not working when he entered Provision Supply soon started. Anyone already working began working a little harder.

All he could see was orange jumpsuits, which surprised him. Two of the captain's deputies were also supposedly investigating Mr Coyle's death. He'd expected to find them here, questioning the dead man's colleagues, but he could see no sign of them. Perhaps they had other leads they were keeping from him.

Or perhaps they had been hypnotised and were now in the thrall of the vampire.

It was all nonsense of course. It had to be, but part of him wouldn't leave the idea alone. He also found himself thinking about the fact that Tolland Coyle was not the only cadaver on board the Terra Firma. A further four hundred lifeless corpses were laid out in long airless bays in the depths of the ship.

Of course, the shareholders wouldn't appreciate them being described in that way. Technically, they were cryogenically frozen. There was another glossy brochure on the topic, piles of which were left unread at the launch centre back on Earth. The copywriters for the brochure had been given strict instructions to

avoid any terms that might make people think that a body with
no heartbeat and frozen beyond minus two hundred degrees
centigrade was actually dead. Terms like "vitality pause" and
"calming cessation" were used more than once.

In a way, the semantic coyness was understandable. It had
been presented as a painless routine procedure mainly to quell
any fears within the crew, who were all scheduled to have their
"vitality paused" at some point in the next few years. The idea
was to rotate everyone in and out of cryogenic suspension over
the decades ahead. It had all been carefully planned out to eke
out supplies and ensure that no one died of old age.

The breakthrough in cryogenic suspension had arrived just in
time to save humanity. It had been considered unworkable for
decades. The suspension part of the equation was never the issue.
Freezing a body and keeping it that way was easy enough. It was
the resurrection side of things that caused all the headaches.
Cellular damage seemed impossible to avoid. They'd tried
replacing the blood with various different fluids, freezing the
bodies fast, freezing them slow, even attempting the process using
just severed heads - all to no avail.

Then along came Uniten, headed by Casper Reeger,
billionaire tech wunderkind, declaring that he'd perfected the
process. Demonstrations were given, bodies resurrected after
weeks, then months of stasis. Interstellar travel, with its decade-
long journey times, was suddenly viable, just in time to escape the
ailing Earth.

Four hundred corpses, thought Dr Polker. Lying in darkness.
Asleep, yet not. Dead, yet not. What does that sound like to you?

It sounds like vampires.

He'd done a quick web search on vampire traits as he walked
there. Just to pass the time, you understand (which didn't explain
why he felt the need to run the query through a dummy account
with no connection to him). He'd ignored all of the fiction and
gone back to the folklore, hoping to find some common thread,
but he'd been disappointed, finding instead a mass of
contradictions. Generally speaking, vampires were undead
creatures who drank the blood of the living. Except when they

didn't, and were, in fact, alive and absorbed spirits instead. They only travelled at night, except when they didn't. And so on.

If vampires had ever been real - and that was a big "if" - he had to assume that their biology was markedly different from a human's. Different enough to show up in a thorough medical examination, which everyone on board had gone through, including all of those currently frozen in the cryo bays.

For this supposed difference to have been overlooked, four hundred times, would require a cover-up of mammoth proportions. Every doctor in the launch centre, their bosses, the crews manning the induction centre, and so on. All in on it. All threatened or bribed or blackmailed into silence.

It reminded him of Flat Earth Theory, which was patently nonsense; but even putting that aside, the sheer number of people needed to keep quiet about the "truth" would have made it totally unworkable. Every employee of every space agency around the globe, ditto airlines, ditto astronomers, and so on. Thousands of people, all keeping quiet about the flat truth and insisting the world was round, with no leaks, no exceptions.

The frozen bodies in the cryo bays were human. The alternative was a conspiracy so large as to be ridiculous. True, the bodies had a certain superficial passing resemblance to vampires in their resting state, but it was a creaking floorboard mistaken for a burglar. In his current hypervigilant mode, he'd created connective tissue where there was none. It was a pattern recognition misfire. Nothing more.

It didn't explain where the captain's deputies had got to. Still, it seemed far more likely that they were simply slacking off somewhere, rather than lying drained and inert, stuffed in some closet.

Well, if they weren't going to do their job, perhaps he'd just have to do it for them.

He approached a knot of workers, intending to ask after the dead man's colleagues. It was only as he drew closer that he spotted a crew member in civilian clothing, a woman whose face he vaguely knew. It took him a second to place her before he realised that it was the woman who had found the body, looking awkward and out of place. She appeared to have been actively doing her best to keep out of his sight, behind one of the vats. He caught her eye and beckoned with a finger.

There was an office to one side that seemed to double up as a storage unit. Teetering stacks of boxes loomed over a desk and a couple of chairs, but there was enough space between them for it to be workable. Polker took a seat and gestured for her to do the same. Before he could ask a single question, the woman began to speak.

Mary Cranmer wasn't sure if the doctor was part of the cover-up or not. Either way, she wasn't about to share what she suspected regarding the death of Tolland Coyle. If and when she made her demands, it was going to be to someone of significantly higher rank. Until then, she would keep her powder dry. The more people that know a secret, the less use it is as leverage. She was sure of that much.

So, she fed him the lie she'd prepared. That she was on compassionate leave. That she'd gone for a walk to try and clear her head of the horrible sight she'd seen. That she came to the man's work station to try and make sense of it all. She rambled along on that theme until she could see she was boring him. He dismissed her with a couple of words she could tell he intended to be comforting. She reacted as if she'd found them so.

She then left the protein vats, but instead of returning to her quarters or the floral bays, she followed signs to the command section. Although, by any measure, her evidence was flimsy and based primarily on a split-second of panic glimpsed in a girl's face, she decided it was enough. She was convinced she'd found her killer. Accidentally or otherwise, Jen had killed Tolland Coyle. She'd stake her life on it.

She negotiated several airlocks, followed curves and T-junctions until she found herself in the rarefied air of those who led them. Whether intentional or not, there was a sense of heightened comfort in the corridors she now passed through. They seemed slightly wider, the fixtures a little more refined, the lighting scheme more subtle. Here, black jumpsuits were the norm. Mary felt like an oddity, an intruder, although in truth none of the officers gave her a second look.

She had intended to go straight to the captain with her suspicions, but fate intervened. Mr Culver, her former interrogator and deliverer of veiled threats, appeared before her, stepping from a knot of officers who continued without him. He stared at her without curiosity, with a kind of blankness that Mary found unsettling. She decided that Culver was probably high enough in the chain of command to serve her purposes.

"I'd like to have a word," said Mary. "In private."

Culver nodded, as though he'd been expecting as much, and beckoned for Mary to follow him into a nearby office. It was empty bar a desk and two chairs. No touches of personalisation, or indeed signs that anyone had ever worked here. He closed the door behind them.

Mary took her seat first, deciding it was a move that showed confidence. As soon as Mr Culver had taken his seat, she began to speak.

"Tolland Coyle didn't kill himself," said Mary, "and I have a pretty good idea who did. Now, there's no reason this has to go any further than me. You should know I can be trusted to keep my mouth shut, for a little consideration."

Mary had intended to go on, to outline potential ways they could make her life on ship easier - a bigger cabin, a lighter workload - but she found the words dying in her throat.

Mr Culver was smiling.

Had it been a smile of amusement, or even one tainted with the bitterness of defeat, Mary may well have continued. But this was something else entirely. Mary had seen smiles of contempt before, of delight in another's downfall, another's pain, or at least she thought she had. Culver's smile showed such open malice, it was as though he had struck her. It was so extreme that it seemed as though his face was contorting around his mouth. Mary abruptly became gripped with the feverish notion that he was no longer in control of his own face. Some demonic puppeteer had yanked on the wire that drew back the lips, exposing the teeth.

All of the teeth.

"Do you know how many units of blood are in the average human body?" said Mr Culver.

Mary really didn't want to know. She didn't want to be in that room anymore, or even on that ship. She realised then that she'd made a terrible, terrible mistake in coming there.

Then Mr Culver told her the answer to his question, and exactly why it was important. And the puppeteer controlling his face pulled even harder on the wire leading to his mouth.

And Mary began to scream.

Dr Polker was about to pull the "we're all fucked" emergency ripcord.

Unsurprisingly, that was his own personal shorthand for the protocol and not its official title. In the Exo Liaison training module, it had been titled the "Last Resort Backstop".

He remembered the morning he received that particular briefing. The instructor, a drawn-looking woman in her sixties that Polker strongly suspected was ex-CIA, explained the process in great detail with a sombre air. Both of them were fully cognisant of the dire straits the ship would have to be in for him to ever consider using it.

The protocol, in a nutshell, was a method to safely and securely send a message home with as much useful detail as possible about the presumably terminal crisis the ship was facing. A message in a bottle from a doomed and sinking vessel. For it to be in play, the captain and other senior staff were presumed to be either dead or in some way compromised by an alien infiltration.

There were several hidden terminals on board the ship from which these messages could be sent. The location of the terminals and, indeed, the existence of the protocol itself, were kept from the captain and other senior officers, for obvious reasons. They no doubt had their own version of the protocol, but redundancy made a lot of sense.

Even within this action of last resort, there was a further layer of precaution: a terminal connected directly to the communications array, with no possibility of interception or interference. As accessing this final terminal would require walking across the outer hull, it was explained to Polker that he should only use it if he feared for his own safety on board the ship, or had reason to believe that the secret terminals had been compromised.

Which is why Dr Polker was currently jammed inside a sweaty vacuum suit, breathing heavily as he lumbered across a gantry bolted to the outer skin of the Terra Firma.

A lot had happened in the last twenty minutes.

Twenty minutes ago, he'd been in Provision Supply, gradually becoming convinced that he was wasting his time.

He'd questioned Tolland Coyle's co-workers, but none appeared to know anything useful. He was surprised to learn that they all thought Coyle had killed himself. On one level, he could understand the need for misinformation. A suicide on board was less likely to cause panic than a murder, vampiric or otherwise, but it would have been nice of the captain to keep Polker in that particular loop.

The woman who found the body, Mary something, had been an odd fish. Her answers all seemed perfectly reasonable, but Polker had the sneaking suspicion that he was watching a performance. Could she be the killer? Pretending to have discovered the body to draw attention away from herself? Then ruining it all by hanging around the dead man's work station.

Yeah. Didn't make a whole heap of sense.

He'd filed her under "odd, probably nothing" and set off for the ship's main medical bay. He was drawn there for a couple of reasons. If there really was a vampire on board then they had somehow slipped through the rigorous medical tests they'd all undergone. He wanted to see exactly how that might be achieved. He also wanted to ask about any blood plasma they had in storage. For a crew of their size, they had to have a stock in case of emergencies.

Wouldn't that be a draw for a vampire?

It was all guesswork, in turn based upon the flimsy foundation of the supposed existence of an imaginary creature. Polker was well aware of that, but he went anyway. He had no idea where his questions would lead him. Ideally, the doctors in charge would just be clearing up after a bizarre break-in, during which their entire stock of blood had been stolen.

The main med-bay was just down the corridor from the command section. Polker was sure there were very sound logistical reasons for that, but you could also draw some uncharitable conclusions about the officers wanting to be as close as possible to the best medical care on board.

The treatment room itself was wide and brightly lit. Utilitarian gleaming white monitors and examination bays were tempered a little by holographic views of forest glades.

Polker did his best to ignore the gently spinning suppository advertisements.

The physician in charge, a Dr Omandi, had a smooth paternal air marred only by his tic of blinking a little too often. He welcomed Polker as though they were old friends and nodded sagely when Tolland Coyle's murder was brought up.

"Terrible business. Any ideas who might have done it?"

"Not a one," lied Polker.

Dr Polker acted as though he was clutching at straws even coming there. He wondered how much of that was an act. He noticed that Omandi had a small plastic action figure upon his desk. It was brightly coloured, with cape and staff. Did it belong to one of his children? Or did they give it to the younger patients to keep them distracted? It felt as though it came from another world, a world without death, where throats were never cut and blood was never drained.

Omandi fielded his questions about the medical screening process with a bemused air. Polker implied that he suspected someone had managed to join the crew while hiding a life-threatening condition. Which he supposed technically vampirism was, he just didn't specify whose life was being threatened.

Dr Omandi confessed that he couldn't think of any way that such a condition could be hidden.

"Even if they managed to get on board," he said, "with, say, terminal cancer, medicals are compulsory every month. And they are quite thorough. Can I ask what's prompted--"

"You have blood plasma on board?" asked Polker.

Dr Omandi blinked three times before answering. That was interesting.

"Of course," he said.

"How easy would it be to steal?"

"That's a very odd question," said Dr Omandi. "Can I ask why--?"

"Have you done an inventory recently?" asked Dr Polker.

Dr Omandi smiled, hands held wide. Nothing to see here.

"I can assure you, our plasma is perfectly safe," he said. "It's kept under the same rigorous security as our other - as our pharmaceutical narcotics."

Dr Polker acted as though he was satisfied with the answer, then confessed that he felt like he was chasing his tail with this case. That it wasn't even his assignment really, but that it felt good to be involved. Good to keep busy.

Dr Omandi relaxed a little. He nodded and blinked some more, walked him to the door and shook his hand as he left. Only when the door had closed between them did Polker allow his face to show the fear he was now feeling.

There had been a single moment in their conversation that had chilled Polker to the core. It was either a simple momentary slip of the tongue, or the key to the death of Tolland Coyle and a hint at something much larger and more terrible.

Dr Omandi had said that the blood plasma was kept under the same rigorous security as their pharmaceutical narcotics. He almost said something else, but stopped himself. He almost said that the blood plasma was being kept under the same rigorous security as their *other* pharmaceutical narcotics.

Which implied that he considered addiction to blood a possibility.

Polker remembered walking away from the med-bay, no real destination in mind, with a heavy stone of dread in his stomach. Since the death of his mother, hadn't he always known this day would come? That the shapeless chaos clawing at the fringes of his world would eventually break through. True, he'd never expected it to wear this face, but wasn't part of him relieved that the torturous wait was finally over?

He tried to organise his scattered thoughts. To give form to his fears. What did he suspect was actually going on?

A vampire had killed Tolland Coyle.

The command staff were attempting to cover that up. Wiping the CCTV footage. Telling everyone it was a suicide. Not even bothering to do any further investigation. Dr Omandi was colluding in that. He knew that vampires find blood addictive.

Which implied what?

What else could he deduce from that?

Was he even sure that anything was going on? The web of suppositions and implications swirling around the death of Tolland Coyle seemed, at times, gossamer thin. Could he justifiably raise the alarm based on what little he had seen and heard? What he suspected felt so huge and monstrous, it could almost be rejected on those grounds. It was too much to be true.

It's possible he might have talked himself down from that ledge, convinced himself that it was all just another pattern recognition misfire, had he not crossed paths again with Mary, the woman who had found the body.

He had just reached a T-junction and paused when he saw her. She was walking down the corridor that led away from the command section, which in itself was a surprise. She was a long way from both her work station and quarters. Polker initially thought that perhaps she'd been summoned for further questioning.

Then he saw her face.

Far away and a lifetime ago, Polker had been one of the first people on the scene of a car accident. A boy racer going too fast through a busy market street. He'd spun out, the back end of his car swiping through a crowd. Three people were killed outright, a dozen more injured. Polker remembered the face of a middle-aged man who had, seconds earlier, been happily shopping with his wife. Now he was a widower, holding the limp hand of a woman who would never move, never smile, never speak again.

He saw echoes of that face in Mary. Her eyes wide, focussed

on nothing; lips moving almost soundlessly, as though in prayer; eyebrows raised high in the centre, beseeching the universe. She seemed almost unaware of her surroundings, walking on auto-pilot back towards her section.

Then her eyes fell upon the motionless Dr Polker, waiting at the T-junction.

It was as though a switch had been flipped. Her face contorted in fear and she began to babble, hissed entreaties. He noticed she had tears in her eyes.

"I won't tell," she whispered. "I swear I won't. You can trust me."

She passed him with her back pressed close to the wall of the corridor, keeping out of reach, as if afraid he might lunge. He watched her as she backed away, a pressure door opening at her approach. His view of her was finally cut off as the door closed.

Dr Polker considered for all of two seconds, walked briskly to the nearest emergency airlock, hurriedly pulled on a vacuum suit and clambered out into the void.

Polker was almost at the communications array. It had been in his field of view for much of the last ten minutes, growing from a silver splinter in the distance that marred the gentle curve of the hull, until now it loomed above him. A dense cluster of aluminium dishes and cabling were all centred around the cannon-like barrel of the laser, doing it's best to keep a constant lock with a receiver back on Earth.

It would have undoubtedly been quicker to make much of the journey inside the ship, but something within him - some primal need to flee - had propelled him through that airlock.

Mary had been threatened. That much was clear. It was also fairly obvious that Polker's black officer jumpsuit had triggered the memory of that threat. She had assumed that Polker was part of it. All of which were useful new puzzle pieces, but ultimately what tipped the scales for him was what she'd been murmuring as she approached. He only caught a second or two of it, but it was enough.

"Ten units," she had been mumbling. "Ten units. Ten units."

Over and over.

There were ten units of blood in the human body. Polker knew that much. It was the final kick he needed to spur him to action, to finally raise the alarm. Since then the words had become an earworm, a mantra, rattling endlessly around his mind as he walked. Giving rhythm to his steps.

Ten units. Ten units. Ten units.

It was such an oddly specific way to threaten someone.

"I am going to drink your blood. All ten units of it."

There was something else about it. A reason the words wouldn't leave him. Something relevant to all of this at the edges of his thoughts, a connection he hadn't yet made.

He was sure it would come to him.

The mic in the suit helmet had automatically paired with his wrist tab as soon as he put it on, which allowed him to record his report to send back home en route. He'd couched it in dry official terms that almost made him sound sane. He stated that he believed Tolland Coyle had been drained of blood by a creature on board that was not human. He also stated that he believed this same creature had, in some way, compromised the command staff, who were actively covering up its existence and threatening witnesses.

He tried to keep his voice even as he spoke. He wondered if he sounded desperate or unhinged.

In theory, the command staff of the Terra Firma could send their own competing messages, paint him as deluded, attempt to undermine his account. But Tolland Coyle was still dead. His blood was still missing. Their attempts to explain away these facts would surely expose them.

Polker knew that even if his message was ultimately believed, it would still bring no help. The engines of the Terra Firma had pushed it far out of the range of any potential rescue vessel from Earth. All he was doing was improving the chances of the ships to come, ships that would hopefully have a little more rigorous medical screening.

Assuming that any more were ever built.

The Terra Firma was the first of a planned fleet of

colonisers, but there had been disquieting rumours of supply chains collapsing in the last few days before launch. The mines for the raw materials and metals vital for any further construction finally running dry.

Polker hoped there was no truth to these stories. For if there was, if no further ships were even possible, raising the alarm was worse than futile. Worse because those trapped on the dying Earth currently still had hope that the mission would work, that humanity would live on through the Terra Firma. Polker wasn't totally sure what was happening on board his ship, but somehow he couldn't picture it ending with one big happy colony decades from now.

He did his best to push those worries from his mind, prepared the audio file for transmission and carried on walking.

Much of the Terra Firma was continually spinning, centrifugal force standing in for gravity. It resembled a series of vast drums, with the inner curves experiencing roughly three quarters of Earth gravity, lessening as you climbed decks, with zero gravity in the centre.

All of which meant that a conventional space walk was impossible, as the centrifugal force would simply throw you off into space. To solve this, the ship's architects had kindly provided a lattice of metal gantries bolted to the hull, allowing maintenance access without needing to stop the spin.

A lovely theory, terrifying in practice.

From Polker's perspective, the ship towered above him with no apparent support, a huge curved mass threatening to crush his tiny body. Below him stretched the endless void of space. The only thing between him and falling into oblivion was a fragile length of gantry, which was hanging from the hull by the slenderest steel rods he had ever seen. To further save on weight, the gantries themselves were made of gridded metal, with a support railing on only one side. He felt as though he were walking along a cheese grater, providing dizzying glimpses of the abyss beneath him. Nausea and vertigo were never far away.

He estimated he was a minute or so from the array when he heard the voice.

"We only wanted to survive," said the voice. "Just like you."

Polker almost cried out with shock before he realised that it was his in-suit radio. He should have turned it off, but there had been a few other things on his mind.

The voice was deep, but clipped and a little sing-song, in a manner you could tell the owner thought was charming. Or perhaps it was meant to intimidate, mock jollity before the fall of the axe. The accent surprised Polker. He'd been subconsciously expecting something European or Slavic, instead it was clearly American, somewhere Midwest.

"Who is this?" said Polker.

"The captain. The *real* captain. Call me Coombs."

Polker looked back along the gantry. Currently empty for hundreds of metres. The only possible route to reach him. Coombs was probably inside the ship rather than hurrying here to stop him. Even so, Polker ran the last few feet to the array.

"Pleased to meet you, Captain Coombs," said Polker. "Can I help you with something?"

As he talked, he brushed ice crystals from an interface panel and flipped it open to reveal a keyboard and monitor, both currently dead. A single button was lit up red and Polker pushed it.

"How much do you think you've figured out?" said Coombs.

"Well, I wasn't entirely sure until now," said Polker. "Something of a relief to hear from you, to be honest."

He realised Coombs was chuckling. It was not a nice sound.

A retinal scan left a blooming spot on Polker's vision and caused the monitor to spark into life. He rattled in his password, tugged an interface cable from his suit and plugged into a waiting slot.

"I'm genuinely curious," said Coombs. "How much do you know?"

Polker had no need to show his hand, to reveal just how little he knew, but he also felt the need to keep Coombs talking. To stall whatever he was planning.

"OK. How does this sound," said Polker. "You realised Earth was toast, so you hid aboard the ship, threatened the crew.

Maybe turned some of them, or whatever you call it. Is that how it worked?"

"You're not thinking large enough," said Coombs.

Ten units. Ten units. What was it about those words?

"How many of you are there?" asked Polker.

"Hundreds," said Coombs.

Polker could hear the smile in his voice.

He was lying. He had to be.

There were currently one hundred and sixty active crew on the Terra Firma, not counting the four hundred cryo frozen. For "hundreds" of that number to be vampires would imply a conspiracy so large as to be ridiculous. His earlier logic still held. One or two sneaking aboard, especially if they had a doctor on side, he could just about believe. But hundreds? No.

Polker's message was uploaded in seconds. He attached the autopsy report, the only piece of actual evidence he had. The array began to compress and convert the message into a format that the laser could send. A progress bar appeared on the screen, gradually depleting. It was moving so slowly.

"We don't want to kill you," said Coombs.

"Comforting," said Polker. "What about Tolland Coyle? Did you want to kill him?"

"That was an unfortunate mistake," said Coombs. "One of our number allowed their hunger to get the better of them. It won't happen again. Just think about it logically. Your blood is our food source. If we kill you all, what are we going to eat?"

The idea didn't exactly comfort him, even if it was true. He also wondered why this conversation was even happening. They'd connected to his vacuum suit, which meant they knew he was outside. They had to know what he was trying to do. When being briefed about this terminal, Polker had been assured that it couldn't be blocked from within the ship, but he was beginning to wonder.

He suddenly felt so very tired. He wondered what fate awaited him when he returned within. He was momentarily gripped by the idea that he was the lone human left on board. The instant he cleared the airlock, dozens of the creatures would pounce, their mouths biting, gouging, sucking.

He peered briefly over the edge of the gantry, down into the infinite darkness below him. Would that be a better death? Falling into the void until his oxygen ran out and carbon dioxide overwhelmed him? He'd read somewhere that it wasn't like drowning, that you simply pass out. Perhaps it would be just like going to sleep.

"We're quite happy to let you live," said Coombs, as though reading his thoughts. "You can still live a long, relatively happy life on the ship, just like everyone else. We only ask you keep our secret a little longer. We plan to reveal ourselves in time. But the rollout of information has to be carefully managed. Panic could be very dangerous."

"Does it ruin the flavour?" said Polker.

Coombs didn't like that. There was a new hardness in his voice when he next spoke.

"You should be grateful we are even here," he said. "All of you."

The progress bar hit seventy per cent. The gantry behind him was still empty.

"Grateful?" said Polker. "I can't wait to hear this."

"They weren't even going to build a ship until we came forward. Cryogenic technology was a dead end, and without that, a journey this long--"

"Are you saying you *solved* the cryo problem?" said Polker.

Ninety per cent. Come on. Come on.

"Not at all. It *still* doesn't work. Probably never will. On humans at least. Thankfully our, *gifts* make us very resilient. Heartbeats have always been kind of optional and resurrection is baked into the deal. Faced with the choice of humanity dying on Earth or an alliance with us, it was really no choice at all."

It was quite a story. If it was true, Polker was wasting his time. They weren't stopping him sending his little warning because all the people at the launch centre back home knew exactly who he was sharing a ship with.

It was a lie. Had to be. A distraction to make him doubt his mission. Because the alternative was madness.

147

He abruptly became aware of a growing prickly sensation on the back of his scalp - his primitive early warning system telling him that he was not alone. He turned to look back along the gantry. Still totally empty.

The array fed a chime through his internal speaker. It had completed its compression. It just required a final approval from him to send the message. It was almost over.

Ten units. Ten units.

As he turned back to the array, by complete chance he happened to glance out on to the curved surface of the hull. He'd paid no attention to the view beyond the gantry, as anyone attempting to approach him that way would have immediately been thrown off into space by the spin of the ship.

Dozens of vampires were standing on the hull watching him.

Polker felt the breath catch in his throat. What he was seeing was so chilling and impossible on so many levels that it stopped him dead. He could see men, women, and - dear God - children. Standing staring like the souls of the dead. None of them was wearing a vacuum suit. What skin he could see was as white as marble, giving them the appearance of statues.

From his perspective, they were all standing upside down, which made their expressions impossible to read, but their mouths were wide - my God, so wide. Ready to swallow the world.

The small part of his mind that wasn't paralysed with fear idly mused on how they were so brazenly defying physics. His eyes drifted to their feet, all of which were bare. Below their ankles, the skin contorted and rippled, the feet ending in monstrous talons akin to those of an eagle or vulture, the claws of which were all puncturing the hull with a firm hold. They were not ignoring physics at all, instead hanging on like enormous bats. Part of him wanted to laugh at the idea, but he feared he might never stop.

He decided that if any of them moved any closer, he would leap off into space.

One of them, a young woman in an orange overall, gestured towards the array. Even upside down, he could read her intent, comically polite in the circumstances. She was, in effect, asking him to please, go ahead.

He had totally forgotten about his mission.

The screen on the array was blinking politely, awaiting his final permission before sending the message, sounding the alarm to the world.

And the vampires didn't care.

Even more chilling, they were actively encouraging him to send it. Underlining its futility.

And then he understood.

The terrible shape of it, finally clear to him.

He realised why ten units had rung a bell.

Coombs' story had all been true. The vampires hadn't infiltrated the ship, they'd helped build the damn thing. Without them and their ability to survive cryo, humanity would have been stuck on the dying Earth. Out of options and facing extinction, those in charge back home had accepted the vampires' help, knowing full well what it would mean. Now the human race, if it had a future at all, was merely as a food source. Nothing more.

The Terra Firma was a ship of the damned.

Whenever Polker had pictured chaos breaking through, he imagined it would bring an end, and with it the release of death. But this was a nightmare with no end in sight. As cryo didn't work on humans, they would experience the whole journey in real time. Decades growing old and dying, their offspring maturing only to take their place as walking blood banks. Only there to feed their masters.

Perhaps more ships would follow, but Polker was willing to bet that if and when they did, they would be just as infested as this one.

Maybe their offer to let him live was genuine. Maybe he could simply walk back inside and rejoin the rest of the cattle, as long as he kept his mouth shut.

Ten Units.

The arrogance of it. The vampires had hidden the truth in plain sight. Their true nature, their true desire encoded within the name of their corporation.

Ten Units.
Uniten.
Polker almost smiled as he stepped off into the void.

I Shall Bring
A Purging Fire

IT is a sacred space. A space of quiet contemplation.

The only sound is the hiss of thirty-one planchettes gliding across stone tablets. Like distant whispers, the noise reverberating and echoing around the great hall.

Anyone who enters must do so barefoot. All conversation is forbidden. A priest may risk a murmured word or two of instruction to a novice, but anything beyond that must be confined to the anterooms.

Thirty-one planchettes gliding across thirty-one stone tablets. In turn, resting upon thirty-one circular stone tables.

Around each table are seated three conduits, each facing inwards with a hand resting upon the moving planchette. Ninety-three conduits in all, to symbolise the ninety-three bolts that held the gibbet cage closed as the Kindest Soul burned.

There is, of course, a cage in the centre of the great hall. It is the centrepiece of the altar, and is indeed a cage of dazzling splendour, fashioned in delicately filigreed gold and set with ninety-three jewels of varying sizes. In excellence it rivals, in my view, the gibbet cage of High Host Temple. Which is only proper, given that this chamber is central to our faith.

Should not the cage at its centre be the most exquisite in the empire?

The conduits' chairs and tables are themselves just as much works of art, each chair back, leg and table intricately carved -

the chairs from oak, the tables from sandstone. The carvings themselves depict various pivotal moments from the Books of the Faithful. It has become an accepted shorthand to refer to each conduit by the scenes depicted on their chairs. Thus, a conduit whose chair carvings depicted, say, The Shaming of Belhalla, would be known to the novices as Belhalla, regardless of their actual gender.

Our job as novices is to tend to the conduits' every physical need. Below each chair is a special compartment, opened by means of a hidden latch. Contained within is a sealed vessel into which the waste and urine of the conduit pours through a series of rubber tubes. At least three times a day, the vessel is removed, emptied and replaced. A similar compartment is built into the headrest. Here, we refill a vessel containing liquefied food, which passes, using simple gravity, down through another tube into the conduit's stomach. We also regularly bathe the parts of their bodies we can reach, using water heated by fires in the anterooms.

Once a week, the conduits' heads are shaved. When I began my duties here, I was told this was to avoid lice infestation, but I have come to believe that this is not the whole reason. For shaving their heads in this way also makes their lobotomy scars very easy to see, serving as a potent reminder of their supreme sacrifice.

My understanding of the full process is limited. I do know that the automatic bodily functions - such as breathing, heart rate and digestion - are regulated by a relatively small area of the brain. Also necessary is the area of the brain that controls motor functions. Every part not vital to these processes is cut away.

Throughout all of our duties - changing, feeding, washing and shaving the conduits - the motion of their hands holding the planchettes never ceases. Hissing across the stone tablets at speed, from letter to letter. Spelling out words and messages from beyond the veil. Prophecies, warnings, admonishments, instructions. The oil that keeps the machinery of our empire running.

Not that I, personally, have ever read one of these messages. Such a thing would be unthinkable for a mere novice. That privilege is reserved for hierophants only. For this reason, the conduits' stone tablets are hidden from common view. This is achieved by a combination of two precautions. The first is a long, hollow stone column suspended above every table. This tube is the same width as the table beneath and terminates barely six inches above, just high enough to allow the hands of the conduits to reach the planchettes within. The second precaution is a short, beaded curtain hanging from the base of these columns, which prevents a novice from even accidentally witnessing the miracle in flow.

At the top of each hollow column, I am informed there is - although I of course have never observed - a window to the floor above. These windows are apparently set with some kind of magnifying lens and are monitored at all hours by hierophants, in order to catalogue the words streaming down to us from the aether.

And in this way, the words and wisdom of the Host are transcribed and translated, before being disseminated to all corners of the empire.

Working in the great hall, tending to the needs of the conduits, is a great honour. Every novice that I encounter within the temple is filled with awe when they discover my responsibilities. To many, it is seen as the pinnacle of a novice's potential duties and in many ways, of course, it is. To be in the same room as this miracle occurs, and continues to occur, is breathtaking. Spellbinding.

But I am dissatisfied.

This is something I would admit to no one. No confessor, high priest or confidant will ever hear these words pass my lips. It is a shameful, prideful secret that I will carry to my grave. The fact that I know the exact reason for my restlessness brings me no comfort at all. For you see, I have not always lived in the novice quarters of the temple, or indeed the citadel at Collbrae. The first twenty-five years of my life were spent on various frontiers of

155

the empire, as an apprentice to Master Gideon Foll. He was, and is, a shining light, a pioneer in the realm of outreach and education. Bringing the manifold truths of the Host to the many lands and peoples less fortunate than our own. In this work, I saw humanity at its lowest ebb, but with Master Foll's guidance and teachings, we strove together to raise those poor lost souls to a higher path.

It was exhilarating, fulfilling work. Each day brought a new challenge, a new vista, a new group of vessels waiting to be filled with the Truth. I met and broke bread with the wind-scarred nomads of the Crawsand Wastes, introduced the sullen wanderers of the Broken Hills to the chronicles of the Kindest Soul and left replica gibbet cages with the painted widows of the Silver Coast.

I felt it to be my true vocation and Master Foll agreed. I would have been more than content to live out my life within his group as one of his wandering missionaries, but it appeared the Host had other plans for me. Something in my behaviour or outlook had drawn their attention and led to a wax-sealed message, arriving directly from the temple at Collbrae. No details were given, I was simply to return to the citadel as fast as I was able.

Two months later, still caked with the grime of my journey, I met with the high priest who had sent the summons, apparently transcribed directly from a conduit's table. He informed me that, as of that moment, my duties would be limited to the physical care of the conduits within the temple at Collbrae. All other duties were to be relinquished, all possessions given over to the temple. He informed me that the Host had offered no reason for my summons, or indicated the expected length of my servitude.

That was three years ago.

Initially, I was ecstatic. Knowing that from the thousands of novices across the empire, I was one of a mere handful chosen personally by the Host to care for their physical representatives. It was an undeniable, incredible honour for which I still, to this day, am deeply and humbly grateful.

And yet…

I still think fondly of my other life as a missionary, perhaps a little too often. Learning at the hem of Master Foll's robe, meeting some new group of travellers on the road and introducing them to the Truth. It was such a rich and varied way to live and express our devotion to the Host. How could I not miss it? Is my shame ill-founded? Perhaps this is all some great test of devotion, or lesson in the strength of humility, or dangers of pride, hidden in the everyday forms around me.

I must meditate upon it.

I walked a dark path,
Beset by tribulation,
Yet I heard a chorus,
And it steeled my step,
The Host is calling. Will you answer?
The Host can lead you. Will you follow?
The Host will guide you, out of the darkness.
The Host will chide you, if you stray from the path.

I had known the song since childhood, we all had, but the baker was delivering a stirring rendition. From my vantage point, I couldn't see the singer, but I was very familiar with his rich tenor. It was well known to everyone who worked in the market, which is why it drew so little praise or attention - although, in my view, it was certainly worthy of both. Instead, it was left to compete with the other noises of trade in the square - the hubbub and haggle of stallholders and servants, the calls of the spiced-meat vendors, the squeak of passing cartwheels, the cluck of caged chickens.

I was sitting on the flat roof of the novice washrooms, which afforded me a good view of the crowds several storeys below. Market day at temple always made for a good spectacle. I myself had walked through the throng many times, but infinitely preferred viewing it from above. At ground level, it could be a jostling trial of patience. As an elevated witness, distanced from the scrum, the discomfort of others took on a pantomime air, some raucous play enacted purely for my benefit. A dozen petty arguments, boasts and jokes playing out in mime before me. Here, a guard leching at a passing hand maiden, totally failing to notice a beggar stealing from a fruit stall. There, a rotund butcher angrily rejecting an insultingly low offer from a Bachean servant. Beside them, two stallholders enjoyed what felt like a long-running joke, conveyed purely in shouts and florid gestures, across a wide moving river of crowd.

The smells up high were better too. Down amongst the faithful, it seemed the stink of sewage and unwashed flesh was never far away. Up here, due to some fortunate quirk of air currents I didn't pretend to understand, it seemed that only the scents of the food on sale below could be detected. Baking bread, cooked meats of various stripes and cinnamon crusted apples were the delights on today's menu.

Meditating while watching the square below in this way, on market day or not, was one of my favourite ways to spend any free moments. They were few and far between in my duties. I did not pay much attention to the activities of my fellow novices. I was aware that some of them would gamble in their free time, or visit brothels, neither of which were forbidden in the books of the faithful. Nevertheless, I could not help but think that their time would be better spent in study, or meditating on the mysteries of the Host.

My observation of the square was interrupted by the familiar ringing of a nearby Messenger Bell. It sounded three times, the peal echoing around the market. A sudden respectful silence descended. All transactions and arguments ceased, as did all movement, save for the hurried clearing of the central thoroughfare. Seconds later, the messenger for the Host and his horse galloped through, his distinctive plumed helmet and gold-fringed armour shining in the sunlight. In his saddlebags, one, or two, or twenty messages from the Host. Spelled out by the conduits, transcribed by the hierophants and now destined to be carried far and wide across the empire. In his saddlebags were words that could turn a battle, or begin one. Words that could end a life, or spare one. The words of the Host, the very blood in the body of our faith, passing through the veins and arteries, the lanes and roads of this fair land.

The messenger's path cut from left to right from my viewpoint. As was customary, those on that path had turned their faces away as he passed, just as King Gorran spurned the Kundites. This meant that half of those on that path were facing in my direction.

One of them I recognised.

It was a fellow novice called Samuel, who I had not seen for three years. He had been a fast friend of mine during my service with Master Foll, a service I had assumed Samuel was still continuing. To see him here, at the heart of the empire rather than at its borders was quite a surprise. Added to this was his clothing - no longer the tight tunic of a missionary, he now wore the simple robes of a temple novice.

I stood and held up a hand. My movement caught the eye of many in the crowd, including Samuel, and he reacted in happy surprise.

Ten minutes later, we were catching up in the temple kitchens. Samuel explained that I was not the last novice to be called away from Master Foll's happy band. In the month after I left, a further four of my companions received new orders from the Host, all calling them away to other duties, with three summoned to this very citadel. More may have followed, but Samuel was the last of the four to be reassigned, which is where his account ended.

I expressed surprise that the Host should have different plans for so many of us. A strange expression came over Samuel's face.

"If it was the Host," he whispered.

It was rare but not unheard of. Every few years, a group of enterprising blasphemers would attempt to forge some message from the Host, usually ordering the release of gold from distant provinces. Sometimes it even worked, but whenever these crimes were uncovered, the empire would rouse from its slumber and respond with definitive and disproportionate severity. The criminals responsible would be found, tortured and executed, followed by their families and any others with even the slimmest tangential connection to the crime.

Ultimately, faking a message from the Host came to be viewed as a suicidally reckless act. But Samuel was inferring that just such a thing had happened here. He claimed to have heard the accusation directly from the mouth of Master Foll. Even more distressing, Foll had claimed that the brace of messages that had robbed him of his best novices were *all* fakes.

Five faked messages from the Host.

The idea was unthinkable.

Much as it pained me to view my former mentor in such a light, I had to conclude that he was in the grip of some mania. I did not share this thought with Samuel and our meeting ended shortly afterwards. I returned to my duties that afternoon with a troubled mind and a heavy heart, mourning the great Gideon Foll for the man he used to be.

Three days later, everything changed.

The morning began much like any other, with myself and three other novices cleaning and feeding the conduits, taking over duties from those that had tended to them during the night. There was nothing unusual to report. No illness or conduit cessation, which is the accepted term for their passing. Just the quiet hiss of the planchettes acting as a soothing accompaniment to steady, wholesome work in the service of the Host.

We had just completed the first half of our morning duties when a change occurred in the atmosphere of the room. I noticed that my fellow novices were looking beyond me and I became aware of an approaching presence.

It was Master Hayden, the high priest in charge of the entirety of the novices in the temple. I had spoken to him only once, on the day I was given my duties in the great hall. He was a thin, cadaverous man with what I tended to think of as a permanent half-smile on his face.

Well, there was no sign of that smile today. He looked deadly serious as he approached, gestured for me to follow and turned on his heel. I shared looks of shock with my fellow novices before leaving them and following.

I assumed that as soon as we had left the great hall, Master Hayden would offer some word of explanation, but once he had confirmed I was at his heel, he simply continued to walk. We passed out of the anterooms and along several all but empty corridors. We reached two temple guards on either side of a narrow stone staircase that I knew all too well. The steps lead up to an area forbidden to all but the highest servants of the Host.

Master Hayden did not even pause, walking straight past the guards. I followed his lead, half-expecting them to bar my way, but they did not even look at me.

At the top of the stairs were a suite of rooms I had never visited. They were much larger and more lavishly furnished than any other in the temple. We passed hanging tapestries depicting the Trials of Hella and the Forging of the Iron. There was also a golden tableau depicting the Repentance of the Woodsman. I would have loved to tarry and study the treasures, but Master Hayden did not slow his pace.

At the end of these chambers, we reached a large stone door, again guarded. Master Hayden gestured that I was to pass through the door, then turned and left without a word. I watched his back as he retraced his steps through the chambers, then looked to the guards. They were both studiously avoiding my eye. I tentatively knocked on the door before me, which swung inwards at my first knock. I surmised it was counterweighted in some ingenious fashion. Beyond it, a short chamber and another stone door. It appeared that the second door would not open before the first was fully closed. I was familiar with the principle and had seen it used on smaller doors. Prying eyes and ears would find it impossible to glean anything from the room beyond.

I closed the first door and the second swung open. Beyond, two further guards and a long, high-ceilinged chamber were revealed, well-lit but plainly a place of work and industry, in contrast to the rooms I had just left. Workbenches and tools were in evidence, along with a handful of cracked and broken conduit tabletops leaning against the walls, with their unmistakable grids of dark letters. I had never seen outside any conduit table outside of the great hall, but they were not what captured my attention.

Four hierophants were sitting in the room.

I had seen many of the high priests before, of course, at public ceremonies. At every yearly Forgiving of The Flint, at least seven would be in attendance, but it was one thing to see them from a distance, across the floor of a crowded hall, and quite another to stand before them.

They were not in their full regalia, naturally. The gilded bars of their crowns and charred staffs were no doubt stored elsewhere, but their silver braided tunics and robes were unmistakable.

Another aspect that was very different was their posture. There was not a straight back amongst them, slumped as they were in a loose cluster of wooden chairs. They had the air of men defeated after a long argument in which no ground had been won on either side. It was very odd to see such grand, important men in such slovenly positions.

I bowed before them, then kept my head low. I said nothing.

"You are the novice known as Fenlow Anaville?" asked one of the priests. "Former apprentice to Gideon Foll?"

He was an old man, perhaps sixty years of age. Totally bald, with a short grey beard. He had an anger in his eyes that made me wary. I believed his name was Master Fallow.

"I am, my lord," I replied.

He was on his feet in a second, striding across the floor between us. He struck me twice, once with the back of his hand across my face and again with a closed fist to my stomach. I fell to my knees, winded, terrified. What could I possibly have done to offend him so? What dereliction in my duties had I allowed to fester to such a degree?

"How did you do it?" he demanded.

"My lord, I don't--" I began, before he struck me again.

"Let the boy speak," said another of the priests, who sounded tired. I thought I recognised him as Master Daydus, the youngest and most well-fed of the group. Master Fallow took a step back, but everything in his posture said that another blow might soon follow.

I stayed on my knees as I spoke, doing my best to gather my

scattered thoughts.

"My lords, I am unaware of any failing in my duties," I said, "but I swear upon the Kindest Soul--"

Master Fallow advanced on me, raised his hand again and I flinched away.

"Fallow, please," said Master Daydus, which seemed to halt the blow, for the moment.

"He seems, to my seasoned eye at least, to be an innocent in this, whatever this transpires to be," continued Master Daydus.

"Or he wears a false face to hide his true intent," retorted Master Fallow.

"Perhaps we should put him to the question," said another priest - a man with long dark hair tied up in a top-knot and narrow, calculating eyes.

"Perhaps we should at least make him aware of what he is accused of," said the last priest, who was rubbing his temples, eyes closed. He had the air of a man annoyed at being awoken from a nap.

None of the others offered an alternative, so Master Daydus stood and gestured for me to follow. I gladly moved towards him, being careful to keep out of reach of Master Fallow as I did so.

The workshop was connected to another room by way of an arch. The circular chamber beyond had not drawn my attention, being mainly lost to shadow, but as I gingerly followed Master Daydus, the shapes within became gradually clearer. He lit a torch and my suspicions were confirmed.

In the centre of the space sat three motionless conduits around a stone table, hands resting upon a planchette. It had long been rumoured that there were other conduits in the private quarters of the hierophants, and here was proof. Not only that, but the table's familiar grid of letters had no stone column or curtain to obstruct the view. Had the planchette moved, I could have been witness to the words of the Host arriving in our world. I immediately averted my eyes to avoid even the chance of this unthinkable transgression for a lowly novice.

Master Daydus was watching me carefully, no doubt guessing the reason for my discomfort.

"Look at the table," he said.

I decided that a larger transgression would be to disobey his order, so I did as he asked. I became aware that the other priests had followed us into the room.

Master Daydus gestured at the planchette.

"At some point in the early hours of this morning, this planchette began to move. It was heard, then witnessed by myself and Master Clemens, who called for Master Fallow and Master Poltice. All four of us witnessed its movement and read its message, before it finally ceased some hours later."

I looked between the priests. They were watching me intently. It was not my place to ask questions, so I said nothing.

"Do you know what the message was?" asked Master Fallow.

"No my lord," I said.

"It was your name," he replied. "Over and over again."

Communications from the Host could sometimes be confusing, cryptic or contradictory. I had heard a tale of a message from the Host sent to a general, ordering his army to attack, long after that army had been routed and slaughtered. I had heard other tales of Host messages sent with news of missing family members, declaring them dead, only for the missing to return days later.

The ways of the Host are not our ways,

The designs of the Host are not ours to know,

Trust in the Host.

These were the thoughts I meditated upon as I stood before the hierophants, in an attempt to calm the confusion in my mind. In all the varied cryptic messages from the Host I had heard tell of, I had never heard of a message so short, without instruction or context. One name, repeated. *My* name, repeated. The attitudes of the hierophants were also confusing - angry or suspicious of me for reasons I couldn't even begin to fathom.

I realised that the priests were speaking amongst themselves, but making no effort to hide their words from me. Not that they needed to, as so little of what they were saying made any sense to me at all.

"Look at him. He is an innocent," said Master Daydus.

"He is no innocent," said Master Fallow. "He was trained by Gideon Foll. Which, by the way, I am still certain has bearing on this whole business."

"Foll has been declawed. He is no longer a threat,"

"Then what are we saying?" asked Master Fallow, with a mocking sneer. "That this is the *Host?* No. This is trickery by some method we have not yet ascertained."

Master Daydus was staring at me, tapping his chin with a fingertip.

"I feel our young friend here still does not understand what he is being accused of," he said. "I propose we tell him everything."

The other hierophants gestured dismissively. It seemed they did not care one way or the other. Their focus had abruptly shifted from me and I was thus rendered invisible. Master Daydus gestured for me to follow him back into the original room. The other hierophants continued to argue around the conduit table.

I had already noticed various conduit table tops dotted around the workshop, but Master Daydus led me instead toward what I had initially taken to be the exposed innards of some vast clock. Four sets of rods, perhaps four feet long, had been assembled in a square, like the legs of a table. They supported a flat array of cogs, joints and further rods. Master Daydus approached this assembly, crouched and began to turn a handle below. This, in turn, caused the cogs and rods to smoothly and silently move. The ultimate aim of this machine seemed to be the swift movement of a small square of metal, attached to a short rod set slightly above the main assemblage of the machine. This metal square darted hither and thither as the handle was turned, seemingly without further reason or purpose.

Master Daydus ceased turning the handle. He could see the confusion in my face and held up a finger. The demonstration was not over. He reached out for the metal square, which he pulled free with a little effort.

"This is a magnet. You are familiar with magnets, yes?" asked Master Daydus.

I nodded. The magnets I had seen were the preserve of children's toys, but I was conversant enough with the principle.

Master Daydus seemed satisfied with my response and strode across the room towards a cracked conduit table top, leaning against one of the walls.

"If you would be so good as to examine this table," he said.

I was beginning to feel like some conjurer's accomplice in a travelling fair, but I did as he asked and carefully tilted the broken table top away from the wall. As expected, it was a familiar wide stone circle, around six inches thick but I was surprised to discover a deep rectangular hollow cut into the underside, directly below the grid of letters.

Master Daydus then produced a planchette which he held against the letter grid of the tabletop. He used his other hand to press the magnet into the hollow at the back of the table, then released the planchette.

Even though the table was almost vertical, the planchette did not fall, held in place by the magnet. Master Daydus moved the magnet, and the planchette moved with it, across the board of letters, seemingly propelled by an invisible hand. He looked to me to ensure I was following, then removed both magnet and planchette.

"So you see, when the tabletop and mechanism are combined, the illusion is complete," he said. "The conduits' hands are attached to the planchette, and the handle is turned from the floor below."

I began to grasp the intent behind this demonstration. A method by which messages from the Host might be counterfeited. An unthinkable blasphemy, one that I could only assume this room and the tools within it were devoted to detect and stamp out.

"You understand?" asked Master Daydus.

I nodded. I thought I did, but I had many questions.

"The table through there," he said. "Where the conduits spelled out your name, is usually where the machines are tested. It currently has no such mechanism installed, that we can detect, but the possibility exists that some new method, of which we are unaware, has been used to spell out the message. Do you know of any such method?"

I was confused again. They suspected trickery at the heart of the message? Whatever had led them to this suspicion?

"My lord, forgive me my ignorance, but what reason do you have for suspecting trickery? If no machinery is attached, could the message not simply be from the Host?"

Master Daydus looked pained for a second. He sighed.

"Every table in the great hall, every planchette, is currently connected to and moved by a machine identical to the one I have just shown you," he said. "There has not been a genuine message from the Host in living memory."

When I travelled with Master Gideon Foll, as pupil and missionary, many of the peoples we encountered on our travels were not interested in our teachings. We would often find ourselves spurned, sometimes gently, sometimes with overt hostility.

On these occasions, Master Foll, a model of pragmatism, would always lead by example. Patience and restraint were his watchwords. As he would often remind us, a single ally in the Host is worth all the riches of a king's chambers. Our sufferings in our ministry were as nothing to the agonies endured by the Kindest Soul. In his name, we would not cease in our attempts to bring the ignorant into the light of the Host's knowledge. Even if the rebuffs grew to the point of physical harm for one or more of our company. Only after six days of honest, open attempts to bring more lost souls into the comfort of the Truth, only after all our attempts had failed, would Master Foll declare the soil barren, the well dry.

For that steadfastness, and countless other minor demonstrations of his strength of character, I felt secure in my judgement of Master Foll as a kindly, wise man, with all the patience in the world for those following misguided or heretical beliefs.

And the hierophants in that room had conspired against him. With what I now knew, I could confirm Samuel and, indeed,

Master Foll's suspicions. I felt shame at my dismissal of him as a delusional old man. He was instead possessed of a keen insight into the rotten truth of the matter. If no genuine messages were being received from the Host then it stood to reason that any orders leaving the temple were based solely upon the desires of men. The desires of the hierophants, four of which were in this room. And what those men desired, in part, confessed from their own mouths, was the "defanging" of Master Gideon Foll, achieved by the ordered reassignment of myself and my fellow novices, away from his tutelage and care.

This was surely the least of their crimes. No messages from the Host in living memory. Which meant that since well before my birth, every order, summons, or piece of advice, every adjustment to the Books of the Faithful, or insight into the story of the Kindest Soul, flowing from the temple in an unending stream, were all the work of fallible and self-serving men.

I pictured their words, their lies, spreading out from the citadel like blackened cancerous veins, corrupting the body of the empire. Carried in good faith by riders, couriers and sailors, across oceans of sand and sea, protected to the dying breaths of soldiers and guards, revered as holy words of the brightest Host.

How many soldiers of the faithful had died in service to this false Host? How many needless wars and brutal skirmishes had been set in motion by the whims of these men and their hollow lies, that now lay bitter upon my heart?

Was I now expected to simply return to my duties? Tending conduits that I now knew were mere mindless puppets, arms jerking not at the behest of a higher power, but of mere clockwork and trickery?

No. I could not.

Then what other course lay open to me?

Master Daydus, having casually ripped my world asunder with a mere sentence, could sense the turmoil his words had caused within me. I seem to recall he spoke some further words of comfort, but my memories of those moments are not clear, consumed as they were with anguish. He left me alone with my roiling thoughts and returned to his bickering companions. I believe I sat on a chair in the workshop and considered the shape of this new world I found myself in.

I must confess that my faith in the Host was tested. Unsurprising, given the massive and long-running deception that had been revealed to me, but I could not forget the reason that I had been summoned to those chambers. The conduits that had spelled out my name, seemingly without magnets or clockwork to guide them. The hierophants were convinced some other trickery was responsible and I could understand that need on their part, but I myself had a need to believe otherwise, that this was indeed the Host, asking for me by name. I clung to this hope as a drowning man clings to driftwood. I still had no idea why I should be summoned in this way, but I took comfort in it, nonetheless.

I realised, with a start, that these hierophants - long considered the most reverent and pious of all men - did not actually believe in the Host at all. In many ways, they were the worst kind of non-believer, deceiving with every word, with every false affirmation of their faith.

Beside me was a selection of stoneworking tools. I selected a large chisel.

My mind kept returning to Master Foll, always so patient in his dealings with non-believers. Six days of honest attempts to elevate lost souls with the teachings of the Host. Six days of enduring whatever slights and injuries the ignorant and misguided could bring our way. And at sunset on the sixth day, when all hope of conversion was lost, only then would Master Foll declare those unbelievers past redemption. It was then considered our sacred duty to free their eternal souls from the cages of their earthly bodies and deliver their essence to the comforting embrace of the Host.

The two guards beside the door from the workshop were paying me scant attention. The one nearest to me met his end with my chisel deep in his neck.

We would never, as has been alleged in some quarters, hurry to this part of our missionary work. It was always seen as a regrettable final act after all other options had been exhausted. Having said that, it was still a vital and necessary part of our calling.

As the guard staggered, bewildered, blood pulsing, blooming through the white of his doublet, he released his halberd, which I caught before it fell.

We were steadfast in our determination to bring all those we encountered into the service of the Host, either in this world or the next. To this end, for each hour I spent studying the Books of the Faithful, and the life and legacy of the Kindest Soul, I would spend another hour honing my skills with the blade and shield. Both sides of our ministry were seen by Master Foll as equally important in bringing the lost masses of this world to the joy of the Host.

The remaining guard was slow to respond, to even realise I was a threat, and this was his undoing. He died with his head almost severed by the keen edge of his companion's halberd.

Very rarely, in some distant province, we would encounter blasphemy. Some distortion of the Host or its principles. In some cases, this was down to an innocent misinterpretation, easily corrected with counsel. But sometimes the blasphemy was intentional, with blatant disrespect for the Host or mockery of the Kindest Soul. In these rare cases, and only in these cases, Master Foll would broker no room for discussion or debate. A purging fire, a burning out of the corruption, was the only course of action our beliefs would allow.

Neither guard had shouted out. There had been no ringing of steel to indicate battle. The loudest noises had been the falling of two bodies and the second guard's weapon.

I could still hear the hierophants bickering in the other chamber, unaware.

I steadied my grip on the halberd and approached.

There has been no true message from the Host in living memory.

Save one.

A message repeating my name. Of all the ranks of the

faithful, across the whole empire, I alone have been chosen. To what end, at first I did not know. I could not see the wisdom of my summons.

Now I understand.

Others called up in my stead might well have faltered in their duty, have allowed the robe of the hierophant to cloud their mind, stay their hand. Been cowed by the weight of authority, or tradition, or any of those other convenient lies we tell ourselves to excuse the inexcusable.

But I saw only faithless men, in robes they were not fit to wear. I saw lost blasphemers, knowingly enacting a blatant corruption of the Host. If I had encountered such a thing on the borders of empire, I would have reached for my sword without hesitation. To find such a travesty festering here, at the heart of temple, deserves no less of a response.

I am alight with a purging fire. I feel the Host, the *true* Host moving within me, guiding my hands to glory. Hands now wet with the blood of those gaudy pretenders, the false priests who squirmed and squealed beneath my blade like the bloated pigs they always were.

My steps lead me on from the abattoir in my wake, down a new staircase, to further rooms. I find oblivious artisans, working diligently at rows of benches, feeding the clockwork monstrosity at the heart of the lie.

They are not fighters. They barely resist as I bring them to the Host. None of them even attempt to flee and they fall before me like wheat. Only as I leave do I notice the chains holding them to their seats.

I feel no shame, no regret. Unwilling or not, they still maintained this abomination. Any true men of faith would rather have taken their own lives.

A noise reaches me, the echoes of some distant chanting, but all I can hear is conspirators bearing false witness, intoning sacred words they do not believe.

This temple now feels soiled, unclean. A place of shadows hiding filth.

How many more?

How many more liars and defilers mock me from the darkness?

How many more must fall before this temple is cleansed, and worthy of the name once more?

The rot must be burned out, root and branch.

Some innocents may well fall along the way, and they will be mourned - but, as always, I am guided by the words of the Kindest Soul: *Better a hundred honest men are brought to the Host, than a single blasphemer given leave to flourish.*

I will trust in the Host to guide my blade.

Titus
And The Vase

THE ability to tune out any distraction was a talent that Simone had never really valued until the day of the crash.

It was just a part of her, something she had never actively considered, like the colour of her eyes or her shoe size. It probably originated from having to study in a bedroom shared with two brothers, both of whom seemed to spend their time either playing their favourite music at competing levels of volume or arguing the merits of said music. If Simone had not developed the ability to create her own internal bubble of silence, her studies, her education - hell, her whole life - would have no doubt taken a very different shape.

It was an ability she certainly valued now, as she watched the other passengers cry and scream and pray as the plane plummeted. She sat serenely amongst them, running through what she was almost certain would be her last thoughts, taking stock of her life and preparing for the end.

She was probably in shock as well, she reflected. That was no doubt part of it. She was grateful for that too. She decided that she would rather die in a calm, quiet bubble of traumatised paralysis than in blind screaming panic.

In hindsight, there had been warning signs. The plane had sat on the tarmac for a full forty-five minutes before they even taxied to the runway. They were told at various points they were: awaiting fuel, baggage to be loaded, a slot to open up and clearance to be given. At one point, through her window, Simone had seen one of the ground crew - a stocky man in a fluorescent vest with ear protectors around his neck - arguing with someone out of her eyeline. The man was gesturing at the plane and shaking his head as if he couldn't believe what he was being told. Ultimately, he shrugged and gestured dismissively. Simone knew that gesture. It basically translated as "I'm not being paid enough to care."

Thirty minutes into the flight, the plane had begun to buck unexpectedly, in a clear sky with no clouds. Simone had seen a look pass between two stewardesses, smiles frozen but eyes worried. They knew the signs of turbulence and this wasn't it. One of them hurried towards the cabin. The "fasten seatbelts" sign flicked on and, ten seconds later, the plane dropped out of the sky like a stone.

Several untethered people slammed into the ceiling. The nearest one to Simone was a fragile-looking man in his sixties with obvious dyed black hair and eyeliner. He was returning from the toilet, wearing a Jesus And Mary Chain t-shirt and no shoes, when the plane dropped about fifty feet in half a second. His head caught the edge of an overhead compartment and he was knocked unconscious. For a second, his flopping body was pressed against the ceiling, then as the dive began in earnest, everything grew weightless. Several people below him reached up and pulled his body down towards them. He ended up sprawled across several passengers' laps, bruises blooming at his temple, groggily struggling to get up.

Simone remembered the man from the tedium of check-in. She'd decided he used to be a roadie and to amuse herself she'd gone further, inventing a whole fictional back story. He'd worked mainly for The Rolling Stones, had seen the world and lived a full life until his career was sadly cut short due to a back injury caused by falling from a gigantic amp.

At the time, she'd smiled at the image, but now, watching his disorientated face struggle to understand what was happening to him, she felt ashamed of the fun she'd had at his expense, however mild.

The dive continued. Occasionally, gravity would return somewhat, but only for a second or two, causing a sickening lurch in Simone's stomach. She presumed this was due to the pilot attempting some new tactic to slow their descent, but it appeared futile.

The sunlight bathing one side of the plane abruptly cut out. They were passing through clouds now. How many thousands of feet had they fallen? How long before they hit the ground?

Simone was surrounded by people variously screaming, babbling prayers or repeating inanities such as "This isn't happening" and "Is it terrorists?"

She hadn't even wanted to come on this dumb flight. It clashed with an open-air festival in her local park that she'd been looking forward to for months. But then her older brother Marcus had decided that his new child's first birthday was going to be a "thing" and that "We'd really appreciate it if you could come." The kid was one year old, for God's sake. He'd remember nothing of the day by the time he was five. They could pin a picture of Simone's face to a broom for the amount it would register.

But, of course, it wasn't about that. It was about building bridges and showing willing and trying to repair the broken flapping thing that was Marcus and Simone's relationship. A relationship that would now be frozen in amber the moment the plane crashed, locked in the state it had been for most of their lives, with old grievances still festering and petty scores still unresolved.

She imagined Marcus getting the news she'd died. Feelings weren't really his thing, but it would have to register, especially since she was only on this flight because of him. Was it wrong of Simone to want him to suffer just a little? Probably.

Why in hell was she wasting time thinking about Marcus? These were probably her last minutes alive. It felt like a waste of thought.

Unbidden, an image of Titus came into her mind. The brother that died. The brother that no one mentioned anymore. Little surprise in a family as emotionally stunted as theirs. She supposed his presence in her thoughts was understandable, given the circumstances.

Titus had died when Simone was only five, which meant her memories of him were few and fragmented. He was two years older than Simone, the closest to her in age of all her siblings - a fact that made them closer emotionally too. Her few memories of him mainly concerned the stupid games he'd play with her, pulling faces and doing silly voices, laughing until they were both giddy.

Then one day he was gone and no one would tell her why. It was as though he never existed. Simone's questions were met with deflection and dismissal. She'd been judged too young to deal with the truth, that he'd simply stepped out into traffic. Simone supposed it was an attempt to protect her from that harsh reality, but the deflection caused its own trauma. She vividly recalled her own hysteria at the brusque wall of silence around his death. They even took his bed and toys away immediately, as though afraid of the questions they would raise.

She couldn't even remember how she eventually found out that he'd died. Wasn't that odd? That was surely a moment that would have stayed with her. Being sat down and spoken to in sombre tones, probably by her mum or gran. Or maybe she accidentally overheard the grim news, sitting on the top step as adults talked downstairs. But there wasn't even the flicker of such a scene in her memory.

She did remember, in the wake of his death, dire warnings being given at school to not cross any road unsupervised. But she also remembered that Titus was present at that assembly, pulling faces whenever she looked his way, which was obviously impossible.

Memories are made of shifting sand, especially those from childhood. Details blur and fade. What you wish had happened or wish you'd said or done can sometimes grow like a weed until the truth is lost in its shadow. An anecdote you were once told and imagined vividly could, in time, morph into a memory of something you would swear happened to you.

For example, Simone had vivid memories of seeing Titus die.

Seeing him walking, happy and oblivious, into the road. The blur of a car, not even braking before the impact. A crunch of metal and bone, Titus spinning and sprawling. Blood pooling beneath his head as his twisted body lay inert.

But, of course, she wasn't there, couldn't have seen any of that. It was simply how she'd imagined he died, every time she thought of it. The fantasy had eventually been carved into her memory through sheer repetition.

What was true is that Titus' death had given Simone nightmares for years and led to a life-long fear of cars. She had never been able to even stomach the idea of learning to drive. The various therapists she'd employed over the years had all pinpointed her family's continued silence around his death as the root of Simone's ongoing trust issues.

In many ways, Titus' death had shaped Simone's life.

The plane emerged abruptly from the clouds. She could see a vast patchwork of fields below them, tilted at a sickening angle, but she wasn't sure of the scale and didn't know how far away the fields were. The sight caused a new chorus of screams around her, as though the blindfold of cloud had allowed some people to kid themselves this wasn't actually happening.

Simone's ability to tune out distractions, good though it was, was not perfect. A repeated chanting of The Lord's Prayer broke through. It was coming from a balding man sitting on the row in front of her, his eyes clenched shut, head bowed and nodding.

She wished he'd shut up. Simone supposed her wish for silence would be granted long before his appeal to a higher power, if indeed that is what he was doing. It sounded more like the prayer form of a comfort blanket, which Simone could understand in the circumstances.

It chimed perfectly with her views on religion in general. Opium for the masses, as Marx put it. She tended to view belief in any form of religion or spirituality as a childish character weakness. Several promising relationships had floundered on the rocks of that issue over the years, partly because it all seemed so damn egotistical. It was never *"There is a god but we're like ants to him. He doesn't give a damn about any of us"*, instead it was always

"There is a god who watches over me and has steered my path over the years", which struck Simone as not only narcissistic but borderline pathological. Seven billion humans on the planet and yet the invisible Sky-Daddy has taken a personal interest in you? Well, aren't you special!

Sure, there was a time when Simone believed, when she was too young to know any different, but that was a very long time ago. She idly wondered when that was. When was the last time she prayed and actually meant it?

Ah yes. When she broke the vase.

Simone felt a sudden involuntary flicker of panic and shame at the idea of revisiting the memory. She inwardly rolled her eyes.

You're on a plummeting plane, about to die and this is what scares you?

Grow up, girl. The past can't hurt you here.

She hadn't thought about the vase in such a long time. How old had she been? Four? Five? Skipping happily around her granny's old flat in Hastings, giddy at the momentary freedom of no supervision. Her gran had nipped next door for five minutes - "You'll be alright won't you love? You've got your colouring." She could picture the room now - the sagging paisley sofa, the tall, dark wooden dresser filled with carefully placed ceramic ornaments that had so fascinated her. Where had her mum been? She didn't remember. Off doing one of the many jobs she'd juggled in the early years.

The giggling hysteria of freedom had ended in tragedy, as she began to run in circles, lost her balance and careened full-speed into the dresser. She'd watched in horror as a large ruby-red vase, in her memory almost as big as her, fell from its shelf on the dresser and broke like an egg on the tiled floor. It exploded with a crash that surely signalled the end of her childhood.

She remembered standing in silence, staring at the fragments, some of which were still slowly spinning. Most were still close to the area of impact, but some had skittered to the far corners of the room. She started to gather up the shards into a little pile, as though that would somehow lessen her punishment. She was already crying, mumbling snotty pleas for clemency to the empty room. Then she cut her finger on one of the shards and began the deep shuddering sobs of despair known only to children who are really going to get it when their parents find out.

In desperation, she fell to her knees, put her little hands together - now smeared with her own blood - and prayed.

She remembered, at the time, she viewed prayers as existing somewhere on the wish continuum. Much less certain to come true than wishes to genies, who had to obey whoever rubbed the lamp. Prayers were more of a long shot, because God was a very busy man and had millions of people praying to him every day. But sometimes, very rarely, you might get lucky.

So Simone prayed. Not, as she recalled, for something potentially reasonable like a lesser punishment, or for her mum not to find out. No, Simone prayed for the vase to become whole again.

Simone prayed for a miracle.

And why not? The chances of God picking her prayer out of all the others was highly unlikely - but if he did pick hers, Simone thought she might as well ask for something big.

That was where Simone's recollection of the day got a little muddy, because she had no memory of her punishment, which was odd. Surely her mum would have hit the roof. Did gran cover for her?

Why was she spending so much time thinking about the vase anyway? Was that really what she wanted her last thoughts to be?

She could smell vomit. Someone close to her had definitely thrown up. Probably more than one, given the circumstances. The plane had tilted so that the window on Simone's row showed nothing but sky. She was grateful, in a way. Perhaps not knowing how close the ground was would be a blessing.

Simone tried to steer her thoughts elsewhere but they kept returning to the vase. Why did she have initial panic at the memory of it? She'd assumed it was because of the awful punishment she'd received for breaking it, but now she couldn't even remember that. Was she looking at some sort of repressed memory? Had her mother gone overboard, perhaps hit her? She'd certainly come close a couple of times.

She replayed the events over in her head.

She was praying over the shards of the vase, begging, willing, yearning for them to be whole again.

And then they were. The vase was once again on the shelf.

She was misremembering, of course. She had to be. It was an earlier image of the dresser and vase, appearing out of order in her mind. She ran through the sequence of events again and ended up with the same odd disconnect. The vase made whole, the prayer answered.

What utter nonsense.

And yet… that was where her drawing away from religion began. Over the years, it solidified into a mocking, scathing dismissal. But it wasn't always that way. For years, the idea of God had scared her, a fear rooted in the events of that day. Why fear? Why was she having such a hard time remembering what actually happened?

The fear calcified into dread as the veil lifted.

The realisation that she could remember exactly what had happened. That she had already seen it in her mind's eye. She was just refusing to accept it because it was impossible. And because it was impossible, she had avoided thinking about it and deliberately repressed the memory for nearly thirty years.

Simone was never punished because on that day her prayer had been answered. The vase had been made whole again and returned to the shelf.

Simone looked around at her doomed companions. Some catatonic, some sobbing, some serene. She wondered how many of them, like her, were having last-minute conversions.

Is that really what you're telling us here, Simone? That you've suddenly decided that God is real after all? That he cared enough about you when you were five to replace a broken vase?

Do you think he'd get you off this plane if you asked him nicely?

Is that really what she *was* saying? What she remembered? She had been all of five years old. How sure could she really be of *anything* from that long ago? She knew from her experience with the death of Titus how unreliable her memories could be. Was this more of the same? Some fiction that her immature brain had forged into a memory?

Let's say that's true. If so, then why the fear? Why did her brain immediately panic at the idea of revisiting it, if it was mere fiction?

Because there was a price, said a voice in the back of her head.

Because it wasn't just the vase that was changed.

Now that she was facing the unexamined memory head on, other connections were tumbling into focus. Something about the wallpaper? Yes. The wallpaper.

Her childhood lounge had been wallpapered in a rich green flock. Simone had spent many an hour spotting faces, even giving names to the characters she could see in the riot of whorls and curlicues. She knew that wallpaper very well. Better, she would wager, than any adult passing through the room.

The day of the incident with the vase, she and her mother had returned home from gran's and Simone noticed that the wallpaper had changed. It had been replaced with sombre brown stripes. She asked Mum why she'd changed it and Mum just looked at her oddly and told her to go and play.

She had pretended to play, but whenever Mum looked away or left the room, Simone would study the new wallpaper - this interloper. She resented the new stripes immediately. They had no rich detailing, ripe for invention or fantasy, they were just boring stripes.

It went further than that, though. Simone could tell that the striped wallpaper was not new. It was peppered with all the weathering and dings that the old wallpaper had acquired over years of use. A concave dent caused by a doorknob, a scratch from a wooden chair back, a dozen scuffs and stains from its location in the heart of the house. The wallpaper was giving a very good impression of having been there for years, but Simone knew for a fact that it had not been there that morning.

She instinctively knew that the wallpaper was connected to

the vase. Two miracles had occurred in one day. One good; one, if not bad, then at least weird. She hoped this would be the end of it.

And it was. Wasn't it?

Wasn't it?

Simone stared, unseeing, her eyes welling with tears as a flurry of fresh connections were made, old protective assumptions cast aside. New terrible knowledge landing with a heavy certainty.

Titus.

That was the day Titus died.

Simone heard a commotion somewhere in the rows behind her, someone arguing with a stewardess. They were angrily insisting that they needed to "storm the cabin". The stewardess sounded past caring, her usual buoyant façade nowhere to be seen. She was trying to explain that it was not terrorists, it was a mechanical problem. Getting into the cabin wasn't going to help. The arguing man didn't seem able to process that idea. Others were chipping in, shouting him down. The argument culminated in a deep, ragged voice bellowing from a totally different area of the cabin.

"Shut up and let us die in peace!"

The day of the vase was also the day that Titus disappeared, the day that every question about him was met with a wall of seeming indifference that eventually led to Simone's hysterical breakdown.

His death. That she doesn't even remember being told about.

But they moved his bed and toys.

No. You assumed they had. No one spoke about it. His bed and toys disappeared along with him.

Simone took a mental step back. She felt she was close to the truth of it all.

When she was five, she broke a vase and prayed to God to fix it. She willed reality to shift to save her from the wrath of her mother, and it did. But there were side effects: the wallpaper, the disappearance of Titus, his bed, his toys.

And her five-year-old brain had done what little it could to make sense of it all. She was afraid of cars long before he disappeared. The assembly where they warned us all, he *was* there. If she was going to invent a death to explain his absence...

Simone had only a passing familiarity with science fiction. An old boyfriend who'd been something of a fan - mostly *Star Trek*, playing unseen in the background as they made out. But she did understand the idea of the road not taken, a fork in the path where a simple choice could lead to a vastly different life.

She'd seen *Sliding Doors*.

Could this be that? Could her naive young prayer, her yearning, her dire need, have somehow allowed her to jump tracks into a whole new world? A world with an unbroken vase, yes, but also with different wallpaper and no Titus.

A world where Titus was never even born and any questions about him were understandably ignored.

For the sake of argument, let's say that's what happened. And now the sixty-four-thousand-dollar question, probably the very reason why her subconscious wouldn't leave this topic alone, even though she only had minutes to live:

Could she do it again?

Could she do it now?

The plane banked again and Simone could see the ground once more, still at a sickening angle. Jesus, that's close. The patchwork of fields near enough to make out shining ribbons of rivers and roads. How long till impact? A minute? Less?

Simone took a deep breath, closed her eyes and focussed.

Part of her mind was screaming that this was insane, that she was delusional. She pushed the thought aside. If you're wrong, you'll die anyway, but if there's a chance...

She tried to recollect her state of mind when she brought back the vase.

No, not brought it back. That isn't what she did.

She'd shifted into another world where the vase had never been broken.

Now all she needed to do was shift into another world where she wasn't on a crashing plane.

Easy.

She imagined her feet on the ground, clear sky above her. Another Simone, who never took this flight. Who told Marcus to do one. Who went to the festival instead. There had to be a world where that happened.

Simone strained, got nothing and panicked. She didn't have time to ease into this. It either happened right now or not at all.

When it happened before, when she was a child, what had been different?

Oh yes.

Terror.

She embraced her panic, turned off her filter and let in all the screams and sobs and hysteria of the people around her. She absorbed their fear, their desperation. She felt her heart rate rise, her breath catching in her throat. She started to shake.

She was five again, on her knees before the broken vase, crying, hands clasped together, begging the universe to spare her. Straining, eyes clenched shut.

Yes. Something.

On the edge of her perception, a barrier, a shimmering membrane in the corner of her mind's eye. Was this the way? Was this the key? She had no other options. She sensed it was delicate, diaphanous, but there was no time. She rushed at it, attempted to push through.

And nothing happened.

She tried again. Still nothing.

There was a roaring in her ears. A man across the aisle was bellowing "I'm sorry! I'm sorry!" over and over. Through the window, all she could see was ground. Seconds away now. She wanted to be on that ground. Standing still and calm. Not here. Anywhere but here. Please.

Holding the desperate need in her mind, she rushed again toward the barrier with all her heart.

And punched through.

Reality splintered. Simone tried to gasp, but no longer had a mouth. She was a point of perception with no physical form. She struggled to make sense of what she was experiencing. She was dimly aware that she hadn't escaped. She was still anchored to her physical body, currently sitting on a plummeting plane. She had to be quick.

She had emerged from one of a thousand glowing points of light, rising in a glittering spiral, like a helix of DNA suspended in a void. She pulled back further and could see that the spiral curved, seemingly stretching to infinity in each direction. The sheer scale of it all threatened to overwhelm her. Vertigo, awe and panic all pinballed around her mind.

She forced herself to focus. Somehow, the act of willing drew her closer to a section of the lights. They were oscillating, dilating and contracting as though alive, like cells under a microscope. And they were not just lights, they were *windows*. Clearly visible through each one, she could see views into presumably different worlds.

No. Not different worlds. Different Simones.

Each window showed a view through her eyes. And all of them were subtle variants on the crashing plane she had just left.

No. There had to be more. There had to be Simones that would *live*.

She willed her point of view to move up the spiral. The windows were soon flickering past below her in a blur. All still showing panicking passengers and seat backs. The questions "How am I moving? Am I flying?" surfaced and were dismissed. No time to think about any of that.

She noticed that some of the windows were now black. Shrivelling. Fading.

A moment's thought gave her the reason why.

The planes were crashing.

One after another. More and more, swathes of them winking out. Minute differences in altitude and angles of descent giving some planes and Simones a second or two more life.

It had to be now.

The second the flurry of plane views ceased, Simone plunged headlong into the first window showing something else. Anything else.

Colours flared. A vertiginous headlong fall. The physical returning with a jolt.

Simone blinked and swayed. Distorted reggae was playing, with a bass line so deep she could feel it in her bones. Big speakers, not that far away. The smell of fried batter and cinnamon filled the air. She looked around with confusion. For a second she was aware of two sets of memories jostling for space in her head, some flatly contradictory. Part of her was still in shock over what she'd just been through on the plane. Another part of her was startled by the abrupt arrival of these new memories.

What plane? Was she having a stroke?

She was standing in a short queue for a churro stall. It was one of a dozen or so food trucks in a loose circle around a collection of benches and chairs in the centre of a flattened patch of grass and mud. Crowds milled around; families with toddlers on shoulders, young lovers hand in hand, teenagers in fluorescent prints laughing and mock-fighting.

Beyond the food court, she could see the crowds thickening nearer the stage. She couldn't see who was playing, didn't recognise the song.

She had come to the festival. Of course she had.

She looked down at her clothes. A long beige lace-fringed dress, walking boots and a tote bag. She simultaneously had never seen the clothes before and could remember exactly where she bought each item. Two sets of contradictory memories throwing off sparks as they collided.

"Screw it," said a nearby voice. "I'm gonna have one."

She turned to face the man standing next to her. Too close for a stranger, but then, of course, he was anything but. He was large, with a face like a friendly bear, and wearing a bodywarmer and a Kangol hat. A touch of early grey in what little afro she could see at his temples. Just like dad.

He totally misread her look and laughed. He spread his hands wide and said "I'm a weak man, sis."

Simone pulled him into a hug and he looked surprised.

"Titus," she said - a name she hadn't said aloud for years.

"Yes?" he answered, confused, waiting for the joke.

Simone shook her head, smiling through tears. She said nothing and held on to him.

The Bomb Of Tears

Chapter I - The General

THE scent of the piled bodies in the courtyard could not be denied.

It defied filters, airlocks and aircon, permeating the very stones of the palace. The grand suite itself was supposed to be airtight, a guard against viral agents. But even here, every meal was tainted with the smell.

As he washed down his last mouthful of roast chicken with a glass of wine, General Korlov reflected that he would not have to suffer the smell for very much longer. The bomb was ready. The moment the rebels breached the inner bailey wall, it would be activated in a final act of defiance against the traitorous scum who had challenged the Ascendancy. The blast would consume the entire city, loyalists and rebels alike.

The general knew that, in principle, he should feel regret for the innocent civilians and Jorran fighters who would perish, but he felt nothing but contempt. Any civilians still in the city were fools for not evacuating weeks ago and the loyalist fighters, supposedly trained and equipped to a far higher standard than the enemy, had failed utterly in their orders to contain the rebellion. In his considered opinion, they all deserved nothing but oblivion.

He sat back from the table, belched and almost gestured for a waiter to remove his plate, before remembering that all the servants had gone. Some had fled, no doubt to join the rebels, and the rest had been shot, now part of the pile in the courtyard. He idly wondered if any particles from their decaying bodies were circulating in the air of the room, ruining the meals they had once served.

The larders were still full, which he supposed was comfort of a sort. The siege had not lasted long enough for rationing to begin, or to bring less savoury options on to the menu.

Unbidden, the image of a mountain goat, frozen in place as though stuffed, came to mind. What the hell was that again? Ah yes, one of Dr Beltram's more exotic experiments. As Korlov remembered it, it had been an attempt to extend the lifespan of the army's rations using some variant of cryogenic suspension. Korlov had pulled funding when he realised just how much money the good doctor was wasting on that speculative nonsense. Only Dr Beltram's expertise in munitions had saved him from demotion and a potentially more severe punishment.

A low bass thud shook the room, rattling the cut-glass decanter. His own artillery, captured and turned on the palace. He had given orders to sabotage the guns to avoid this very outcome, but all in vain. Incompetence or cowardice, it didn't matter at this stage. The guns had been draining the shield wall around the palace grounds for the last hour. It had to be close to failing.

The general realised that he had no idea if it was day or night. The windows of the grand suite had been bricked up after the second assassination attempt. He gestured in the air and his display informed him that it was three fifteen in the morning. So. Still dark out. Did that change anything?

He became aware of someone saluting at his elbow. It was Colonel Dunnell, promoted after the death of Colonel Tranter, who in turn had replaced Colonel Reems. *We are all standing on the bones of those who came before.* Who was it who had said that? Someone famous, no doubt. Famous and probably dead.

As always, Colonel Dunnell's dress uniform was immaculate, the creases in the trousers sharp, the epaulettes gleaming. Only his face betrayed the truth, his eyes bloodshot and unfocussed. These past weeks had aged him, that was plain. Korlov stood and returned the salute. As he drew closer, he could smell alcohol on the man. He'd been drinking, heavily. The idea of disciplining him momentarily occurred to Korlov and almost made him laugh. They would both be dead within the hour. What would be the point?

Wordlessly, he followed the colonel out of the suite and into the echoing corridors of the palace. They both knew their destination and did not tarry, their heels clacking on the polished marble floors. They walked swiftly past exhausted soldiers on guard at various doorways, who saluted in their wake. Hand-picked men with loyalty beyond reproach, all of whom would soon be ash.

They reached the status hub, the supposed nexus of battlefield data flowing in and out of the palace, back when that still mattered. A bank of monitors displayed feeds from various cameras in the city - the massed ranks of rebels gathered in the streets, the burning hulks of the last tanks, the shield wall shimmering and fritzing as it neared its end. All subtle variations on the same theme: your time is up.

The hub was usually a hive of activity, with soldiers manning radios and passing on orders to various commanders. Commanders all now dead or captured, rendering the room obsolete. The staff of the hub had all gone, either to man the battlements or desert. The only soldier left in the room, sitting before the monitors as he had done since the siege began, was Corporal Solomon. He was a little less attentive than usual, missing, as he was, most of the side of his head. The pistol he had used rested on the floor beside his chair.

The general supposed it was as good an exit as any other.

Despite himself, General Korlov paused. One of the camera drones had zoomed in on a section of the frontline of the rebel army. A nearby house burned steadily, providing enough light to see the faces of the enemy. They were standing waiting for the artillery to finish its work, all eyes fixed on the shield wall. Their stillness was eerie. There was a lot of hate in those eyes.

Korlov could count dozens of draft-worthy age in the crowd, but there were also elderly men and women, even children, carrying weapons and wearing armour, most of which had plainly been looted from Jorran corpses then repainted in rebel colours. Several of the soldiers carried homemade flags of the rebel sigil - a fist holding feathers, symbolising the crushing of the Ascendancy Angelus.

Korlov instinctively bristled at the brazenness of it, then caught himself. This ragged army had done worse than wave the rebel flag. Far, far worse. But it demonstrated how quickly things had collapsed. Just three short months ago, mere possession of that symbol, in any form, had been a crime punishable by death. Now a row of them fluttered in the breeze outside the palace.

Another shell hit the shield wall and the room shuddered with the impact. A blaring alert sounded from the console. Korlov didn't need to look at the monitors to know what it meant, but he did so anyway.

The shield wall had finally failed.

Korlov silenced the alarm and watched with dead eyes as the pulsing green glow keeping the hordes outside flickered and died. The frontline of the rebel army broke into a cheer, fists aloft. The monitor was silent, but Korlov could hear it even here - a roar of massed voices that sounded like an animal in pain.

The general half-expected the frontline to surge forward and charge towards the palace, but they weren't stupid. They had other physical walls left to breach and a reckless advance at this stage would be costly. The many minor victories in battle that had led them here demonstrated that they had some canny tactical minds in their ranks.

There was a momentary pause in the artillery barrage, as the guns realigned, before they fired again. The shield wall had acted to deaden all noise from the city. With it gone, the artillery became deafening thunder, trumped only by the monstrous roar of the shell's detonation. Their target was now the south gate, which they missed by only a few metres, destroying a section of the parapet. A camera feed showed a cloud of dust and debris billowing into the ornamental garden.

Korlov realised that he had been standing staring at the monitors, at the Ascendancy's impending defeat, for far too long.

He gestured to Colonel Dunnell and they walked briskly on.

Two seconds later, an artillery shell destroyed the entire room they had just left.

Korlov only realised this in retrospect, of course. At the time, the blast wave knocked him unconscious and threw him twenty feet down the corridor. He awoke, covered in dust and disorientated. His medical alert display informed him that he had been unconscious for seven seconds and had a probable concussion.

Colonel Dunnell, who had been two steps behind him, was nowhere to be seen, which surprised Korlov. Desertion didn't seem his style.

Korlov coughed grimly and pulled himself to his feet. He'd assumed that the rebels would breach the walls then use their infantry to take the palace. The idea that they might simply flatten the whole building had never occurred to him.

Korlov walked gingerly back along the corridor to survey the damage. Just before he reached the room, he noticed Colonel Dunnell's body partially flattened under a metal support beam.

That made more sense.

The building shook as another shell hit, then another. It was hard to tell, but these new impact sounds seemed to be coming from the east wing.

The status hub was a sprawl of shattered burning monitors and smoking rubble. The shell had punched a large hole in the south wall, which was now open to the night sky. He could hear the crack of rifle fire from the parapets near the gate. Another boom of a shell impact followed by a cheer from the rebels. Did that mean the outer gate was down?

Korlov realised he was running.

As he headed towards the council chamber, he reassessed his assumptions. The hub was a tactically important location, or at least it had been when there was still an army to direct. The first shell to hit the building had not destroyed that room by chance. But the rebels were still firing at least one of their guns at the south gate, which meant they still intended to breach and enter at some point.

They weren't trying to flatten the palace, just disable it.

If their positions were reversed, where would he target next? The barracks? The armoury? The generators?

The room shook with another impact and, as if to confirm his theory, the lights flickered and died. A second later, red emergency lighting kicked in.

Korlov ran on.

The council chamber had suffered a direct hit.

A shell had destroyed a structural wall, causing the partial collapse of the floor above. Illuminated in jerking torchlight, Korlov could see that a pile of smoking rubble at least ten feet high had buried the grand table, the lectern and most of the benches. Dazed soldiers and priests staggered through the dusty space of the chamber. Shouts for help and cries of the wounded filled the air, along with the chant of a priest who was standing in a corner, uselessly intoning the First Sightings.

Korlov was relieved to see, through one of the now broken high windows, that the silhouette of the temple bell tower appeared to be intact. It had no strategic importance as far as the rebels were concerned. It overlooked no gates and there were far higher towers in the palace into which you could place snipers.

As indeed Korlov had.

As long as the tower remained, the bomb remained. The plan could still work.

His voice was lost in the chorus of cries in the room as he called out for Dr Beltram, with no response. He could well be buried under the rubble, along with half the Ascendancy council, which could pose a problem.

Korlov's arrival had been noticed by one of the surviving priests, Father Rawlins. He had something of the ghost about him, white with masonry dust from head to toe, an image marred only by a single red smear of blood across one cheek.

At the sight of Korlov, he raised an accusing hand to point and advanced.

"You!" he said. "You have brought us here. To this end."

This was quite a departure for Father Rawlins. He was not someone that Korlov thought he had ever heard raise his voice in session, being as he was one of the grey, second-tier priests who would nod wisely at the words of others, but never add to them. He was the sort who would pull you aside after council for a private word or two. A subtle manipulator, who had achieved his position through back-room deals and the exchange of under-the-table favours.

Well, that table was now under a pile of rubble and it seemed to have broken something in Rawlins. He stood before Korlov and continued to rant his accusations, attempting to pin the blame for the fall of the Ascendancy squarely on the general's shoulders. His spittle was flying, his eyes wide and rolling, his jabbing finger inches from Korlov's face.

Korlov decided that if that finger touched him, he would draw his service pistol and shoot Rawlins in the mouth.

As for the accusations, they had some merit, as far as they went. The Ascendancy Council in place before Korlov's coup had been weak and soft, allowing open rebellion to flourish, punishing only the most egregious examples and then only with financial penalties.

Korlov had put a stop to all that.

An argument could be made that he had gone too far. That even as the purges, the mass executions and the ghettoes decimated the rebel cause, they also served to turn public opinion in the rebels' favour. He knew from reading interrogation transcripts that, for some previously blameless civilians, the excesses of his regime had been the tipping point that persuaded them to help and eventually join the rebellion.

Fine. He'd accept that his methods had perhaps swelled the rebel ranks somewhat. He'd take that one on the chin, but the rest of it - the military defeats, the routs, the captured armouries and artillery - none of that was down to his methods or leadership. He could place all of that at the door of a poorly equipped and ill-disciplined military, starved of funding for weapons and training by the very people in this room.

Either way, he wasn't exactly in the mood to debate any of

his potential failings with a shell-shocked priest.

Father Rawlins jabbing finger lightly pressed Korlov's cheek. The general smoothly drew his service pistol and shot him in the face.

As the priest's body fell, Korlov was gratified to note that he had indeed managed to hit him directly in his open mouth.

There was a moment of stunned silence and every eye in the room turned to him.

"Where is Dr Beltram?" he asked with a tone that promised further violence. He kept his pistol in his hand.

The question was met with shared looks of fear and confusion. Minister Piker stepped forward and bowed minutely. Even now, at the end of everything, he somehow maintained an air of pompous detachment. As though everything that was happening was somehow beneath him. Korlov noted, with no small satisfaction, that Piker's robe was torn and bloodstained.

"My General," began the minister, "I myself have not seen the doctor for perhaps an hour. It is possible he has fallen…"

He gestured apologetically to the pile of rubble in the centre of the room, as though it was of some minor inconvenience.

Korlov was about to retort when he became aware of someone standing beside him. One of Dr Beltram's lackeys, he didn't know her name, but he recognised her face from some of the doctor's earlier demonstrations - possibly the one with the frozen goat. She was wordlessly holding out a circular clamshell case about the size of a dinner plate. She looked distant, possibly in shock.

Korlov re-holstered his pistol and accepted the case.

"Is he dead?" asked the general quietly.

"I don't know," she replied. "Does it matter?"

The case was sealed with a DNA and handprint scanner. Korlov pressed his hand upon it and a second later the top surface unfolded smoothly and geometrically, like the petals of a flower.

Typical Beltram, thought Korlov. Over-engineered for the sake of it.

Inside the case was a small, black ceramic grip handle set into a foam cut-out. Korlov removed the handle and tossed the case aside. There was a spring-loaded red button at one end of the handle, protected by a guard that could be flicked back with a thumb. It was a radio trigger, extensively used by the military to remote-detonate explosives. Korlov doubted that one had ever been connected to a payload of this size, tuned as it was to the fifty kiloton nuclear device placed in the bell tower by Dr Beltram.

There had been a total of five people at the closed meeting where this course of action had been decided. Korlov could see two of them in the chamber and expected no interference from them, but he had to assume that word had leaked elsewhere. He had made sure that his back was to a wall when he removed the detonator and had his other hand resting on his service pistol.

He considered simply pressing the button, but felt he should at least say something. Those in the room that knew of the plan had fallen silent and those not in the know could sense something was afoot.

What should he say? A few things sprang to mind.

That he regretted nothing? That all he had done was in order to protect the principles of the Jorran Ascendancy, principles that he felt his predecessors had betrayed? That was all true, as far as it went, but if he was honest, he considered most of the people in this very chamber to be just as feckless as the ministers and priests they had replaced. They had come to this dead end through their own selfishness, their own greed, their own venal stupidity.

None of the words he considered felt right. The very act of speaking itself, to a group of people he had so little respect for and that would all soon be vaporised, felt worse than redundant.

Korlov detected motion in his peripheral vision and instinctively drew his pistol and fired. A council guard, midway through raising and aiming his rifle. Korlov's first bullet found his chest, the second took out his throat. He fell, gargling.

Korlov could hear the rifle shots of the palace guard echoing down the corridor leading to this very chamber. The rebels had breached the building.

"Fuck it," said Korlov and pulled the trigger.

He had specifically requested no countdown. No opportunity for second thoughts or defusing. The detonation should have been instant. But nothing happened. He pulled the trigger again, then again, eyes fixed on the silhouette of the bell tower.

Others in the room had started to become alarmed. He was dimly aware of two factions - one struggling to reach him, the other to protect him.

There was a familiar three-note fanfare behind him. The first notes of "Tinfoil Wings", the forbidden rebel anthem. Korlov turned to discover a ten-feet-wide hologram of a flapping rebel flag suspended in the air above the chamber. A holo projector, hidden somewhere in the room. This seemed to be all that the trigger had activated.

Dr Beltram had betrayed him.

But perhaps there was still time. They had other, smaller nuclear devices in their basement arsenal. Detonated at ground level, the impact would not be as great, but perhaps Dr Beltram's assistant could--

Korlov became aware of a new sound, carried on the wind through the broken windows.

It was coming from the bell tower.

A rising whine, a machine charging. Korlov realised that he had heard it before, at one of Dr Beltram's demonstrations, but he couldn't remember which one. There was plainly no nuclear device in the tower, but the trigger had activated something, some other machine of Beltram's.

Jesus, it wasn't the one that froze the goat, was it?

He became aware that he was laughing. Suddenly it all felt slightly ridiculous, his hubris and Beltram's betrayal, the goat-freezing machine in the tower, the dust-choked survivors in the council chamber scuffling with each other to wrench a trigger from his hand that had already done its work. And even beyond that, he was suddenly taken with the folly of all of it; the Jorran Ascendancy itself and the rebellion that looked likely to end their rule. All of them scrabbling for what little--

The device in the tower detonated.

At the speed of light, a wave of energy spread out from the epicentre, consuming the palace and the buildings beyond in an instant. Observers at the time reported the appearance of a blinding white dome, six miles across, obscuring everything in the city.

All in total, baffling silence.

When the light faded, less than a minute later, survivors outside the blast radius discovered that the city was all still there, just as before. For the device had not emitted a blast wave. It had not caused the city's destruction.

If anything, it had ensured its preservation.

Chapter II - The Boy

THE sign was sun-bleached and faded to the point of illegibility in places, hidden in weeds and lying halfway down the bank. It read:

"Warning: Do not progress any further. You are close to the real-time boundary surrounding Lumin City. Progressing any further automatically releases the local authority of any and all liability should injury or death befall you. Trespassing within the city also incurs an automatic $500 fine."

Jake found the sign kind of interesting and, as someone who worked in the city most days of the week, he also found the sign pretty funny.

One evening, when it got dark, he went back to the boundary wall, wrestled the old sign free of the weeds and dragged it home. He thought his parents would find the sign interesting and funny too, but his mum said they didn't have room for it in the caravan. His father did call it a "fascinating bit of history" but agreed that they couldn't keep it.

Jake ended up dumping it behind the communal bins. Two days later it had gone.

The current sign at the border wall was also pretty faded and old, but felt very different in tone. It read:

"Welcome to Lumin, the famed City Of Statues. Please keep to the

designated pathways between attractions to avoid injury."

The rest of the sign was taken up with a small-scale map to the gift shop and visitor centre. There was also some tiny writing at the bottom about legal liability for death and injury, which was similar to the old sign.

Jake accepted that the city could be a dangerous place, if you didn't know what you were doing. There was always some story doing the rounds about a bone-headed tourist wandering off the path to go exploring and ending up impaled on something or other. Even people who had lived and worked within the city all their lives would be very careful when leaving the designated "safe" zones.

The problem was that none of it looked dangerous. Visitors would arrive from the outside world with a bunch of baked-in assumptions about how things behaved and by the time they realised those assumptions were worse than useless in Lumin, they were being either bandaged up or carted off in an ambulance.

Grass was a good example.

If you saw a blade of grass out in the world, you would step on it without a second thought. Grass traditionally has give. A child could roll through a field of the stuff without injury.

Not so, the grass in Lumin.

In Lumin, a single thin blade of grass, standing alone in the centre of a muddy path, was as rigid and immobile as a knife made of diamond. More so, Jake would argue, as a knife can be moved, dug out or pushed down into the earth.

None of those things could be done to a blade of grass frozen in time.

A field of grass, of which there had been many caught within the blast radius, was really a field of knives in disguise. The only safe way to cross such a field was via a raised platform, built after the blast.

That was before you even considered the elements frozen in mid-air: bullets, shrapnel, fragments of masonry. All locked in place, hard to spot and waiting to impale the incautious wanderer.

When Jake was very young, his parents had told him a story that terrified him, about a bumble bee frozen in time by the bomb, around three feet from the ground. Easy to miss and at just the right height for an incautious child to run into, losing an eye.

That story had given Jake nightmares until he realised that the city had been frozen in the middle of the night. What had a bee been doing out in the dark? He questioned his parents and they gave him some hogwash about bee sleeping patterns being disturbed by the war, but he was on to them.

As he grew a little older, he understood the point of the story. Better a few nightmares than an injured child. And it had worked - throughout his childhood, he had kept to the paths outlined in safety stripes whenever he went into the city, viewing the areas beyond with a shudder.

Not that the warnings were even necessary for the longest time, as for many years Jake was held in his parents' arms whenever they walked through a frozen zone. Over time, this transitioned into a firmly held hand, until finally he was trusted with walking the route to and from the family pitch alone. It was only recently, in his fourteenth year, that he had felt confident enough to explore beyond. To go into those forbidden areas outside the safety stripes.

His parents would kill him if they found out, of course.

But most of the time, his route through the city was identical. It began on the river bank to the east, where a sallyport had been built into the border wall. The wall itself had been constructed around the entire city and was a perfect circle, six miles in diameter. In most places, it was a ten-feet-tall affair made of concrete slabs, spray-painted in the ubiquitous bright red and pale blue stripes that indicated real-time items and safe zone borders.

Here, the wall was showing its age - the stripes faded, the concrete stained and crumbling. As this sallyport was only ever seen by workers that staffed the city, Jake didn't think the council was in any hurry to repaint it.

Once the guard had scanned his work permit, Jake would then be cleared to walk through the sallyport and down a concrete slope on to the river, which felt a little like walking on ice, but it was never slippery or cold. The path across the river had been carefully plotted years ago to avoid eddies around rocks, which had thrown water droplets up from the surface. The drops hung in the air like diamonds and could cut you just as keenly as any knife.

Leading up from the river was a real-time wooden platform, built over a tangle of shattered boat hulls and ripped netting. The platform gave way to a slope, which finally led down into the streets.

The east side of the city had not seen the worst of the destruction, but even so, charred piles of rubble that used to be houses were dotted everywhere.

Here Jake would pass his first "statues". It was a shorthand that everyone who visited the city used, even though most people who worked there said they found it disrespectful. Most of the statues on Jake's route to work were corpses when the city froze. Slumped against walls or sprawled over the cobbles. A couple of Ascendancy uniforms but mainly civilians. Bodies that would never, could never, be buried or even moved. If a body had landed face down, with the face obscured, then that face would never be seen again.

There were only five statues on the route that had been alive when the Bomb Of Tears was activated. They were all civilians and had all been frozen mid-run.

Jake knew them all intimately, having passed them at least twice a day during his working week for the past five years. As a young child, he'd found them all fascinating, but now, with a little more of a seasoned eye, he could see why none of the five had been deemed worthy of inclusion in the guidebooks.

They had no clear narrative.

Obvious narratives accompanying memorable clear images were what the tourists liked. If the five had been running in terror, carrying piled possessions in their arms, then their story would have been compelling. As it was, the runners were carrying nothing and their expressions varied between exhaustion, annoyance and blankness. One of them had even been caught mid-blink. They were like bad photos of themselves, that they would have asked to be deleted.

Ten minutes from the river, Jake would turn left at a T-junction. He was now on a secondary tourist route, which appeared in all the guidebooks and led straight to the palace. Here, there were many more statues and tableaux but all the good ones had small real-time huts built around them and charged entry fees. They were called pitches and, five minutes along this route, Jake would reach the pitch that his family had rented for the last three generations.

Their pitch was centred around a dead soldier that Jake's family all called Dusty. Jake was seven before he realised that this wasn't his real name, they all just called him that because his uniform had been dusty when he died.

He remembered feeling stupid when he realised.

The city was full of things that weren't called by their real names. Even Lumin City itself was rarely called that. Most people called it Statue City, or even shortened it to Stat.

The Bomb of Tears wasn't its real name either. Jake had read up on it. Ninety-eight years ago, back when the city first froze, scientists had a theory that it had been caused by something they called a "Cryogenic Bomb". They thought it used the same technology that froze the old colonists on their long journey from Earth to New Refuge. The public started shortening Cryogenic Bomb to Cry Bomb, then eventually that became The Bomb Of Tears.

By the time the scientists realised that their theory was wrong and that they didn't really have any idea how Lumin had been frozen, the name had stuck. Bomb Of Tears it was.

At a guess, it had been Jake's grandfather that had first called the soldier Dusty. He was the one who first claimed the pitch, decades ago, much to the confusion of the Lumin Tourist Board. For you see, when Jake's grandfather first found him, Dusty had no clear narrative at all. He was just another dead soldier in a city full of them. He was sitting with his back to a crumbling wall staring sadly at the ground, with a hole in his chest the size of Jake's fist.

If Dusty had been frozen mid-throw of a grenade or clutching his chest and falling just before he reached cover, *that* would have been a narrative. That would have been worth paying to see; but as it was, no-one could see why anyone would care, all of which made renting the pitch very cheap indeed.

But Jake's grandfather had vision. As was customary, he built a small hut around Dusty's body and, three days later, revealed his new narrative:

A love-sick soldier staring at a photograph of his sweetheart.

It was something of a cliché and didn't have the dynamism of some of the pitches, but it spoke to people and the tourists warmed to it. Dusty rapidly became a popular stopping point on the way to some of the bigger, more impressive tableaux at the palace.

The fact that Jake's grandfather had simply attached a fake arm to the corpse, made of twisted coat hanger and papier-mâché and holding a random photograph, was - depending on your point of view - either a stroke of genius or a cynical exploitation of the dead.

Jake's family had replaced the arm and photograph many times over the years, refining and improving the original design. The sleeve was now a perfect replica of the Jorran Ascendancy uniform, complete with historically accurate buttons and gold thread, scuffed and dusted to match the rest of the body. A short, starched cape had also been added to hide the fact that Dusty's real arm had been twisted behind his body as he fell against the wall.

Jake knew Dusty as well as the members of his own family. The sweat beading on his forehead, as hard as armoured glass; the loose thread hanging from his collar, now as sharp as a needle. He looked so young, no older than twenty. There was no way to tell. He probably had dog tags around his neck, but they were beneath layers of a uniform that would never, could never, be moved again.

Every morning, Jake and his father would unlock the hut

surrounding Dusty, reattach the fake arm, ensure that the photograph was positioned perfectly to meet his blank gaze, check that the hole in his chest was fully obscured and then open the doors to the public.

They charged three dollars for a photograph and five dollars for a private viewing.

Every pitch had a title in the official guidebook for the city. Dusty's was "One Last Look at Lydia", which was supposed to be the name of the woman in the fake photo. A few years ago, Jake's family started writing "Love Lydia" on the back of the fake photo, but it didn't seem to do anything for visitor numbers either way.

Some tourists could get quite emotional viewing Dusty staring at his fake photograph. Thinking about the lover that he would never see again. Jake used to find it exciting, knowing the secret truth behind it all, that they were fooling the tourists. Now he was slightly older, he found it all a little sad. Photograph or not, Dusty was dead. Someone had no doubt mourned him and he probably had someone he missed, even if he wasn't holding their photo when he died.

Sometimes, when he was alone in the hut with him, Jake could believe that Dusty really was looking at Lydia rather than simply staring at nothing.

The money they made from Dusty wasn't their only income. Jake's mother picked vegetables in the farms far outside the city, from fields that hadn't been frozen by the bomb. Sometimes she would bring home bags of sprouts and sweet potatoes, then cook up huge vats of soup. As he dished it up, Jake's father would make up a song about all the wind it was going to give them. Jake's mother would smack him, but she would be laughing too.

Jake and his parents lived in a caravan park just outside the blast radius. There were twenty caravans in all. Most were rented by staff of other tourist attractions, but none of the big ones up at the palace. The workers who ran the tableaux there commuted in and lived in proper houses. Their attractions drew most of the tourists, which meant that the palace earned most of the money.

Some of the tourists went straight to the palace, ignoring the streets around it entirely.

Jake thought that was very unfair.

Sometimes, a vacancy would open up in the palace, but it was never offered to any of the people that Jake knew. Not that they would take it if it was. Working there was, for some reason, seen as shameful, but Jake couldn't figure out why.

Whenever his father saw workers from the palace, he would shake his head and say that working in the building was "rubbing off on them" and that they "had ideas above their station".

Jake would shake his head too. He didn't quite know what his dad meant, but he could tell it wasn't a good thing.

Secretly, Jake quite liked the idea of working at the palace. All their tableaux were already exciting. They didn't need papier-mâché anything. They also got paid more, which Jake liked the sound of. He didn't tell anyone, but he decided that when he was old enough, he would try really hard to get a job there. And when he did, he would make sure that the building didn't rub off on him, or get ideas above his station, so that his dad would still like him.

All the families in the caravan park knew each other well. Some of them had been renting the same pitches for generations, much like Jake's family. They could all be trusted to cover for one another in times of illness or emergency. As an unspoken agreement, they could all view each others pitches for free, but they never did.

When Jake found this out, he was five years old. He spent a giddy weekend viewing all the other pitches, dragging his apologetic mother behind him. He didn't understand at the time why she was so embarrassed. He did now. The proper way to behave around the frozen bodies was respectful. If you laughed and gawped and pointed, you were no better than a tourist.

Now, if he ever covered another worker's pitch, he would barely smile and only look at the bodies if there was no one else around.

He knew them all well by this point. Their official names in the guidebook suggested their supposed narrative. Things like

"Crafty Nap" for a sleeping corporal, "The Coward" for a private holding a gun to his temple, or "Sweet Relief" for a captain having a piss.

Many of them employed tricks much like Dusty's. Jake's mother confided in him that the corporal taking a "Crafty Nap" had a visible and undoubtedly fatal head wound that had been covered with a fake helmet placed at a jaunty angle. Likewise, "The Coward" had an entirely fake arm holding a replica pistol to his temple.

That one took Jake a while to realise. He'd done a full shift covering it before anyone told him, looking into the soldiers sad, broken eyes and imagining how desperate he must have been to want to kill himself. The next morning, he helped set up the pitch with the owner and watched in shock as the fake arm and gun were attached.

The renters of "The Coward" were an Erghan family, headed by a fierce matriarch called Gemma. She showed Jake that the soldier originally only had one arm, the other blown off at the shoulder and heavily bandaged. This made the illusion much easier to sell. There was no need to hide the original arm and the new arm had a series of uniform-coloured cloth flaps to hide the bandages.

Gemma then went on to tell Jake that, for many years, "The Coward" had been called something totally different, with no fake arm at all. She showed Jake a really old faded copy of the map of attractions in the tourist guide, where the coward's pitch was marked as "Going Home". The look on the private's face in that context could be read very differently. He had lost an arm, but as a consequence he would no longer have to fight.

Tessa explained that, at the time, tourist visitor numbers to "Going Home" were not high and they were considering giving up the pitch. Just before they did, Jake's grandfather unveiled Dusty. Inspired by this, Tessa's grandfather built a fake arm and gun and relaunched "Going Home" as "The Coward". Visitor numbers spiked and they had been steady ever since.

Jake didn't like to think about what that meant about people.

"Sweet Relief" didn't employ any tricks. It depicted a portly rebel soldier urinating against a half-demolished bakery. He was frozen mid-stream with one hand resting on the wall. Predictably, this was a very popular pitch for posed photos with stag or hen parties. However, he was cordoned off so that no one could reach his penis.

"Sweet Relief" was rented by a man called Henry, unusual in that he ran it alone, with no other family to help him. When Jake was old enough to understand, his parents explained that Henry's family had all been Disappeared after going on a protest march. This meant that the Goodmen had either imprisoned them or, more likely, killed them.

Jake's father told him that the Goodmen were called that because of an old requirement for juries, which was "twelve good men and true". The Goodmen began as an alternative to the courts, but even back then they weren't good or true.

Jake regularly had nightmares about the Goodmen coming to Disappear him. Because they were dreams and didn't have to make sense, sometimes Disappearing meant that they were going to erase Jake's face. But the worst dreams were the ones where they came for Jake's family as well, like they had with Henry's.

Henry was a quiet, thin man with a distant smile. Jake enjoyed covering Henry's pitch because he thought that a man who had lost so much deserved all the help in the world. Sometimes Jake would bring him cakes or food and just sit with him. Once or twice, when Henry didn't know he was watching him, Jake would catch an expression on his face of such intense pain that it made him want to cry.

Henry's story also made Jake realise how lucky he was. He had a mother and father who loved each other and loved him, which he knew was rare. They also never went hungry, although the caravan could get very cold in the winter.

As is often the way, because he'd never known anything else, he used to view his childhood as the norm, if he ever stopped to consider it at all; but he'd recently come to realise that it was anything but. This was prompted primarily by the news feeds. His family used to stop him from watching them as he was too young, but recently they'd begun to watch them all together as a family, answering any questions Jake might have at the end.

To begin with, Jake didn't understand a lot of it and found much of the footage upsetting. This led to one of the rare arguments that he could remember between his parents, with his father saying that Jake was too young and his mother disagreeing. Jake found their arguing more upsetting than watching the news. He broke their deadlock by insisting that he could handle it, but privately he wasn't sure. He told himself that watching upsetting things was part of becoming a man, which he was determined to do.

He'd been watching the news every few days for the past six months now. He still had lots of questions, which his parents did their best to answer, and his questions and their answers became more detailed every time. The main thing that he took away from the news was that the bubble of stability he and his family enjoyed was rare and to be treasured.

He saw lots of families on the news who were not enjoying their lives. Fighting for a loaf of bread in food riots, on the run from the Goodmen or appearing on missing posters as they joined the ranks of the Disappeared. Jake's father said that the Goodmen were gradually taking more and more control of the media and the internet. He said that if they ever had full control, things would immediately get much worse because no one would be watching them.

Jake had also come to realise that he and his family owed all of their good fortune to the frozen city. Had it not been there, had grandfather not seen the potential of Dusty, they could well be on the news too, fighting for food in distant towns along with everyone else.

The city had been frozen ninety-eight years ago. Some people said it would be frozen forever, others said the effect would eventually wear off and the statues would all move again.

That idea terrified Jake.

Much as he felt for the plight of all those poor frozen people, he also realised that if they came to life again then all the pitches would disappear. Dusty would be revealed as the corpse he always had been and Jake's family's livelihood would disappear overnight.

He knew it was selfish, but he hoped that the city would stay frozen forever, keeping his family fed and safe and warm. Away from all the bad things he saw on the news.

Chapter III - The Scientist

DR Julius Beltram could pinpoint the exact moment when the veil fell away and he realised that he was working for a madman.

It was the day Thomas died. Shot through the head, on the orders of General Korlov, for an infraction so minor it made Beltram weep to think of it. The fact that Dr Beltram had somehow managed to overlook the thousands of innocents that had died on Korlov's orders before that point, filled him with a profound shame.

"The death of one man is a tragedy. The death of millions is a statistic."

And so it was with Beltram. He had been dimly aware of the mass rebel executions, the growing number of de-programming camps, the riots that eventually grew into a fully fledged rebellion, but all of this had been filed under "someone else's department" in Beltram's head. It took the death of a man he had known well, a man he'd worked with every day for the past twelve years, to finally open his eyes. To finally make him face the fact that he was chief scientific advisor to a murderous psychopath riding the Ascendancy into the abyss.

Before that day, the amount of attention that Beltram paid to politics within the Jorran Ascendancy was minimal, and grudging at that. This was admittedly an odd position for someone to hold, embedded as he was at the heart of governance, but it all felt so irrelevant to his real goal. Put simply, Dr Beltram had devoted his life to scientific advancement and tended to view everything through the prism of that aim. Thus, the events that occurred within the council chamber were either a route to more funding or a distraction from his work, in which case they could be pointedly ignored.

By and large, the other council members had achieved their positions by some combination of nepotism, trading favours, bribery or blackmail. Beltram was guilty of none of these things, rising to the council solely on the back of his scientific accomplishments. He was there purely because he was very good at what he did. He remained there for the same reason - refusing, for the most part, to be drawn into any scheming or plotting, which seemed to be rife within the chambers. For these reasons, his fellow counsellors viewed him as an unfathomable and unpredictable oddity. Why wasn't he spending every waking hour calculating how best to hang on to or increase the power and status he had achieved? What long game was he playing?

Very occasionally, when he could predict that nudging a situation would ultimately lead to more funding flowing into his division, he would enter the fray, usually to the complete shock of his fellow councillors. This, in turn, only added to his reputation as an unpredictable maverick.

But, for the most part, he kept his head down and delivered whatever scientific advancements he'd made to whomever happened to be in power at the time. He'd outlasted three Premiers using these tactics and, even though General Korlov took power in a coup, at first glance his policies didn't seem that different to those of his predecessors.

Beltram really should have been paying more attention.

But, as always, the work was all-consuming. Most recently, every waking hour had been devoted to his groundbreaking advances in quantum shifting, which had reached a pivotal milestone. He had managed to freeze several large animals for over twenty-four hours before returning them to real time, with no apparent ill effects.

The potential applications he could see were immense, everything from medical triage to deep-space exploration. The effect also appeared scalable, the math supporting freezing of a much larger area. Beltram imagined it deployed on a battlefield, like a massive pause button that would allow any conflict to be resolved by politicians and pens rather than bullets.

Looking back at his own naivety for even holding these thoughts in his head, Beltram felt physically sick. To think he came close to giving this technology to Korlov. He didn't even want to imagine the general's reaction to the gift of a frozen battlefield. He had got as far as planning a presentation, was actually on his way to the meeting with the general to outline his breakthrough, when he discovered that Thomas had been killed.

Thomas Delling had come with the building. His official title had been caretaker of the workshop and he had held that position for over twenty years before Beltram's arrival. He had an open face, never far from a curious smile. He wore a stained overall that had been endlessly patched and reinforced at elbow and knee, along with a frayed cloth cap, his white hair tucked beneath it. He walked with a stoop, but with purpose in his step, and rarely seemed to be at rest. There was always something in the workshop that needed cleaning or repairing or replacing.

When he'd first arrived, Beltram, who openly acknowledged that he could be something of a science snob, had looked past Thomas for weeks. The man wasn't a scientist, he merely emptied their waste paper bins, ergo he could be ignored. However, he soon came to realise that Thomas knew everything worth knowing about the equipment at their disposal, from the smallest centrifuge to the largest of the scanning chambers.

Beyond the equipment in it, he knew the building. He knew how to restart the temperamental boiler when it invariably died in the depths of winter; and in summer, when the equally temperamental air-con failed, he knew precisely which windows to open for optimal air circulation.

Very occasionally, he could be found at rest in his tiny office, which was half taken up with cleaning supplies and spare parts. The only concession to personalisation or decoration was a thin shelf crowded with tiny doodles on scraps of paper.

One day, a month or so into his time at the workshop, Beltram went looking for Thomas. They'd fried a power breaker and were in search of a spare. As Beltram approached, he could see Thomas through the open door of his office. He was sitting in his armchair, presumably on his lunch break, as he opened a greaseproof packet of sandwiches. Unaware he was being watched, Thomas removed a small folded slip of paper from the sandwiches, smiled as he studied it, kissed it and placed it on the shelf with the others.

He finally spotted Beltram, stood and put the sandwiches to one side. Even before the doctor had finished speaking, Thomas had located the exact model of power breaker they needed from the pile of spares beside him and had handed it over.

As Beltram walked back to the testing bay, he considered what he'd seen. What he'd taken to be random doodles seemed to be love notes from Thomas' partner.

Beltram returned later to examine the shelf more closely.

Some of the notes were intricate drawings of hearts or doves. Sometimes a few lines of verse. Thomas later confirmed, when he grew to know Beltram a little better, that he'd been receiving one a day, every day, for the past twenty years. When the shelf got too full, he would retire the older notes to a drawer.

Beltram was inexplicably jealous.

He'd had relationships in the past, some years long, but all had foundered on the rocks of his obsession with science. None had felt like love. None had felt like this thing that Thomas had. It was, of course, possible that Thomas and his partner argued incessantly at home, that Beltram was imbuing these love notes with far too much significance, but he somehow doubted it.

He began to draw Thomas into conversations, to subtly probe his intelligence. He wanted to hate him, or discover that he was an idiot, which would instantly solve his jealousy. But Thomas was no fool. To do his job effectively and safely, he needed at the very least to have an in-depth understanding of the machinery he was servicing, which was no small ask. But beyond that, Thomas had spent twenty years working at the shoulders of the finest scientific minds of the Jorran Ascendancy.

And he had been paying attention.

Beltram's questions became ever more specific and arcane. Thomas' answers, in turn, became ever more impressive. At a certain point, he began to get the answers wrong, but in such a specific way that Beltram could tell that he was playing dumb. He gave three wrong answers in a row regarding supposedly harmless chemical compounds that would have led to sizeable explosions had they been acted on, which in itself was impressive. His wrong answers demonstrated far more technical knowledge than the right answers would have done.

Beltram was amused by his contrariness and the game that they both knew he was playing. He eventually concluded that Thomas easily exceeded several of his apprentices in technical knowledge and offered him a job on the spot. He was stunned when Thomas turned him down.

He was initially cryptic with his reasons, but over time Beltram came to understand. In his position as caretaker, Thomas flew far under the radar of the Ascendancy council. He knew how to do his current job well and, providing he kept the machines in the workshop in good repair, he would never be judged for the failure or successes of any teams working there.

Joining Beltram's team would change all that. The supposed benefits - the extra money, the prestige - none of that seemed to interest him. He had found contentment in his position and had no burning desire to make a name for himself or change the world through science, or indeed expose himself to repercussions should he fail.

Beltram's original aim of finding something to dislike about Thomas quickly faded, as did his jealousy, to be replaced with a growing respect and ultimately a great fondness. Whenever Beltram spotted him working around the workshop, he would wander over, mug of coffee in hand, and pass the time of day at his elbow for a few minutes. He also began regularly "popping by" his office.

The unspoken conceit, which was part cover story and part running joke, and which they both played to the hilt, was that Thomas was not very smart and was totally oblivious to the experiments going on around him. However, occasionally Beltram would ask for Thomas' input on his work. To keep this fact secret, and again, without any prior verbal arrangement, Beltram would pointedly hand Thomas a waste paper basket containing the issue in question on a screwed-up paper ball. The next morning, the basket and paper ball would be back beside Beltram's desk. When the ball was unfolded, Beltram would find Thomas' usually brilliantly insightful notes and observations below the problem in question.

In short order Beltram came to consider Thomas the most valuable member of his staff. Uniquely, of anyone in the workshop, Beltram could be sure that his opinion was untarnished by either ambition or fear of repercussions, which made his analyses invaluable.

For twelve years, their odd little friendship continued. Beltram sensed that what they had was fragile, so they never socialised beyond the workshop, never bought each other gifts at birthdays or Christmas. There was also the gulf in terms of rank to consider. Beltram was Chief Scientific Advisor to the Jorran Ascendancy. Thomas was a caretaker. The idea of them going out for a night drinking together would have raised quite a few eyebrows.

They both knew the rules of the game, even though neither of them had ever, nor would ever, speak them out loud.

And then one crisp morning, on the way to give Korlov an experimental demonstration, Beltram spotted Thomas' blood-stained body sprawled on the growing pile in the courtyard.

Beltram only pieced together the full story later. The reasons behind the bullet hole in his temple, the end of his friend's life. At the time he was numb, reeling in shock, allowing himself to be hurried along to a demonstration that he no longer had any interest in.

Apparently, Thomas had been shepherding a fresh consignment of supplies from the palace loading dock to the workshops when he had happened to cross paths with a couple of soldiers dragging a screaming chambermaid out into the courtyard to be shot.

Understandably, he had questions. The soldiers had no interest in answering them, but those nearby informed Thomas that the chambermaid's name was Kelly Reems. Her brother, Johann Reems, had reportedly abandoned his role as carpenter and joined the rebellion. In Korlov's mind, this was apparently sufficient cause to have his sister shot for treason.

Thomas made the mistake of protesting at this injustice. Not only that, he happened to do it within General Korlov's earshot.

A few moments later, both he and the chambermaid were dead.

On his more charitable days, Dr Beltram had opined that General Korlov had retained the face and bearing of the soldier he had once been. A more accurate description, sometimes whispered between his rivals in the council chamber, was that he looked like a thug wearing the uniform of a general he had just murdered.

The dress tunic always looked somehow wrong on him, an affectation he endured because his position made it necessary. This impression was reinforced by the fact that he kept the uniform as free of adornment as was permissible and, since the coup, he had removed every single medal but one, reputedly the first one he earned.

His scalp and face were perpetually shaven, far from the current fashion in chambers and, combined with his hanging brow and jutting jaw, it gave him a brutish, brooding look. Many of his rank and position had allowed their physical fitness to slip, often sliding fully into obesity. But not Korlov. You only had to look at the man to see that he was as fit now as the day he left basic training.

On the morning of the presentation, Korlov's lone medal caught the lights from the stage, glinting as he sat in the darkness. When it was over, he called for the lights and sat brooding for a long minute.

He did not look happy and Beltram didn't blame him.

Beltram later wondered how events would have transpired had Thomas lived. Would his eyes have been opened by some other tragedy? God knows, there were enough to choose from. Or would he have remained loyal, blinkered and oblivious to the bitter end, shot by the rebels as they stormed the palace?

As it was, the death of Thomas set in motion a chain reaction of events that culminated in Beltram's total betrayal of General Korlov and arguably the Ascendancy itself. It was the epiphany that made him finally raise his head from his work and realise that his house was burning down.

In the short term, it totally changed the nature of the demonstration that he gave to the general. He had planned to outline, in detail, the potential tactical uses of the quantum shifting technology, but in the twenty minutes that Korlov kept them waiting, Beltram faced some painful home truths about his own wilful ignorance regarding his employer. An employer that he realised should never, in any circumstances, have access to technology this powerful.

So Dr Beltram lied. Much to the confusion of his team, who were waiting in the wings, he stood in the spotlight of the virtually empty auditorium and massively undersold the technology. It would have been too suspicious to totally sabotage the demonstration, so he allowed the quantum generator to power up and freeze the goat, at which point he ad-libbed some waffle about using the technology to preserve soldiers' rations. He went on to imply that it was merely an advancement in cryogenic freezing, but that to make it stable would require further funding, to add to the eye-watering amount it had already cost.

At the end of his faltering, apologetic presentation, he watched General Korlov carefully. If he'd misjudged the general's tolerance or his own value to the council, he could well be joining Thomas in the courtyard. As it was, Korlov looked more weary than angry.

"You're lucky I don't have you shot for wasting Ascendancy time and money," he said, "Your funding for this farce is hereby revoked. Get back to making me bombs."

And with that, he left the auditorium. Beltram breathed out

and began packing up the presentation. His confused team was full of questions, but Beltram said nothing. Instead he pointedly led them all through the courtyard and paused beside Thomas' body before declaring, "I don't know what came over me."

Now that the shield wall was down, the cheer of the rebels massed in the city was suddenly audible. Noise could reach the palace from the outside world, which meant that the next time the artillery fired was a thunderous cacophony, the impact of the shells doubly so.

Beltram was gratified to see the guard jump.

"I think they're going to need every gun they can find on the battlements," said Beltram.

He didn't expect his ruse to work, as the guard had, up until that point, been stubbornly sticking to his post. He'd spent the last thirty minutes insisting that it was Beltram's duty to tend to the bomb and he had very specific orders to ensure that he did just that, refusing to allow him to leave the tower.

But with the shield wall failing, things had suddenly changed. The fall of the palace was no longer theoretical, it was happening around them. Rebels were about to breach the building and Beltram could now see fear in the guard's eyes.

He made a meal of considering Beltram's words carefully before saluting briskly, turning on his heel and leaving. Beltram listened to his boots hurrying down the spiral staircase. He doubted very strongly that the guard was en route to aid his brothers-in-arms fighting the rebels. It was always the way with the barrack room lawyers. Eager to come down on minor infringements and exercise what little authority they wielded, but first to crumble in combat. He suspected the guard would attempt to escape the palace, perhaps shedding his uniform even now.

By torchlight, Beltram examined the bomb one last time. The casing told the world that this was a fifty-kiloton nuclear device attached to a radio-activated trigger. There was nothing on the exterior to hint at the quantum shift device hidden within.

The rebel artillery continued its barrage, shaking the tower and lighting up the night with each impact. Pummelling the outer walls and gates was to be expected, but Beltram was sure he sensed explosions from other directions, deeper within the palace. He was tempted to peer out at the rooftops from the stone windows, but resisted the impulse. He had a job to do.

Satisfied with the bomb, Beltram closed and snapped shut the casing and left the circular viewing floor. At the top of the stairs, he locked the heavy wooden door behind himself and broke the key off in the lock before working his way carefully down the spiral stairs, pointing the torch at his feet.

He was keenly aware that time was running out. The rebels were close to breaching the palace, which meant that at any moment Korlov could activate the trigger, at which point - assuming the math of Beltram and his team was reliable - the palace would be frozen in time and the city saved from destruction.

There were a lot of annoying variables, not least of which was the stability of their calculations. The largest trial they'd attempted had been in the palace's abandoned tennis court, where they'd successfully frozen a sphere thirty feet in diameter. This was encouraging in some ways, but worrying in others, as they'd only intended the sphere to be twenty feet wide.

Still, there was nothing to be done about it now. Using the quantum shifter had been the best of a set of bad options. Once Korlov gave the order to Beltram to help him level the city, the clock had been ticking. Beltram's team had discussed numerous alternatives to the shifter, all of which quickly fell by the wayside. Leaking Korlov's plan to the rest of the council was rejected as too risky a strategy. They didn't know what percentage of the council would prefer oblivion to capture. Sabotage of the bomb was also rejected on the grounds that there was an arsenal in the cellar full of the things. They couldn't defuse them all without arousing suspicion.

One suggestion, which held favour for quite a while was to rig a smaller device within the bomb casing, to just destroy the palace and prevent further bombs being activated. This would at least spare the city, if not the vanguard of the rebels. But it could still mean the death of hundreds, which none of them was happy with.

Their final plan had a lot of moving parts. The rest of Beltram's team should, by now, have made their way out of the palace. All were carrying small jury-rigged field neutralisers in their knapsacks. These devices would allow them to both pass through the shield wall and reset the quantum shift, once it had frozen the palace.

Their instructions had been to all attempt to escape in different directions, wave a white flag at the rebel forces and apprise them of the situation, then hopefully be allowed - or assisted - to move even further away from the supposed blast radius.

Beltram's delay at the hands of the jobsworth guard meant that he doubted very strongly that he would even make it to the palace wall before the device was activated. Nevertheless, he continued to behave as they had planned, shrugging his own knapsack on to his back, hurrying out of the tower and across the deserted quad.

He was heading broadly north through the grounds and his journey was punctuated by regular artillery impacts behind him, the shells seeming to land in different areas of the palace.

Abruptly, all the lights around him died.

They'd taken out the generator, either by luck or judgement. Red emergency light flicked on from a few nearby windows, but nothing outside. He was now dependent on his torch, which made him feel like a target in the darkness. He tried turning it off, hoping his memory of the route would get him through, but within three steps he'd collided with a wall. He had no time to wait for his eyes to adjust and simply turned the torch back on.

He could soon hear sporadic gunfire behind him. They had come in through the south gate, as predicted, and Beltram soon became convinced that he could hear gunshots and sounds of fighting coming from within the palace.

The rebels had breached the building. Time was almost up.

He rounded the brooding silhouette of the hedge maze and hopped over a low rope, which indicated the unofficial border of the cultivated grounds of the palace. A fallow field, peppered with high weeds, sloped down to a copse of trees against the north-east wall of the grounds. He slid a little on a patch of rotting leaves and slowed his pace. Rushing was futile at this stage.

Halfway across the field, a shot echoed from the copse and Beltram heard the bullet impact at his feet. Rebels? He threw himself to the ground, landing awkwardly on his side. He heard an ominous crack from the knapsack. The field neutraliser? If he'd broken that, his usefulness to the plan was over.

Another shot. This time he heard the bullet whiz over his head.

"Wait!" he shouted, finally finding his voice.

He scrabbled in the knapsack for the white flag they'd all packed, then winced, shielding his eyes from a sudden light.

His initial thought was that someone was pointing a torch directly at him, but as his eyes became acclimatised, he realised that it wasn't directed at him. It was all around.

It was daylight.

Beltram was crouched in an empty field in direct sunlight, with clear blue skies overhead. He had the merest moment of confusion before realisation dawned. Time had skipped. Therefore, Korlov had activated the quantum shifter and the palace had been frozen. And subsequently unfrozen, at the very least a few hours later.

No. His scientific training kicked in and he corrected himself. He was making too many assumptions. All he could be sure of was that he himself had been released from the quantum shift. Everything else was supposition.

He was still hyperventilating and jittery, at any moment expecting another shot from the copse of trees. He couldn't assume the rebels had gone. He hurriedly unravelled the white flag from his knapsack, which was attached to a telescopic rod. He extended the rod and planted it in the ground, then stared at the copse.

"I surrender!" he shouted.

He didn't detect any reaction and couldn't see anything but leaves.

Beltram thought a little more about his situation. The field neutralisers he and his team carried were short-range only. The plan had been to selectively release allies from the grip of the quantum shift, but Beltram could see no one else in sight. Which meant what? That the shift field had collapsed on its own over time? Some larger device had been built and utilised?

He reached into his rucksack again and removed his own field neutraliser. It was a metal sphere around a foot across, suspended in a tight lattice of electrical wire. Hanging below it and attached by a ribbon connector was a control box, a customized remote from some other device that they had cannibalised.

Beltram could see that the control box was cracked, with one of the switches hanging loose by its wire. Upon closer inspection, Beltram could also see a patina of rust across the sphere that had not been there when he placed the device in the bag.

New theory: this field neutraliser had indeed been broken in the fall, leading to it unlocking an area of real time around itself for long enough to cause rust. It had then further deteriorated, causing it to unlock a larger area, including Beltram.

The rust worried him greatly. For it to be on the device, the quantum shift field must have lasted weeks, possibly longer. Which implied that every other member of his team had failed in their mission. If even one of them had been able to use their device to free the others, they would have done so. Something must have stopped them.

He needed more information.

He put the device back in his knapsack and reclaimed the white flag before standing and setting back off up the hill, a journey that he'd made mere minutes ago, from his perspective. He wondered how long ago it had been in real terms.

He'd taken perhaps ten steps when he abruptly tripped and fell flat on his face, suddenly in blinding pain. He felt something sharp and unyielding jab in and under his ribs. He rolled away from the pain, back down the hill, and lay there panting. He could feel other cuts stinging on his hands and legs.

After recovering for a few seconds, he gingerly pulled himself to his knees and peered at the area that had caused him such pain. He was half-expecting to see barbed wire or discarded weaponry of some sort, but all he could see was grass and weeds, some now dripping with his blood.

Grass frozen in time. Immobile. Unyielding.

He felt like an idiot.

He unfurled the white flag from his knapsack and ripped it from its pole, then used it to wipe the cuts on his hands. One of the longer stalks had gone in under his ribs, he couldn't tell how deeply, but there wasn't much pain. He bunched up the flag, shoved it inside his shirt to cover the wound and considered his next move.

The field neutraliser had enough charge left to clear a path to the top of the hill. A swathe of grass, which a second ago had stabbed his flesh, was soon waving happily in the breeze. He carefully climbed over the low rope beside the gravel path bordering the hedge maze. There was a new boundary before the entrance to the maze - a low wooden fence painted in red and blue stripes.

Fences took time to build. The paint was also sun-bleached in certain areas and, as Beltram drew closer, he could see that the bottom of the wood was rotting in places.

His estimation for how long he'd been frozen was rising by the second.

He clambered over the new wall, holding his stomach in pain, and found himself on the gravel path that led back to the quad. He could see the very top of the temple bell tower containing the quantum shifter peeking over the library wall. Everything felt comfortingly familiar, yet utterly alien.

It was here that he encountered his first tourists.

He didn't realise what they were at first, of course. A sun-damaged couple in their fifties, wearing shorts and rain capes, bickering over the most time-effective route around the palace attractions. They were so deep in their argument that they barely looked at Beltram as they passed him.

Lacking any better options, he decided to follow them.

They led him past the maze, along one side of the quad, and directly to the courtyard where Korlov had dumped Thomas' body. Some part of Beltram's mind expected to find the space cleared of corpses and was shocked to find them all still there, exactly as they were the last time he saw them.

No, not exactly the same. The perspex walls around them were new, as was the slowly moving line of tourists.

Head reeling at the implications, Beltram drew closer to inspect a brass plaque mounted to one side. It read:

"The Shame Of the Ascendancy"

In the final weeks of the Jorran Ascendancy, the collapsing regime began to execute ever more of it's own citizens. Some were accused of collaboration with the rebel forces, others killed for more arbitrary reasons. Here we see a group of rebels, having just breached the palace, reacting to this grim discovery.

Beltram hadn't noticed, due to the angle he approached, but there was indeed a loose knot of rebel soldiers also inside the perspex box. They too were frozen, guns in hand as they looked in shock at the pile of bodies.

One of them, a woman in her fifties with a rifle on a strap across her back, had just fallen to her knees. Her face was locked in an expression of torment, eyes brimming with frozen tears as she stared at one of the bodies in the pile, no doubt a relative. Suspended forever in the moment of realisation that all hope was lost.

Beltram wondered if this was Thomas' partner. If she had been the one to write him the infinite notes of love.

He found his eye drawn to the line of tourists as they filed past. Most of them were quietly respectful, but here and there he noticed the distracted or bored. A slack-jawed man with a shaved head picked his nose as he peered intently at his guidebook. A child of perhaps six hummed to himself as he dragged his hand across the perspex wall, oblivious to or uncaring of the horrors within.

Something about it felt like madness. The fact that the body of Thomas still lay sprawled in that pile, his face bloated and discoloured. Beltram's own grief at his death, the shame that followed, emotions still raw within him, now felt distant and trivial, their subject reduced to a carnival attraction, some obscene sculpture to be gawped at or ignored en route to more popular spectacles.

An eddy of wind blew up a handful of litter and leaves, which swirled around Beltram's feet. Flapping amongst them was a discarded map to the palace, which he managed to pin with his foot. He leaned down to retrieve it.

It was split into two sections, the largest covering the frozen tableaux to be found within the palace grounds - given names such as The Storming Of The Gate, The Executioner's Lament and The Dance Of Death. A litany of tragedies reduced to a menu of attractions. The second section covered the wider city, at which point Beltram's heart sank. There was a clear indication that the entire city had been frozen. A perfect circle, six miles across.

Something within the math or stability of the device they had massively misjudged. Which explained what happened to his team - they had all been caught within the blast radius, as he had been, and unable to complete their mission.

He peered closer at the small print on the map, searching for the print date. He sagged when he found it.

If the date was correct, the city and the palace had been frozen for at least a hundred and forty-seven years.

Up until that point, Beltram had had some half-formed plan in his mind to make his way back to the workshops to repair and recharge his field neutraliser. He could then have begun the task of locating and releasing his team, speeding up the process of defrosting everyone else. But their mission began a century and a half ago. What relevance or urgency did any of it have now?

History was hardly Beltram's field of expertise, but even he could see that after this length of time, the issue of whether or not the rebels had won was likely moot. A century and a half was time enough for a fragile empire to rise and fall and for the fast-moving world of politics to cycle through dozens of ruling parties and systems of government.

At best, all that lay ahead of Beltram now was a rescue mission, releasing the hundreds, perhaps thousands, of poor souls in the city that his invention had inadvertently imprisoned. Awaking them into a world that had to be massively different to the one they left.

They had saved the city, but at what cost?

The implications were sobering, but they did not slow him down. They merely reframed what he needed to do, as apparently he was the only one with the knowledge and ability to do it. Had science really progressed so little in a hundred and fifty years that what they had achieved here had been viewed as an impenetrable marvel?

But before he set about his task, there was something else, something nagging at him about the plaque describing the bodies in the square.

At no point did it mention General Korlov.

He returned to the map, searching it for any mention of his name. He found only one, referring to a tableau in the council chamber.

He was already in motion.

Access to the chamber was afforded by means of a raised walkway leading through a jagged hole high in the wall. The walkway then branched in two, becoming a circular viewing platform lining the walls of the domed roof. From there, the tourists could look down at the frozen tableau below from any angle.

The room was busy, murmuring voices echoing from the dome above. A knot of school children sat drawing on tablets, carefully comparing their results to the scene below. Beltram joined the constant flow of humanity circling the room and made a full circuit of the walkway, his eyes rarely leaving the scene below, before pausing in front of a brass plaque mounted on the railing. It read:

"Korlov's Triumph"

*Here we see the moment that General Korlov heroically gave his life,
detonating The Bomb Of Tears and revealing his true nature as a rebel
agent. Having spent years doing his best to curb the cruel excesses of the
Jorran Ascendancy from within, he realised the only way to save the city from
destruction was to freeze it forever in time.*

As long as New Haven exists, he will be remembered.

Beltram read the inscription on the brass plaque twice and
then sank down on to one of the benches that lined the wall. He
could still see much of the tableau below from his position. He
tried to empty his mind of what he knew about Korlov and his
crimes, tried to see the image anew.

He failed.

He had too much history with the man. But he could see why
the false narrative suggested by the tableau had power, why it had
taken hold. A dusty bedraggled group of priests and councillors
all struggling to reach the dynamic thrusting figure of General
Korlov, who stood laughing in their faces, pistol in one hand,
bomb trigger in the other. Above his head, a fluttering hologram
of the rebel flag.

Of course he was the hero of the story. The lone rebel
standing strong against a corrupt regime.

Beltram felt like weeping.

The hologram of the flag had not been his idea, but he didn't
resist its inclusion. It was a trivial grace note to the plan, a final
defiant gesture of no real consequence. Now it was the bedrock
of a fiction whitewashing the legacy of a monster.

The idea that Korlov had been an unwilling participant
rather than the architect of his own brutal policies was such a
breathtaking lie, but Beltram could understand why it had
endured. The Ascendancy had been notoriously secretive and
most, if not all, of the people who could testify as to Korlov's true
character were currently frozen in the palace.

And Beltram and his team were going to defrost them all.

He wondered if people would welcome the truth. How many people actually cared, after all this time. Would the correction be anything more than a historical curiosity?

Beltram imagined the route from this chamber back to his workshops. It suddenly seemed a very long way. He had a growing feeling of drowsiness and soon discovered why. The white flag pressed against the wound in his ribs was soaked red with his blood. The grass or weed or whatever the hell it had been had obviously penetrated a lot deeper than he supposed. His black suit jacket hid the truth for now, but he plainly needed medical help, and soon.

He noticed a member of staff watching him, a portly man in his sixties overseeing the walkway, hands clasped behind his back. At first, Beltram was convinced that the man had noticed his condition, but he approached Beltram with a kindly smile.

"First time?" asked the attendant.

Beltram should have shown him the blood, the flag, the wound, asked for help. But he did none of these things. Instead, he nodded minutely.

"It can sometimes be a little overwhelming," said the attendant, then considered, as though choosing his words.

Beltram had the feeling the attendant was about to say something he considered wise. Beltram just wanted him to leave, but instead he sat beside him on the bench.

"Do you know he's become a verb?" said the attendant.

Beltram had no idea what he was talking about.

"To 'korlov'. It means 'to secretly undermine something from within'."

Beltram just stared at him, but the attendant wasn't done.

"I'm old enough to remember The Goodmen. They used to terrify me as a child. Thought they'd Disappear me in the night. But just like all the liars and fascists that came before them, they were brought down by the people."

The attendant nodded sagely. They watched the crowds shuffle by for a moment.

"I think," continued the attendant, "and I'm not alone, that it was because of this place. Because of the example it sets. A lesson, frozen forever, that everyone can visit and see with their own eyes. That the little man can make a difference. Working quietly, diligently, from within."

The attendant gestured towards Korlov to bring his point home, then pulled himself to his feet, nodded goodbye to Beltram and sauntered out of the gallery.

Beltram stared at the tableau for a long moment.

General Korlov as inspiration to the oppressed. Inciter of rebellion, for evermore.

Beltram found himself smiling.

Korlov would have fucking hated that.

And maybe that was enough.

For a moment, he had a glimpse of the totality of it. The boiling churn of history, ideas rising from the darkness to be championed for a spell, then falling from favour, only to rise again centuries later wearing a new face and a new name. An endless cycle with a rhythm like a glacially slow heartbeat.

The insight washed over him then passed in an instant, leaving him breathless and dizzy.

He decided it was just blood loss. That was all.

It was time to get up and make the journey to his workshops.

And he would do. Any minute now.

They found Doctor Beltram's body an hour later, still slumped on the bench, eyes locked on the tableau below.

His wounds, when examined by the medics on site, were familiar enough. Time-frozen grass caused seventy per cent of the wounds they treated. Still, deaths from it were relatively rare. Beltram was dismissed as just another reckless tourist claimed by The City of Statues.

He had no ID on his person and no one claimed his body, so a month later - as was customary in those cases - he was cremated in Crosswind, the nearest real-time town. He was listed in their records as John Doe 432.

The knapsack and field neutraliser were erroneously deposited at the palace cloakroom lost and found. As per their policy, six months later they were donated to a charity, where the neutraliser was logged as "machinery?" before ultimately being broken down and sold for its scrap-metal value.

Jake, the boy who secretly dreamed of one day working at the palace, eventually got his wish and was employed there until he was sixty-three years of age. He retired early, blaming himself for failing to notice the injuries of a tourist who later died.

He spent the rest of his days tending his family's pitch.

Leaving
Tumblethorn

THERE were three men in the alley.

I judged that I could probably have taken them in a fight, but the person I was pretending to be couldn't.

Which meant I might have to take a beating.

They were big, dressed in battered, mismatched armour panels, their faces deeply tanned and scarred - all features common to settlers on this planet, but their boots were caked with fresh mud. Which meant they'd been outside the settlement. No one went outside unless they had to, and workers with official business outside wore better armour than theirs.

Which meant they were probably smugglers.

That may well have been their main source of income, but they seemed keen to supplement it with a little light robbery, looming as they were over a woman half their size. It was plainly a mugging in progress, or worse. I couldn't see the woman's face from this angle, but her body language told me the whole story.

I mentally flipped through a dozen potential personas and hopeful outcomes, before settling on a plucky white knight with dated ideas of chivalry, out of his depth but unable to leave a woman in peril.

"Is there a problem here?" I asked from the mouth of the alley, and their attention turned to me.

Their leader looked like a wrestler. Six-five if he was an inch, a barrel of a chest and a tangle of black curly hair framing a

241

truly memorable face. I had never seen eyes so deeply set, beneath a brooding, heavy brow. This would have lent him a naturally menacing air, even had his nose been complete. The tip had been replaced with a plug of scar tissue, perhaps lost in a fight, perhaps from tumblethorn.

His two companions were less distinctive, though no less haggard-looking. Both had shaved heads, accentuating their various scars. They also had tattoos on their scalps, reduced to faded blue smears from this distance. No visible weapons, which was something.

"Best walk on, pally," said the big guy. "None of your concern."

"What if I made it my concern?" I said.

I made my voice tremble a little. Didn't want to oversell it. The big guy smiled and gestured between himself and his companions, as if to say, *you have noticed there's three of us?*

"Let the woman go," I said.

The big guy sagged and sighed at this dreadful inconvenience. He gestured for me to come closer, impatiently, as though he had something important to tell me.

I didn't move. They were in the alley, I wasn't. I had no intention of changing that situation. They'd have to come to me, which would bring them on to a main thoroughfare and within the eyeline of the local bar and any potential cameras. I hoped that might be enough to give them pause.

It didn't. They began to lope towards me, mock casual, sizing me up.

The woman didn't move. The alley was a dead end. She'd have to get past them to escape, which meant she was trapped until this was resolved, one way or the other.

She looked totally blank, in shock.

They surrounded me in a rough triangle. Their bodies were covered in bone armour, which meant any blows below the neck would be futile. I kept my eyes on the big guy and, as expected, the first punch came from tattooed thug number one, who was just on the edge of my eyeline.

I could have dodged the blow easily, but I forced myself to

accept it. It wasn't a bad punch, as it goes, snapping my head to one side and setting my left ear ringing. I allowed its momentum to knock me sprawling towards tattooed thug two. Apparently by accident, I jabbed my thumb deep into his eye as I grappled with him. He yelped, pushed me away and I allowed myself to fall headlong on my belly back toward, tattooed thug one. My shoulder hit his calves at speed and he went down.

We were both on the floor, scrabbling to get up, him punching me as I tried feebly to protect myself. Another accidental disabling would have been a little much, so I rode out his blows as well as I could, looking for an opening.

He rolled away and got to his feet, as I sensed the big guy moving in. His first kick grazed my ribs, his second took the wind out of me, but I had been braced for it. I planned to grab his leg the next time it passed my way, but it never came. I was aware of shouts from the direction of the bar, running feet. I pulled myself upright in time to watch the smugglers making a hasty getaway, darting into the maze of pre-fab narrows.

A settlement marshall, trailing a few looky-loos from the bar, was doing a half-run towards us. It was the run of a man who would rather avoid the paperwork that catching the smugglers would bring. He passed us with a minimal nod, hand on his holstered pistol.

The woman was leaning against the wall, watching me. She looked wary rather than thankful. I limped over to her and held out a hand.

"Are you okay?" I asked.

She considered, then accepted my hand and nodded.

"Are you?" she replied.

I snorted a feeble laugh, then feigned dizziness, gripping her hand tighter for support as I slid down the wall beside her.

"I don't usually do this sort of thing," I said, eyes closed and hyperventilating. I was still holding her hand.

"You couldn't tell."

She was teasing me, but squeezed my hand in what I took to be a gesture of thanks.

I was taking long, slow breaths, out through my mouth and in through my nose. I was hoping it would read that I was going into shock, or a panic attack. Anything to keep her there, keep her holding my hand.

She patted my head, asked if she should call a doctor. I shook my head.

"I'm sure it'll pass," I said.

The interface in my pocket vibrated minutely, indicating that the tiny scanner built into my finger ring had done its work. It had successfully cloned the ID chip implanted beneath the skin of her wrist.

"I think I'm feeling a little better now," I said, and let go of her hand.

The woman's name was Vienna Holden and she was coms tech on a freighter currently berthed less than five miles away. In just under eight hours, the freighter would be leaving the planet, having just been filled with cargo for export. The security around the spaceport was imposing, but the ID chip that I had just copied would hopefully circumvent much of it.

I fully intended to be on board that freighter when it left.

The type of ship was irrelevant, as was the destination. I just needed to get off planet. The reasons for this desire were varied, but can be summed up in five words:

I fucking hated the place.

The alley in which I disrupted the mugging was underground, as was much of the settlement. This was partly due to the incessant gale-force winds on the planet's surface. The settlement had been named Chicago, after the windy city on Earth, which was the closest the locals ever got to humour.

You may begin to see why I couldn't wait to leave.

How I ended up stuck there is a whole other story. My name, my *real* name, which I rarely go by, is Callum Brandish. Other names come and go, adopted and discarded when necessary. Broadly speaking, I guess you'd call me a confidence trickster. I make a living by persuading the gullible and easily led to give me their money. Or at least I did, until I picked on the wrong group of people.

I read them as high rollers blowing thousands at a casino - they were actually gangsters casing the place. They caught me and I was braced for a bullet to the head when I realised they were arguing. A couple of them had a grudging respect for the scam I'd pulled, but the consensus was that I still needed punishing. They knocked me out and I came to on the supply shuttle to this world.

At times over the next year, I wondered if the bullet might have been kinder.

To understand why I am so keen to leave this godforsaken armpit of a world, it might be an idea to start with the story behind the planet's name. Not its original name, which I believe is some dry string of letters and numbers, but the name that the settlers began to call it fairly soon after arriving. They called it Tumblethorn, after a particular carnivorous plant that dominates the planet's surface.

It begins as a bush, a spherical tangle of vines, bristling with serrated thorns about a foot long. Brushing past one without care will cut through most clothing and the flesh beneath, no problem. At which point, any blood on the thorns is absorbed into the plant for sustenance.

Immediate nightmare fuel, am I right?

For obvious reasons, any area where they grow is to be avoided. And they grow absolutely everywhere, which would be bad enough, but that's not even the worst part. Because when tumblethorns reach maturity, the roots beneath them wither and die and the plants become mobile. Or, to put it more accurately, the buffeting winds that seem to scour the planet at all times rip them free and turn them into deadly footballs, rolling in their thousands across the plains.

They basically turn into killer tumbleweeds.

This is no exaggeration. If you're not wearing full armour at all times when outdoors, you take your life in your hands. Everyone who lives here has tumblethorn stories and scars. Can name someone who died because they went outside dressed poorly. Old timers dine out on their scars and stories of the early days.

It's fair to say that the plants have affected every aspect of colony life, even the architecture. Early settlers learned the hard way - if you can bury your house or build it on stilts, do it. If you can't, make your buildings low with ramps for walls. Better to have tumblethorns pass over your roof and leave town than risk them piling up outside your door or clogging the streets. Even then, every ground-level wall and roof is riddled with pockmarks and bristling with broken thorns, ripped free from passing plants.

Most of the modern settlements here are built underground. The rattling sound of the tumblethorns passing, as their thorns clack and scrape against the roofs and walls, is the soundtrack to life in the colony. The noise keeps off-world visitors awake, but locals barely notice it anymore. Some people are proud of that fact, claim that they can't sleep without a recording of the plants passing. Personally, I just saw it as one more item on my long list of reasons why I had to get the hell out of there.

More awfulness is to be found in the other life on display. Most of it has plainly evolved to avoid the tumblethorns. The creatures that could evolve to burrow underground or climb up trees, did so. Anything that decided to tough it out on ground level had to come up with some impressive strategies or very thick armour plating. Often both.

Which brings us to the wedgehorns.

Imagine a bison. Now cover that bison in a thick horn-like carapace of bone plate, like a tortoise. The finishing touch is a wide tail - I'm talking three feet wide, similarly armoured - that ends in a flat edge and is commonly pressed to the ground. This creates the wedge that gives them their name and forms part of the strategy they have evolved for coping with the tumblethorns. In the wild, the beasts sense the direction of the wind and rotate to allow any approaching hell-weeds to roll up their tail, along their back and away.

Not that I've ever seen a wedgehorn in the wild. Any spotted roaming loose are immediately corralled and brought in to the nearest settlement, either for breeding or slaughter. Pretty much every element of the wedgehorn's carcass is in demand and forms the basis for the economy of the entire planet. The best armour for resisting tumblethorns can be fashioned from its carapace, the remaining hide provides excellent leather, and its tender, oddly spicy meat is considered a delicacy on all other worlds.

Wedgehorn meat is a relatively cheap dish on Tumblethorn. You'd pay fifty times the price anywhere else in the galaxy. The first week I was here, I ate nothing else, devouring it with gusto. It was only when I tried to vary my diet that I realised there *was* nothing else. No other palatable meat on the planet. Now, a year later, I can't even smell it cooking without feeling nauseous.

The mass breeding and butchery of wedgehorns is the primary industry on Tumblethorn. Every settlement is centred around the battery farms and slaughterhouses, with ancillary services catering primarily to the workers there. Housing, bars and transport hubs are all measured in terms of proximity to the nearest wedgehorn processing facility. It's where everyone is going, sooner or later.

When I was dumped here, I had enough cash hidden in the heel of my boot to keep me alive for a month, but nowhere near enough for a ticket off-world. All of the bank accounts I could remotely access, under various aliases, were in the red. In addition, I couldn't think of a single contact, a single person who would be willing to come to my aid. I could, however, think of plenty of people who would happily drop everything to come and kill me, or cheer and eat popcorn while someone else killed me, but no one who liked or trusted me enough to help me out.

At thirty-two years of age, that was quite a depressing realisation.

Lacking any other option, I needed to get a job. The only vacancies going were - surprise surprise - up at the nearest slaughterhouse. Even then, the wages were pitiful. Working there full-time, I calculated that I'd be able to afford a ticket home by the time I was eighty. Assuming I didn't eat and slept outside.

I took a job there anyway, as my money was fast running out. They started me off working the bolt gun, which uses compressed air to drive a steel bolt into the brain of the wedgehorns, killing them instantly. The bolt gun has a metal spreader, like calipers, attached to the barrel, to pull back a section of bone plate, exposing the hide beneath, otherwise the bolt would have no chance.

Working the bolt gun is a rite of passage for the new guys. It's not the most physically demanding job in the slaughterhouse, but killing hundreds of animals a day sure takes a mental toll. A good night's sleep soon becomes a distant memory. I can still hear their rumbling bellows of panic, see their swivelling eyes, smell their musk as they strain against the steel bars that hold them in place.

I lasted just shy of a week on the bolt gun before calling in sick, but the regulars considered that enough to prove my mettle. I was then put on rotation, learning the other duties in the factory. The butchery was beyond me initially, but six months in I was gutting, skinning and filleting like a pro.

The money from my job there bought me a room at a nearby hostel, barely more than a bunk and a shared shower. Felt a little like a prison, with scratched graffiti from previous occupants on the wall beside me - *"Billy is a wedgehorn fucker"* was a particular favourite. At weekends, my co-workers would be spending what little spare money they had at The Horn O'Plenty, our local bar. I sometimes joined them, but I had plans for my extra funds.

The name of the freighter I intended to escape on was *Join The Family 763*, being the seven hundred and sixty third ship of that name. "Join The Family" had been the slogan of the Waking Dream Corporation for the past seventy-three years. It appeared on everything from drinks coasters to flamethrowers. And, indeed, freighters, named with an unwavering adherence to corporate dogma.

The freighter itself was an old dirty workhorse. It had originally been painted in the corporate livery of powder blue and sunflower yellow, but that was clearly years ago. Its story since had been spelt out in the scorched metal of atmospheric burn, the grime of retro exhaust and the dents and patched holes of micro asteroid impacts.

It was far from the longest ship Waking Dream owned, but it cast a long shadow over the spaceport. It was perhaps three hundred metres from prow to stern. Fifteen decks, seven cargo bays of varying sizes and a crew of eight in living quarters based in the top three decks.

It reminded me of a dry-docked ocean liner. Something about the shape, the towering bulk of it. It spent ninety-nine per cent of its life in a vacuum, but they'd still made an attempt at aerodynamic lines. Not all modern ships did, but in the era when it was built, sweeping curves had been all the rage, with spiked clusters of sensor barbs and communications arrays doing their best to spoil the aesthetic here and there.

It was currently berthed on the largest landing platform Tumblethorn offered, which said a lot about the planet. The platform was composed of thick steel plate, in turn supported by a lattice of girders and pylons, elevating it a good fifty feet above the ground, and any rolling hazards. They'd also raised a curtain of seventy-foot-high metal netting around the ship. I personally had never seen tumblethorns propelled that high, but I'd heard stories. They were taking no chances.

The ship was currently being loaded with a literal fortune in wedgehorn meat and hide, which would be later sold for astronomic sums on other worlds - a fact not reflected in the wages of the staff loading it. Nor, indeed, the wages of anyone on Tumblethorn. The Waking Dream Corporation, who had staked their claim to this planet decades ago, made sure of that. Anyone who worked there would never save up the means to leave, which was just how the company liked it. A captive workforce.

I had a variety of high-end surveillance tech hidden in my clothing when I arrived on-world, all of which was useless without a receiving tablet. It took me ten months of hoarding my slaughterhouse wages to save up enough for the most rudimentary of computer interfaces. I considered running some con tricks or thievery to speed up the process, but didn't want to risk being caught. Being run out of town on Tumblethorn would effectively have been a death sentence.

Once my interface had arrived and was synced with my gear, my escape plans began to take shape. I could eavesdrop on most coms in Chicago, the settlement I was most interested in, as it bordered the planet's largest and busiest spaceport. My evenings and weekends were now spent probing their security systems for holes, scouring flight plans and personnel lists.

The main stumbling block was obtaining a valid ID chip to get me past the various checkpoints. An ideal chip to clone would be that of a crew member, which would get me all the way on to a ship. The only problem with this idea was that the crews rarely ventured further than the spaceport, which was off-limits without - you guessed it - a valid ID chip.

The crews stayed in the spaceport for a few reasons. There were obviously no tourist attractions or breathtaking views on Tumblethorn. One look through any window at the hellscape beyond would tell them that. In addition, I'd seen CCTV feeds of the palatial bars and living quarters set aside for visiting crews. Venturing any further into town would have been a downgrade on every level.

It was all beginning to feel a little like a dead end, so I switched tack. While it was true that spaceports were the only places on the planet where ships were legally permitted to land, it wasn't the only place they landed. They just did it elsewhere illegally.

Unregistered wedgehorn farms and smuggling rings were a continual problem for the authorities on Tumblethorn. With something as valuable as wedgehorn meat in play, the potential earnings were astronomical. Every few months, we'd hear of some new farm being busted, usually kilometres from any settlement. Smugglers had their own ships, no need to file flight plans or ask permission. They also had no reason to offer me a bunk and every reason to shoot me to keep their secrets.

However, I was reasonably confident that my skillset could prove useful. I had already hacked into the settlement's crime-logging system, which would offer advance warning of any raids. My loose plan was to offer access to this information in exchange for a ticket off-world.

Now I just had to find some smugglers, which meant hanging around a lot of dodgy bars on the edge of town. My evenings were soon filled with neon, distorted sound systems and barely nursed whiskies. I weathered three propositions, two pick-pocketing attempts and a rather well-told sob story from an obvious fellow con-artist before I struck lucky, but not in the way that I'd hoped.

The bar was called The Globe, notionally nostalgia-themed for the home planet, but I'd bet good money on the designer having never been to Earth. The theme translated into a few oddly named cocktails (*Niagara Falls Over* anyone?) and a faded mural of national landmarks; the Eiffel Tower, the Pyramids, Mount Rushmore. All seemingly on the same continent.

The bar was constructed of five or six shipping containers welded together, the default cheap building material on colony worlds. How well this fact was hidden is usually a good indicator of the quality of neighbourhood. It was telling that in The Globe, all the weld seams between containers were clearly visible and you could still read the spray-paint-stencilled consignment numbers over the urinals.

It was a low-lit grimy hole of a place, filled with scowling, grumbling settlers. The night I chose to visit, it seemed surprisingly busy for such a shit-hole, until I realised how close it was to an exit gate. It was the first bar anyone would encounter upon entering the settlement, the first watering hole after kilometres of gales and rolling hell-spikes. One drink would become two and then inertia could well turn the bar into a regular haunt.

Looking around the other patrons, it was a theory that seemed to make sense. Most of them had the battered over-scarred look of years spent outside the larger settlements. Many of them wore patches, uniforms or armour pieces to confirm it. It would also, I hoped, be the first bar any incoming smugglers would visit.

One face stood out in the crowd, a woman of perhaps thirty in an oversized colony overall. I only caught a glimpse of her face as she left, but something about it seemed oddly familiar. It took me a moment to realise that she was a crew member of a freighter currently in port. I was still habitually checking the crew roster of ships as they docked, a practice that owed as much to OCD as anything else. That, and a large dash of not being able to let my earlier plan go.

Quite why coms tech Vienna Holden felt the need to slum it in a bar like that is probably a question for another day. Maybe because she *was* slumming it, way outside the safe cordon of the space port. I could imagine that cocoon of protection might feel a little stifling after a while.

As soon as I realised who she was, I hurried out after her. My plan of connecting with smugglers was immediately jettisoned. My original plan, of cloning a crew member's ID chip, was suddenly feasible. All I had to do was somehow hold my hand close to hers for approximately ten seconds and let the scanner built into my ring work its magic.

I am ashamed to say that when I caught up with her and realised she was about to be mugged, my heart leapt. It would be much easier to hold the hand of someone grateful for rescue. Spotting signs that the muggers were also probably smugglers was a nice irony, but I didn't waver in my change of plan. In the second I had open to me before I was spotted, I refined my approach and persona. I would be the plucky amateur, almost fainting after the fight, hopefully comforted by Vienna's hand.

And thus it transpired. I clumsily thwarted the muggers, with a little timely help from a passing marshal, and the ID chip was duly copied, clearing the way for me to make my excuses and leave - both the alley and, hopefully, the planet. I still had a lot of issues to resolve before the freighter left and time was tight. It made no sense at all to stay with Vienna for one second longer than I had to. No sense at all.

I could blame my following tardiness on a few things. For a start, Vienna wasn't from Tumblethorn. She represented a wider universe that I hadn't tasted for almost a year. That was part of it. Her reaction after the mugging was impressive too. I would have expected anyone to be in shock, or panic, but she seemed to be completely calm and entirely devoted to my well-being. From her perspective, I had tried to help her, shambolic though my efforts had been, and she seemed to recognise that. Now I appeared to need her help and she wasn't about to abandon me.

At any point, I could have shaken off my fake swoon, thanked her and left. Instead, I allowed her to steer us back to the bar. It was a little more empty than when we left. An educated guess would say that the appearance of the marshal had cleared out the more disreputable element.

She led me into an empty booth, ordered herself a light beer and me a glass of imported whisky, the good stuff. She watched me carefully as I knocked it back.

"You're not from here, are you?" she asked.

"The accent?" I asked and she nodded, sipping her beer.

I inwardly cursed but kept my face affable. There was a subtle but distinctive local burr, a rolling of the "Rs" and flattening of the vowels that I'd not bothered to mimic. Rookie error. I mentally revised the character I was playing, gave him a fresh back-story that was already in place even as I opened my mouth.

From her point of view, I hadn't paused at all.

"I'm from all over," I said. "but mainly Hunterhigh."

Which was true, to a point. There was enough Hunterhigh in my normal accent for that to scan. It was an old colony world, with millions of inhabitants. A good place to hide - or to construct a back-story around.

"So how does a Hunterhigh boy end up here?" she asked.

I tried to read her expression. She didn't seem suspicious, or flirtatious. She also didn't really seem that interested in any answer. I decided she felt obligated, keeping me company until I'd got my wind back.

I stole the sob story of one of my co-workers at the slaughterhouse. He'd been told that there was a fortune to be made on Tumblethorn, being the planet where Wedgehorn meat originated. Only when he got here did he realise the stranglehold that Waking Dream had on the world and, consequently, the hourly wage.

I was halfway through painting myself as a gullible loser when I could see something shift in her face. A decision made. I assumed that she was about to thank me and leave. Instead she said:

"So, want to go somewhere and fuck?"

I shouldn't have followed her. I should have said I was still too shaken to even think of sex. It fitted my character and the situation perfectly, would have allowed me a smooth exit.

That's what I should have done.

I read it as her way of saying thank you. For disrupting the mugging. For saving her. Which technically I did.

But that wasn't my real motive for being there that night. And sure, I could tell myself that had I chanced upon the mugging, with no other motive in play, I would still have intervened. A hypothetical I clung to, a fictional testimony to my supposed moral fibre that was unravelling with every step I took.

Vienna paid for a room a few streets over. There were cheaper motels that charged by the hour, blatantly for the use of hookers and their johns. The one she chose was a little classier. You paid for the night, though I'm sure the desk clerk could tell we wouldn't be there that long.

The bed was three times the size of the bunk I'd been sleeping in for the past year. The smell of disinfectant fighting air freshener. Low musak and low lighting. She kissed me hungrily and I responded in kind. She undid my trousers, reached inside with a knowing smile. I decided gratitude and passivity was in character for me. For her part, she seemed happy to lead the way.

At a certain point, she took full control and something changed in her eyes. She was looking through me now. I realised I had been wrong. This was never a thank you. She was on a mission, she was scratching an itch. Perhaps the very reason she'd been slumming it in that neighbourhood in the first place. I was simply a means to get her there.

I might have been insulted had I not been pretending to be

someone else.

In the afterglow, I decided that my character would be smitten and more than a little needy. I would ask her where she was staying, if I could see her again. I imagined that would get me ejected fairly quickly.

I said nothing.

I watched her in the half-light. She was staring at the ceiling, thoughts elsewhere. She'd already moved on from me mentally, the physical surely soon to follow. We could both hear the faint but distinctive sounds of another couple having sex in a neighbouring room. A steady rhythm of moans. I wondered if that couple had heard us earlier. If our sounds had spurred them on, encouraged them.

Vienna turned to look at the man I was pretending to be.

"Can I see you again?" I said.

Five minutes later, I was out on the street.

Two hours after that, I was wearing a totally new persona, that of gum-chewing landing pad technician. My shoulders were slumped, my eyes suitably slow to focus. My new character had been doing this job for fifteen years and was bored to tears. My wedgehorn armour had all the accurate flashing and hazard stripes of my role, painstakingly copied from freeze frames of hacked CCTV. Strapped to my wrist was a slightly adapted copy of Vienna's ID chip, a magic wand that caused checkpoints to open before me in a rolling wave.

I passed through the echoing empty service corridors of the spaceport. Any guards on duty looked straight through me, barely pausing in their conversations. A clattering elevator took me from just below ground level up inside the strutwork of the landing platform. The wind above the spaceport hit the lift like a fist. It was so long since I'd been outside, I'd almost forgotten the sheer force of it. The whole platform was shuddering and creaking in the gale.

The lift finally reached the platform, I put my helmet on and stepped out into the buffeting air. The freighter loomed above me like a curved cliff, suspended on ten immense hydraulic feet, each the size of a bus. Dozens of similarly dressed landing pad techs were busy working beneath the ship, uncoupling anacondas of cable and pipes that had apparently finished replenishing the freighter's supplies. I ignored them all, sticking to the walkway on the edge of the platform. I tried to keep my step slow and steady, staying in character. My helmet hid my identity, but a hurried walk could still give me away.

None of the workers so much as looked my way.

A hundred feet on and the number of technicians had thinned considerably. I waited for a moment when their attention was elsewhere, then abruptly turned from the walkway and darted in under the body of the ship. I took shelter from the wind behind one of the freighter's feet, an imposing lattice of metal and rubber taller than me. I held my wrist up to a grease-smeared ID panel. It chimed and a metal hatchway clicked open. Within, a hollow containing a narrow service ladder bathed in red emergency lighting, leading up inside the hollow strut of the foot.

I clambered inside the hatch, closed it behind me and began to climb the ladder. Thirty feet in, I reached another sealed hatch and another scanning panel. It too beeped obediently and the hatch slid back with a hiss, revealing that it was at least two-feet thick. The outer skin of the ship. My ears popped from a slight change in air pressure. The schematics I had studied listed the room beyond as "Support Platform Maintenance Access". It was poorly lit, grimy and cold, but at that moment I couldn't have cared less.

I was in.

Stowing away on a modern system-hopping freighter isn't easy.

Ideally, you want the crew to arrive at their destination totally unaware you were ever aboard. Everything you do, every decision you make, is ultimately in pursuit of that aim.

Flight length is, of course, a factor. The longer you are on board pilfering food, water and air, the more chance there is of you being discovered. According to the logs, my new ship's destination was Silver's Folly, a well-connected world. But the ship wasn't going to be touching down there for another two months.

It was going to be quite the logistical challenge.

Should I be discovered, one of two things could happen. The crew could take pity on my plight and simply arrest me and throw me in the brig, in which case I'd still reach Silver's Folly, only in handcuffs and facing jail. Or the crew could just throw me out of an airlock and pretend I was never there.

A stowaway does not look good on a crew's record.

Having a copy of Vienna's ID chip gave me a big advantage going in, but it wouldn't last long. If she tried to board the ship with my fake ID active, alarms would sound. That was a problem that needed solving straight out of the gate.

The moment I boarded, my interface tablet began talking to the freighter through the chip. It happily informed me that I was currently the only crew member on board. I needed to take advantage of that fact while I could.

I emerged into a gun-metal grey service corridor, utilitarian and lined with pipework. I'd loaded a copy of the ship's blueprints on to my tablet. They told me that this corridor ran the length of the ship and would usually only be accessed for repairs. I hurried along it, bulkhead doors opening as I approached and closing behind me. I could have taken an elevator straight to the flight deck, but was paranoid the elevator's deck change might later be noticed. Instead, I climbed up fourteen decks worth of service ladder and popped open a wall hatch in the living quarters.

The difference in décor was startling. Lots of soft recessed lighting, rounded corners and carpeting. Bare walls had been given over to holographic murals, usually rotating slideshows of paradisal vistas. Soothing scents pumped through the air con. I hurried past doors marked GYM and CANTEEN and the elevator I'd been afraid to use before entering the flight deck.

It was circular, the focal hub being a central pillar of interfaces and holo projectors surrounded by eight suspension couches, all with their own interface stalk and array. Vienna already had pretty high clearance, but I needed more. I used her chip to handshake me in, connected my tablet to the nearest array, and activated my suite of cracking software.

Twenty minutes later, I had deactivated my copied Vienna chip and created a new one for myself that would give me free rein of the ship, but not appear on any system. I had also installed a backdoor patch.

The process was thirty seconds from being completed when my tablet happily informed me that three other crew members had just come aboard.

The main crew airlock to the freighter, which was their logical entrance, led directly to the elevator I'd avoided, which would deposit them in the corridor right outside the flight deck. If that was the case, they were mere seconds away from this room. If I unplugged my tablet and made a run for it, I could probably make it back to my hatch before they arrived.

I did not want to unplug my tablet.

The process it was currently running would enable me to spy on many of the ship's systems from my hiding place. If I unplugged it before the backdoor patch was completed, I would effectively be deaf and blind for the whole journey. The chances of me being caught would become immeasurably higher.

When the lift doors opened, if the three crew members turned left, they would enter the flight deck. Turning right would lead them to their living quarters. I was banking on the idea that their first instinct would be to go to their rooms. They would likely have luggage from their stay on Tumblethorn, changes of clothes. All would need to be returned to their rooms.

I decided to risk staying in the room, based solely on that supposition.

If I was wrong and even one of them took a left, I was screwed. I could have made a good fist of bluffing my way out, but no one from the landing pad crew should have been anywhere inside the ship, let alone on the flight deck. My journey would have been over before it began.

I watched the seconds tick down on my tablet as the patch

took hold. It reached zero, I was rewarded with a tick and a satisfied chime. I unplugged the tablet and pocketed it. I heard the lift doors open in the corridor outside. Chatter. Laughter. I instinctively crouched down behind the nearest suspension couch. It offered little cover, but was better than nothing. A couple of seconds passed. I became convinced that my guess had been correct. The crew had all turned to the right.

Then a crewman walked into the room.

I recognised him as Colton Spivey, the navigator. Young, maybe twenty-five, still had that little cocky bounce in his step. Still thought he was invincible. He had a small suitcase on wheels in one hand and was wearing a Waking Dream branded flight suit. This threw me, as I was expecting some sort of body armour, before I remembered that the crew had a covered walkway leading up from the spaceport straight to the airlock. For most of them, the winds and dangers outside were something they'd only heard about.

"You miss me baby?" he asked the room, arms held wide with a grin.

The room didn't reply. Colton didn't seem to care.

He walked over to the central pillar, punched up a few interfaces and checked a few readings. He was chewing something. He'd left his suitcase in the doorway.

If he simply turned his head to one side, he'd see me.

The seconds ticked by. The other crew members had gone to their rooms, that was plain. But would they just dump their cases and come to the flight deck? Were they merely changing their clothes?

Apparently satisfied, Colton returned to the doorway and left, wheeling his suitcase behind him. I risked peering down the corridor at his receding back as he left. No one visible but him. Now or never.

I walked out into the corridor and called the elevator. The doors opened immediately, the car still on this floor. I got inside and pushed the button marked five. The doors closed and the elevator began to descend.

The freighter had thirty escape pods on board. While this might have seemed overkill for a class of ship that was traditionally crewed by eight people, the design of the freighter was modular. Most of the cargo bays could be refitted with passenger living quarters. The design of the escape pods was less forgiving, built as they were into the hull. It was less hassle to just leave them where they were when the ship was running pure cargo.

All of which was great news for me. If you knew what you were doing, escape pods were a perfect place for a stowaway to hide. You were always guaranteed some quantity of food and water, a basic suspension couch and, if you were lucky, a chemical toilet. Getting in or out of them without setting off alarms was the tricky part, but the system backdoor I had installed would head those issues off at the pass.

There was a bank of pods just off the flight deck and living quarters, which I ruled out for obvious reasons. The logical choice seemed to be a cluster of pods in the belly of the ship, far astern. But there was something about their location that felt a little hemmed in, too much like a dead end.

Ultimately, I picked a row of five pods on the starboard side. They were in a sealed corridor that I hoped none of the crew would have any feasible reason to visit. As an added precaution, I intercepted the feed from the CCTV overlooking the pods and replaced it with a ten-minute loop of an empty corridor. I then did a similar thing to cover my earlier tracks, replacing the footage of my entry to the ship with shots of empty rooms and hallways. It wouldn't pass a forensic analysis, but if we got to that point I was toast anyway.

Until the pods were ejected from the ship, they shared it's air supply. Over two months, an extra set of lungs might cause a big enough dent in the oxygen levels to raise an eyebrow. I'd have to keep an eye on it, fudge the numbers if I had to.

The pods weren't much bigger than the suspension couch they surrounded. Broadly egg-shaped, they still smelled of new plastic and fake leather. The chemical toilet was built right into the seat cushion, survival rations stacked in curved lockers, water from a hanging tube in the ceiling. Once I'd used up the supply of one, I could move to the next in line.

I picked a pod at random, strapped myself into the couch, made sure the shock absorbers were active and allowed myself to finally breathe out.

The freighter *Join The Family 763* left the planet known as Tumblethorn just under five hours later. I leached a feed from an exterior camera, so I could watch that hell-hole get ever smaller in the rear-view mirror.

Now I just had to stay quiet, keep myself to myself, and remain undetected for the next two months.

I managed three weeks.

Over those weeks, I had full access to their media library, which had an impressive collection of old Earth shows and movies. I watched some old favourites, took a punt on a few I'd never heard of, then chanced upon a gem - a 2030s sit-com called *Man Overboard*. It concerned a hapless homeowner called Walter and his continually foiled attempts to sell his beach-front property before rising sea levels claimed it.

It had run for three seasons.

I watched them all, in frank admiration that such a bad taste, one-note premise had been stretched so far.

I would try to spend at least an hour a day exercising in the corridor outside my pod. This wasn't as risky as it sounds. My system back door was keeping tabs on the crew's location at all times and would warn me if they came anywhere near.

Three weeks in, halfway through my morning exercise, my tablet chimed an alarm.

Not to indicate nearby crew, but to tell me that there was a problem with the ship. I'd set up a basic alert for any deviation from course, expected speed or behaviour. For some reason, we were slowing down.

I got back in the pod, fired up my interface and began to investigate.

There was apparently some problem with the engine, though the computer was having a hard time locating it. The cold fusion core appeared to be intact and running at full efficiency, but somehow that power was not translating into propulsion. It was intermittently cutting out, which was a big issue.

We were still a week from the jump point, a locked sphere of thin space in close orbit around and powered by the sun of the Tumblethorn system. We plainly couldn't risk traversing thin space with an intermittent failure of this nature. The crew decided to slow the ship down and park us in orbit around the nearest planet while they ran diagnostics.

We were soon in a high orbit around the system's equivalent of Mercury, a dead burned world that had no name beyond its log number. I viewed its airless cliffs and chasms roll below us through an exterior camera for a while, then returned to the bigger issue.

The crew were running diagnostics. On a computer system I'd been tampering with.

The jig could be up.

I used my backdoor to track the software, as the crew searched for errors. Luckily, the systems they were checking were not anything I'd messed with. I hoped they'd find and solve the problem before looking any deeper.

I leached a feed from the flight deck, listened to their chatter, watched them stroll around. No suspicions so far, it seemed. One of them suggested returning to Tumblethorn if they couldn't locate the problem.

I wondered how long I'd survive on the airless charred rock below us. Because I sure as fuck wasn't returning to Tumblethorn.

Vienna wasn't on the flight deck. I pinged her chip. She was two decks down, her tablet plugged into an engine manifold port. I accessed the camera for that area and saw her for the first time since the night we'd met. She looked intense, absorbed in her work. I found myself staring at her face, remembering how it looked above me in the light of the motel room.

I snapped myself out of it, feeling more than a little like a stalker. I killed the feed to that camera and decided that it was in my best interests to fix the engine problem. Not exactly my area of expertise, but an extra set of eyes couldn't hurt.

Twenty minutes later, no closer to solving the problem, another alert sounded on my tablet. I was about to silence it, assuming it'd be telling me something I already knew, when I realised it was actually a proximity alarm.

Another ship had just docked with us.

My initial impulse was to panic. The ship's appearance within sensor range, any coms exchanged and the instigation of docking procedures should all have caused alerts on my tablet. The fact that I was only informed on its final approach meant that something was very wrong somewhere.

Could my backdoor hack have been discovered and disabled? This would have explained the lack of warning. Perhaps the crew had made a distress call and this was the answer. The new ship was here to help with repairs.

I tentatively attempted to access my system backdoor. It all appeared to be functional.

I rewound the cameras and sensor cloud, viewed the mystery ship emerge from the other side of the planet below us, swiftly moving to match our speed and heading. It was roughly a third of our size, a sleek black knife of a ship with no identifying beacon. It loomed ever closer before handshaking with one of our port airlocks.

It didn't move as though it was here to repair anything.

As soon as the new ship rounded the planet, our freighter should have set off automated queries for identity and intent. Had the answers been found wanting, our rail gun and missile turrets would have automatically fired. Modern space warfare relies on the speed of AI, with battles often all but over before the human pilots are aware they've even begun.

I called up logs from the flight deck. There were no records of any recent identity queries. In fact, there were no records of the new ship at all. As far as the flight deck readouts were concerned, it didn't exist. Camera and monitor feeds showed that the crew were oblivious, still engrossed in their search for the engine issue. Laughing and chatting without a care in the world, their interfaces all green, happy and deceived.

I appeared to be the only one on board who knew the ship existed.

I was aware that these were all educated guesses, but our failing engines suddenly didn't feel like an accident. The mystery ship had presumably activated some field or jamming device, which had glitched the engines just enough to force a stop here. More jamming of our ship's defence and warning systems, which my backdoor had only evaded because it shouldn't have been there.

Everything about the new ship and its behaviour said pirates.

I considered my options. If I did nothing, the pirates would in all likelihood surprise and kill the crew. The sleek knife ship didn't appear large enough to carry the cargo, so they'd have to commandeer this one. They'd no doubt change the freighter's ID beacon, fly it to some market world and sell the wedgehorn cargo at an insane profit.

As for my own well-being, the pirates had just as much chance of finding me as the current crew. Less, in fact. They wouldn't be as familiar with the ship's systems. Were less likely to work out what I'd done.

One very twisted, selfish way of looking at this was that if I did nothing, I would be simply upgrading my crew for one less likely to find me and one random destination for another.

On the other hand, if I stuck my head above the parapet and got involved, the likelihood of my own death, or at the very least imprisonment, increased exponentially. Even if the crew, with my help, managed to repel the boarders - a by no means certain outcome - I doubted that this would endear me to them enough to pat me on the head and look the other way. The smart play was to sit this one out.

I never said I was a smart man.

I routed my call through the flight deck. Made it appear to be from one of her crew members, so Vienna answered without suspicion. She was still near the engine.

"Any luck?" she asked.

"You need to move fast," I said. "A rogue ship has somehow managed to dock on your port side."

I was watching her on the camera feed. She frowned. Knew the voice, but also knew it wasn't one of her crew.

"Who is this?" she asked.

"You met me on Tumblethorn," I said. "In an alley."

She looked confused, then angry. I couldn't blame her. Looking at her wrist, where the chip was implanted. Starting to put together how I got aboard.

"Worry about me later," I said. "You have bigger problems. I am not joking about that ship. I think they're pirates. They've killed the cameras near that airlock."

She began frantically working on her tablet. Frowning. Seeing what I said was true.

"I've locked down every door between them and the flight deck," I said. "It'll slow them down, but you need to move. You have the chance to be a hero here, but keep me out of it. I get found, this does not reflect well on you."

I killed the call, watched her fume in its aftermath, then turned off the camera feed. I'd given her all she needed to save the day. And hopefully provided some insurance for myself. The fact that Vienna had slept with someone who then appeared as a stowaway on her ship was not a good look for her.

It was a shitty card to play, but then again I'm kind of a shitty guy.

I switched to the feed of the flight deck. Waited for the crew to react to her alert. Instead, the camera feeds all died. Not totally unexpected. Vienna was playing it smart. If the pirates could kill cameras, maybe they could use them too. Made sense to pull the plug.

My backdoor was still functioning, but the systems and sensors I could access were steadily winking out as Vienna rolled out a system-wide block. It felt like overkill. Did she really think the pirates had access to everything? Or was this purely aimed at me?

I was soon totally system blind, which felt unnerving. I now had no idea where any of the crew were, if they had engaged with the pirates or were, in fact, hurrying to my pod. The only exceptions were the exterior cameras, which I found I could still access. Perhaps this was just an oversight on Vienna's part, or perhaps she ignored them because they were no use to me at all, unless everyone started taking short cuts across the hull.

I tried to stay calm. I had tipped off the crew, now I just had to let it play out. They had weapons on board, they had to have trained for this kind of thing.

Weapons on a spaceship have historically been a very tricky thing to get right. If you're fighting close to the outer hull, you risk explosive decompression; but even deeper in, so many vital systems could be a mere wall away from any battle. Traditional guns, propelling chunks of metal at speed, are an absolute last resort and are usually banned from any legally approved vessel.

Pirates, of course, would have no such rules, but they'd have many other options to choose from that were a lot less likely to destroy the ship. Given what was currently in vogue, I imagined they'd be carrying either sonic or flechette cannons. Maybe both. Whatever they carried would have built in AI, making everyone a sharpshooter as they locked on to human heat signatures and shapes. And refusing to fire if they could find neither, which avoided the aforementioned "holes in the hull/exploding ship" scenarios.

I'm sure it would be a great comfort to the crew to know that they were being killed by the safest guns ever designed.

I sat in the cocooned darkness and silence of my escape pod, apparently motionless and serene, but my mind was running through dozens of potential scenarios, most of them negative. Occasionally, there would be a slight vibration, an almost imperceptible tremor running through the skin of the ship. Perhaps the echo of an airlock blowing, or an explosive used to breach a door.

Or the beginning of a core meltdown that would doom us all.

I lasted ten minutes before cracking. I couldn't just sit there while my fate was decided in a battle I could well turn. My wedgehorn armour had been hanging in a netting bag in one of the spare escape pods since the day I arrived. I retrieved it and put it back on.

I still had no weapons. In theory, my ID chip would open the nearest armoury locker. They were dotted throughout the ship for just such an eventuality, but I worried it might set off an alert, give away my position. I had an idea where I might find some less secure weaponry, but I would need to traverse quite a bit of the ship. The interior camera feeds were all still down, which would hide me. For the moment.

I left my little escape pod corridor for the first time since I'd arrived. It had been roughly fifteen minutes since I'd warned Vienna.

The bay had the feel of a brewery I'd once visited. Rows of stainless steel vats and angled pipework, here mainly containing distilled water. There were also pallets of dried food, canisters of flour and milk. It housed roughly a third of the food stores on board, ensuring redundancy should one of the three bays become spoiled, or exposed to a vacuum.

There was a wide path, outlined in hazard tape, bisecting the bay. Traversing it using that method would have taken mere seconds, but it felt way too exposed. Which is why I found myself crouched on a narrow metal walkway, hidden in the shadows of the ceiling, fifteen feet above the bay floor.

There was a loose network of such walkways distributed throughout the ship. Ostensibly for maintenance access, they were usually confined within their own narrow ducts, but in some rooms they appeared, as here, suspended from the ceiling on rows of metal struts.

Traversing the ship using only this network had been awkward and slow. For some reason known only to the ship designers, there was never more than four feet of clearance between any walkway and the ceiling. I had to adopt an odd shuffling crouch as I moved along them, head occasionally glancing off a protruding pipe or valve. It was taking me twice as long to get anywhere and by the time I reached the food storage bay, I was feeling slightly foolish. Had I used the normal corridors, I could have been back in my pod by now. I had seen no one, heard no sounds of battle. Whatever had happened was surely long over.

When I reached the food storage bay, I considered climbing down. Surely I could make this last section of my journey walking upright? Stubbornly, I decided that I had come this far crouching and wincing. I would continue in a similar fashion to the bitter end.

It was this decision that ultimately saved my life.

I had almost reached the exit from the bay, which for my walkway was a hatch two feet square. It was mounted into the wall, around six feet above the main door to the bay.

Which abruptly hissed open below me.

I froze in position, peering down. A man wearing a Waking Dream jumpsuit backed into the bay. One hand was clutching a wound in his gut, the other holding a wavering rifle. As he moved further into the bay, I got a clearer look at his face. It was Colton Spivey, the navigator, the bounce in his step apparently ground down by the events of the past half-hour. He was trailing blood as he came, almost collapsing behind a rack of tinned goods. He was breathing heavily, keeping the bobbing barrel of his rifle pointing roughly in the direction of the door he'd just come through.

He didn't thumb his lapel mic. Didn't call for help. Didn't warn the rest of the crew. All of which were not good signs.

The door hissed opened again. A second later, a pirate stepped through.

She was wearing a vacuum suit inset with armour panels. Looked like a stolen combat model, but I couldn't place the corporation. It didn't help that the suit had been resprayed with rebel tags and other obscene graffiti. Her face was hard, her hair shaved to the scalp. A thick white war paint X covered her face from forehead to chin, a rebel fashion at least three years out of date. Maybe no one told her. Maybe she didn't care.

She looked relaxed. Calm. A battered flechette-spitter loose in one hand.

Colton raised his gun and pulled the trigger. An error noise sounded. Again and again. Was it out of juice? I didn't recognise the model, but it had a hell of a battery, which probably meant some form of plasma cutter.

The pirate walked slowly towards him, shaking her head. Milking the moment.

"Come on," she said, "We're all friends here. Even your gun knows that."

It wasn't out of juice. It was reading her as a friendly and refusing to fire. Which meant what? The pirates had run another hack? Were now identified as crew?

Colton kept pulling the trigger, kept getting the error noises. Hoping that reality would somehow reconfigure and let him live. The pirate crouched down before him.

I considered intervening but decided against it. Even if I was victorious in a fight against the pirate, I didn't know how Colton's gun would view me. I could well end up sliced in two the moment I landed.

The pirate reached out and gently pushed the barrel of Colton's gun to one side, raised her flechette pistol and pulled the trigger. The pistol hissed percussively and Colton convulsed, his chest now bristling with black metal flights. His rifle clattered to the floor.

The pirate stood, cricked her neck and tapped a com unit on her shoulder.

"Poll here. Got the last one," she said.

"Any sign of the stowaway?" a tinny speaker replied.

"I'll let you know. Heading portside," she said and killed the connection.

She began to stroll casually back to the door.

The pirates knew about me. Which was a problem, but it wasn't my first thought.

She'd said Colton was the last one. Which meant the rest of the crew were dead.

Which meant Vienna was dead.

I had miscalculated massively.

I had barely known her, had no loyalty to her. If anything, I had wronged her, abused her trust to get into her bed and on to this ship. And now she was dead. She would have no doubt died had I been aboard or not, but perhaps if I hadn't sat on my ass, had joined the fight out of the gate, we could have beaten the pirates. She and the crew would still be alive.

Happy and smiling as they pushed me out of an airlock.

Even so, I felt I owed her something.

Killing her murderers would be a start.

I jumped down on top of the pirate as she passed beneath me. Some noise must have given me away and her reaction times were impressive. She'd almost managed to raise her pistol in the split second before my boots connected with her shoulders, but my full weight impacting at speed caused her to buckle and fall immediately. I heard something snap and she screamed. Shoulder blade? Ankle?

I landed sprawled partially over her, my focus obviously on her pistol. I managed to get both hands around her wrist and wrenched it backwards. She yelped, the pistol came free and I tossed it across the room.

It wouldn't fire pointed at her anyway.

It became a messy close quarters fight. Both armoured as we were, the focus was blows to each other's heads. I clumsily blocked one with my forearm, but let another through that broke my nose. As my head snapped back and blood sprayed, I yelled out in what I hoped sounded like panic.

It was all, of course, theatre. Distraction from what my other hand was doing. I'd noticed from above that some of her armoured panels were not fully secured, simply having been tucked within elastic webbing. I managed to prise one free from her midriff. I now had a thin slab of hardened polymer hidden in my right fist. I attempted a punch with my left and she blocked it, clearing the way for me to ram the armoured panel into her windpipe, crushing it.

Air was immediately cut off. She continued to attempt to land punches but her face was turning red, eyes bulging. She began to claw at her own throat, a futile attempt to clear the blockage.

Within a second or two, her blows were weak enough to be safely ignored.

She was dying, which meant I had to work fast.

I retrieved the tablet from within my armour and set the hacking suite running. My ring had already begun its work the moment she was in range. As soon as her heart stopped, her ID chip would notify everyone else on the network before erasing itself. I needed to copy and disable it before that happened.

I made it with seconds to spare.

My ID chip now showed me as Pollyanna Hadrian, first officer on The Barbed Reply, which turned out to be the name of the mystery knife ship. I removed the com patch from her collar and her holo wrist terminal, which was about ten times more powerful than my tablet. I then dragged her body off the central aisle and shoved it behind a vat of water. Wedged Colton beside her. Someone walking through the bay hopefully wouldn't spot them.

I called up a holo map of the freighter on my new wrist display. By default, it showed all of Polly's pirate "friendlies" as green dots. Six left alive. I didn't look too closely at their locations, I just wanted a headcount and to make sure that they were nowhere nearby. The closest was three floors away.

Even so, it felt unnerving to know that they could now see me as a green dot on their displays, even though they thought I was someone else. I activated a digital ghost of Pollyanna, which I sent walking randomly in the opposite direction I intended to take.

Thus comforted, I set off again, stopping only to pick up Colton's rifle and the flechette pistol. Both currently useless, but maybe I could do something about that. Knowing I was alone on the deck, I allowed myself the luxury of normal doors and corridors. I was also less careful about noise, moving at speed.

Within five minutes, I had reached my destination, one of the larger cargo bays. Pollyanna's chip opened the sliding pressure door and a billow of freezing air washed over me. Motion-activated lights flickered on, revealing towering stacked pallets of boxed wedgehorn meat. Monolithic titans in rows, held firm with thick fabric straps bolted to the deck. Roughly half of the cargo on board. The whole bay was refrigerated, at least -10°c, every surface glinting with a thin sheen of ice crystals. I walked down the central aisle, instinctively covering corners with my useless rifle. Illogical but oddly comforting.

I was searching for a particular crate belonging to a company called Wedgecutters. They had a distinctive logo of crossed axes beneath a stylised wedgehorn tail. By the time I found it, I was shivering. Neither my armour nor the jumpsuit beneath were particularly well-insulated.

It was an old-school wooden crate, nailed shut, logo and serial numbers stencilled on, about a third of the size of the wedgehorn meat stacks and apologetically lashed to the back wall. I used the butt of my rifle to pry open the front of the crate, hoping there would be something, anything inside that I could use.

Wedgehorn meat and armour had a certain cachet in the wider universe. Every now and again, a company would settle on Tumblethorn and attempt to extend that cachet to other products. Bankruptcy and failure were certain to follow. The only exception to this rule, that I was aware of, was the company Wedgecutters, which had, for the past ten years, been selling perfectly ordinary blades of various designs at an eye-watering mark-up, purely because they were forged on Tumblethorn. The inference presumably being that these were the blades that had despatched and butchered the mighty, and mighty expensive, Wedgehorn.

It was true enough, in a way. Most of the tools at my slaughterhouse had been made at the Wedgecutter forges. Sold to us at close to cost, because they had yet to receive their Wedgecutter branding, which would have magically made them twenty times more valuable.

After a few seconds of straining and levering, the front of the crate was sufficiently loose for me to wrench it free. A torrent of packing foam pellets spilled around my ankles. Within, six identical wooden cases, each around five feet long. I pulled one of them out. It was made of dark polished wood, held shut with brass clasps and branded with a gold filigree Wedgecutter logo. It looked tacky as hell. I undid the clasps and hinged it open.

Jackpot.

At a guess, it was a retail display case. Inside, set within black foam indents, were around twenty blades of various shapes and sizes: machetes, cleavers, hatchets, carving, filleting and paring knives. A selection box of sharp edges. I chose a short utility knife and a long chef's knife. Slid both into my belt. I also tucked a paring knife into my boot.

You never know.

There were other shapes protruding from the packing foam. I dug them out. A tethered bundle of wedgehorn hide, which, when unfolded, turned out to be a promotional poncho branded with a Wedgecutter logo so large it was embarrassing.

I put it to one side. I wasn't *that* cold.

Also in the box, an old friend. A chrome-plated bolt gun, complete with a Wedgecutter-branded compressed air cannister. I tried to imagine a slaughterhouse of sufficient luxury to justify it and failed.

Could I use it? Sure. As long as my enemy stayed perfectly still on their knees in front of me.

I left it where it was.

I began to head out of the cargo bay. I now at least had some functioning weapons. True, they were poor at anything less than close quarters. But, on the plus side, they had no inbuilt AI. They couldn't refuse to stab or slice.

I was still badly outnumbered. I needed to thin the herd somehow.

I'm not a bad fighter, but I'm a much better manipulator. Maybe with a little misdirection, I could sow a little division, get them fighting amongst themselves. I had no idea of the group dynamics at play, but I'd encountered plenty of mercenaries and pirates over the years. Nine times out of ten, greed was the glue holding a group together, which meant that paranoia and fear of betrayal would be good buttons to push.

I got out of the cargo bay and hid myself in a ladder access shaft. It had hard seals between decks, but would grant me quick escape routes to other floors.

I blew on my numb fingers and went to work.

Pollyanna's coms unit had ongoing passive recording, an archive of everything she'd said while wearing it. I connected it to my fancy new wrist terminal and ran an illegal deepfake voice app. What would have taken at least a half-hour on my old tablet was done in thirty seconds.

I could now speak using an accurate copy of Pollyanna's voice.

Time to pick my marks.

I'd been checking my map periodically to ensure I was alone. I checked it again. Two of the pirate green dots had stayed on the bridge of The Barbed Reply. One was manning our bridge and the other three were moving together. With a jolt I realised they were on my deck. They didn't appear to be moving towards me. I pulled up more details of their location. It was another refrigerated bay, much the same size as the one I'd just left, and also stacked with wedgehorn meat. At a guess, they were viewing the spoils of war.

Three of them. In one location. With a wide airlock to aid loading.

I shelved Pollyanna's voice for the moment. A new possibility had arisen, but I had to work quickly. There were quite a few safety lockouts to stop someone doing what I was attempting, but a combination of my backdoor and Pollyanna's cloned ID gave me a lot of clout.

Ten seconds later, all the doors leading out of their bay were sealed.

A second after that, I blew the main airlock.

There was a second of garbled panic through the shared coms, then I felt the ship shudder.

I called up an exterior camera view, watched the pressure difference blow tumbling stacks of wedgehorn meat out into space. Millions of dollars worth. Other shapes were caught spinning in the light.

They might have been bodies.

On the map, I watched the three green dots drift steadily away from the ship and then wink out one by one as the vacuum claimed them.

"What the fuck just happened?" said a gruff voice over the coms.

The map told me his name was Houser. He was on the bridge of The Barbed Reply, around ten feet from another green dot - a pirate called Lannier.

Thinking fast, I called Lannier directly.

"Three down, two to go. You think you can handle Houser?" I said in Pollyanna's voice.

I was guessing they'd all have the same coms system, which meant that my words would have sounded from a small speaker on Lannier's collar. Tinny, but definitely audible from ten feet away. I was sure Houser would hear. But would he take the bait?

There was a long beat of silence. I called up the exterior camera with the best view of The Barbed Reply. A dark slice of menace latched on to our hull, silent and still.

"Houser," said Lannier finally. He sounded worried. "I don't know what she's talking - wait! Wait!"

Good old Houser.

I heard the mic blow out. Some sort of weapon discharge. Sounded loud, not spaceship-friendly, whatever it was. On the camera, I saw light flash in one of the windows near the top of the ship. Had to be the bridge. The sounds of a struggle followed, then another blast of weaponry. Another flash of light in the window.

Then the whole port side of The Barbed Reply erupted in fire.

I don't really know what happened. I don't suppose it really matters. I can assume that a bullet pierced something flammable, which led to a chain reaction, but that's all it is - an assumption. An abject lesson in the folly of using projectile weapons on a spaceship.

A series of explosions tore down the port side, which was closest to the freighter. There was a good fifty-metre gap, but the side of our ship was still peppered with shrapnel. I saw the tell-tale gusts of debris indicating multiple breaches in our hull. I initially viewed that as disastrous, but soon saw how things could have been much worse.

The thrust caused by the explosions wrenched The Barbed Reply free of our airlock and sent it spinning away. Had the explosions occurred on their starboard side, the ship would have been pushed into us instead of away, possibly taking us down with them.

I watched the doomed ship tumbling down towards the planet, throwing out debris as it fell, lights flickering and gouting gas as it died.

I had just killed two people and their ship with a well-told lie.

My wrist tablet was chiming and flashing with alerts regarding the hull damage we'd just suffered. Emergency systems had immediately kicked in, sealing bulkheads and venting areas at risk of fire, but no major systems seemed to have been impacted. We could still fly and weren't about to explode. I silenced the alerts and took a breath.

A few minutes ago, I'd been facing six enemies. Through a combination of social engineering, technological prowess and blind luck, I'd managed to wipe almost all of them out. I can't deny I was feeling pretty pleased with myself.

I really should have been paying more attention.

According to my tablet, only one pirate remained alive. Their green dot showed that they were still on the freighter's flight deck. The ID tag was a blank placeholder. I didn't know what to make of that. They'd also not spoken an entire word since the chaos began. That should have been a big clue. Opening a com line might have given away background noise. Sounds of exertion. Echoes that didn't fit the flight deck.

I didn't know it, but I was watching a digital ghost.

That's always the problem with conjuring computer illusions, faking data. It's easy to forget that you are just as susceptible to those illusions. When you start relying on readouts rather than the evidence of your eyes and ears.

It was my ears that saved me, oddly enough. They picked up the merest whisper of a hatch sliding open on the floor above me. Which should have been impossible. I was alone in this area of the ship.

Wasn't I?

My movements were instinctive. I didn't allow myself time to reason it out, opening the door beside me and throwing myself through it, even as the hatch above the ladder slid open and the plasma beam lanced down. I felt a searing pain in my left leg and collapsed into a roll, trying desperately to move out of the eyeline of the hatch.

I got to my feet, almost screaming with the pain, opened the nearest doorway and limped through. It slid shut behind me. I was back in the frozen cargo bay. I could smell my own burning flesh, see my own panicked breath clouding the air. Was there another way out? The holo map was still open, floating above my wrist as I limped further in. There were other doors, but they all opened on to that corridor and certain death.

I'd not heard the door open again. My pursuer had not followed. Yet.

But they didn't have to. They could just seal me in and blow the airlock, do exactly what I'd done to their fellow pirates.

Would they, though?

I'd already cost them dearly. Half of the potential profit of this heist, by my reckoning. Most of the rest of it was in this room. If they blew the airlock, they'd get nothing. I had to count on their greed to keep me alive.

Which meant that, sooner or later, they were coming in after me.

The plasma beam had cut through the wedgehorn armour on my thigh and carved a deep furrow in the muscle beneath. The wound had partly sealed from the heat of the beam but I could feel warm blood pooling in my boot. My face and hands felt numb with the cold.

This was not looking good.

My map died, along with the tablet. Blocked and useless. I wondered how long they'd been feeding me lies. I began to toss anything that could be used to track me. My old tablet, new holo display, com patch, even my hacking ring. Couldn't trust any of it now.

I wasn't really paying attention to my route, just trying to quickly get away from the doors. I found myself back at the Wedgecutter knife crate. Could something from here help me? Perhaps the extra knives? Could I set some sort of trap? I knew it was desperation, but I had a half-formed idea. I gathered up what I needed and walked on.

Thirty seconds later, I tripped over the bodies.

They were both coated in a thin layer of frost, partly hidden in the deep shadow of a monolithic stack of meat. They must have been here the last time. If I'd chosen a different aisle, taken a left rather than a right, I would have seen them.

One I recognised immediately as Sol Hollander, captain of the freighter. His chest was peppered with flechette barbs, a dark frozen puddle of blood beneath him. Lying beside him was a dead pirate, a presumption I made because of his graffiti-tagged vacuum suit, a la Pollyanna. His head was shaven and tattooed, his neck twisted at an impossible angle, turning his face away from me. Their positions and causes of death didn't immediately suggest a narrative. Perhaps others were involved. It hardly mattered now.

I moved past them, glancing at the pirate's face as I did. Then I stopped dead, turned. Stared.

I knew his face. And the implications of who he was changed everything.

Five minutes later, I heard a door leading into the bay finally slide open.

I was sitting with my back to the main airlock, a vast metal door between the bay and open space. I was now wearing the

Wedgecutter poncho, which made me look like a little tent with a head, but it wasn't enough to keep out the cold. I was still bleeding and I could feel my core temperature dropping rapidly.

They didn't hurry to me. I'm sure they had the cameras back on by now. Knew exactly where I was. I heard their slow, steady footsteps as they walked down the central aisle. I was sure my reasoning as to their identity was sound, but it was still a shock when they rounded the stacks and stood staring at me.

Vienna.

Alive and well, holding a plasma rifle loose in one hand.

"You fucking piece of shit," she finally said.

The first domino to fall had been the frozen pirate. A distinctive scalp tattoo and a face I'd last seen in the alley the night I rescued Vienna. One of her would-be muggers, whose presence here and now made me replay that whole night, questioning every assumption I had made.

They'd not been mugging Vienna. They'd been meeting with her, planning the raid on her ship. That's why she left the safety of the spaceport. She wasn't slumming it on the bad side of town for kicks, she was there to meet her contacts.

The mystery engine failure? Vienna's sabotage, surely. It would also be easy for her to ensure that The Barbed Retort approaching and docking wouldn't trigger any alerts.

And then I came along and screwed it all up.

I thought I was saving her life by warning her about the pirates, when in reality all I'd done is paint a big fat target on my back. She'd moved to the flight deck and stayed there, being the most familiar with the ship's systems, trying to root me out, as I - more by luck than judgement - managed to wipe out every single one of her allies.

I thought back to the night of her "mugging". No wonder she was calm in the aftermath. She'd been in no danger at all.

She'd been playing a role, just as much as I had been.

"Do you know, it strikes me," I finally said, " that this is the first time we've actually met."

Vienna did not look in any mood to discuss the fragile nature of identity, but her plasma rifle was still pointing at the ground. For the moment.

"Do you know how much you've cost me?" she said.

"That's not the way to look at this, surely," I said. "With every pirate I killed, your share went up. Fifty per cent of everything in this bay is still a lot of money."

Vienna managed a hollow laugh.

"Oh, you want to *split* it?" she said. "Is that what you're saying?"

"Seems fair," I said. "It was a lot of work. Be easier to fly the ship with two of us."

"Do you really think you can talk your way out of this?" she said.

"I've just killed six people. And a ship," I said. "But I'm feeling generous. I'll let you live."

Despite herself, Vienna seemed to be enjoying my performance.

"You'll let me live?"

"Call it loyalty to the person I thought you were. I'm guessing you didn't have particular allegiance to the pirates. Unless you're telling me they were all your brothers or something."

She shook her head, looked as though she was considering my offer, but I could tell it was an act. A feint before an attack.

"Do you want to know something funny?" I said. "The only reason I went after the pirates is because I thought you were dead. I thought I was avenging you."

"That is funny," said Vienna.

She raised the rifle and pulled the trigger.

I knew she'd have wiped all my ID clearances. The gun would no longer view me as a friendly. I found out later that she'd also set up a damping field. Wanted to be sure that the only piece of technology working in the whole bay was the rifle in her hands. It was a smart move. She knew I'd got hold of guns, thought I might have been able to hack them into working.

I hadn't. I was thinking in totally different directions.

The plasma rifle she was using was not brought on board by the pirates. It was ship's issue, which meant that its spacial awareness of the freighter's hulls, bulkheads and airlocks was always in play. Sitting with my back to a main airlock would hopefully make the AI very cautious about firing. I was also hoping that the poncho would present enough of a non-human silhouette to add more caution. Lastly, my facial temperature was so low, I could no longer feel my nose or lips.

If she'd adjusted its thermal settings to target a man dying of hypothermia, I'd have been screwed.

As it was, the rifle chirped an error noise and did nothing. Vienna looked stunned. Pulled the trigger again. More error noises. She tilted the gun to view its interface panel, which meant the barrel was no longer pointed at me.

I raised the Wedgecutter bolt gun from beneath the poncho and pulled the trigger.

In its usual operation, the metal bolt immediately retracts after firing. There are quite a few safety brackets and pins in place to stop the bolt from flying from the end of the gun.

I'd removed all of them.

The metal bolt, roughly six inches long and two in diameter, was pneumatically propelled from the end of the gun at seventy-five metres per second. Had it hit Vienna in the face or chest, it could well have killed her. As it was, she took the bolt in her left forearm. I heard a bone break and she was knocked from her feet as if hit by a bowling ball.

She was still holding her rifle.

I sprang to my feet, or at least tried to. I was favouring my right leg, but the cold and my wound was making me sluggish. Crossing the floor felt like an eternity.

Vienna was stunned, gasping, lying on her back, clutching her broken left arm to her chest but still trying to bring the rifle to bear on me with her right. It could still fire. Now standing, my silhouette was clearer, the body beneath the poncho surely a few degrees warmer than my face.

I lunged for the rifle, falling across her. She screamed hoarsely. My full weight had landed on her broken arm, the rifle now pressed between us.

I reached for the knives on my belt.

The flight deck was full of corpses. It looked like most of the crew had died there. A couple had been shot in the back.

I wondered how many Vienna had killed personally.

The ship's med bay was well equipped. I pumped myself full of painkillers, boosted my red blood cell count and sprayed my leg wound with a sealant cast. I should have rested it. Instead, I spent a good hour using the elevators and a hydraulic loading trolley to ferry the bodies of the crew to a refrigerated bay. It was exhausting work.

The bodies of the pirates I threw out of an airlock.

The hull damage to the freighter looked worse than it was. Auto-patching units had been busy and sealed the worst of it. The rest could wait until drydock.

I did a tally of the surviving cargo. Selling it on the black market would take a hefty chunk of profit, but I would still make a small fortune. I could retire, if I wanted to.

If I wanted to.

Once I'd managed to circumvent the various computer lockouts Vienna had put in place, I purged the entire network and booted from scratch. It meant another six hours sitting in orbit, but I didn't want any surprises. By the time I left the system, I was reasonably certain I was the only living thing on the ship. And that the core wasn't about to blow without at least warning me.

I set a course for a market world and turned on the autopilot. I then moved into the captain's cabin and slept for twenty-four hours.

I'm not totally sure why I didn't kill Vienna. I was fully prepared to when it was a question of survival, but as soon as that survival seemed assured, the desire left me.

I had a knife in my hand, I had just sliced through the power cables linking the battery to the body of her rifle, rendering it useless. It would have been a moments work to slit her jugular, pierce her heart. I did neither, throwing my knives away, clinking into the shadows, out of her reach as well as mine. I saw confusion in her eyes.

It was possibly in my eyes too.

I pulled back a little, moved my weight off her. Winced as I got up on my knees, holding up both hands in a gesture of good faith. I gently reached out, pulled the now-useless rifle from her and she didn't resist, assuming I was going to throw it aside. Instead, I brought it back and smacked her in the face with the steel butt.

She came to in an escape pod, already accelerating away from the ship. With just enough food and water to make it back to Tumblethorn.

I realise that my actions weren't really logical on any level. She'd tried to kill me more than once and struck me as the sort that would definitely hold a grudge. In keeping her alive, I was simply creating a headache for myself further down the line. Once she'd recovered, she'd come after me. Of that I had no doubt.

I threw some roadblocks in her way. Once she got to Tumblethorn, she could have spun any story she liked about the pirates and me. She could have been on the next supply shuttle out of there, which wouldn't be ideal, so I sent a message to Waking Dream outlining her role in the heist. I also sent a copy of the message to Vienna's pod.

Now her real ID was a liability. She'd maybe have some friends in the smuggling and piracy world she could lean on. And maybe those friends would be hesitant to trust someone who'd bungled their last job so completely.

Maybe she'd have to get a job. Maybe she'd end up working in a familiar slaughterhouse, counting the days until she'd earned enough to leave.

It was a thought that amused me.

I had spent a year trapped on Tumblethorn, before finally pulling free of its terrible gravity. I liked the symmetry of sending back another in my place, a symbolic offering to balance the

books.
　　I wondered how long it would take her to escape.

Where Were You When They Burnt The Mother Trees?

*TRANSCRIPT of host Michael J Steel from the 'America Is Burning'
podcast, episode 547:*

MJ Steel: Mother Nature has entered the housing market, ladies
and gentlemen, and she has undercut pretty much everyone. You
see this piece in the *New York Times* talking about worried
landlords? Heh. I'll just bet they are. This is market forces at
work, my friends. Why pay three quarters of your wages to some
bloodsucking landlord when you can just sleep up a fucking tree?
I mean, sure, you're losing out on some creature comforts, but
did I mention that it's free?

Now you know in the past I have been accused of
sensationalism, in some cases justifiably. I hold my hand up. But I
want you to mark the date and time on this. The mother trees are
not going to go away. And they are going to change everything.

....

*Extract from article on "The Delver" website: "Mother's Warm Embrace"
By Josh Reynolds (contains the earliest online mention of the term
"Mother Tree")*

Billy tries his best to not look homeless, figures it's his best chance
of getting off the streets. So he dresses as if he's going for an

interview, in suit and tie, white shirt and black brogues. But look a little closer and you notice that the suit is shiny at the knees, the shoes scuffed and dirty.

He knows the streets well. He knows which cops will pat you down and which ones will pass you by. He knows when the bakeries start throwing out unsold produce. He also knows which will toss some bread or cake your way and which will threaten you before padlocking their dumpster.

He also knows about The Mother Trees.

You probably do too, although I doubt you call them that. They began sprouting up all over, about six months ago, like twitch grass, seemingly anywhere there was soil. The press at the time called them anything from Spike Weed to Devil's Cactus. You may remember a parade of botanists on various news channels, theorizing as to their origin, enthusing about their intriguing DNA or their odd placement in the hierarchy of plant classification. More likely, you recall farmers and gardeners cursing them and the depths of their root system.

It's doubtful you ever saw one grow to its full size.

There is a cluster of the trees growing in the wasteland behind an abandoned factory on the outskirts of the hollowed-out garment district. Billy takes me to see them as dusk is falling. We push our way through a rusting chain-link fence, past rotting tyres and layers of sun-bleached trash. Round a corner and there they are, tall and brooding, half in shadow from the crumbling factory.

Those of you familiar with them at earlier stages of growth may think you know their shape and structure, but when they reach maturity - at around six feet in height - their form changes remarkably. They begin like a closed umbrella, planted in the earth, point down. Now picture that umbrella opening slowly, gradually forming a concave bowl, revealing a central trunk. The visual comparison breaks down at that point, because the sides continue to open until they are flat with the ground, forming a kind of thick lily pad, a circle around twelve feet across, with the trunk in the centre. A behaviour and shape that, I am reliably informed, does not occur in any other plant or tree in nature.

Once the trees grow higher than six feet or so, the structure repeats. Another thick lily pad "floor" is grown along with a section of trunk, and so on. Obligingly, the mother tree provides a series of short stubby branches protruding from the central trunk at regular intervals, which can be used as a staircase of sorts to access the higher floors.

The largest trees behind the factory have three floors of lily pad and are over twenty feet tall. Resting on each lily pad, we find several of what Billy calls "bunks". These are shrivelled pod-like objects, around six feet long, with openings in one end, swathed in leaves and a vein-like network of roots. These "bunks" look to all the world like organic sleeping bags, radiating from the trunk like spokes on a wheel.

And tonight, Billy and I plan to sleep in them.

No one is sure who first attempted this, but it is an open secret amongst the homeless in this area. As we clamber on to the lily pad base of the nearest mother tree, Billy grunts a greeting and I realise that one of the bunks already contains a figure. Disconcertingly, all that's visible is a disembodied head protruding from the pod, a young woman who identifies herself as Kath. She doesn't say much, but Billy vouching for me carries weight.

I wriggle inside my bunk, feet first. The sleeping bag comparison continues, the interior pliable and soft. There is a vague smell of soil and decay, but it is not unpleasant. I am braced for cold and damp, but am surprised by dryness and warmth enveloping my legs. Billy meets my eye. He's smiling and nodding. I feel as though I am being inducted into some secret society.

Soon I am almost totally cocooned. If I push a little with my feet, I can feel the bark of the central trunk through the elastic wall enveloping me. It's oddly comforting. I stare up at the rapidly darkening sky and we continue to talk as night falls. Billy says that the mother trees have been a lifesaver for many homeless people in the city, in some cases literally. They seem to respond to the outside temperature, warming their occupants on cold nights and cooling them in the height of summer.

I hear the nearby rattle of a freight train and the distant sound of barking dogs, banal sounds at odds with the surreal nature of the experience. At one point, I become aware of nearby laughter and new voices. I sense other people climbing up the central trunk to take their place in other bunks. I feel momentarily vulnerable, but soon silence has returned to our tree.

I don't know if I'd feel safe sleeping here as a woman, alone. I quietly mention this to Billy and he nods, thoughtful, before pointing out that women sleep alone on the streets every night. Are the mother trees any less safe than a shop doorway?

Billy had warned me about the next stage, but it still startles me. Almost imperceptibly at first, I feel my bunk tipping, moving gradually to the vertical, raising my head and lowering my feet. I instinctively tense, then force myself to relax. Billy had explained that every night, as the sky darkens, the mother trees all close up, naturally pulling all the bunks and their occupants to a vertical position. The bunks are then enclosed within the now-vertical shield of concertinaed lilly pad, held in that protective embrace until morning.

Even forewarned, being enveloped in this way is highly disconcerting, especially in near darkness. The only sounds are the rustle of leaves and the creaks of the tree as it reconfigures itself. I doubt anyone with claustrophobia could weather the experience.

Once the transformation is complete, my eyes begin to adjust and I realise there must be a slight luminescence to the interior, which allows me to see the trunk, standing just a few inches from my face. We appear to be totally enclosed, with no sign of the night sky above us, although I never feel short of breath. I am now suspended in a roughly standing position and initially worry that I might slip down, but the gentle embrace of the bunk and mother tree keep me in place. I feel warm and comfortable and am soon struggling to stay awake, then remember that I am here to sleep, after all. I surrender and go under, to a night of drifting calm and unremembered dreams.

I am awoken by the sensation of gentle movement. Our

mother tree opening once more, unfurling to reveal the misty dawn to its sleeping children. Billy and I wriggle free of our bunks and he reveals yet another wonder hidden within our new host. The "staircase" of short stubby branches protruding from the central trunk have another use, which Billy demonstrates to me. If one of the branches is pushed up with a firm motion, a section of bark on the other side of the trunk is forced open, like a pointed scale of armour, giving access to a chamber within. He instructs me to push up one of the branches and I hear him rummaging within the trunk. He emerges triumphantly brandishing two fruits roughly the size and shape of large mangoes, but beige in colour.

"Breakfast!" he announces.

The fruit of the mother tree is tangy and mildly sweet. It's closest in flavour to a sweet potato and very filling. We sit eating in silence as the world awakes around us. Other people descend from their bunks, often clutching the same fruits. There is a feeling of jubilance and fellowship, a sense that we are all now part of some secret wonder.

After we've eaten, we sit in a contemplative silence. I had planned to hurry back to my apartment this morning. I have appointments to make and errands to run, but they all seem like distant worries. It's as though I'm now viewing them all through the filter of the mother tree. Even visually, the world is now framed by her lily pad floors, above and below me.

Billy tells me that many in the homeless community want to keep quiet about the trees. They think if word gets out, it could ruin what they have.

"But you don't agree?" I ask.

"It might cause problems, to begin with. But long term…" Billy trails off. I can see he's thinking it through, trying to organise his thoughts. I am happy to wait until he's ready to speak.

"I don't tend to remember the dreams I have in the trees. A lot of people don't. Except for one a few weeks back… in the dream, everyone in the world was sleeping in the mother trees. It had become so popular that people had started building houses without bedrooms. Then they stopped building houses altogether."

As Billy talks, I can sense other conversations around me in the tree have ceased. Listening to Billy talk.

"It was the happiest dream I'd ever had," says Billy. "But if we don't spread the word and tell the rest of the world about the trees, it can never come true."

I nod and smile as he continues, outlining a world where humanity literally returns to nature. Part of me knows it's naive and hopelessly romantic - but sitting in the shade of that miraculous tree, the ridiculous suddenly seems a little more possible.

I don't know if I really want Billy's dream to come true. I like living in a house. I like sleeping in a bed. But for those of us that have neither, a mother tree is a timely blessing.

....

Graffiti seen on a subway train, New York, 2032:

ON YOUR NECK IS THE RICH MAN'S KNEE
THE MOTHER TREE WILL SET YOU FREE

....

Leaked transcript from the Pentagon. Closed session between H (redacted) and K (redacted)

H: What the fuck is this? We asked for the dumbed-down highlights.

K: I know, I know. Dr Kleiner can be diff--

H: It's over two hundred pages long - have you read it?

K: I've tried. Maybe--

H: As someone without a degree in whatever she has, could you give me the cliff notes here?

K: Okay. Okay. Broadly she agrees with Dr Paulson. It's seeming more and more likely that the trees were designed rather than, uh, evolving.

H: Does she mention a country? Are there any smoking guns in the DNA?

K: She doesn't mention any country. She does say that the genetic engineering knowhow required to produce something as complex as a mother tree is decades beyond anything in the West.

H: Which implies what? Russia? China?

K: It's widely agreed that even their dark labs are, at most, months ahead of us at any given time.

H: Come on. Those trees are literally socialism with leaves on. And it's not the Chinese?

K: Current understanding is that they couldn't do it if they tried.

H: So whoever designed them is decades ahead. Of everyone?

K: That is her conclusion.

H: So who does that leave us with, Tony? Little green men?

K: I'm just passing on her findings.

H: I have another report on my desk a whole lot thinner. On the nutritional value of the fruit. You read that one?

K: I have.

H: "A single fruit from a mother tree supplies" blah blah blah "an almost perfectly balanced blend of vitamins and nutrition" - you could literally live on them. Some people already are. If people figure this out, if word gets out--

K: Well, we'll just have to spin it before it does.

....

Leaked email from Republican think-tank Guided Light.

Carl,

I know it was a blow that the fruit sailed through the FDA testing. Some hallucinogens or carcinogens would have really helped us out there. We're looking at ways to trademark them, ideally so that no one can promote them or advertise them without us suing, which would be a start.

Currently it's not illegal to climb the trees, sleep in them or eat their fruit. Terry obviously has legal teams looking at ways to change all that. A few actual injuries or deaths because of the trees would really strengthen our position on that front.

You would imagine the fact that they're still regularly used by the homeless would give us a plethora of ODs in and around the trees, but official reports have been frustratingly light in that area. Whenever an incident occurs within a few blocks of a mother tree, we do our best to imply a link through our usual outlets.

We really need to get ahead of this and get some beefy anti-tree content out there. Get some traction on our preferred narratives. I suggest starting with safety. Stories and tweets about people breaking their necks falling from the trees, suffocating inside them, becoming poisoned by the fruit. Stories about people being attacked while they slept in the trees. Mike's got some great new bot scripts we can utilise for this.

Paranoia about the origin of the trees, their true nature, what exposure could do to you. Worry about all of that is there already to a degree, we just need to piggyback and amplify. Were they grown in a lab? If so, where? We can have simultaneous contradictory chaff threads running with all the usual suspects: deep state, Russia, China, North Korea. Were they sent here as a socialist infiltration tool? To weaken our economy? Could exposure make you sterile?

Amongst certain groups, the mother trees have gained a certain cachet. The words "mysterious" and "cool" scored big in our focus studies, particularly with the under-thirties. We need to undermine that and the obvious angle is social mobility. The trees already have strong associations with the homeless community, let's lean into that. Imply that use of the trees is a social signifier of poverty and failure. "If you sleep in a mother tree then you've failed at life." That kind of thing. Think-pieces around this topic from the writers or outlets we own.

Let's talk again on Friday,
Paul.

Article from issue 43 of Shrift magazine,
"The New Net" by Millie Hoffstead.

When I was in my twenties, I worked behind a bar in a theatre. It was no better or worse paid than any other bar work in town, but it had one great advantage. For most of the evening, while the performance was on, the bar was empty. True, you had to weather the chaos before the curtain rose, and again at the interval, but this was more than made up for by the calm that surrounded it. It was, in many ways, a supremely cushy job which I valued a lot at the time.

Then we gained a new manager - let's say her name was Lily. Almost overnight, Lily turned what had been an easy job into a living nightmare. She openly resented the fact that, for much of the evening, there were no customers to serve. Any staff member found doing nothing was berated, often at volume. The new rule was that if you were not serving, you were cleaning. And if you're picturing a mere sweep of the floor or perfunctory wipe down of the bar, think bigger. Imagine removing every bottle of spirits from a shelf twenty feet long and wiping it clean. Every. Single. Night.

She micromanaged and criticised every order she witnessed. She talked a lot about the "values and image" of the theatre, which apparently didn't include being overweight or dyeing your hair any colour other than blonde. Younger, more brittle staff were brought to tears. Many quit within the first month.

I couldn't afford to. I had rent to pay and was just scraping by with a mix of three part-time jobs. I desperately needed the money and reasoned that, even with Lily, it was still easier work than any other bar in town.

That resolution lasted six months before I jumped ship, deciding that, ultimately, I'd rather work in a bar crammed to the rafters with punters from opening till close than spend another minute with Lily breathing down my neck.

They say that people don't quit bad jobs, they quit bad bosses. But many people can't afford to do either. It was true twenty years ago, when I finally gave my notice at the theatre and it's doubly true now. But things could be changing. The great resignation in the wake of Covid, the anti-work movement, the massive increase in union membership have all been framed by some commentators as a tipping point. A fundamental change in the shape of capitalism, of the relationship between employer and employee.

I hope so. God knows, it's been a long time coming.

The Black Death, the plague that swept across Europe in the fourteenth century, is reputed to have killed somewhere between thirty and sixty per cent of the population. The Covid pandemic obviously occurred under a very different set of circumstances, but there are some interesting parallels. In the wake of the Black Death, simply put, there were not enough workers left alive to go round. This meant that the surviving peasants were able to negotiate higher wages for their services. This was a practice that was fought tooth and nail by the government and landlords of the time, but it is widely agreed that the Black Death ultimately led to the end of the feudal system and a massive increase in social mobility. For the first time, the power was in the hands of the workers.

In the wake of the Covid pandemic, things are not nearly as clear-cut. For one thing, a lot fewer people have died. But there is a new factor in play, an ace in the hole that should offer dissatisfied workers the world over a ray of hope.

The mother trees.

If allowed to flourish and proliferate, the mother trees, for the first time, offer a universal safety net. No matter who or where you are, being penniless and homeless no longer means that you are at risk of starvation or lack a bed for the night. Furthermore, fear of falling into that state no longer holds quite the same sting that it once did.

It used to be one of the unspoken assumptions of taking a low-paid job that you had few other options open to you. Both you and your boss always knew that there was a long line of potential hires waiting to take your place. This knowledge would embolden awful managers to take advantage of their workers in a variety of ways that we hardly need to list here.

Not anymore. The line of potential new hires has shrunk massively, for a variety of reasons, and with the new options on the table that the mother tree provides, many low-paid workers are simply dropping out of the workforce and rental market altogether. Sleeping in and eating from a mother tree has moved in public perception from the desperate preserve of the homeless to a viable option for anyone wanting to save money. And there is growing evidence that young professionals on higher salaries are also hearing the call of the wild.

Needless to say, this all has a lot of employers and landlords very worried.

In some places, the backlash has been pronounced and obvious. Trees torched in towns and cities all over the world, often by "angry public mobs" that invariably turn out to be in the pay of local landlords or business owners. Attempts to draft legislation in various courts, outlawing the trees and their fruit, thus far thankfully unsuccessful. There have also been less obvious attempts to turn public opinion against the trees. Concerted social media campaigns, pumping out horror stories about deaths caused by the trees, spreading rumours about their origin. Whenever these stories are examined with any rigour, they dissolve like mist, but the sheer number of them is very telling.

A lot of very rich people want those trees gone.

On the flip side of the equation, some cities have welcomed the trees with open arms. Predictably, those with the largest homeless populations are leading the way; New York, Los Angeles, Seattle and San Francisco, all of which have passed local legislation of some sort, protecting the trees. To quote the mayor of San Francisco, Dan Plumpton: "Each tree can feed and 'house' dozens of homeless, if allowed to grow to several 'floors', which eases the budgetary drain that a large homeless population traditionally causes."

Which is hardly the most altruistic angle we could hope for, but it's a start.

....

Extract from article on "The Delver" website:
"The Miracle of The Mother Trees"
By Josh Reynolds

We meet in the same coffee shop as before, by my reckoning almost a full year since Billy first showed me the mother trees. He's no longer wearing his interview suit, which is the first surprise - dressed instead in a denim jacket over a T-shirt. He explains that he's managed to get a job as a programmer, which predictably has no dress code, and for the most part no need to go into an office. He holds up a cheap laptop.

"I can work anywhere with wi-fi."

I ask him if he liked the first article. He laughs.

"You made me sound like a hippy. But it got the word out."

I assume he's not renting an apartment and my assumption is correct. He's still sleeping in the mother trees.

"I could afford an apartment in the city. Just. If I budgeted like crazy. And washed in cold water."

He shrugs with a smile. His largest monthly expense is gym membership, to provide showers and washrooms. He explains that some canny gyms have begun providing large permanent lockers as an attraction to mother tree users. The market adapting.

We've already discussed the rough plan for today over email, basically a catch-up on how things have changed with the mother trees and the homeless community, ending with a night in the same tree we first slept in.

Billy explains that that might be a problem, but won't elaborate until we've reached the trees, so I follow him along a familiar route through what used to be the garment district. Even before I reach the grove, I can sense something is wrong. Charred debris is strewn across the road in front of the abandoned factory, the chain-link fence flattened, the waste ground leading to the trees churned into mud, crossed with tyre-marks and bootprints.

I round the factory and discover that the grove has been

reduced to a few blackened stumps, the smell of gasoline still in the air.

"The fire was set in the middle of the night," says Billy.

"Were the trees empty?" I ask.

"No. They were full. And the people that did this, had to know that."

But Billy is smiling. Holding on to some secret joke he has yet to share.

"Did they all get out?" I ask.

"No," he answers. "The trees remained sealed as they burned. No one got out."

"Then why are you smiling?" I ask.

I am beginning to feel that something within Billy has broken.

"I was inside one of the trees as they burned," he says. "And I was utterly oblivious to it all. In the morning I awoke, my tree opened and I discovered that I was now in a totally different tree, two miles away."

....

Email recovered from a CIA server
(George Bush Center for Intelligence, Langley, Virginia.)

Terry,

We're keeping a policy of denial and deflection in place while we get our ducks in a row, but just to get the team up to speed, here's the latest revelations out of the labs.

If you are sleeping inside a mother tree when it is attacked or threatened with destruction, there is a good chance that a defence mechanism will be activated and you will be transferred, through some method that we don't yet understand, to another tree, usually within a few miles of the threatened tree.

We're going to call it teleporting for the sake of brevity - but as I say, we still don't know exactly what occurs.

Now that in itself would be alarming enough and raises all kinds of questions about the technology behind the trees, a potential guiding intelligence and the increasing likelihood that the trees have an extraterrestrial origin. But believe it or not, it's not even our biggest worry at the moment.

Extensive testing in our labs has confirmed that this "teleporting" ability can be activated when the trees are not under threat. Certain individuals, through focussing on a particular destination whilst falling asleep, can "persuade" the tree to teleport them to other locations, in some cases hundreds of miles away.

Needless to say, the joint chiefs shit a brick when they learned about this particular wrinkle.

The one upside is that there appears to be some sort of filter in place to stop anyone and everyone from using it. The boys in the lab have dressed it up in a lot of university language, but boiled down, it seems to be simply this:

The trees detect intent.

Teleporting armed soldiers seems to be impossible. The only time we've managed to teleport any service personnel at all is when they're unarmed and the destination tree is somewhere they value, such as their home town.

The idea that the trees are, to some degree, reading our minds raises a whole new set of terrifying questions, but at least this "filter" appears to rule out hostile incursions. For the moment, at least, we don't have to worry about, say, a troop of Russian soldiers teleporting into Washington DC.

The lab is working round the clock, attempting to circumvent the filter, and we know the Chinese have similar labs. You can bet they're doing the same. Before someone cracks it, we need to make sure that every one of these trees on US soil is a pile of smoking ash.

···

Where Were You When They Burnt The Mother Trees?
(rebel anthem - author unknown)

I was working all hours to keep myself fed,
Heard on the news that they were all dead,

I was sitting in jail for daring to climb,
Into the arms of this mother of mine,
I was gassing the march,
I was planting the drugs,
I was painting the mothers with babies as thugs,
Where were you when they burnt all the trees?
I was next to the tree with a match
I was next to the tree with a match

....

Extract from article on "The Delver" website:
"Mother Thinks Of Everything"
By Josh Reynolds

I have booked a ticket to travel by tree.

How quickly the miraculous becomes mundane.

Up until a certain point, it feels very much like air travel. The same check-in desks, the same security lines. Everything has a comforting familiarity. This is the new normal. Teleporting thousands of miles in the blink of an eye, by means of a tree that is possibly (who are we kidding - probably) from another world.

The mother trees themselves have been grown inside concrete-walled silos topped with armoured-glass skylights. It feels a little like overkill, but the idea that dozens of armed North Korean soldiers could suddenly swarm out of them is still viewed as eminently possible. Bored-looking soldiers are stationed just outside. They look as though they'd be glad of the distraction.

The designers have done everything they can to round the edges of the brutalism on display, with pastel shades and mood lighting, but the mother tree still looks as though it's in prison. As I draw closer, I hear soft musak and the sounds of a jungle piped in from hidden speakers, squawks of parrots and chittering insects, but all it does is make me wish we were truly outside.

I reach the lily pad floor I've been assigned by means of an escalator and a short extendible walkway. Another echo of air travel. Another attempt to sanitize and formalise something that

301

will always seem insane and bizarre to me. The walkway smells vaguely of antiseptic and hot rubber, overpowering the soft peat scent of the tree itself.

I dutifully climb into my bunk and wait for the tree to close. I have watched the briefing video on how to focus my mind on my intended destination. I have also signed the legal waiver stating that I will not be refunded if my attempt to travel fails and that transit to any unsanctioned tree carries severe penalties, up to and including imprisonment.

The circle of sky visible through the skylight darkens, the extendible walkways retract and the tree smoothly closes, tilting my bunk to the vertical. I clear my mind, focus on my intended destination and allow sleep to take me.

The tilted opening of my new tree awakens me. I can hear surf crashing and smell seaweed and salt. For a moment, I think it's more musak and illusion, but opening my eyes reveals the truth.

My new mother tree sits on the edge of a swathe of scrubby vegetation bordering a long arc of apparently deserted sandy beach. I wriggle from my bunk to get a clearer view and discover dozens more mother trees bordering the beach, some five or more storeys high. Behind them, the vegetation gives way to thicker jungle, rising to what looks like a dormant volcano. The surf is booming like a cannon, hissing as it falls.

At first glance, it looks like paradise. Even this early in the morning, the air is warm and there's not a soul in sight. I can't hear anyone else in the tree either, which is a first and oddly disconcerting. My lily pad is two storeys up, so I carefully clamber down to ground level and walk out on to the beach, leaving the shade and cool of the tree. I expect to see others emerging from their trees, but there is still no one else in sight. My uneasiness rises.

As I move on to the sand, I realise that the beach is far from the unspoiled haven I first took it for. The tide line is marked with what I'd initially taken for shells, but instead turn out to be thousands of small pieces of plastic garbage, some bleached white by the sun and sea, others still proclaiming cut-prices and special offers. More are being washed ashore with each crash of the waves. I can see larger pieces bobbing further out. Plastic crates and tangled netting forming floating islands.

I wonder where I am.

This may seem an odd thing to ponder, emerging from a new mother tree, but one of the lesser-known wrinkles of tree teleportation is that you can also be transported to individual people rather than just locations. The process is much the same - intensely focus on them as you fall asleep, picture awaking in or near their tree and there's a good chance it will happen.

Assuming you don't want to do them harm and that they want to see you.

Mother really does think of everything.

The man I have come here to meet is a wanted fugitive for various offences, all of them connected with the now-illegal "unlicensed growing and protection of mother trees". When I first met him, six years ago, both he and the world were in very different places. He was homeless, one of many I'd met in order to write a small social-interest piece on the community's plight in our city. He showed me the mother trees, we spent a night under their protection and, in the morning, we ate their fruit.

The small article that resulted from that meeting was the most widely read of my career and is cited, in some quarters, as the start of the global awakening to the potential of the trees. During our second interview, he claimed that the mother trees could teleport their charges to safety in times of danger - an idea that I not so subtly mocked at the time, before scientists the world over confirmed his insane claim, and then some.

I can't wait to see what he reveals in our third meeting.

Billy, or William S Montague as the FBI refer to him, appears around five minutes later, calling out to me as he emerges from a tree a little further down the beach. As he approaches, I take in his appearance. He's wearing sandals, linen shorts and a loose, billowing shirt. He's allowed his hair and beard to grow long. He looks, in short, as though he's about to rent me a jet-ski. Or start a cult.

Some might argue that he already has. The attention that my columns brought led to him becoming something of a celebrity in the mother tree community. He also became a target for the anti-tree right, experiences that no doubt hardened his already steadfast resolve to champion and protect the mother trees. What began as wholesome activism was rendered illegal by the far-reaching and, some would argue, draconian Hammond Act two years ago. He's been off the grid ever since.

We exchange hellos, nothing too effusive. We don't really know each other that well. I think we like each other, but in total we've only spoken for a handful of hours over the past six years.

He hands me a fruit from the trees with a smile, a call back to our first meeting. We both sit cross-legged on the edge of the beach and eat as we watch the surf roll in and out. I express regret at all the garbage in the sea, a comment I intended as throwaway before we start the interview proper, but Billy immediately leads us into deeper waters.

"We've broken the planet," he declares evenly.

I don't reply and he pauses for a long time, staring out at the booming surf. I know his rhythms, so don't hurry him. I count cycles of the surf booming and receding. I reach five before he speaks again.

"Within a century, probably less, most of the world will be too hot for us. For most of the year. The survivors will migrate north, settle where they can, until eventually even that becomes impossible."

I've heard similar proclamations of doom from various quarters. Some have also opined that the mother trees appearing at this moment in history is no coincidence - Mother Earth providing a tidy little rescue package to save us from ourselves, if only we'd take it. I wonder if Billy is about to make a similar claim, but he pauses again. I count three cycles of surf before he continues.

"I know what the mother trees are. Why they are here. What they're for."

Another pause. Two cycles of surf. A seagull lands and begins pecking at a sprawled mass of netting nearby. It distracts me. I worry it will get tangled.

"They are here to help us escape. Escape from the world we have broken."

"How do you know that?" I ask.

"Because I've already done it and come back. I've met with the makers of the mother trees."

. . . .

Transcript of host Michael J Steel from the "America Is Burning" podcast, episode 975.

MJ Steel: There's no great mystery to any of this. It's just a bunch of loafers, who couldn't handle an honest day's work for an honest day's pay, so they dropped out, hopped up a mother tree and they're now sunning themselves on a beach somewhere. It's not the "great disappearance". It's the "great drop-out".

And this latest fairy story doing the rounds on liberal media - which, by the way, is an insult to everyone's intelligence, but I'm going to give it a little time here, just to thoroughly debunk it, then we can move on.

So. This story some outlets are peddling, with a straight face, is that the mother trees can also - drum roll, please - teleport you into space! To another planet! No doubt full of rainbows and puppies. Or hookers and blow, depending on your preferences. But only if you wish really hard and have love in your heart. Which apparently rules out most of the right. Because we broke the planet and now only lefties with tie-dye underwear get to leave.

And, of course, there's no evidence of any of this, no one is coming back with any proof, it's just another flimsy attempt to guilt-trip the right. Well, my friends, you are going to have to try a little harder and smarter than that.

Because that's what this is really about. Who we get to blame. Who's really at fault for the cities on fire and the droughts and the starvation and the wars. Of course, it's the SUV-driving NRA member who never recycled. Isn't it always?

OK then. I'll play. Let's say that's true. Let's say every little thing that's collapsing right now - and there is quite a list - is all down to us. Let's say we're heading towards the end times and we're the ones to blame.

Well then, what I say to you is this: so what? So fucking what? At least we had fun living our lives. While the left were all failing to save the whales and eating tofu. That's what it came down to. We were free and you weren't. We had fun and you didn't.

I can live with that. Hell, more than that. I can celebrate it. Give me a bullhorn and get me to the roof.

. . . .

Partial transcript of conversation between Josephine and Hester Grant, recovered from server within bunker designation Cerberus, situated six hundred miles from the north pole.

Josephine: I've stopped doing my exercises. The visualisations.

Hester: Why? If you don't -

J: Because it's a waste of time. If it was going to happen it would have happened.

H: You don't know that. There's still a chance.

J: No. I think the trees have made their choice. I think everyone that's going to be allowed to leave has already left.

H: People are leaving all the time. Jordan left last week.

J: No, Jordan *disappeared* last week. Which means he was either banished, executed--

H: You don't know that.

J: I know he didn't sleep in the trees. Not once, according to the guards.

H: That can't be right.

J: I think the trees know who we are. Deep down. And they've made their choice. And I don't think we're going to change that by meditation or prayer or fake charity. It's too little too late. I think Mitch has the right idea.

H: Mitch is a drug addict. And a pervert.

J: And he's not hiding it. He's not pretending to be a saint, hoping to fool the trees.

H: That's not what I'm doing. Do you think that's the only reason--?

J: All I'm saying is, I'm done wearing the hair shirt. I'm going to spend whatever time we have left here, enjoying myself, in any way that I can.

H: Well that's your choice of course.

J: Ma, look around you. How do you think this is going to end?

H: What do you mean?

J: You really see us all being alive this time next year?

H: We've got enough food and water--

J: I'm not talking about that. I'm talking about who we're sharing this place with. How much we trust them.

H: How can you say that? They're some of the most respected business leaders---

J: Do you know the percentage of CEOs with psychopathic tendencies?

H: Psychopathic--?

J: Just makes them better at business. Cuts empathy out of the equation.

H: You're talking nonsense. You really think--

J: That's amongst *normal* CEOs. But the people in here? Happy to pay millions for a bed in a bunker? While the world burns and starves outside? That takes a special kind of broken.

H: Your father worked night and day to get us a bed in here.

J: To get *himself* in here you mean. Do you really think if they'd said "You can't bring your family", he'd have paused for a second?

H: You shouldn't speak ill of the dead.

J: You deserved better, Ma. We both did.

(five second pause)

H: Have you eaten today?

J: What?

H: You always get cranky when you don't eat.

J: Seriously?

H: Come on. Come to the commissary with me. Bacon and eggs. That's what you need.

J: That's your take away from all this? That I need feeding?

H: No, I'm sure you're making very valid points. Including that one about enjoying ourselves in what little time we have left.

J: You liked that one did you?

H: It's growing on me.

J: Ha. Tell you what I *am* enjoying - watching all these withered old bastards gradually come to realise that they can't buy their way out of this. It must be eating them up.

H: I think I might go with pancakes.

J: All those years spent exploiting everyone and everything to get these vast fortunes. And the mother trees just don't care. They know exactly who they are and what they've done. And escape is not for sale.

H: Or maybe waffles. What do you think?

(three second pause)

J: Waffles sounds good Ma. Lead the way.

Printed in Great Britain
by Amazon

20912184R00180